PUFFIN CLASSICS

THE COUNT OF MONTE CRISTO

ALEXANDRE DUMAS (1802–70) was born near Paris, the son of a general in Napoleon's army. He received little formal education and started his adult life in a series of minor clerical jobs, which he got due to the beauty and clarity of his handwriting. But in 1829 he achieved great success with a historical melodrama about the French king Henry III. He had found his forte, and over the next ten years he wrote a series of extremely successful action-packed plays for the theatre.

In about 1840, however, he turned his vast imaginative talents to novel-writing. He was even more successful as a novelist than he had been as a playwright. Two of his books became just about the most widely read books of the nineteenth century. These were *The Three Musketeers* and *The Count of Monte Cristo*. Both were originally serialized in newspapers (which is why each chapter tends to end in a cliff-hanger) and astonishingly, both were written in the same year, 1844–5.

Dumas went on turning out lengthy adventure stories, including such famous books as *The Black Tulip*. Nowadays, his novels are generally considered too long, which is why this Puffin edition has been abridged. In addition to his novels, he wrote travel books, biographies, reminiscences of his huge menagerie of pets, children's books – and even a cookbook! His output seems too large to be possible; and indeed he was helped by a series of collaborators, who sometimes amounted to a staff of writers. However, Dumas always supervised the work, and provided the plots, the imaginative details, and the twists and turns of the thrilling adventures.

In keeping with the man's nature as a prodigy, Dumas earned an enormous amount of money from his writing, but was extraordinarily extravagant, dying in near poverty.

ALEXANDRE DUMAS

The Count of Monte Cristo

Abridged by

ROBIN WATERFIELD

PUFFIN BOOKS

PUFFIN BOOKS

Published by the Penguin Group
Penguin Books Ltd, 80 Strand, London WC2R 0RL, England
Penguin Putnam Inc., 375 Hudson Street, New York, New York 10014, USA
Penguin Books Australia Ltd, 250 Camberwell Road, Camberwell, Victoria 3124, Australia
Penguin Books Canada Ltd, 10 Alcorn Avenue, Toronto, Ontario, Canada M4V 3B2
Penguin Books India (P) Ltd, 11 Community Centre, Panchsheel Park, New Delhi – 110 017, India
Penguin Books (NZ) Ltd, Cnr Rosedale and Airborne Roads, Albany, Auckland, New Zealand
Penguin Books (South Africa) (Pty) Ltd, 24 Sturdee Avenue, Rosebank 2196, South Africa

Penguin Books Ltd, Registered Offices: 80 Strand, London WC2R 0RL, England

www.penguin.com

First published in 1844
This abridged edition first published in Puffin Books 1996
20

Set in Monophoto Plantin
Filmset by Datix International Limited, Bungay, Suffolk
Printed and bound in Great Britain by
Mackays of Chatham plc, Chatham, Kent

British Library Cataloguing in Publication Data
A CIP catalogue record for this book is available from the British Library

ISBN 0–140–37353–5

1

On the 24th of February 1815, the watch-tower of Notre-Dame de la Garde signalled the arrival of the three-master *Pharaon*, from Smyrna, Trieste, and Naples.

The usual crowd of curious spectators immediately filled the quay of Fort Saint-Jean, for at Marseilles the arrival of a ship is always a great event, especially when that ship belongs to a shipowner of their own town.

Meanwhile the vessel drew on, and was approaching the harbour under topsails, jib, and foresail, but so slowly and with such an air of melancholy that the spectators, always ready to sense misfortune, began to ask one another what ill-luck had overtaken those on board. However, those experienced in navigation soon saw that if there had been any ill-luck, the ship had not been the sufferer, for she advanced in perfect condition and under skilful handling; the anchor was ready to be dropped, the bowsprit shrouds loose. Beside the pilot, who was steering the *Pharaon* through the narrow entrance to the port, there stood a young man, quick of gesture and keen of eye, who watched every movement of the ship while repeating each of the pilot's orders.

The vague anxiety that prevailed among the crowd affected one of the spectators so much that he could not wait until the ship reached the port; jumping into a small boat, he ordered the boatman to row him alongside the *Pharaon*.

On seeing this man approach, the young sailor left his post beside the pilot, and, hat in hand, leant over the ship's bulwarks. He was a tall, lithe young man of about twenty years of age, with fine dark eyes and hair as black as ebony; his whole manner bespoke that air of calm resolution peculiar to those who, from their childhood, have been accustomed to face danger.

'Ah, is that you, Dantès!' cried the man in the boat. 'You are looking pretty gloomy on board. What has happened?'

'A great misfortune, Monsieur Morrel,' replied the young man, 'a great misfortune, especially for me! We lost our brave Captain Leclère off Civita Vecchia.'

'What happened to him?' asked the shipowner. 'What has happened to our worthy captain?'

'He died of brain-fever in dreadful agony. Twenty-four hours after we left Naples he was in high fever, and died three days afterwards. We performed the usual burial service.'

'Well, Monsieur Edmond,' said the owner, 'we are all mortal, and the old must make way for the young, otherwise there would be no promotion. And the cargo . . .?'

'Is all safe and sound, Monsieur Morrel, take my word for it. It has been a voyage that will bring you in a good twenty-five thousand francs!'

As they were just past the Round Tower the young man shouted out: 'Ready there! Lower topsails, fore-sail, and jib!'

The order was executed as promptly as on board a man-of-war.

'And now, Monsieur Morrel,' said Dantès, 'here is your purser, Monsieur Danglars, coming out of his cabin. If you will step on board he will furnish you with every particular. I must look after the anchoring and dress the ship in mourning.'

The owner did not wait to be invited twice. He seized a rope which Dantès flung to him, and, with an agility that would have done credit to a sailor, climbed up the ladder attached to the side of the ship, while the young man, returning to his duty, left the conversation to the individual whom he had announced under the name of Danglars, and who now came towards the owner. He was a man of twenty-five or twenty-six, of unprepossessing countenance, obsequious to his superiors, insolent to his subordinates; and besides the fact that he was the purser – and pursers are always unpopular on board – he was personally as much disliked by the crew as Edmond Dantès was beloved by them.

'Well, Monsieur Morrel,' said Danglars, 'you have heard of the misfortune that has befallen us?'

'Yes, yes, poor Captain Leclère! He was a brave and honest man!'

'And a first-rate seaman, grown old between sky and ocean, as a man should be who is entrusted with the interests of so important a firm as that of Morrel and Son,' replied Danglars.

'But,' replied the owner, watching Dantès at his work, 'it seems to me that a sailor need not be so old to understand his business; our friend Edmond seems to understand it thoroughly, and to require no instructions from anyone.'

'Yes,' said Danglars, casting a look of hatred on Dantès, 'yes, he is young, and youth is never lacking in self-confidence. The captain was hardly dead when, without consulting anyone, he assumed command of the ship, and was the cause of our losing a day and a half off the Isle of Elba instead of making direct for Marseilles.'

'As captain's mate, it was his duty to take command, but he acted wrongly in losing a day and a half off Elba unless the ship was in need of repair.'

'The ship was as right as I am and as I hope you are, Monsieur Morrel; it was nothing more than a whim on his part that caused the delay off Elba.'

'Dantès,' called the owner, turning towards the young man, 'just step this way, will you?'

'One moment, monsieur,' he replied, 'and I shall be with you.' Then turning to the crew, he called out: 'Let go!'

The anchor was instantly dropped and the chain ran out with a great rattle. In spite of the pilot's presence Dantès remained at his post until this last task was accomplished, and then he added: 'Lower the flag and pennant to half-mast and slope the yards!'

'You see,' said Danglars, 'he already imagines himself captain.'

'And so he is,' said his companion. 'Why should we not give him the post? I know he is young, but he seems to be an able and thoroughly experienced seaman.'

A cloud passed over Danglars' brow.

'Your pardon, Monsieur Morrel,' said Dantès, approaching. 'Now that the boat is anchored, I am at your service. I believe you called me.'

Danglars retreated a step or two.

'I wished to know the reason of the delay off Elba.'

'I am unaware of the reason, monsieur; I only followed the last instructions of Captain Leclère, who, when dying, gave me a packet for the Maréchal Bertrand.'

'And did you see the Maréchal?'

'Yes.'

Morrel glanced around him and then drew Dantès on one side.

'How is the Emperor?' he asked eagerly.

'Very well, so far as I could see. He came into the Maréchal's room while I was there.'

'Dantès,' Morrel said, 'you were quite right in carrying out Captain Leclère's instructions and putting in at the Isle of Elba, though if it were known that you delivered a packet to the Maréchal and talked with the Emperor you might get into trouble.'

'How so?' said Dantès. 'I don't even know what the packet contained, and the Emperor merely made such inquiries as he would of any newcomer. But excuse me, monsieur, for one moment. Here are the medical and customs officers coming on board.'

As the young man departed Danglars approached.

'Well,' said he, 'it would seem that he has given you good reasons for dropping anchor off Porto Ferrajo?'

'Most satisfactory ones, dear Monsieur Danglars.'

'So much the better,' replied the purser, 'for it is never pleasant to see a comrade neglect his duty.'

'Dantès certainly did his, and there is nothing more to be said on the matter. It was Captain Leclère who ordered him to call at Elba.'

'Talking of Captain Leclère, hasn't Dantès given you a letter from him?'

'No, was there one for me?'

'I think that, in addition to the packet, Captain Leclère gave him a letter.'

'What packet do you mean, Danglars?'

'The one Dantès delivered at Porto Ferrajo.'

'How do you know that he had a packet for Porto Ferrajo?'

Danglars turned red.

'I was passing the captain's door, which was ajar, and saw him give Dantès the packet and the letter.'

'He has not mentioned a letter to me, but if he has one I have no doubt he will give it to me.'

'Then, Monsieur Morrel, pray don't mention it to Dantès. Perhaps I am mistaken.'

Just then the young man returned and Danglars retreated as before.

'Well, Dantès, have you finished now?'

'Yes, monsieur.'

'Then you can come and dine with us?'

'I beg you to excuse me, Monsieur Morrel. I owe my first visit to my father. All the same, I greatly appreciate the honour you pay me.'

'You are quite right, Dantès. I know you are a good son. But after this first visit has been paid, may we count on you?'

'Once more I must ask you to excuse me, Monsieur Morrel. There is yet another visit which I am most anxious to pay.'

'True, Dantès; I had forgotten that there is at the Catalans someone who is awaiting you with as much impatience as your father – the fair Mercédès.'

Dantès smiled.

'Well, well!' said the shipowner. 'Now I understand why she came to me three times for news of the

Pharaon. Upon my word, Edmond, you are to be envied: she is a handsome girl. But don't let me keep you any longer. You have looked after my affairs so well that it is but your due that you should now have time to look after your own. Are you in need of money?'

'No, thank you, monsieur, I have all my pay from the voyage; that is nearly three months' salary.'

'You are a careful fellow, Edmond.'

'Say rather that I have a poor father.'

'Yes, yes, I know you are a good son. Off you go to your father. I too have a son, and I should be very angry with anyone who kept him away from me after a three months' voyage.'

'I have your leave, monsieur?' said the young man, saluting. 'But that reminds me, I shall have to ask you for a fortnight's leave.'

'To get married?'

'First of all, and then for a journey to Paris.'

'Very well, take what time you need. It will take us quite six weeks to unload the cargo, and we shall not be ready to put to sea again for another three months. But you must be back in three months, for the *Pharaon* cannot sail without her captain,' he added, patting the young sailor on the back.

'Without her captain, did you say?' cried Dantès, his eyes sparkling with joy. 'Oh, if you really mean that, monsieur, you are touching on my fondest hopes. Is it really your intention to make me captain of the *Pharaon*?'

'If it depended on me alone, my dear Dantès, I should give you my hand saying, "It is settled," but I have a partner. But half the battle is won since you already have my vote. Leave it to me to get my partner's for you. Now, off you go; I shall remain here awhile and go over the accounts with Danglars. By the by, were you satisfied with him on the voyage?'

'That depends on what you mean by that question. If you mean as comrade I must say no, for I do not think he has been my friend ever since the day I was foolish enough to propose to him that we should stop for ten minutes at the Isle of Monte Cristo to settle a little dispute. I never ought to have made the suggestion, and he was quite right in refusing. If you mean as purser I have nothing to say against him, and I think you will be satisfied with the way in which he has discharged his duties.'

Thereupon the young sailor jumped into the boat, seated himself in the stern and ordered the oarsmen to put him ashore at the Cannebière. With a smile on his lips M. Morrel glanced after him till he saw him jump ashore.

On turning round the shipowner saw Danglars standing behind him. The latter, who appeared to be awaiting his orders, was in reality, like him, following the movements of the young sailor. But how different was the expression in the eyes of each of these two men as they gazed after Dantès' retreating figure!

2

Let us leave Danglars struggling with his feeling of hatred and trying to whisper some evil insinuation against his comrade into their master's ear, and let us follow Dantès, who, after having run along the Cannebière, turned down the Rue Noailles. Here he entered a small house situated to the left of the Allées de Meilhan, ran up the four flights of dark stairs, and, trembling with excitement, stopped before a half-open door which revealed the interior of the little room.

It was the room which Dantès' father inhabited.

The news of the *Pharaon*'s arrival had not yet reached the old man, who was mounted on a chair, and, with a hand trembling with old age, was busy staking some nasturtiums that, intermingled with clematis, climbed up the trellis before his window. Suddenly he felt an arm thrown round him, and a well-known voice called out:

'Father, my dear old Dad!'

With a cry of joy the old man turned round and saw his son; pale and visibly trembling, he threw his arms round him.

'What ails you, Father?' the young man anxiously inquired. 'Are you ill?'

'No, no! my dear Edmond . . . my boy . . . my son . . . not at all, but I was not expecting you, and the joy at suddenly seeing you again has given me rather a shock.'

'Well, calm yourself, Father, it is really I. They say that joy never harms anyone, so I came in without any warning. I have come back and we are going to be happy together.'

'That's right, my boy,' replied the old man, 'but in what way are we going to be happy? You are not going to leave me any more? Come, now, tell me how you have fared.'

'May God forgive me that I should rejoice in good fortune brought about by another's death! Goodness knows, I never sought it. It has happened and I have not the strength to regret it. Our good old Captain Leclère is dead, Father, and it is probable that with Monsieur Morrel's assistance I shall take his place. Do you understand, Father? A captain at twenty, with a salary of a hundred louis, besides a share in the profits! Isn't it really more than a poor sailor like me could hope for?'

'Yes, my son, yes, it certainly is,' said the old man.

'With my first pay I shall buy you a little house with a garden where you can plant your clematis, your nasturtiums, and your honeysuckle. But, Father, what *is* the matter? You don't look well.'

'It is nothing, it will soon pass,' said the old man; but his strength failed him and he fell backwards.

'This will never do!' exclaimed the youth. 'A glass of wine will soon put you right. Tell me where you keep it,' he continued, opening one cupboard after another.

'It is useless to look for it,' said the old man. 'There is no wine.'

'What? No wine?' said the young man, turning pale and looking first at the old man's sunken and pallid cheeks and then at the bare cupboards. 'No wine? Have you been in want of money, Father?'

'I have not wanted for anything now that you are here,' said the old man.

'Yet,' stammered Edmond, wiping the perspiration from his brow, 'yet when I went away three months ago I left you two hundred francs.'

'True enough, but you forgot a little debt you owed

to our neighbour Caderousse. He reminded me of it, and told me that if I did not pay it for you he would go to Monsieur Morrel for the money. Fearing that might do you harm, I paid it for you.'

'But,' cried Dantès, 'I owed Caderousse a hundred and forty francs. Do you mean to say that you paid him that sum out of the two hundred francs I left you?'

The old man nodded.

'So that you have lived for three months on sixty francs?'

'You know that I require very little.'

'May God forgive me!' cried Edmond, throwing himself on his knees before his father. 'Here, Father, take some money, take some and send for something good to eat and drink.' So saying, he emptied the contents of his pockets on to the table – a dozen pieces of gold, five or six crowns, and some smaller coins.

His father's face brightened. 'Whose is that?' said he.

'Mine . . . yours . . . ours! Take some, buy some provisions and be happy, for we shall have some more tomorrow.'

'Gently, gently,' said the old man, smiling. 'If you don't mind, I shall spend your money warily. If people see me buying too many things at a time, they will think I have had to wait for your return before buying them. But hush! Here comes someone; it is Caderousse, who has no doubt heard of your arrival, and has come to welcome you home.'

At that moment Caderousse entered. He was a man of five- or six-and-twenty, with a mass of black hair. He carried in his hand a piece of cloth which, in his capacity of tailor, he was going to turn into a coat-lining.

'So you have come back, Edmond?' he said with a strong Marseilles accent, and with a broad smile that disclosed teeth as white as ivory.

'Yes, as you perceive, neighbour Caderousse, and ready to serve you in any way,' Dantès answered, but ill concealing his coldness by these civil words.

'Thank you. Happily I am not in need of anything; it is sometimes others who have need of my assistance.' Dantès made a slight movement. 'I don't mean that for you, boy; I lent you money and you returned it. That was but a neighbourly action and we are now quits.'

'We are never quits with those who oblige us,' said Dantès, 'when we no longer owe them money we owe them gratitude.'

'Why speak of it? What is past is gone and done with. Let us talk of your happy return. It would appear that you have had a stroke of luck and are already well in Monsieur Morrel's good books.'

'Monsieur Morrel has always been very kind to me.'

'In that case you were wrong to refuse to dine with him.'

'What? Refuse to dine with him!' exclaimed old Dantès. 'So he asked you to dinner, did he?'

'Yes, Father,' returned Edmond, with a smile, 'because, you know, I wanted to come to you as soon as possible.'

'I don't suppose your dear kind Monsieur Morrel was over-pleased at that,' said Caderousse, 'and of course when a man aims at being captain he mustn't offend his employer. You should butter him up a bit.'

'Oh! I hope to be captain without doing that,' replied Dantès.

'Capital! That will please your old friends, and I know someone who won't be sorry to hear it.'

'Do you mean Mercédès?' said the old man.

'Yes,' Edmond replied. 'And now that I have seen you, Father, and assured myself that you are well and want for nothing, I will ask your permission to leave you for a time. I am anxious to see Mercédès.'

'Go, my son, go,' said old Dantès. 'And may God bless you in your wife as He has blessed me in my son.'

Edmond took leave of his father, nodded to Caderousse, and went out. Caderousse waited a few minutes, and then he also descended the stairs and joined Danglars, who had been waiting for him at the corner of the Rue Senac.

'Well,' said Danglars, 'did you see him?'

'I have just left him,' said Caderousse.

'Did he speak of his hopes of becoming captain?'

'He spoke as if it were quite settled.'

'Patience,' said Danglars; 'it seems to me he is in too much of a hurry.'

'But I believe Monsieur Morrel has even promised him the captaincy.'

'Pooh!' said Danglars. 'He is not captain yet! Is he still in love with the beautiful Catalan?'

'Head over ears! He has just gone to see her, but if I am not greatly mistaken there is a storm brewing in that direction.'

'What do you mean?'

'I do not know anything for certain, but I have seen things which make me think that the future captain will not have it all his own way up at the Vieilles-Infirmeries.'

'What have you seen?'

'Every time that Mercédès has come to town lately, she has been accompanied by a tall young Catalan with black eyes and red complexion who seems very attentive to her, and whom she addresses as cousin.'

'Really! And do you think he is making love to her?'

'I suppose so. What else would a man of twenty-one be doing with a beautiful young girl of seventeen?'

'And you say Dantès has gone to the Catalans?'

'He left before me.'

'Let us go in the same direction; we can turn in at La Réserve and await events over a glass of wine.'

3

About a hundred paces from the spot where the two friends were sitting sipping their wine the village of the Catalans rose behind a bare hill, exposed to the fierce sun and swept by the biting north-west wind.

One day a mysterious colony set out from Spain and landed on the narrow strip of land which they inhabit to this very day. No one knew whence they came or what tongue they spoke. One of their chiefs who could speak a little Provençal solicited from the commune of Marseilles the bare and barren promontory on which they, like the sailors of ancient times, had run their boats ashore. Their request was granted, and three months later, there arose a little village.

We would ask our readers to follow us along the only street of this little hamlet and enter with us one of its tiny houses. A young and beautiful girl, with hair as black as jet and eyes of the velvety softness of the gazelle, was standing leaning against the wall. Three steps away a young man of about twenty years of age was sitting tilting his chair and leaning his elbow on an old worm-eaten piece of furniture. He was looking at the girl with an air which betrayed both vexation and uneasiness; his eyes questioned her, but the girl's firm and steady gaze checked him.

'Mercédès,' said the young man, 'Easter is nearly round again, and it is just the right time for a wedding. Give me an answer, do!'

'I have answered you a hundred times, Fernand. I really think you must be your own enemy that you should ask me again. I have never encouraged you in your hopes, Fernand. I have always said to you: "I am fond of you as a brother, but never ask anything more of me. My heart belongs to another." Haven't I always told you that, Fernand?'

'Yes, I know, Mercédès. I know that you have always been cruelly frank with me.'

'Fernand,' Mercédès answered, shaking her head, 'a woman becomes a bad housekeeper and cannot even be sure of remaining a good wife when she loves another than her husband. Be satisfied with my friendship, for, I repeat it once more, this is all I can promise you.'

Fernand rose from his seat, walked round the room, and returned to Mercédès, standing before her with scowling brows.

'Tell me once more, Mercédès; is this your final answer?'

'I love Edmond Dantès,' the girl answered coldly, 'and none other shall be my husband.'

'You will always love him?'

'As long as I live.'

Fernand bowed his head in defeat, heaving a sigh resembling a groan, and then, suddenly raising his head, hissed between his clenched teeth:

'But if he is dead?'

'If he is dead I too shall die.'

'But if he forgets you?'

'Mercédès!' cried a gladsome voice outside the door. 'Mercédès!'

'Ah!' the girl exclaimed, blushing with joy and love. 'You see he has not forgotten me since here he is!'

And she ran towards the door, which she opened, calling:

'Here, Edmond, here I am!'

Fernand, pale and trembling, recoiled like a wayfarer at the sight of a snake, and, finding a chair, sat down on it.

Edmond and Mercédès fell into each other's arms. The fierce Marseilles sun which penetrated the room through the open door covered them with a flood of light. At first they saw nothing around them. Their intense happiness isolated them from the rest of the world. Suddenly Edmond became aware of the gloomy countenance of Fernand peering out of the shadows, pale and menacing, and instinctively the young man put his hand to the knife at his belt.

'I beg your pardon,' said Dantès, 'I did not perceive that there were three of us here.' Then, turning to Mercédès, he asked, 'Who is this gentleman?'

'He will be your best friend, Dantès, for he is my

friend. He is my cousin Fernand, the man whom, after you, I love best in the world. Don't you recognize him?'

'Ah, so it is!' Edmond said, and, still keeping Mercédès' hand clasped in his, he held the other one out in all friendliness to the Catalan. Instead, however, of responding to this show of cordiality Fernand remained mute and motionless as a statue. Edmond cast an inquiring glance at the agitated and trembling Mercédès, and then at Fernand, who stood there gloomy and forbidding.

This glance told him all, and his brow became suffused with anger.

'I did not hasten thus to your side to find an enemy here, Mercédès.'

'An enemy?' Mercédès cried, with an angry look at her cousin. 'An enemy in my house, did you say, Edmond? You have no enemy here. Fernand, my brother, is not your enemy. He will grasp your hand in token of devoted friendship.'

So saying, Mercédès fixed the young Catalan with an imperious look, and, as though mesmerized, he slowly approached Edmond and held out his hand. Like a powerless though furious wave his hatred had broken against the ascendancy which this girl exercised over him.

But no sooner had he touched Dantès' hand than he felt he had done all that was within his power; he turned tail and fled out of the house.

'Oh!' he cried out, running along like one demented and tearing his hair. 'How can I get rid of this fellow? Poor, wretched fool that I am!'

'Hey, Fernand, where are you running to?' a voice called out.

The young man suddenly stopped, turned round, and perceived Caderousse seated at a table in an arbour of a tavern with Danglars.

'Why don't you join us?' said Caderousse. 'Are you in such a hurry that you cannot wait to pass the time of the day with your friends?'

'Especially when those friends have got a full bottle before them,' Danglars added.

Fernand looked at the two men as though dazed, and answered not a word. Then he wiped away the perspiration that was coursing down his face, and slowly entered the arbour. The cool shade of the place seemed to restore him to calmness and brought a feeling of relief to his exhausted body. He uttered a groan that was almost a sob, and let his head fall on to his arms crossed on the table.

'Shall I tell you what you look like, Fernand?' said Caderousse, opening the conversation with that frank brutality which the lower classes show when their curiosity gets the upper hand of them. 'You look like a rejected lover!' And he accompanied his little jest with a coarse laugh.

'What are you saying?' said Danglars. 'A man of his good looks is never unlucky in love. You've made a bad shot this time, Caderousse!'

'Not at all. Just listen to his sighs. Come, Fernand, raise your head and give us an answer. It is not polite to give no reply when friends inquire about your health.'

'I am quite well,' said Fernand, without raising his head.

'Ah, you see, Danglars,' Caderousse said, winking at his friend. 'This is how the land lies. Fernand, whom you see here and who is one of the bravest and best of the Catalans, to say nothing of being one of the best fishermen in Marseilles, is in love with a pretty girl called Mercédès; unfortunately, however, this fair damsel appears to be in love with the mate of the *Pharaon*, and as the *Pharaon* put into port today . . . well, you understand.'

'And what of it?' said Fernand, raising his head and looking at Caderousse as if he would vent his anger on him. 'Mercédès is tied to no man, and is free to love anyone she likes, isn't she?'

'Of course, if you take it like that, it is quite a different matter, but I thought you were a Catalan and I have always been told that a Catalan is not a man to be supplanted by a rival; it has even been said that Fernand is terrible in his vengeance.'

'Poor fellow!' Danglars exclaimed, pretending to feel a great pity for the young man. 'You see, he did not expect Dantès to return in this way without giving any warning. Perhaps he thought him dead or even faithless.'

'When is the wedding to take place?' asked Caderousse, on whom the fumes of the wine were beginning to take effect.

'The date is not yet fixed,' Fernand mumbled.

'No, but it will be, as surely as Dantès will be captain of the *Pharaon*, eh, Danglars?'

'Ah, well,' said Danglars, filling the glasses, 'let us drink to Captain Edmond Dantès, husband of the beautiful Catalan!'

Caderousse raised his glass to his mouth with a trembling hand and emptied it at one gulp. Fernand took his glass and dashed it to the ground.

'Look there!' hiccuped Caderousse. 'What do I see on the top of the hill yonder near the Catalans? I seem to see two lovers walking side by side and clasping hands. Heaven forgive us! They have no idea we can see them, for they are actually kissing!'

Danglars did not lose one agonized expression on Fernand's face.

'Do you know them, Monsieur Fernand?' he asked.

'Yes,' the latter answered in a husky voice. 'It is Monsieur Edmond and Mademoiselle Mercédès.'

'You don't mean to say so!' said Caderousse. 'Fancy my not recognizing them! Hallo, Dantès! Hallo, fair damsel! Come here and tell us when the wedding is to be, for Monsieur Fernand is so obstinate that he won't say a word.'

Danglars looked first at the one and then at the other of the two men: the one intoxicated with drink, the other mad with love.

'I shall not get any further with these two fools,' he murmured. 'Dantès will certainly carry the day; he will marry that fair damsel, become captain, and have the laugh over us, unless . . .' – a livid smile was seen to pass over his lips – 'unless I set to work.'

'Hallo,' Caderousse continued to call out, half out of his seat and banging on the table. 'Hi, there! Edmond, don't you recognize your friends, or are you too proud to speak to them?'

'No, my dear fellow, I am not proud, but I am in love, and I believe love is more apt to make one blind than pride is.'

'Bravo! A good excuse!' Caderousse said. 'Good day, Madame Dantès!'

Mercédès curtsied gravely and said: 'That is not yet

my name, and in my country it is looked upon as bringing bad luck when a girl is given her sweetheart's name before he has become her husband. Call me Mercédès, if you please.'

'I suppose your wedding will take place at once, Monsieur Dantès?' said Danglars, bowing to the young couple.

'As soon as possible, Monsieur Danglars. All the preliminaries will be arranged with my father today, and tomorrow or the day after at the latest we shall give the betrothal feast at La Réserve here, at which we hope to see all our friends. You are invited, Monsieur Danglars, as also you, Caderousse, and you of course, Fernand.'

Fernand opened his mouth in answer, but his voice died in his throat and he could not say a single word.

'The preliminaries today . . . tomorrow the betrothal feast . . . to be sure, you are in a great hurry, captain.'

'Danglars,' Edmond said smiling, 'I repeat what Mercédès said to Caderousse just now. Do not give me the title that does not yet belong to me. It brings bad luck.'

'I beg your pardon. I simply meant that you seemed to be in a great hurry. Why, there's plenty of time. The *Pharaon* won't put out to sea for another three months.'

'One is always in a hurry to be happy, Monsieur Danglars, for when one has been suffering for a long time it is difficult to believe in one's good fortune. But it is not selfishness alone that prompts me to press this matter. I have to go to Paris.'

'You are going on business?'

'Not on my own account. I have a last commission

of Captain Leclère's to execute. You understand, Danglars, it is sacred. But you can put your mind at rest. I shall go straight there and back again.'

'Yes, yes, I understand,' said Danglars aloud. Then to himself he said: 'To Paris? No doubt to deliver the letter the Maréchal gave him. Better and better! This letter has given me an excellent idea. Ah, Dantès, my friend, you are not yet entered in the *Pharaon*'s log book as number one.' Then, turning to Edmond, who was moving away, he called out, '*Bon voyage!*'

'Thank you,' Edmond replied, turning round and giving him a friendly nod.

Then the two lovers went on their way, peaceful and happy, while the three men continued their interesting conversation.

4

The next day was gloriously fine. The sun rose red and resplendent, its first rays tinting the fleecy clouds with many delicate and brilliant hues. The festive board had been prepared in a large room at La Réserve, with whose arbour we are already acquainted. Although the meal was fixed for noon, the tavern had been filled with impatient guests since eleven o'clock. They consisted chiefly of some of the favoured sailors of the *Pharaon*, and several soldier friends of Dantès'. In order to do honour to the happy couple they had all donned their finest clothes. To crown all, M. Morrel had determined to favour the occasion with his presence, and on his arrival he was greeted with hearty cheers from the sailors of the *Pharaon*. Their owner's presence was to them a confirmation of the report that Dantès was to be their captain, and, as he was popular with them all, they wished to show their owner, by this means, their appreciation of the fact that by a stroke of good luck his choice coincided with their wishes on the subject.

No sooner had the bridal party arrived than the dishes were handed round. Arles sausages, brown of meat and piquant of flavour, lobsters and prawns in brilliant red shells, sea-urchins whose prickly exteriors resemble chestnuts just fallen from the trees, cockles esteemed by the epicure of the South as surpassing the oyster of the North, in fact every delicacy which the sea washes up on to the sandy beach, and which the fishermen call sea-fruit.

'What a silent party!' old Dantès remarked as he caught a whiff of the fragrant yellow wine that old Pamphile himself had just put before Mercédès. 'Who would think there are thirty light-hearted and merry people assembled here!'

'A husband is not always light-hearted,' Caderousse replied.

'The fact is,' said Dantès, 'at the present moment I am too happy to be gay. If that is what you mean by your remark, neighbour Caderousse, you are quite right. Joy has that peculiar effect that at times it oppresses us just as much as grief.'

Danglars looked at Fernand, whose impressionable nature was keenly alive to every emotion.

'Well, I never!' said he. 'Are you anticipating trouble? It seems to me you have everything you can desire.'

'That is just what alarms me,' said Dantès. 'I cannot help thinking it is not man's lot to attain happiness so easily. Good fortune is like the palaces of the enchanted isles, the gates of which were guarded by dragons. Happiness could only be obtained by overcoming these dragons, and I, I know not how I have deserved the honour of becoming Mercédès' husband.'

'Husband?' said Caderousse, laughing. 'Nay, captain, not yet.'

'It is true,' Dantès said, 'that Mercédès is not yet my wife, but . . .' here he pulled out his watch – 'she will be in an hour and a half. Yes, my friends, thanks to the influence of Monsieur Morrel, to whom, after my father, I owe all I possess, every difficulty has been removed. We have got a special licence, and at half-past two the Mayor of Marseilles will be awaiting us at the Hôtel de Ville. As it has just struck a quarter-past one I think I am quite right in saying that in another hour and thirty minutes Mercédès will have changed her name to Madame Dantès.'

Fernand closed his eyes, for they gave him a burning pain; he leant against the table to save himself from falling, but in spite of his effort he could not restrain a groan, which, however, was lost amid the noisy congratulations of the company.

'This feast, then, is not in honour of your betrothal, as we supposed, but is your wedding breakfast?'

'Not at all,' said Dantès. 'I leave for Paris tomorrow morning. I shall be back again in nine days on the 1st of March. We will have our real wedding breakfast the very next day.'

At this moment Danglars noticed that Fernand, on whom he had kept an observant eye and who was seated at the window overlooking the street, suddenly opened his haggard eyes, rose with a convulsive movement and staggered back on to his seat. Almost at the same moment a confused noise was heard on the stairs. The tread of heavy steps and the hubbub of many voices, together with the clanking of swords and military accoutrements, drowned the merry voices of the bridal party. The laughter died away. An ominous silence fell on all as the noise drew nearer, and when three peremptory knocks resounded on the door, they looked at each other with uneasy glances.

'Open in the name of the law!' cried an authoritative voice.

The door opened, and a police commissary entered, followed by four armed soldiers and a corporal.

'What is all this about?' the shipowner asked, advancing toward the commissary, whom he knew. 'I fear there must be some mistake.'

'If there is a mistake, Monsieur Morrel,' the commissary replied, 'you may rest assured that it will be promptly put right. In the meantime I am the bearer of a warrant for arrest, and, though I regret the task assigned me, it must nevertheless be carried out. Which of you gentlemen answers to the name of Edmond Dantès?'

Every eye was turned on the young man as he stepped forward, obviously agitated, but with great dignity of bearing, and said:

'I do, monsieur. What do you want of me?'

'Edmond Dantès, I arrest you in the name of the law.'

'You arrest me?' said Dantès, changing colour. 'Why, I pray?'

'I know not, monsieur. Your first examination will give you all the information on that score.'

Resistance was useless, but old Dantès did not comprehend this. There are certain things the heart of a father or a mother will never understand. He threw himself at the officer's feet and begged and implored, but his tears and supplications were of no avail.

'There is no call for alarm, monsieur,' the commissary said at last, touched by the old man's despair. 'Perhaps your son has but neglected to carry out some customs formality or health regulation, in which case he will probably be released as soon as he has given the desired information.'

In the meantime Dantès, with a smile on his face, had shaken hands with all his friends and had surrendered himself to the officer, saying:

'Do not be alarmed. You may depend on it there is some mistake which will probably be cleared up even before I reach the prison.'

'To be sure. I am ready to vouch for your innocence,' Danglars said as he joined the group round the prisoner.

Dantès descended the stairs preceded by the police officer and surrounded by soldiers. A carriage stood at the door. He got in, followed by two soldiers and the commissary. The door was shut, and the carriage took the road back to Marseilles.

'Goodbye, Edmond, oh, my Edmond! Goodbye!' Mercédès called out, leaning over the balcony.

The prisoner heard these last words sobbed from his sweetheart's breast, and, putting his head out of the window, simply called out: '*Au revoir*, my Mercédès!'

The carriage then disappeared round the corner of Fort Saint-Nicholas.

'Await me here,' M. Morrel said to the rest of the party. 'I shall get the first carriage I can find to take me to Marseilles, and shall bring you back news.'

The guests, who had been making merry but a short time before, now gave way to a feeling of terror. They feverishly discussed the arrest from every point of view. Danglars was loud in his assertion that it was merely a trifling case of suspected smuggling: the customs officials had been aboard the *Pharaon* during their absence and something had aroused their suspicion. But Mercédès felt, rather than knew, that the arrest had some deeper significance. She suddenly gave way to a wild fit of sobbing.

'Come, come, my child, do not give up hope,' said old Dantès, hardly knowing what he was saying.

'A carriage! A carriage!' cried one of the guests, who had stayed on the balcony on the look-out. 'It is Monsieur Morrel. Cheer up! He is no doubt bringing us good news.'

Mercédès and the old father rushed out to the door to meet the shipowner. The latter entered, looking very grave.

'My friends,' he said, with a gloomy shake of the head, 'it is a far more serious matter than we supposed.'

'Oh, Monsieur Morrel,' Mercédès exclaimed. 'I know he is innocent!'

'I also believe in his innocence,' replied the shipowner, 'but he is accused of being an agent of the Bonapartist faction!'

Fernand, who had now become the horror-stricken girl's only protector, led her home, while some of Edmond's friends took charge of the broken-hearted father.

'Would you have believed it, Danglars?' M. Morrel asked as he hastened to the town with his purser and Caderousse in the hopes of receiving direct news of Edmond through his acquaintance, M. de Villefort, the Deputy of the Procureur du Roi.

'Why, monsieur, you may perhaps remember I told you that Dantès anchored off the Isle of Elba without any apparent reason. I had my suspicions at the time.'

'Did you mention these suspicions to anyone but myself?'

'God forbid,' exclaimed Danglars.

'Poor Dantès!' said Caderousse. 'He's the right sort, and that's a fact.'

'Quite agreed,' said M. Morrel, 'but in the meantime the *Pharaon* is captainless.'

'We cannot put to sea for another three months,' Danglars added, 'and it is to be hoped that Dantès will be released before then.'

'No doubt, but in the meantime . . .?'

'I am at your service. You know that I am as capable of managing a ship as the most experienced captain. Then when Dantès comes out of prison, he can take his post and I will resume mine.'

'Thanks, Danglars, that would be a way out of the difficulty. I therefore authorize you to assume command of the *Pharaon* and superintend the loading of the cargo. No matter what misfortune befalls any one of us, we cannot let business suffer.' So saying, he proceeded in the direction of the law courts.

'So far everything is succeeding wonderfully,' Danglars said to himself. 'I am already temporary captain, and if that fool of a Caderousse can be persuaded to hold his tongue, I shall soon have the job for good and all.'

5

Young M. de Villefort was not the Procureur du Roi, though as the Deputy he expected to succeed to that position before long, especially since his fiancée, Mademoiselle de Saint-Méran, was not only a rare beauty but came from an influential royalist family. The Procureur du Roi was absent, however, when the anonymous letter accusing Edmond Dantès of a Bonapartist conspiracy was delivered to his office; it was opened by his secretary and then taken round to the house where young Gérard de Villefort was also enjoying his betrothal party. Villefort made his excuses and left the party, promising to return as soon as possible. Meanwhile the prisoner was escorted to the young lawyer's house.

M. Morrel met Villefort on the street outside the house.

'Ah, Monsieur de Villefort,' he cried, 'I am very fortunate in meeting you. A most extraordinary and unaccountable mistake has been made: the mate of my ship, a certain Edmond Dantès, has just been arrested.'

'I know,' Villefort made answer, 'and I am on my way to examine him.'

'Oh, monsieur!' M. Morrel continued, carried away by his friendship for the young man. 'You do not know the accused, but I do. He is the gentlest and most trustworthy man imaginable, and I don't hesitate to say he is the best seaman in the whole mercantile service. Oh, Monsieur de Villefort, with all my heart I commend him to your kindly consideration.'

'You may rest assured, monsieur, that you will not have appealed to me in vain if the prisoner is innocent, but if, on the contrary, he is guilty – we live in a difficult age, monsieur, when it would be a fatal thing to be lenient – in that case I shall be compelled to do my duty.'

As he had just arrived at his own house beside the law courts, he entered with a lordly air, after having saluted with icy politeness the unhappy shipowner, who stood petrified on the spot where Villefort had left him.

The antechamber was full of gendarmes and policemen, and in their midst stood the prisoner, carefully guarded.

Villefort crossed the room, threw a glance at Dantès, and, after taking a packet of papers from one of the gendarmes, disappeared. His first impression of the young man was favourable, but he had been warned so often against trusting first impulses that he applied the maxim to the term impression, forgetting the difference between the two words. He therefore stifled the feelings of pity that were uppermost in his heart, assumed the expression which he reserved for important occasions, and sat down at his desk with a frown on his brow.

'Bring in the prisoner.'

An instant later Dantès was before him. Saluting his judge with an easy politeness, he looked round for a seat as if he were in M. Morrel's drawing-room.

'Who are you, and what is your name?' asked Villefort, as he fingered the papers which he received from the police officer on his entry.

'My name is Edmond Dantès,' replied the young man calmly. 'I am mate of the *Pharaon*, owned by Messrs Morrel and Son.'

'What were you doing when you were arrested?'

'I was at my betrothal breakfast, monsieur,' the young man said, and his voice trembled slightly as he thought of the contrast between those happy moments and the painful ordeal he was now undergoing.

'You were at your betrothal feast?' the Deputy said, shuddering in spite of himself.

'Yes, monsieur. I am about to marry a woman I have loved for three years.'

Villefort, impassive though he usually was, was struck with this coincidence; and the passionate voice of Dantès, who had been seized in the midst of his happiness, touched a sympathetic chord in his own heart. He also was about to be married, he also was happy, and his happiness had been interrupted in order that he might kill the happiness of another.

'Now I want all the information in your possession,' he said. 'Have you served under the usurper Bonaparte?'

'I was about to be drafted into the marines when he fell.'

'I have been told you have extreme political views,' said Villefort, who had never been told anything of the kind but was not sorry to put forward the statement in the form of an accusation.

'Extreme political views, monsieur? Alas! I am almost ashamed to say it, but I have never had what one calls a view. I am barely nineteen years of age.

I know nothing, for I am not destined to play any great *role* in life. The little I am and ever shall be, if I am given the position I desire, I owe to Monsieur Morrel. My opinions, I do not say political, but private, are limited to these three sentiments: I love my father, I respect Monsieur Morrel, and I adore Mercédès. That, monsieur, is all I have to tell you. You see for yourself that it is not very interesting.'

As Dantès spoke, Villefort looked at his genial and frank countenance, and, with his experience of crime and criminals, he recognized that every word Dantès spoke convinced him of his innocence.

'This is indeed a charming young man,' Villefort said to himself, but aloud he said: 'Have you any enemies?'

'Enemies, monsieur? My position is happily not important enough to make me any enemies. As regards my character, I am perhaps too hasty, but I always try to curb my temper in my dealings with my subordinates. I have ten or twelve sailors under me: if you ask them, monsieur, you will find that they love and respect me, not as a father, for I am too young, but as an elder brother.'

'Perhaps you have no enemies, but you may have aroused feelings of jealousy. At the early age of nineteen you are about to receive a captaincy, you are going to marry a beautiful girl who loves you; these two pieces of good fortune may have been the cause of envy.'

'You are right. No doubt you understand men better than I do, and possibly it is so, but if any of my friends cherish any such envious feelings towards me, I would rather not know lest my friendship should turn into hatred.'

'You are wrong; you should always strive to see clearly around you, and indeed, you seem such a worthy young man that I am going to depart from the ordinary rule by showing you the denunciation which has brought you before me. Here is the paper. Do you recognize the writing?'

So saying, Villefort took the letter from his pocket and handed it to Dantès. Dantès looked at it and read it. His brow darkened as he said:

'No, monsieur, I do not know this writing. It is disguised and yet it is very plainly written. At any rate it is a clever hand that wrote it. I am very lucky,' he continued, looking at Villefort with an expression of gratitude, 'in having you to examine me, for there can be no doubt that this envious person is indeed my enemy.'

And the light that shone in the young man's eyes as he said this revealed to Villefort how much energy and deep feeling lay concealed beneath his apparent gentleness.

'Very well, then,' said the Deputy, 'answer me quite frankly, not as a prisoner before his judge, but as a man in a false position to another man who has his interest at heart. What truth is there in this anonymous accusation?'

'It is partly true and partly false, monsieur. Here is the plain truth. I swear it by my honour as a sailor, by my love for Mercédès, and by my father's life! When we left Naples, Captain Leclère fell ill of brain-fever; as we had no doctor on board and as he would not put in at any port, since he was very anxious to reach Elba, he became so very ill that towards the end of the third day, feeling that he was dying, he called me to him.

"My dear Dantès," he said, "swear to me on your honour that you will do what I bid you, for it is a matter of the utmost importance."

'"I swear it, captain," I said.

'"After my death the command of the ship devolves upon you as mate; take command, head for the Isle of Elba, go ashore at Porto Ferrajo, ask for the Maréchal and give him this letter. You may be given another letter and be entrusted with a mission. That mission was to have been mine, Dantès, but you will carry it out in my stead and get all the glory of it."'

'What did you do then?'

'What I was bound to do, and what everyone would have done in my place. In any circumstances the requests of a dying man are sacred, but with a sailor a superior's request is an order that has to be carried out. So I headed for Elba, where I arrived the next day. I gave orders for everybody to remain on board while I went ashore alone. The Maréchal gave me a letter which he charged me to deliver in person at an address in Paris. I gave him my promise in accordance with the last request of my captain. I landed here, rapidly settled all the ship's business, and hastened to my betrothed, whom I found more beautiful and loving than ever. Finally, monsieur, I was partaking of my betrothal breakfast, was to have been married in an hour, and was counting on going to Paris tomorrow, when owing to this denunciation, which you seem to treat as lightly as I do, I was arrested.'

'I believe you have told me the truth,' was Villefort's answer, 'and if you have been guilty it is through imprudence, an imprudence justified by your captain's orders. Hand me the letter that was given you at Elba, give me your word of honour that you will appear directly you are summoned to do so, and you may rejoin your friends.'

'I am free, monsieur!' Dantès cried out, overcome with joy.

'Certainly, but first give me the letter.'

'It must be in front of you, monsieur. It was taken along with my other papers, and I recognize some of them in that bundle.'

'Wait a moment,' the Deputy said as Dantès was taking his hat and gloves. 'To whom was it addressed?'

'To Monsieur Noirtier, Rue Coq Héron, Paris.'

These words fell on Villefort's ears with the rapidity and unexpectedness of a thunderbolt. He sank into his chair, from which he had risen to reach the packet of letters, drew the fatal letter from the bundle and glanced over it with a look of inexpressible terror.

'Monsieur Noirtier, Rue Coq Héron, number thirteen,' he murmured, growing paler and paler. 'Have you shown this letter to anyone?'

'To no one, monsieur, on my honour!'

Villefort's brow darkened more and more. When he had finished reading the letter his head fell into his hands, and he remained thus for a moment quite overcome. After a while he composed himself and said:

'You say you do not know the contents of this letter?'

'On my honour, monsieur, I am in complete ignorance of its contents.'

Dantès waited for the next question, but no question

came. Villefort again sank into his chair, passed his hand over his brow dripping with perspiration, and read the letter for the third time.

'If he should know the contents of this letter,' he murmured, 'and if he ever gets to know that Noirtier is the father of Villefort I am lost, lost for ever!'

Indeed it was true. Villefort's father had been an enthusiastic revolutionary, and had taken the name Noirtier in preference to his former aristocratic title.

Villefort made a violent effort to pull himself together, and said in as steady a voice as possible:

'I cannot set you at liberty at once as I had hoped. I must first consult the Juge d'Instruction. You see how I have tried to help you, but I must detain you a prisoner for some time longer. I will make that time as short as possible. The principal charge against you has to do with this letter, and you see –' Villefort went to the fire, threw the letter into the flames, and remained watching it until it was reduced to ashes.

'You see,' he continued, 'I have destroyed it.'

'Oh, monsieur,' Dantès exclaimed, 'you are more than just, you are kindness itself!'

'But listen,' Villefort went on, 'after what I have done you feel you can have confidence in me, don't you? I only wish to advise you. I shall keep you here until this evening. Possibly someone else will come to examine you: in that event, repeat all that you have told me, but say not a word about this letter.'

'I promise, monsieur.'

'You understand,' he continued, 'the letter is destroyed, and you and I alone know of its existence; should you be questioned about it, firmly deny all knowledge of it, and you are saved.'

Villefort rang and the commissary entered. The Deputy whispered a few words into his ear, and the officer nodded in answer.

'Follow the commissary!' Villefort said to Dantès.

Dantès bowed, cast a look of gratitude at Villefort, and did as he was bid.

The door was hardly closed when Villefort's strength failed him, and he sank half fainting into his chair.

After a few moments he muttered to himself: 'Alas! Alas! If the Procureur du Roi had been here, if the Juge d'Instruction had been called instead of me, I should have been lost! This little bit of paper would have spelt my ruin. Oh! Father, Father, will you always stand in the way of my happiness in this world, and must I eternally fight against your past!'

Suddenly an unexpected light appeared to flash across his mind, illuminating his whole face; a smile played around his drawn mouth, and his haggard eyes became fixed as though arrested by a thought.

'The very thing!' he said. 'Yes, this letter which was to have spelt my ruin will probably make my fortune. It will be I who reveals to the king that Bonaparte is planning to leave Elba. Quick! To work, Villefort!'

6

It was four o'clock when Dantès was taken to his cell, and, as it was the 1st of March, the prisoner soon found himself in utter darkness. With loss of sight, his hearing became more acute: at the least sound he rose quickly and advanced toward the door in the firm conviction that they had come to set him free; but the noise died away in another direction and Dantès sank back on to his stool.

At last, about ten o'clock, when Dantès was beginning to lose all hope, he heard steps approaching his door. A key was turned in the lock, the bolts creaked, the massive oak door swung open, and a dazzling light from two torches flooded the cell.

By the light of these torches, Dantès saw the glittering swords and carbines of four gendarmes.

'Have you come to fetch me?' Dantès asked.

'Yes,' was the answer of one of the men.

In the belief that they came at the Deputy's orders, Dantès calmly stepped forward and placed himself in their midst. A police van was waiting at the door, the coachman was on the box, and a police officer was seated beside him. The door of the carriage was opened and Dantès was pushed in. He had neither the power nor the intention to resist and he found himself in an instant seated between two gendarmes, the other two taking their places opposite, and the heavy van lumbered away.

The van stopped at the quay, the officer got down from the box, and opened the locked door with his key; whereupon Dantès stepped out and was immediately surrounded by the four gendarmes, who led him along a path lined with soldiers to a boat which a customs-house officer held by a chain near the quay. The soldiers looked at Dantès with vacant curiosity. He was given a place in the stern of the boat and was again surrounded by the four gendarmes, whilst the officer stationed himself at the bows. The boat was shoved off, four oarsmen plied their oars vigorously, and soon Dantès found himself outside the harbour.

His first feeling on finding himself once more in the open air was one of joy, for did it not mean freedom? But the whole proceeding was incomprehensible to him.

'Where are you taking me?' he asked.

'You will know soon enough.'

'But . . .'

'We are forbidden to give you any explanation.'

Dantès knew from experience that it was useless to question a subordinate who had been forbidden to answer any questions, and he remained silent.

As he sat there, the most fantastic thoughts passed through his mind. It was not possible to undertake a long voyage in such a small boat, so perhaps they were going to take him a short distance from the coast and tell him he was free; they had not attempted to handcuff him, which he considered a good augury; besides, had not the Deputy, who had been so kind to him, told him that, provided he did not mention the fatal name of Noirtier, he had nothing to fear? Had not de Villefort destroyed the dangerous letter in his presence, the letter which was the only evidence they had against him?

Some time later, in spite of the repugnance he felt at putting fresh questions to the gendarmes, he turned to the one nearest him and said:

'Comrade, I adjure you on your honour as a soldier to have pity on me and answer! I am Captain Dantès, an honest and loyal Frenchman, though accused of treason. Where are you taking me? Tell me and on my honour as a sailor, I will submit to my fate.'

The gendarme scratched his ear and looked at his comrade. The latter made a motion with his head which seemed to say: 'I can't see any harm in telling him now'; and the gendarme, turning to Dantès, replied:

'You are a native of Marseilles and a sailor, and yet you ask us where we are heading?'

'Yes, for on my honour I do not know.'

Dantès got up and quite naturally looked in the direction the boat was moving. Before him, at a distance of a hundred fathoms, rose the black, steep rock on which stood the frowning Château d'If.

This strange pile, this prison whose very name spelt terror, rising up so suddenly before Dantès, had the effect on him that the sight of a scaffold must have on a condemned man.

'My God!' he cried. 'The Château d'If! Why are we going there?'

The gendarme smiled.

'You cannot be taking me there to imprison me?' Dantès went on. 'The Château d'If is a State prison, and is only used for important political offenders. I have committed no crime. Are there any judges or magistrates at the Château d'If?'

'As far as I know there are a governor, some gaolers, a garrison, and some good thick walls.'

'What about Monsieur de Villefort's promise?'

'I don't know anything about Monsieur de Villefort's promise; all I know is that we are going to the Château d'If.'

Quick as lightning Dantès sprang to his feet and tried to hurl himself into the sea, but four stout arms caught him before even his feet left the bottom boards of the boat. With a howl of rage he fell back. The next moment a sudden impact shook the boat from stem to stern and Dantès realized that they had arrived. His guardians forced him to land, and dragged him to the steps that led to the gate of the fortress, the police officer following him with fixed bayonet.

Dantès made no useless resistance. He saw more soldiers stationed along the slope, he felt the steps which forced him to raise his feet, he perceived that he passed under a door, and that this door closed behind him, but all his actions were mechanical and he saw as through a mist; he could distinguish nothing.

There was a moment's halt, during which he tried to collect his thoughts. He looked around him; he was in a square courtyard enclosed by four high walls; the slow and measured tread of the sentinels was heard, and each time they passed before the light which shone from within the château he saw the gleam of their musket-barrels.

They waited here about ten minutes, evidently for orders. At last a voice called out:

'Where is the prisoner?'

'Here,' one of the gendarmes replied.

'Let him follow me. I will take him to his cell.'

'Go!' said the gendarme, giving Dantès a push.

The prisoner followed his guide who led him into a subterranean room whose bare and reeking walls seemed as though impregnated with tears. A sort of lamp, standing on a stool, the wick swimming in fetid oil, illuminated the shiny walls of this terrible abode, and revealed to Dantès the features of his guide, an under-gaoler, ill-clad and of a low type.

'Here is your cell for tonight,' he said. 'It is late and

the governor is in bed. Tomorrow, when he has read the instructions regarding you, he may change your cell. In the meantime here is some bread, there is some water in the pitcher over there and some straw in the corner yonder. That is all a prisoner requires. Good night.'

Before Dantès could think of an answer, before he had noticed where the gaoler had placed the bread and the pitcher of water, or looked at the corner where lay the straw for his bed, the fellow had taken the lamp and locked the door behind him, leaving his prisoner to the darkness and silence of the gaol.

When the first rays of the sun had brought some light into the den, the gaoler returned with the information that Dantès was not to change his cell. An iron hand seemed to have nailed him to the spot where he stood the night before; he was motionless with his eyes fixed on the ground. Thus he had stood the whole night long without sleep. The gaoler advanced; Dantès did not appear to see him. He tapped him on the shoulder; Dantès shuddered and shook his head.

'Have you not slept?' asked the gaoler.

'I do not know,' was Dantès' reply.

The gaoler stared at him in astonishment.

'Are you not hungry?'

'I do not know.'

'Do you want anything?'

'I want to see the governor.'

The gaoler shrugged his shoulders and went out.

Dantès gazed after him, stretched out his hands towards the half-open door, but the door was closed upon him.

Then his whole frame was shaken with one mighty sob. The tears which choked him streamed down his cheeks; he beat his forehead against the ground; he remained a long time in prayer, and, while reviewing his past life, asked himself what crime he had committed at his tender age to merit such a cruel punishment.

The day passed thus. He scarcely touched his bread or water. At times he would sit absorbed in thought, at other times he would walk round and round his cell like a wild animal in a cage.

The next morning the gaoler again made his appearance.

'Well,' he said, 'are you more reasonable today than you were yesterday?'

Dantès made no reply.

'Come, now, don't lose heart! Is there anything I can do for you?'

'I want to speak to the governor.'

'I have already told you that is impossible,' the gaoler answered impatiently.

'Why is it impossible?'

'Because the rules of the prison do not allow it.'

'Then what is allowed here?'

'Better food if you pay for it, a walk in the courtyard, and sometimes books.'

'I don't want any books, neither do I want to walk in the courtyard, and I find my food good enough. I only desire one thing and that is to see the governor.'

'Now, look here!' said the gaoler. 'Don't go on brooding over the impossible in this way, or you will go mad before the end of a fortnight.'

'There is one thing you could do for me,' said Dantès. 'If I promise you a hundred crowns, the next time you go to Marseilles, will you go to the Catalans and give a letter to a girl named Mercédès?'

'If I were to take that letter and were found out I should lose my place, which is worth a thousand francs a year in addition to my food, so you see I should be a fool to risk a thousand francs for three hundred.'

'Very well,' said Dantès, 'but remember this. If you refuse to take my letter to Mercédès or at least to tell her that I am here, I shall one day hide behind the door and, as you enter, break your head with this stool.'

'Threats!' the gaoler called out, retreating a step and placing himself on the defensive. 'Luckily we have dungeons at the Château d'If.'

Dantès picked up the stool and swung it round his head.

'That's enough! That's enough!' the gaoler exclaimed. 'Since you insist on it, I will go and tell the governor.'

'That's better!' said Dantès, putting the stool down and sitting on it with bent head and haggard eyes as though he were really losing his senses.

The gaoler went out and returned a few minutes later with four soldiers and a corporal.

'The governor's orders are that the prisoner shall be taken to the dungeon. We must put madmen with madmen.'

The four soldiers seized Dantès, who fell into a kind of coma and followed them without resistance. He descended fifteen steps, the door of a dungeon was opened, and he entered mumbling, 'He is right, they must put madmen with madmen.'

7

Meanwhile, Villefort spent the rest of the day at his office, making urgent plans to go to Paris. Late in the evening he returned home. At his door he perceived in the shadow a white spectre waiting for him, erect and motionless. It was Mercédès. Having no news of Edmond, she had come in person to inquire the reason of her lover's arrest.

As Villefort drew near, she moved from the wall against which she had been leaning and barred his way. Dantès had spoken to the Deputy of his betrothed and he now recognized her at once. He was astonished at her beauty and dignity, and when she asked him what had become of him whom she loved he felt as though he were the culprit and she his judge.

'The man you speak of,' he said abruptly, 'is a criminal, and I can do nothing for him.'

A great sob escaped Mercédès' lips, and when Villefort tried to pass by she again stopped him.

'But tell me at least where he is,' she said, 'so that I may learn whether he is alive or dead.'

'I know not,' was the answer. 'He has passed out of my hands.'

Embarrassed by the straight look she gave him, as also by her entreaties, he pushed by her and entered his house, locking the door after him as though to shut out all sadness. But sadness is not banished so easily. He had no sooner entered his room than his legs gave way under him; he heaved a deep sigh, which was more like a sob, and sank into his chair. For a moment the man was in doubt. He had often passed sentence of death, but the condemned men who owed their execution to his crushing eloquence had not caused him the slightest compunction, for they had been guilty, or at all events Villefort had believed them to be so. But if at this moment the fair Mercédès had entered and had said to him: 'In the name of Almighty God, Who watches over us and is our judge, give me back my lover,' he would have given way and, in spite of the risk to himself, his icy-cold hand would have signed the order for Dantès' release. But no voice broke the stillness, the door opened only to admit Villefort's valet, who came to tell him that his carriage was at the door.

Poor Mercédès had returned to the Catalans, followed by Fernand. Grief-stricken and desperate, she threw herself on her bed. Fernand, kneeling by her side, took her hand, which she did not attempt to withdraw, and covered it with kisses, but she was oblivious to it all.

So passed the night. The lamp went out when the oil was consumed. Mercédès was no more aware of the darkness than she had been of the light. Day broke but she heeded it not. Grief had made her blind to all but Edmond.

M. Morrel did not give up hope: he had learnt of Dantès' imprisonment and had gone to all his friends and all the influential men of the town, but it was already reported that Dantès had been arrested as a Bonapartist, and he met with nothing but coldness, fear, or refusals, and returned home in despair.

Caderousse was restless and uneasy, but instead of trying to do something to help Dantès he had shut himself up in his house with two bottles of wine.

Danglars alone felt no pang of remorse or restlessness: he was even happy, for had he not avenged himself on an enemy and assured for himself the position on board the *Pharaon* he was in danger of losing? He was one of those calculating men who are born with a pen behind their ears and an ink-pot in place of a heart. He went to bed at the usual hour and slept peacefully.

Villefort gained entry to the King in Paris, thanks to his friend M. de Blacas. He had scarcely finished revealing the contents of the letter he had destroyed (though not the name of the person to whom it had been addressed) when the Baron Dandré, Louis XVIII's Minister of Police, burst into the room. On perceiving the Minister's agitated demeanour, Louis violently pushed back the table at which he had been sitting.

'Why, Baron,' he cried, 'what is your trouble?'

'Sire . . .' stammered the Baron.

'Well . . . go on,' replied Louis.

The Minister of Police was about to throw himself in despair at the King's feet, but the latter drew back a step and, knitting his brows, said:

'Well, are you going to speak? I command you to give me your news!'

'Sire, the usurper left Elba on the 28th of February and disembarked on the 1st of March in France, at a little port near Antibes in the Gulf of Juan.'

'The usurper disembarked in France near Antibes

in the Gulf of Juan, two hundred and fifty leagues from Paris on the 1st of March and you report it to me only on the 3rd of March?'

Louis XVIII made a movement of indescribable anger and alarm and drew himself up straight as if a sudden blow had struck him both mentally and physically.

'In France!' he cried. 'The usurper in France! Is he marching on Paris?'

'Sire, I know not. The dispatch only states that he has landed and the route he has taken,' was the Police Minister's answer.

'How did you get the dispatch?'

The Minister bowed his head while a deep colour suffused his cheeks.

'By telegraph, Sire.'

Louis XVIII took a step forward and crossed his arms as Napoleon would have done.

'So,' he said, turning pale with anger, 'seven allied armies overthrew that man; a miracle of God placed me on the throne of my fathers after an exile of twenty-five years, during which time I studied, probed, analysed the men and affairs of this France that was promised me, so that when I had attained my desires the power I held in my hand should burst and break me! What our enemies say of us is only too true. We have learnt nothing and forgotten nothing! If I had been betrayed like him, some consolation would be left to me; but to be surrounded by men whom I have raised to high dignities, who were to watch over me with more care than over themselves, who before my time were nothing, and who, when I have gone, will again be nothing and will probably perish through their own inability and ineptitude! Oh, cruel fate! And now, messieurs,' he continued, turning toward M. de Blacas and the Police Minister, 'I have no further need of you. The War Minister alone can help now.' Then suddenly turning to Baron Dandré, he asked: 'What further news have you in regard to the Rue Saint-Jacques affair?'

'Sire,' the Minister of Police replied, 'I was about to give Your Majesty the latest information on the matter when Your Majesty's attention was attracted towards this other terrible catastrophe; now these facts will not interest Your Majesty.'

'On the contrary, monsieur, on the contrary. It seems to me that this affair may have some direct connection with the other, and the death of General Quesnel will perhaps put us on the direct track of a great internal conspiracy.'

Villefort shuddered at the name of General Quesnel.

'In fact, Sire,' the Minister of Police continued, 'everything goes to show that his death was not due to suicide as was at first believed, but was the work of some assassin. Apparently General Quesnel left the precincts of a Bonapartist Club and disappeared. An unknown man had called on him in the morning and arranged a meeting in the Rue Saint-Jacques.'

While the Minister was telling his story, Villefort, who seemed to hang on his very words, turned alternately red and pale.

The King turned to him. 'Do you not share my opinion, Monsieur de Villefort, that Quesnel, who was believed to be attached to the usurper though he was in reality entirely loyal to me, was the victim of a Bonapartist trap?'

'It is very probable, Sire, but have you no further information?'

'We are on the track of the man who made the appointment with him. We have his description. He is a man of fifty to fifty-two years of age, has brown hair, dark eyes with bushy eyebrows, and wears a moustache. He was dressed in a blue coat, and in his buttonhole wore the rosette of an Officer of the Legion of Honour. Yesterday a man answering to this description was followed but was lost sight of at the corner of the Rue de la Jussienne and the Rue Coq Héron.'

Villefort leaned against the back of a chair; his legs seemed to be giving way under him, but when he heard that the unknown man had escaped his pursuers he breathed again.

'Seek this man out!' said the King to the Police Minister. 'For if, as everything leads me to suppose, General Quesnel, who would have been so useful to us now, has been the victim of a murder, I will have his assassins severely punished, be they Bonapartists or not. I will not detain you longer, Baron. Monsieur de Villefort, you must be fatigued after your long journey; go and rest. You are putting up at your father's house, no doubt?'

Villefort seemed on the point of fainting.

'No, Your Majesty,' he said, 'I am staying at the Hôtel de Madrid, in the Rue de Tournon.'

'But you will see him?'

'I think not, Sire.'

'Ah, of course!' said Louis XVIII, smiling in a manner which showed that all these questions had been put to him with a motive. 'I was forgetting that you are not on good terms with Monsieur Noirtier.

Another sacrifice to the royal cause, for which you shall be recompensed.' The King detached the cross of the Legion of Honour which he usually wore on his blue coat and, giving it to Villefort, said: 'In the meantime take this cross.'

Villefort's eyes filled with tears of joy and pride. He took the cross and kissed it.

Events followed one another very rapidly. Everyone knows the history of the famous return from Elba, a return which, unexampled as it was in the past, will probably remain unimitated in the future.

Louis XVIII made but a feeble attempt to parry the blow. The monarchy which he had but ill reconstructed trembled on its insecure foundation, and a wave of the Emperor's hand brought down with a crash the whole edifice that was naught but an unsightly mass of ancient prejudices and new ideas. Villefort therefore gained nothing from the King but a gratitude which was not only useless but dangerous at the present time, and the cross of the Legion of Honour, which he had the prudence not to display.

Napoleon would, doubtless, have dismissed Villefort but for the protection of Noirtier, who was all-powerful at the Court of the Hundred Days; the Procureur du Roi alone was deprived of his office, being under suspicion of lukewarm support of Bonaparte.

Villefort retained his post, but his marriage was postponed until happier times. If the Emperor remained on the throne, Gérard would require a different alliance and his father undertook to find this for him; if, on the contrary, a second Restoration brought back Louis XVIII, the influence of M. de Saint-Méran and himself would be strengthened and the marriage would be more suitable than ever.

As for Dantès, he remained a prisoner; hidden away in the depths of his dungeon he was ignorant of the downfall of Louis XVIII's throne and the re-establishment of Napoleon.

Twice during this short revival of the Empire, which was called the Hundred Days, had M. Morrel renewed his appeal for the liberation of Dantès, and each time Villefort had quietened him with promises and hopes. Finally there was Waterloo. Morrel did not present himself before Villefort any more; he realized he had done all that was humanly possible for his young friend and that to make any further attempts under this second Restoration would be to compromise himself unnecessarily.

When Louis XVIII remounted the throne, Villefort successfully petitioned for the post of Procureur du Roi at Toulouse, and a fortnight later he married Mademoiselle de Saint-Méran.

When Napoleon returned to France, Danglars understood the full significance of the blow he had struck at Dantès; his denunciation had been given some sort of justification and he called this extraordinary coincidence the Hand of Providence. But when Napoleon reached Paris and his voice was once more heard, imperious and powerful, Danglars grew afraid. Dantès might return any day with full information on the cause of his arrest and eager for vengeance. He therefore informed M. Morrel of his desire to leave the merchant service and obtained a recommendation from him to a Spanish merchant. He went to Madrid and was heard of no more for a long time.

Fernand, on the other hand, could not understand anything. Dantès was absent and that was all he cared about. What had happened to him? He did not know, neither did he care.

In the meantime the Empire made a last appeal to her soldiers, and every man capable of bearing arms rushed to obey the far-reaching voice of his Emperor. Fernand left Mercédès and joined up with the others, but the gloomy and terrible thought preyed upon his mind that Dantès might return now that his back was turned and marry her whom he loved. His devotion to Mercédès, the pity he pretended to have for her in her sorrow, the care with which he anticipated her least desire, had produced the effect that outward signs of devotion always produce on generous hearts: Mercédès had always been fond of him as a friend and this affection was now increased by a feeling of gratitude.

Fernand therefore went off to the army with hope in his heart, and Mercédès was now left alone. She could be seen, bathed in tears, wandering incessantly round the little village of the Catalans; at times she would stand under the fierce midday sun as motionless and dumb as a statue with her eyes fixed on Marseilles; at other times she would sit on the beach listening to the moaning of the sea, as eternal as her grief, and ask herself whether it would not be better to leap down into the abyss below than to suffer this cruel alternative of a hopeless suspense. She did not lack the courage to do this deed; it was her religion that came to her aid and saved her from suicide.

As for old Dantès, he had now lost all hope. Five months after he had been separated from his son, and almost at the very hour at which he had been arrested, the old man breathed his last in Mercédès' arms. M. Morrel paid the expenses of the funeral and the small debts the old man had incurred during his last illness. It required more than benevolence to do this, it required courage. The South was aflame, and to help the father of a Bonapartist as dangerous as Dantès, even though he were on his deathbed, was a crime.

8

Dantès passed through all the various stages of misery that affect a forgotten and forsaken prisoner in his cell. First there was pride born of hope and a consciousness of his innocence; next, he was so reduced that he began to doubt his innocence; finally his pride gave way to entreaty.

Dantès begged to be taken from his dungeon and placed in another one, even though that were deeper and darker. Even a change for the worse would be welcome and would give him a few days' distraction. He entreated his gaolers to let him go for a walk, to give him books, anything to while away the time. All his requests were refused.

In time, his gloom gave way to wrath. He began to roar out blasphemies which made even his gaoler recoil with horror, and dashed himself in a paroxysm of fury against the walls of the prison. Then there recurred to his mind the informer's letter which Villefort had shown him. Each line of it was reflected on the walls in fiery letters. He told himself it was the hatred of men and not the vengeance of God that had thrust him into this dark abyss. He doomed these unknown men to the most cruel torments his fiery imagination was capable of conjuring up, but, even so, the most awful of these torments seemed to him too mild and too short for them, for after the torment would come death, and in death they would find, if not repose, at all events that insensibility which so nearly resembles repose.

Sometimes he said to himself: 'When I was still a man, strong and free, commanding other men, I have seen the heavens open, the sea rage and foam, the storm rise in a patch of sky and like a gigantic eagle beat the two horizons with its wings. Soon the sight of the sharp rocks, coupled with the frightful noise of the waves, announced to me that death was near, and death terrified me. I exerted all my efforts to escape it, and I combined all my man's strength with all my sailor's skill in that terrible fight against God! For to me life was happy then, and to escape from the jaws of death was to return to happiness. Now, however, it is quite a different matter. I have lost all that bound me to life; now death smiles on me as a nurse smiles on the child she is about to rock to sleep; now welcome death!'

No sooner had this idea taken possession of the unhappy young man than he became more calm and resigned; he felt more contented with his hard bed and black bread, ate less, slept not at all, and almost found his miserable existence supportable, for could he not cast it off at will as one casts off old clothes?

There were two ways of dying open to him. One was quite simple; it was only a question of tying his handkerchief to a bar of the window and hanging himself. The other way was by starving himself. Hanging seemed to him a disgraceful thing, so he decided upon the second course.

Nearly four years had passed since he had taken this resolution; at the end of the second year he ceased to count the days.

Dantès had said to himself, 'I will die,' and had chosen his mode of death; he had weighed the matter well, but, being afraid he might go back on his resolution, he had sworn to himself that he would starve himself to death. 'When the gaoler brings me my food in the morning and evening,' he said to himself, 'I shall throw it through the window and he will think I have eaten it.' He kept his word. At first he threw it away with pleasure, then with deliberation, and finally with regret. It was only the remembrance of his oath that gave him the strength to carry out this dreadful purpose. The food which he had once loathed, hunger now made pleasant to the eye and delicious to the smell. At times he would hold his plate in his hand for an hour, his eyes fixed on the morsel of putrid meat or tainted fish and the black and mouldy bread. It was the last instincts of life struggling within him and breaking down his resolution. At length came the day when he had no longer the strength to raise himself to throw his supper away. The next day he could no longer see and scarcely hear; the gaoler thought he was seriously ill. All at once, towards nine in the evening, just as he was hoping that death would come soon, Dantès heard a dull sound on the wall against which he was lying.

So many loathsome animals had made their noises

in his cell that little by little he had grown accustomed to them and did not let them disturb his sleep. This time, however, what he heard was an even scraping noise as though caused by an enormous claw, a powerful tooth, or the pressure of some sharp instrument on the stone. Though weakened, the young man's brain seized on the idea that is ever present to the mind of a prisoner: liberty. The noise lasted for about three hours. Then Edmond heard the sound of something crumbling away and all was silence again.

Some hours later the scraping was continued again, but this time louder and nearer. Edmond's interest was aroused, and the noise seemed almost like a companion to him. 'As it continues even in daylight,' he thought to himself, 'it must be some unfortunate prisoner trying to escape. Oh, if I were only near and could help him! But I must ascertain this. I have only to knock on the wall and if it is an ordinary workman, he will instantly cease working and will endeavour to discover who it is that knocks, and why he knocks; and then, as his work is lawful, he will soon resume it. If, on the contrary, it is a prisoner, the noise I make will alarm him; he will be afraid of being discovered; he will cease his work and only resume it at night when he believes everyone to be in bed and asleep.'

Edmond went to a corner of the cell, detached a stone that had become loosened with the damp, and knocked three times on the wall, just where the sound had been loudest. At the first knock the noise stopped as if by magic. Edmond listened intently all through that day but there was complete silence. 'It is a prisoner,' Dantès said with inexpressible joy.

Three days – seventy-two deadly hours – passed

without a repetition of the noise. One evening, however, after the gaoler had paid his last visit, Dantès, who had his ear to the wall, thought he heard an almost imperceptible sound. He moved away, paced round the cell several times to calm himself, and then returned to the same spot. There could be no doubt about it: something was happening on the other side of the wall. The prisoner had recognized the danger of his previous tactics and had substituted the crowbar for the chisel.

Encouraged by this discovery, Edmond resolved to help the untiring worker. He looked round for some object he could use as a tool, but could discover nothing. He had no knife or sharp instrument; the only iron in the cell was that at the windows, and he had already proved the impossibility of moving the bars.

He had but one resource, and this was to break his pitcher and use one of the jagged fragments. Accordingly he dashed the pitcher to the ground, and, choosing two or three of the sharp, broken bits, hid them under his bed; the others he left scattered about the floor. The breaking of the jug was such a natural accident that it would cause no suspicion.

He had the whole night to work in, but, groping about in the dark, he did not make much headway, and he soon found that he blunted his instrument against the hard stone. He laid down his tool and waited for the morning. Hope had given him patience.

All night long he listened to the unknown miner at his subterranean work. Day came, the gaoler entered. Dantès told him the pitcher had fallen from his hands as he was drinking out of it the previous evening. The gaoler went grumbling to fetch another one without even taking the trouble to pick up the bits of the old one.

The grinding of the lock in the door which had always caused Dantès a pang now gave him inexpressible joy. He listened for the last of the dying footsteps and then, hastily moving his bed away, he saw by the faint ray of light that penetrated his cell how useless had been his work of the previous night in attacking the hard stone instead of the plaster surrounding it.

The damp had rendered the plaster friable, and Dantès' heart beat with joy when he saw it break off in little bits: they were but tiny atoms, it is true, but within half an hour he had scraped away nearly a handful.

In three days he managed, with untold precautions, to lay bare a stone. The wall was made of ashlars, for the greater solidity of which a freestone had been placed at intervals. It was one of these freestones which Dantès had now laid bare, and which he must now dislodge. He used his nails, but they were useless tools; the fragments of the pitcher broke whenever he tried to make them do the duty of a crowbar. After an hour of useless toil, he paused, his forehead bathed in perspiration. Was he to be thus stopped at the beginning, and must he wait, inert and useless, while his neighbour, who was perhaps growing weary, should accomplish all?

Suddenly an idea occurred to him. He stood up smiling; the perspiration on his forehead dried.

The gaoler always brought him his soup in a tin saucepan with an iron handle. It was this iron handle he longed for, and he would have given ten years of his life to get it. The contents of the saucepan were always poured into Dantès' plate; this he ate with his wooden spoon and washed his plate in readiness for the next day.

On the evening in question Dantès placed his plate on the floor, half-way between the door and the table. When the gaoler entered, he stepped on it and broke it to pieces. This time the gaoler could not blame Dantès; it is true he should not have left his plate on the floor, but then, the gaoler should have looked where he was going. He contented himself with grumbling and looked around for some other vessel for Dantès' soup.

'Leave the saucepan,' the prisoner said. 'You can take it again when you bring me my breakfast in the morning.'

This advice suited the gaoler as it spared him the necessity of going up and down the many steps again. He left the saucepan.

Dantès was trembling with delight. He ate his soup and meat hastily, and then, after waiting an hour to make sure the gaoler would not change his mind, he set himself to the task of dislodging the freestone, using the saucepan handle as a lever. At the end of an hour he had extricated the stone, leaving a hole of more than a foot and a half in diameter. Dantès collected all the plaster very carefully, carried it into the corners of the cell and, with a piece of broken earthenware, scraped some of the grey earth from the floor and strewed it over the plaster.

He continued to work all night and at dawn of day replaced the stone, pushed the bed up against the wall, and lay down to sleep.

His breakfast consisted of a piece of bread which the gaoler placed on the table.

'Aren't you going to bring me another plate?' Dantès asked.

'No, you break everything. First of all there was your pitcher, then you made me break your plate. You can keep the saucepan now and your soup will be poured into that.'

Dantès lifted up his eyes to Heaven, joined his hands under the coverlet, and said a prayer of thanks. The piece of iron which had been left him created in him a feeling of gratitude towards God stronger than any he had felt for the greatest blessings in past years.

He worked all day unremittingly; thanks to his new instrument he had scraped out more than ten handfuls of broken stone, plaster, and cement by the end of the day. He continued working all through the night, but after two or three hours he encountered an obstacle. The iron did not grip any more, it simply slid off a smooth surface. He touched the obstacle with his hand and soon recognized it as a beam. It crossed, or rather blocked, the hole that Dantès had commenced. It now meant that he had to dig either above or below it.

'Oh, my God, my God!' he cried. 'I prayed so fervently that I hoped Thou hadst heard my prayer. My God, after having deprived me of my liberty, after having deprived me of the peace of death, and after calling me back to existence, have pity on me and let me not die of despair!'

'Who speaks of God and of despair in the same breath?' said a voice that seemed to come from under the ground and sounded sepulchral to the young man. His hair stood on end and he drew back.

Edmond had not heard any man's voice but that of his gaoler for the past four or five years, and to a prisoner a gaoler is not a man; he is but a living door added to his oaken door; he is but a bar of flesh added to his bar of iron.

'In Heaven's name,' Dantès cried out, 'speak once more, though the sound of your voice frightened me. Who are you?'

'And who are you?' the voice asked.

'An unhappy prisoner,' replied Dantès, who had no difficulty in answering this question.

'Your name?'

'Edmond Dantès.'

'Your profession?'

'A sailor.'

'How long have you been here?'

'Since the 28th of February, 1815.'

'Your crime?'

'I am innocent of any crime.'

'But what are you accused of?'

'Of having conspired in favour of the Emperor's return.'

'What? The Emperor's return? Is the Emperor, then, no longer on the throne?'

'He abdicated at Fontainebleau in 1814 and was banished to the Isle of Elba. How long have you been here that you do not know this?'

'Since 1811.'

Edmond shuddered. This man had been in prison four years longer than himself.

'Dig no more,' the voice continued, speaking quicker. 'Tell me only at what height your hole is.'

'On a level with the floor.'

'How is it concealed?'

'It is behind my bed.'

'Where does your room lead to?'

'To the passage.'

'And the passage?'

'To the courtyard.'

'Alas! Alas!' muttered the voice.

'Oh, my God! What is the matter?' Dantès cried out.

'Only that I have made a mistake, that the inaccuracy of my plans has misled me, that the lack of a compass has ruined all, and that what I believed to be the wall of the fortress is the wall you have been digging!'

'But in any case the fortress would only give you access to the sea.'

'That is what I desired.'

'And if you had succeeded?'

'I should have thrown myself into the sea, swum to one of the islands round the Château d'If, or even to the shore, and then I should have been saved. Now all is lost. Fill in your hole again very carefully, work no more and wait till you hear from me again.'

'Tell me at least who you are.'

'I am – I am number twenty-seven.'

'Ah! You surely mistrust me,' cried Dantès. 'I swear by the living God that I will not betray you. Do not forsake me! You will not leave me alone any more, will you? Come to me or else let me come to you. We will escape together, and if we cannot escape we will talk together, you of those you love, and I of those I love. You must love someone.'

'I am all alone in the world.'

'Then you will learn to love me. If you are young, I shall be your companion; if you are old, I shall be your son. I have a father who must be seventy years of age if he is still alive. I love but him and a girl named Mercédès. I know that my father has not forgotten me, but who knows whether she still thinks of me! I will love you as I loved my father.'

'So be it,' said the prisoner. 'Farewell till tomorrow.'

From this moment Dantès' happiness knew no bounds; he was not going to be alone any more, and perhaps he might even gain his freedom. He walked up and down his cell all day long, his heart beating wildly with joy.

Night came. Dantès thought his neighbour would take advantage of the silence and the darkness to renew conversation with him, but he was mistaken; the night passed without a single sound breaking in upon his feverish waiting. But the next morning, after the gaoler had been, he heard three knocks at equal intervals. He threw himself upon his knees:

'Is that you?' he said. 'Here I am.'

'Has your gaoler gone?' inquired the voice.

'Yes,' replied Dantès, 'and he will not come again till this evening, so we have got twelve full hours of freedom.'

'I can set to work, then?'

'Oh, yes, yes, without delay. This very instant, I beg of you.'

The piece of earth on which Dantès was leaning suddenly gave way; he threw himself back, and a mass of earth and loose stones crumbled into a hole which opened up just beneath the aperture he himself had made; then from the bottom of this hole, of which he could not gauge the depth, he saw a head appear, then a pair of shoulders, and finally the body of a man who crept with great agility out of the hole just made.

9

Dantès drew his new friend towards the window that the little light that penetrated into his cell might reveal his features.

He was short, with hair blanched with suffering rather than with age. His keen, penetrating eyes were almost hidden beneath thick grey eyebrows, and his beard, which was still black, reached down to his chest. His thin face, furrowed with deep lines, and the bold outlines of his characteristic features revealed a man who was more accustomed to exercise his mental faculties than his physical strength. Large drops of perspiration stood on his brow and, as for his garments, it was impossible to distinguish their original form, for they were in rags.

'Now let us see whether we can conceal from the eyes of your gaolers all traces of my entrance,' said the newcomer; and, stooping down to the aperture, he lifted the stone with the greatest ease, in spite of its weight, and fitted it into the hole.

'This stone has been removed very carelessly,' he said, shaking his head. 'Hadn't you any tools?'

'Have you some?' Dantès asked with astonishment.

'I made some. With the exception of a file, I have all I need: chisel, pincers, crow-bar.'

'Oh, I should like to see them.

'Well, to begin with, here is my chisel.'

And he showed Dantès a sharp, strong blade with a handle of beech-wood.

'How did you make that?' asked Dantès.

'Out of one of the clamps of my bed. I have hollowed out the passage, a distance of about fifty feet, with this instrument. To think that all my work has been in vain! There is now no means of escape. God's will be done!'

Dantès looked with astonishment mingled with admiration at this man who renounced with such philosophy a hope cherished for so long.

'Now,' Dantès said, 'will you tell me who you are?'

'Yes, if it interests you.' Then he continued sadly: 'I am the Abbé Faria, a prisoner in the Château d'If since 1811, and previously imprisoned in the fortress of Fenestrella for three years. In the year 1811 I was transferred from Piedmont to France.'

'But why are you here at all?'

'Because in 1807 I meditated the very scheme that Napoleon tried to realize in 1811; because I desired Italy to be one great, strong, and compact empire, instead of a nest of petty principalities each with its weak and despotic ruler; because I thought I had found my champion in a crowned fool, who pretended to share my views so as the better to betray me.'

For a moment Dantès stood motionless and mute.

'Then you abandon all hope of escaping?' he said at last.

'I realize that it is impossible, and that it is tantamount to revolting against God to attempt what is contrary to His designs.'

'Why despair? Why not start afresh?'

'Start afresh! Ah, you little know how I have toiled. Do you know that it took me four years to make my tools? Do you know that for the past two years I have been scraping and digging out earth as hard as granite? I have had to move stones that I once thought it impossible to loosen. I have spent whole days in these titanic efforts, and there were times when I was overjoyed if by night-time I had scraped away a square inch of the cement that age had made as hard as the stones themselves. I have had to pierce the wall of a staircase so that I could deposit all my stones and earth in its well. And I thought I had almost finished my task, and felt I had just enough strength left to accomplish it, when I found that all my plans were frustrated. I assure you, I have known very few successful attempts to escape. Only those have been crowned with success which were planned and worked out with infinite patience. We shall do best now to wait till some unforeseen occurrence gives us the opportunity of making our escape. When such an opportunity occurs, we will seize it.'

'You could well wait,' Dantès said with a sigh. 'Your work occupied every minute of your time, and when you could not work, you had your hope in a brighter future to console you.'

'I accomplished other things besides all this.'

'What did you do?'

'I wrote or studied.'

'Who gave you paper, pens, and ink?'

'No one,' said the abbé. 'I made them myself.'

Dantès looked at the man with admiration; only he could scarcely credit all he told him. Faria noticed this shade of doubt on the young man's face and said:

'When you come to my cell, I will show you an entire volume entitled *Treatise on the Possibility of a*

General Monarchy in Italy, which is the result of the thoughts, reflections, and researches of my whole life.'

'Do you mean to say you have written it?'

'On two shirts. I have invented a preparation by means of which linen is rendered as smooth and glossy as parchment. I also made some excellent quills which everyone would prefer to the ordinary ones if once they were known. I made them from the cartilage of the head of those enormous whiting they sometimes give us on feast-days. Formerly there must have been a fireplace in my cell which was doubtless closed up some time before I came. It must have been used for very many years, for the interior was coated with soot. I dissolved some soot in a portion of the wine they bring me every Sunday, and my ink was made. For notes to which I wished to draw special attention, I pricked my fingers and wrote with my blood.'

'When can I see all this?' Dantès asked.

'Just follow me.'

So saying the abbé re-entered the subterranean passage and disappeared. Dantès followed and found himself at the far end of the passage, into which the abbé's door opened. Here the passage became narrower; indeed there was scarcely room for a man to crawl through on his hands and knees. The abbé's room was paved; it had been by raising one of the flagstones in the darkest corner of the room that he had commenced the laborious task of which Dantès witnessed the completion.

As soon as he entered the cell, the young man examined it very carefully, but at first sight it presented nothing out of the ordinary.

'And now I am very anxious to see your treasures,' Dantès said.

The abbé went towards the fireplace, removed a stone which was formerly the hearthstone, and which hid a fairly deep cavity.

'What do you wish to see first?'

'Show me your work on the Monarchy of Italy.'

Faria took from his cupboard three or four rolls of linen four inches wide and eighteen long which were folded like papyrus leaves. These strips of linen were numbered and covered with writing.

'Here you have the whole of it,' he said. 'I put the word *finis* at the bottom of the seventy-eighth strip just a week ago. I have used for it two of my shirts and all the handkerchiefs I had. If ever I gain my liberty and can find a publisher in Italy who will publish it, my reputation is made.'

He then showed Dantès the quills he had made; the penknife of which he was particularly proud and which he had made out of an old iron candlestick; the ink; the matches, the sulphur for which he had obtained by feigning a skin disease; the rope-ladder, the material for which he had obtained by unravelling the ends of his sheets; and finally the needle. On seeing these ingenious products of an intelligent and highly developed brain, Dantès became thoughtful, and it occurred to him that the man might be able to clear up the mystery surrounding his own misfortune which he himself had been unable to fathom.

'What are you thinking of?' the abbé asked with a smile, seeing his companion's pensiveness, and attributing it to inexpressible admiration.

'I was thinking that though you have related to me the events of your life, yet you know nothing of mine.'

'Your life, young man, is far too short to contain anything of importance.'

'Nevertheless it contains a very great misfortune,' said Dantès, 'a misfortune that I do not deserve, and I would rather attribute the authorship of it to mankind and no longer blaspheme God as I have hitherto done.'

'Tell me your story, then.'

Dantès then related what he called the story of his life, consisting of a voyage to India, two or three voyages to the East, and finally his last voyage, the death of Captain Leclère, the package confided to him for the Grand Maréchal, the letter given him by the latter addressed to a certain M. Noirtier. Then he went on to tell his friend of his arrival at Marseilles, his interview with his father, his love for Mercédès, his betrothal feast, his arrest, his examination, his temporary imprisonment in the Law Courts, and finally his permanent imprisonment in the Château d'If. After this he knew nothing more, not even how long he had been a prisoner.

When Dantès had finished his story, the abbé sat silent, deep in thought. After a time he said: 'There is a maxim with a very deep meaning which says: "If you wish to discover the author of a crime, endeavour to find out in the first place who would derive advantage from the crime committed." You were about to be nominated captain and also to marry a beautiful girl, were you not?'

'That is true.'

'Was it to anyone's interest that you should not be

appointed captain of the *Pharaon*? And again, was it to anyone's interest that you should not marry Mercédès? Answer the first question first; order is the key to all problems.'

'I was very popular on board. If the sailors could have chosen their chief, I am sure they would have chosen me. There was only one person who had any reason to wish me ill; I quarrelled with him some time ago and challenged him to a duel, but he refused.'

'Now we are coming to the point. What was this man's name?'

'Danglars, the purser of the ship.'

'Good. Now who was present at your last conversation with Captain Leclère?'

'No one; we were alone.'

'Could anyone have overheard your conversation?'

'Yes, the door was open, and . . . wait . . . yes, it is true, Danglars passed at the very moment Captain Leclère was handing me the package for the Grand Maréchal.'

'Better still. Now we are on the right track. Did you take anyone ashore when you put in at the Isle of Elba?'

'No one at all.'

'What did you do with the letter the Grand Maréchal gave you?'

'I put it in my portfolio.'

'Had you your portfolio with you then? How could a portfolio large enough to contain an official letter find room in a sailor's pocket?'

'My portfolio was on board.'

'So you did not put the letter into the portfolio until you returned to the ship?'

'No.'

'What did you do with the letter from the time you left Porto Ferrajo till you reached the ship?'

'I carried it in my hand.'

'So that when you went on board, everyone could see that you carried a letter?'

'Yes.'

'Danglars as well?'

'Yes; Danglars as well as the others.'

'Now listen to me and try to recall all the incidents. Do you remember how the denunciation was phrased?'

'Oh, yes, I read it over three times and each word is engraved on my memory.' And he repeated it word for word.

The abbé shrugged his shoulders. 'It is as clear as daylight,' he said. 'You must have a very noble heart and simple mind that you had not your suspicions from the very outset.'

'Do you really think so?' Dantès exclaimed. 'Such infamy is not possible!'

'How did Danglars usually write?'

'He had a good, round hand.'

'How was the anonymous letter written?'

'With a backward slant.'

The abbé smiled. 'I suppose it was a disguised hand?'

'It was too bold to be disguised.'

The abbé took one of his quills and wrote the first two or three lines of the denunciation on a piece of prepared linen. Dantès stood aghast and looked at the abbé in terror, and exclaimed: 'How extraordinarily alike the two writings are!'

'The simple explanation is that the denunciation was written with the left hand. I have noticed that whereas handwritings written with the right hand vary, those written with the left hand are nearly always like. Now let us pass to the second question. Was it to anyone's interest that you should not marry Mercédès?'

'Yes, there was a young man who loved her, a young Catalan named Fernand.'

'Do you think he would be capable of writing the letter?'

'No, he would rather have stuck his knife into me. Besides, he was ignorant of the details stated in the denunciation. I had not mentioned them to anyone.'

'Stay a moment. Did Danglars know Fernand?'

'No. Oh, yes, I remember now. On the eve of my betrothal, I saw them together in old Pamphile's tavern. Danglars was friendly and jocular, but Fernand looked pale and agitated. A tailor, named Caderousse, whom I know very well, was with them. He was quite drunk though.'

'Do you want to know something else?' asked the abbé laughing.

'Yes, since you seem to be able to fathom every mystery. Tell me why I was only submitted to one examination, and why I was condemned without trial.'

'This is a more serious matter,' was the reply. 'What we have just done for your two friends is mere child's play by comparison. You must give me the most precise details. Who examined you?'

'The Deputy.'

'Did you tell him everything?'

'Yes, everything.'

'Did his manner towards you change at all in the course of the examination?'

'He certainly did appear disturbed when he read the compromising letter. He seemed quite upset at my misfortune.'

'Are you quite sure he was so perturbed on your account?'

'At any rate he gave me one great proof of his sympathy. He burnt the letter, my one incriminating document, before my very eyes.'

'Ah! This man may have been a greater scoundrel than you imagine. The Deputy's conduct was too sublime to be natural. To whom was the letter addressed?'

'To Monsieur Noirtier, thirteen, Rue Coq Héron, Paris.'

'Can you think of any selfish motive the Deputy might have had in destroying the letter?'

'I do not know of any, but he may have had some reason, for he made me promise two or three times that, in my own interest, I would not speak to anyone of the letter, and he made me swear that I would not utter the name of the person to whom it was addressed.'

'Noirtier?' the abbé repeated. 'Noirtier? . . . I knew a Noirtier at the Court of the old Queen of Etruria, a man who was a Girondist during the Revolution. What was the Deputy's name?'

'De Villefort.'

The abbé burst into loud laughter. Dantès looked at him in stupefaction. 'What is the matter?' he said.

'Only that I have a clear and complete understanding of everything now. Poor blind young man! This Noirtier was no other than the Deputy's father.'

'His father?' Dantès cried out.

'Yes, his father, who styles himself Noirtier de Villefort,' the abbé replied.

A cry broke from Dantès' lips and he staggered like a drunken man; then rushing towards the opening which led to his cell, he called out: 'I must be alone to think this over.'

Reaching his cell he fell on his bed, and here the turnkey found him in the evening, motionless, his eyes staring into space, his features drawn.

During these hours of meditation, which had passed like so many seconds, he had formed a terrible resolution and taken a fearful oath.

At length a voice roused him from his reverie; it was the voice of Faria, who had come to invite Dantès to have his supper with him. The young man followed him. His face had lost that drawn look it had worn, and instead there was a determined, almost radiant expression which clearly denoted that he had taken a resolution. The abbé looked at him attentively.

'I almost regret having helped you in your researches and having told you what I did,' he said.

'Why?'

'Because I have instilled into your heart a feeling that previously held no place there – vengeance.'

Dantès smiled and said: 'Let us speak of something else.'

The abbé looked at him again and shook his head sadly; but he did what his companion asked him and spoke of other matters.

Dantès listened to his words with admiring attention. At first he spoke of things and ideas of which the young man had no comprehension until later on; like the aurora borealis which lights the navigator of the northern seas on his way, he showed the young man new landscapes and horizons illuminated by fantastic lights, and Dantès realized what happiness it would bring to an intelligent being to follow this exalted mind to those moral, philosophical, or social heights to which he was wont to soar.

'You must impart to me a little of your knowledge,' Dantès said, 'otherwise an ignoramus like myself will only be a bore to you. I am sure that you must prefer solitude to a companion without education such as I am. If you do what I ask, I promise to speak no more of escaping.'

'Alas, my good friend,' said the abbé smiling, 'human knowledge is very limited, and when I have taught you mathematics, physics, history, and the three or four living languages I speak, you will know all that I know. It will not take more than two years to give you the knowledge I possess.'

'Two years?' exclaimed Dantès. 'Do you really think you can teach me all these things in two years? What will you teach first? I am anxious to begin. I am thirsting for knowledge.'

That selfsame evening the two prisoners drew up a plan for the younger man's education and began to put it into execution the next day. Dantès had a prodigious memory and a great facility for assimilation.

Whether it was that the distraction afforded him by his study had taken the place of liberty, or because he adhered strictly to the promise given to the abbé, he made no further reference to escaping, and the days passed rapidly, each day adding to his store of knowledge. At the end of the year he was a different man.

Dantès noticed, however, that in spite of his companionship, the Abbé Faria seemed to lose some of his animation with each succeeding day. It seemed as though there was something on his mind. At times he would become wrapped in thought, sigh unconsciously, then suddenly rise and, with his arms crossed over his breast, gloomily pace his cell. One day, all at once, he ceased his incessant wandering and exclaimed: 'If only there were no sentry!'

'Have you found a means of escape then?' asked Dantès excitedly.

'Yes, provided that the sentry in the gallery is both deaf and blind.'

'He shall be deaf and he shall be blind,' answered the young man in such a determined way that it frightened the abbé.

'No! No!' he cried out. 'I will have no bloodshed.'

Dantès wanted to pursue the subject, but the abbé shook his head and refused to answer any more questions. Three months passed.

'Are you strong?' the abbé one day asked Dantès.

Without replying Dantès picked up the chisel, bent it into the shape of a horseshoe and straightened it out again.

'Will you promise not to kill the sentry except as a last resort?'

'Yes, on my honour.'

'Then we may accomplish our task,' was the reply.

'How long will it be before we can accomplish it?'

'At least a year.'

'Shall we begin at once?'

'Without any delay. Here is my plan.'

The abbé showed Dantès a drawing he had made. It

was a plan of his own cell, that of Dantès', and the passage joining them. In the middle of this passage they would bore a tunnel, like those used in mines. This tunnel would lead the prisoners under the gallery where the sentry was on duty; arrived there, a large excavation would be made by loosening one of the flagstones with which the floor of the gallery was paved; at a given moment the stone would give way under the soldier's weight and he would disappear into the excavation below. Dantès would throw himself upon him before he had recovered from the shock of the fall and while he was still unable to defend himself. He would gag and blindfold him, and then the two prisoners would jump through one of the windows, climb down the outside wall by means of the rope-ladder the abbé had made and they would be saved!

Dantès clapped his hands, and his eyes shone with joy. It was such a simple plan that it was bound to succeed.

That same day the two miners commenced operations with renewed vigour after their long rest.

At the end of fifteen months the hole was made, the excavation was completed under the gallery, and the two prisoners could distinctly hear the measured tread of the sentry. They were obliged to wait for a dark, moonless night for the success of their plans, and their one fear was that the flagstone might give way under the soldier's heavy tread sooner than they desired. To guard against this, they decided to prop the stone up with a kind of beam they had found in the foundations. Dantès was busy putting it into position when he suddenly heard the abbé cry out in pain. He rushed to him and found him standing in the middle of the room, his face ghastly pale, his hands clenched, and the perspiration streaming down his forehead.

'Good heavens!' cried Dantès. 'Whatever has happened? What ails you?'

'Quick! Quick!' the abbé replied. 'Listen to me!'

Dantès looked at Faria's livid face. His eyes had deep lines under them, his lips were white, and his very hair seemed to stand on end.

'Oh! What is the matter with you?' Dantès cried terror-stricken.

'All is over with me! A terrible disease, it may even be mortal, is about to attack me. I feel it coming. I was seized with it the year before my imprisonment. There is only one remedy for it. Run quickly to my cell and raise the foot of my bed. It is hollow, and you will find in it a little glass bottle half filled with a red liquid. Bring it to me. No, I might be found here; help me back to my cell while I still have the strength. Who knows what may happen while the attack lasts?'

In a flash Dantès realized that his hopes of escape were now dashed to the ground; nevertheless he did not lose his head. He crept into the tunnel dragging his luckless companion after him, and with infinite trouble helped him to his cell and placed him on the bed.

'Thank you,' the abbé said, trembling in every limb as though he had just stepped out of freezing water. 'I am seized with a cataleptic fit. It may be that I shall not move or make a sound; on the other hand, I may stiffen, foam at the mouth and shriek. Try not to let them hear me, for if they do, they might change my cell and we should be separated for ever. When you see me motionless, cold, and to all appearances dead, then and not until then force my teeth apart with the knife, and pour eight to ten drops of the liquid down my throat and I shall perhaps revive.'

'Perhaps?' exclaimed Dantès grief-stricken.

'Help! Help!' the abbé cried. 'I am . . . I am dy–'

The attack was so sudden and so violent that the unfortunate prisoner was unable to finish the word. His features became distorted, his eyes dilated, his mouth twisted, his cheeks took on a purple hue; he struggled, foamed at the mouth, moaned and groaned. This lasted for two hours, then stretching himself out in a last convulsion, he became livid and lay as inert as a block of wood, whiter and colder than marble, more crushed than a reed trampled underfoot.

Edmond waited until life seemed to have departed from the abbé's body and he apparently lay cold in death; then, taking the knife, with great difficulty he forced the blade between the clenched teeth. He carefully poured ten drops of the red liquid down his friend's throat and waited.

An hour elapsed and still the abbé made not the slightest movement. Dantès began to fear he had waited too long before administering the remedy, and stood anxiously gazing at him. At last a faint colour spread over his cheeks, his eyes which had remained open in a fixed stare, now began to see, a slight sigh escaped his lips, and he began to move.

'He is saved! He is saved!' Dantès exclaimed.

The abbé could not yet speak, but he pointed with visible anxiety towards the door. Dantès listened and heard the gaoler's footsteps. He jumped up, darted towards the opening which he entered, replacing the flagstone after him, and regained his cell.

An instant later the gaoler entered and, as usual, found his prisoner sitting on his bed.

Scarcely had he turned his back, scarcely had the sound of his footsteps in the passage outside died away, when Dantès, too anxious to eat anything, hastened back to the abbé's cell by the same way he had come a few seconds before. Faria had regained consciousness, but he was still lying stretched on his bed helpless and inert.

'I little thought I should see you again,' he said.

'Why?' asked the young man. 'Did you think you were going to die?'

'No, but everything is ready for your flight, and I thought you would go.'

'Without you?' he exclaimed. 'Did you really think I was capable of such a base action?'

'I see now that I was mistaken. But, alas! I feel very weak and worn.'

'Take courage, your strength will return,' said Dantès.

Faria shook his head.

'My first fit lasted but half an hour, leaving only a feeling of hunger; I could even get up alone. Today, I can move neither my right leg nor my arm; my head feels heavy, which proves a rush of blood to the brain. The third attack will leave me entirely paralysed or else it will kill me.'

'No, no, I assure you, you will not die. When you have your third attack, if you have one, you will be at liberty.'

'My friend,' the old man said, 'you are mistaken. The attack I have just had has condemned me to perpetual imprisonment. Before fleeing, one must be able to walk.'

'Well then, we will wait a week, a month, two months if necessary; during that time you will regain your strength. All is ready for our escape, we have but to choose the day and hour. The day you feel strong enough to swim, we will put our plan into execution.'

'I shall swim no more,' Faria said. 'My arm is paralysed not for one day only, but for ever. Raise it yourself and you will soon know by the weight of it.'

The young man did as he was bid and the arm fell back heavy and lifeless.

'You are convinced now, I expect,' Faria said. 'Believe me, I know what I am saying; I have thought about it unceasingly ever since I had the first attack. I have been expecting this, for it runs in the family. My father, as well as my grandfather, died after the third attack. The physician who prepared this medicine for me has predicted the same fate for me.'

'The physician has made a mistake,' Dantès cried out. 'As for your paralysis, that will not trouble me in the least. I shall swim the sea with you on my shoulders.'

'My son,' the abbé said, 'you are a sailor and a swimmer, and should therefore know that a man could not possibly make more than fifty strokes with such a load on his back. I shall stay here till the hour of my deliverance has struck, the hour of my death. But you, my son, flee, escape! You are young, lithe, strong; trouble not about me . . . I give you back your word!'

'Very well,' said Dantès, 'in that case I shall stay here too!' Rising and solemnly stretching one hand over the old man, he said: 'By all that I deem most holy, I swear that I shall not leave you till death takes one of us!'

Faria looked up at this noble-minded, simple young man, and read in the expression on his face, now animated by a feeling of pure devotion, the sincerity of his affection and the loyalty of his oath.

'So be it,' said the sick man. 'I accept. Thank you.' Then holding out to him his hand, he said: 'It may be that you will be rewarded for this unselfish devotion, but as I cannot leave, and you will not, we must fill in the tunnel under the gallery. The soldier might notice that that particular spot is hollow and call the inspector's attention to it. We should then be found out and separated. Go and do it at once; unfortunately I cannot help you. Spend the whole night on the task if necessary, and come to me again in the morning after the gaoler has made his visit. I shall have something important to tell you.'

Dantès took the abbé's hand and was rewarded with a smile. With a feeling of deep respect, the young man then left his old friend in obedience to his wishes.

10

The next morning when Dantès entered the cell of his friend in captivity, he found him sitting up with a resigned expression on his face. In the ray of light which entered his cell by the narrow window, he held in his left hand, the only one he could use now, a piece of paper which, from being continuously rolled up very tightly, had taken on a cylindrical shape. Without saying a word, he showed it to Dantès.

'What is this?' the young man asked.

'Look at it well,' the abbé said, smiling. 'This paper, my friend – I can tell you everything now, for I have tried you – this piece of paper is my treasure, half of which belongs to you from this day forward.'

'Your treasure?' Dantès stammered.

Faria smiled.

'Yes,' he said. 'You are a noble-hearted lad, Dantès, but I know by the way you shuddered and turned pale what is passing in your mind. This treasure really exists, and though it has not been my lot to possess it, you will one day be the owner of it all.'

'My friend, your attack has tired you, will you not rest a little?' said Dantès. 'If you wish, I will listen to your story tomorrow; today I only want to nurse you back to health, nothing more. Besides,' he continued, 'a treasure is not a very pressing matter for us just now, is it?'

'Very pressing indeed,' replied the old man. 'How do we know that I shall not be seized with the third attack tomorrow or the day after? Remember that then all will be over. But now I tremble at any delay in securing to one so worthy as you the possession of such an enormous buried treasure.'

Edmond turned away with a deep sigh.

'You persist in your incredulity, Edmond,' Faria continued. 'I see you must have proofs. Well, then, listen to my tale. I will keep it brief. I used to work as secretary to Cardinal Spada in Rome, the last descendant of a family which had been fabulously rich. In fact, their wealth was the cause of their downfall. In the time of Pope Alexander VI, the corrupt Pope was desperately in need of money to combat Louis XII.

He poisoned Caesar Spada and his nephew, hoping to lay his greedy hands on the fortune, but all he found – apart from the family houses and silverware – was a will in which Spada left his nephew his library of books, and specifically mentioned his breviary. Alas! Poor Caesar could not have known that the evil Pope was going to kill his nephew at the same time as himself.

'My patron died. He bequeathed to me his library, composed of five thousand books, his breviary, which had remained in the family and had been handed down from father to son, and in addition a thousand Roman crowns with the request that I should have anniversary masses said for the repose of his soul, draw up a genealogical tree, and write a history of his family. All this I carried out most scrupulously.

'In 1807, a month before my arrest, and fifteen days after Count Spada's death, on the 25th of December, I was reading for the thousandth time the papers I was putting in order, for the palace had been sold to a stranger and I was leaving Rome to settle at Florence, taking with me what money I possessed, my library, and the famous breviary, when, tired with my assiduous study and rendered drowsy by the heavy dinner I had partaken of, my head fell in my hands and I dropped off to sleep. This was at three o'clock in the afternoon.

'I awoke as the clock was striking six to find that I was in complete darkness. I rang for a servant to bring me a light, but as no one came I resolved to help myself. Taking the candle in one hand, I groped about with the other for a piece of paper which I intended to light at the last flame flickering in the hearth. However, fearing that in the dark I might take a valuable piece of paper, I hesitated, but suddenly recollected that I had seen in the famous breviary which lay on the table beside me, an old piece of paper, yellow with age, which had probably served as a bookmark and had been kept in the same place for centuries by the different owners. I found this useless piece of paper and, putting it into the dying flame, lighted it.

'But as the flames devoured the paper I held between my fingers, I saw yellowish characters appear, as if by magic; an unholy terror seized me. I crushed the paper in my hand and choked the flame. Then I lighted the candle and with inexpressible emotion opened out the crumpled paper. I recognized that a mysterious, sympathetic ink had traced these characters which could only become apparent when placed in contact with heat. A little more than one third of the paper had been consumed by the flames. And here it is, Dantès. Read it.'

So saying, Faria gave Dantès the paper, and he read this time with great eagerness the following words which had been written with an ink of the colour of rust:

This 25th day of April 1498, be . . .
Alexander VI, and fearing that, not . . .
he may desire to become my heir, and re . . .
and Bentiviglio, who were poisoned, . . .
my sole heir, that I have bu . . .
and has visited with me – that is, in . . .
isle of Monte Cristo – all I pos . . .
els, diamonds, gems; that alone . . .
may amount to about two mil . . .
will find on raising the twentieth ro . . .

creek to the East in a straight line. Two open . . .
in these caves; the treasure is in the farthest cor . . .
which treasure I bequeath to him and leave en . . .
sole heir.

CAES . . .

April 25, 1498

'Now,' continued the abbé, 'read this other paper.' And he gave Dantès a second piece containing the other half of the broken sentences.

. . . ing invited to dinner by His Holiness
. . . content to make me pay for my hat
. . . serve for me the fate of Cardinals Crapara
. . . I declare to my nephew, Guido Spada,
. . . ried in a spot he knows
. . . the caves of the small
. . . sess in ingots, gold, money, jew-
. . . I know the existence of this treasure, which
. . . lion Roman crowns, and which he
. . . ck from the small
. . . ings have been made
. . . ner of the second,
. . . tire to him as my
. . . AR † SPADA

Faria watched him attentively.

When he saw that Dantès had read the last line, he said: 'Now place the two fragments together and judge for yourself.'

Dantès obeyed and read as follows:

This 25th day of April 1498, being invited to dinner by His Holiness Alexander VI, and fearing that, not content to make me pay for my hat, he may desire to become my heir, and reserve for me the fate of Cardinals Crapara and Bentiviglio, who were poisoned, I declare to my nephew, Guido Spada, my sole heir, that I have buried in a spot he knows and has visited with me – that is, in the caves of the small isle of Monte Cristo – all I possess in ingots, gold, money, jewels, diamonds, gems; that alone I know the existence of this treasure, which may amount to about two million Roman crowns, and which he will find on raising the twentieth rock from the small creek to the East in a straight line. Two openings have been made in these caves; the treasure is in the farthest corner of the second, which treasure I bequeath to him and leave entire to him as my sole heir.

CAESAR † SPADA

April 25, 1498

'Well! Do you understand it now?' Faria asked.

'Who reconstructed it in this way?'

'I did. With the assistance of the half of the will I had rescued, I worked out the rest by measuring the length of the lines with that of the paper, and by fathoming the missing words by means of those already in my possession, just as in a vault one is guided by a ray of light that enters from above.'

'And what did you do when you thought you had solved the mysterious script?'

'I made up my mind to leave Rome at once, which I did, taking with me the beginning of my big work on the unity of the Kingdom of Italy. The imperial police, however, had been watching me for some time past, and my sudden departure aroused their suspicions. I was arrested just as I was about to embark at Piombino.

'Now, my dear friend,' Faria continued, looking at

Dantès with an almost paternal expression, 'you know as much as I do; if we ever escape together half of my treasure is yours; if I die here and you escape alone, the whole of it belongs to you.'

'But is there not a more legitimate owner to this treasure than ourselves?' asked Dantès hesitatingly.

'No, none whatever. You can make your mind easy on that score. The family is completely extinct and, besides, the last Count Spada made me his heir; in bequeathing the breviary to me, he bequeathed to me all that it contained. No, if we lay our hands on this fortune, we can enjoy it without any compunction.'

'And you say this treasure consists of . . .'

'Two million Roman crowns and about thirteen millions of money in French coin.'

Edmond thought he was dreaming: he wavered between incredulity and joy.

'I have kept this a secret from you for so long,' Faria continued, 'simply because I wanted to give you proofs, and also because I thought to give you a surprise. Had we escaped before my attack, I should have taken you to Monte Cristo, but now,' he added with a sigh, 'it will be you who will take me. Well, Dantès, are you not going to thank me?'

'This treasure belongs to you alone, my friend, and I have no right to it,' Dantès replied. 'I am not even related to you.'

'You are my son, Dantès,' exclaimed the old man. 'You are the child of my captivity. My profession condemned me to celibacy, but God has sent you to console the man who could not be a father, and the prisoner who could not be a free man.'

Faria held out his one remaining arm to the young

man, who threw himself round his neck and burst into tears.

11

Now that this treasure, which had been the object of the abbé's meditations for so long, could give future happiness to him whom he truly loved as a son, it had redoubled its value in his eyes; daily would he expatiate on the amount, holding forth to Dantès on the good a man could do to his friends in modern times with a fortune of thirteen or fourteen millions. Dantès' face would darken, for the oath of vengeance he had taken would come into his mind, and he was occupied with the thought of how much harm a man could do to his enemies in modern times with a fortune of thirteen or fourteen millions.

The abbé did not know the Isle of Monte Cristo, which was situated twenty-five miles from Pianosa between Corsica and Elba, but Dantès had often passed it and had once landed there. He drew a plan of the island and Faria advised him as to the best means to adopt to recover the treasure. He had kept silent about it for all these many long years, but now it became a daily topic of conversation between the two. Fearing that the will might one day be mislaid or lost, he made Dantès learn it by heart until he knew it word for word.

One night Edmond woke suddenly and thought he heard someone calling him. He opened his eyes and tried to penetrate the darkness. He heard his name, or rather a plaintive voice trying to articulate his name. He raised himself in his bed and listened, his anxiety bringing great beads of perspiration to his forehead. There could be no doubt, the voice came from his companion's cell.

'Great God!' he murmured. 'Could it be?'

He moved his bed, drew the stone away, and rushed to his friend's cell. There by the flickering light of the lamp he beheld the old man clinging to the bedside. His features were drawn with the horrible symptoms which Edmond already knew, and which had filled him with such terror the first time he saw them.

'Ah, my friend,' Faria said resignedly, 'you understand, don't you? There is no need to explain anything. Think only of yourself now, think only how to make your captivity supportable and your escape possible.'

Edmond could only wring his hands and exclaim: 'Oh, my friend, my dearest friend, don't talk like that any more! I saved you once and I will save you a second time.' And raising the foot of the bed, he took the phial, which was still one-third full of the red liquid.

'See,' he said, there is still some of this saving draught.'

'There is no hope,' Faria replied.

A violent shock checked the old man's speech. Dantès raised his head; he saw his friend's eyes all flecked with crimson as though a flow of blood had surged up from his chest to his forehead.

'Farewell! Farewell!' the old man murmured, clasping the young man's hand convulsively. 'Farewell! Forget not Monte Cristo!'

And with these words he fell back on to his bed.

The attack was terrible: convulsed limbs, swollen eyelids, foam mingled with blood, a rigid body, was all that remained on this bed of agony in place of the intelligent being that had been there but an instant before.

Dantès took the lamp, placed it on a ledge formed by a stone at the head of the bed, whence its flickering light cast a strange and weird reflection on the contorted features and inert, stiff body. With staring eyes, he anxiously awaited the propitious moment for administering the saving draught. When he thought the moment had come, he took the knife, forced apart the teeth, which offered less resistance than on the previous occasion, counted ten drops one after the other and waited: the phial still contained double that quantity.

He waited ten minutes, a quarter of an hour, half an hour, and still there was no sign of movement. Trembling in every limb, his hair on end, his forehead bathed in perspiration, he counted the seconds by the beatings of his heart. Then he thought it was time to make the last desperate attempt. He placed the phial to Faria's purple lips – his jaws had remained wide apart – and poured the rest of the liquid down his throat. A violent trembling seized the old man's limbs, his eyes opened and were frightful to behold, he heaved a sigh that sounded like a scream, and then his trembling body gradually reverted to its former rigidity. The face assumed a livid hue, and the light faded out of the wide-open eyes. Dantès knew that he was alone with a corpse.

Then an overmastering terror seized him; he dared

press no more the hand that hung down from the bed: he dared look no more on those vacant and staring eyes which he endeavoured in vain to close several times, for they opened again each time. He extinguished the lamp, hid it carefully and fled from the cell, replacing the stone behind him as carefully as he could.

It was time he went, too, for the gaoler was coming. Dantès was seized with an indescribable impatience to know what would happen in his unfortunate friend's cell; he, therefore, went into the subterranean passage where he arrived in time to hear the turnkey calling for assistance.

Other turnkeys soon arrived; then was heard the tread of soldiers, heavy and measured even when off duty; behind them came the governor.

Edmond heard the bed creaking; he heard too the voice of the governor, who ordered water to be thrown on the face of the dead man, and then, as this did not revive him, sent to summon the doctor.

The governor left the cell, and some words of compassion, mingled with coarse jokes and laughter, reached Dantès' ears.

At the end of an hour or so he heard a faint noise which gradually increased. It was the governor coming back with the doctor and several officials.

The doctor declared the prisoner dead and diagnosed the cause of death. There was more coming and going, and, a few seconds later, a sound like the rubbing together of sacking reached Dantès' ears. The bed creaked, a heavy step like that of a man lifting a weight resounded on the floor, then the bed creaked again under the weight placed on it.

'Tonight, then,' Dantès heard the governor say.

'At what time?' asked one of the turnkeys.

'Between ten and eleven.'

'Shall we watch by the corpse?'

'Whatever for? Lock the door as though he were alive; nothing more is needed.'

The footsteps died away, the voices became gradually less distinct, the grating noise of the lock and the creaking of the bolts were heard, and then a silence more penetrating than solitude, the silence of death, prevailed, striking its icy chill through the young man's whole frame.

Then he slowly raised the stone with his head and cast a swift glance round the room. It was empty. Dantès entered.

12

On the bed, at full length, faintly lighted by a dim ray that entered through the window, Dantès saw a sack of coarse cloth, under the ample folds of which he could distinctly discern a long, stiff form: it was Faria's shroud. All was over then. Dantès was separated from his old friend. Faria, the helpful, kind companion, to whom he had become so attached, to whom he owed so much, existed now but in his memory. He sat on the edge of the bed and became a prey to deep and bitter melancholy.

Alone! He was quite alone once more! Alone! No longer to see, to hear the voice of, the only human being that attached him to life! The idea of suicide which had been dispelled by his friend and which he himself had forgotten in his presence, rose again before him like a phantom beside Faria's corpse.

Dantès, however, recoiled from such an infamous death, and swiftly passed from despair to an ardent desire for life and liberty. 'Die? Oh, no!' he cried out, 'it would hardly have been worth while to live, to suffer so much and then to die now. No, I desire to live, to fight to the end. I wish to reconquer the happiness that has been taken from me. Before I die, I have my executioners to punish, and possibly also some friends to recompense. Yet they will forget me here and I shall only leave this dungeon in the same way that Faria has done.'

As he uttered these words, Edmond stood stock-still, with eyes fixed like a man struck by a sudden and terrifying idea.

'Oh, who has given me this thought?' he murmured. 'My God, comes this from Thee? Since it is only the dead who go free from here, I must take the place of the dead!'

Without giving himself time to reconsider his decision, and as though he would not give reflection time to destroy his desperate resolution, he leaned over the hideous sack, slit it open with the knife Faria had made, took the dead body out, carried it to his own cell, and placed it on his bed, put round the head the piece of rag he always wore, covered it with the bed-clothes, kissed for the last time the ice-cold forehead, endeavoured to shut the rebellious eyes, which were still open, and stared so horribly, and turned the head to the wall so that, when the gaoler brought his evening meal, he would think he had gone to bed, as he often did. Then he returned to the other cell, took the needle and thread from the cupboard, flung off his rags that the men might feel naked flesh under the sacking, slipped into the sack, placed himself in the same position as the corpse, and sewed the sack up again from the inside. If, by any chance, the gaolers had entered then, they would have heard the beating of his heart.

Now this is what Dantès intended doing. If the grave-diggers discovered that they were carrying a live body instead of a dead one, he would give them no time for thought. He would slit the sack open with his knife from top to bottom, jump out, and taking advantage of their terror, escape; if they tried to stop him, he would use his knife. If they took him to the cemetery and placed him in a grave, he would allow himself to be covered with earth; then, as it was night, as soon as the grave-diggers had turned their backs, he would cut his way through the soft earth and escape; he hoped the weight would not be too heavy for him to raise.

He had eaten nothing since the previous evening, but he had not thought of his hunger in the morning, neither did he think of it now. His position was much too precarious to allow him time for any thought but that of flight.

At last, towards the time appointed by the governor, he heard footsteps on the staircase. He realized that the moment had come, he summoned all his courage and held his breath.

The door was opened, a subdued light reached his eyes. Through the sacking that covered him he saw two shadows approach the bed. There was a third one at the door holding a lantern in his hand. Each of the two men who had approached the bed took the sack by one of its two extremities.

'He is very heavy for such a thin old man,' said one of them as he raised the head.

They carried away the sham corpse on the bier. Edmond made himself rigid. The procession, lighted by the man with the lantern, descended the stairs. All at once Dantès felt the cold, fresh night air and the sharp north-west wind, and the sensation filled him at once with joy and with anguish.

The men went about twenty yards, then stopped and dropped the bier on to the ground. One of them went away, and Dantès heard his footsteps on the stones.

'Where am I?' he asked himself.

'He is by no means a light load, you know,' said the man who had remained behind, seating himself on the edge of the bier.

Dantès' impulse was to make his escape, but, fortunately, he did not attempt it. He heard one of the men draw near and drop a heavy object on the ground; at the same moment a cord was tied round his feet, cutting into his flesh.

'Well, have you made the knot?' one of the men asked.

'Yes, and it is well made. I can answer for that.'

'Let's get on with it, then.'

The bier was lifted once more, and the procession advanced. The noise of the waves breaking against the rocks on which the Château is built sounded more distinctly to Dantès with each step they took.

'Wretched weather!' said one of the men. 'The sea will not be very inviting tonight.'

'Yes, the abbé runs a great risk of getting wet,' said the other, and they burst out laughing.

Dantès could not understand the jest; nevertheless his hair began to stand on end.

'Here we are at last!'

'No, farther on, farther on! You know the last one was dashed on the rocks and the next day the governor called us a couple of lazy rascals.'

They went another five yards, and then Dantès felt them take him by the head and feet and swing him to and fro.

'One! Two! Three!'

With the last word, Dantès felt himself flung into space. He passed through the air like a wounded bird falling, falling, ever falling with a rapidity which turned his heart to ice. At last – though it seemed to him like an eternity of time – there came a terrific splash; and as he dropped like an arrow into the icy cold water he uttered a scream which was immediately choked by his immersion.

Dantès had been flung into the sea, into whose depths he was being dragged down by a cannonball tied to his feet.

The sea is the cemetery of the Château d'If.

Though stunned and almost suffocated, Dantès had yet the presence of mind to hold his breath and, as he grasped the open knife in his right hand ready for any emergency, he rapidly ripped open the sack, extricated his arm and then his head; but in spite of his efforts to raise the cannonball, he still felt himself being dragged down and down. He bent his back into an arch in his endeavour to reach the cord that bound his legs, and, after a desperate struggle, he severed it at the very moment when he felt that suffocation was getting the upper hand of him. He kicked out vigorously and rose unhampered to the surface, while the cannonball dragged to the unknown depths the sacking which had so nearly become his shroud.

Dantès merely paused to take a deep breath and then he dived again to avoid being seen. When he rose the second time, he was already fifty yards from the spot where he had been thrown into the sea. He saw above him a black and tempestuous sky; before him was the vast expanse of dark, surging waters; while behind him, more gloomy than the sea and more sombre than the sky, rose the granite giant like some menacing phantom, whose dark summit appeared to Dantès like an arm stretched out to seize its prey. He had always been reckoned the best swimmer in Marseilles, and he was now anxious to rise to the surface to try his strength against the waves. To his joy he found that his enforced inaction had not in any way impaired his strength and agility, and he felt he could still master the element in which he had so often sported when a boy.

An hour passed. Exalted by the feeling of liberty, Dantès continued to cleave the waves in what he reckoned should be a direct line for the Isle of Tiboulen. Suddenly it seemed to him that the sky, which was already black, was becoming blacker than ever, and that a thick heavy cloud was rolling down on him. At the same time he felt a violent pain in his knee. With the incalculable rapidity of imagination, he thought it was a shot that had struck him, and he expected every moment to hear the report. But there was no sound.

He stretched out his hand and encountered an obstacle; he drew his leg up and felt land; he then saw what it was he had mistaken for a cloud. Twenty yards from him rose a mass of strangely formed rocks looking like an immense fire petrified at the moment of its most violent combustion: it was the Isle of Tiboulen.

13

Midway between the town of Beaucaire and the village of Bellegarde in the south of France, there is a small roadside inn, in front of which hung, creaking and flapping in the wind, an iron shield bearing a grotesque representation of the Pont du Gard.

The little inn had been occupied for the last seven or eight years by no other than Dantès' old acquaintance Gaspard Caderousse. He was standing, as was his wont, at his place of observation before the door, his eyes wandering listlessly from a small patch of grass, where some hens were scratching for food, to the deserted road leading from north to south, when suddenly he descried the dim outline of a man on horseback approaching from Bellegarde at that easy amble which betokens the best of understanding between horse and rider. The rider was a priest robed in black and wearing a three-cornered hat in spite of the scorching sun, which was then at its zenith.

Arrived at the door of the inn, he halted. The man dismounted, and, dragging the animal after him by the bridle, tied it to a dilapidated shutter.

Caderousse advanced, all bows and smiles.

'Are you not Monsieur Caderousse?' asked the priest in a strong Italian accent – the priest, whom, after fourteen years in prison, no one would have recognized as Edmond Dantès: the wiry youth with calm, happy features had become a well-built, muscular man with fire and deep sadness in his dark eyes.

'Yes, monsieur,' replied the innkeeper. 'That is my name. Gaspard Caderousse, at your service. Can I not offer you some refreshment, Monsieur l'Abbé?'

'Certainly, give me a bottle of your best wine and afterwards, with your permission, we will resume our conversation.'

When mine host reappeared after a few minutes' absence he found the abbé sitting on a stool with his elbows on the table; he placed a bottle of wine and a glass before him.

'Are we alone?' asked the abbé.

'Oh, yes, all alone or nearly so, for my wife doesn't count as she is always ailing.'

'First of all I must convince myself that you are really he whom I seek. In the year 1814 or 1815 did you know a sailor named Dantès?'

'Dantès? I should think I did! Poor Edmond! Why, he was one of my best friends,' exclaimed Caderousse. 'What has become of poor Edmond, monsieur? Do you know him? Is he still living? Is he free? Is he happy?'

'He died a prisoner, more wretched and more miserable than any prisoner lying in chains in the prison at Toulon.'

The deep red of Caderousse's face gave way to a ghastly paleness. He turned aside, and the abbé saw him wipe away a tear with a corner of the handkerchief tied round his head.

'Poor fellow!' Caderousse murmured.

'You seem to have been very fond of this boy?'

'I was indeed,' answered Caderousse, 'though I have it on my conscience that at one time I envied him his happiness. But I swear to you, Monsieur l'Abbé, I swear it on my honour, that since then I have deeply deplored his lot.'

There was a moment's silence during which the abbé's fixed gaze did not cease to examine the agitated features of the innkeeper.

'Did you know the poor lad?' continued Caderousse.

'I was called to his bedside to administer to him the last consolation of his religion. What is so very strange about it all,' the abbé continued, 'is that on his deathbed, Dantès swore by the crucifix that he was entirely ignorant of the cause of his imprisonment. He besought me, therefore, to clear up the mystery of his misfortune, which he had never been able to explain himself and, if his memory had been sullied, to remove the tarnish from his name.'

The abbé's eyes were fixed on Caderousse's countenance and seemed to penetrate to his very soul.

'A rich Englishman,' continued the abbé, 'his companion in misfortune for a time, but released at the second Restoration, owned a diamond of very great value. On leaving the prison he wished to give his companion a token of his gratitude for the kind and brotherly way he had nursed him through an illness, and gave him the diamond. When on his deathbed, Dantès said to me: "I had three good friends and a sweetheart, and I am sure they have deeply regretted my misfortune. One of these good friends was named Caderousse."'

Caderousse could not repress a shudder.

'"Another one,"' the abbé went on without appearing to notice Caderousse's emotion, '"was named Danglars; the third one," he said, "also loved me though he was my rival, and his name was Fernand; the name of my betrothed was . . ." I do not remember the name of his betrothed.'

'Mercédès,' said Caderousse.

'Oh, yes, that was it,' replied the abbé with a repressed sigh. 'Mercédès it was. "Go to Marseilles," Dantès said, "and sell this diamond. The money obtained for it divide into five parts and give an equal share to each of these good friends, the only beings on earth who have loved me."'

'Why into five parts?' exclaimed Caderousse. 'You only named four persons.'

'Because I hear that the fifth person is dead. The fifth share was for Dantès' father.'

'Alas, it is only too true!' said Caderousse, deeply moved by the contending passions that were aroused in him. 'The old man died less than a year after his son disappeared.'

'What did he die of?'

'I believe the doctors called his disease gastric enteritis, but those who knew him say that he died of grief, and I, who practically saw him die, say that he died of . . .'

Caderousse hesitated.

'Died of what?' the priest asked anxiously.

'Why, of hunger . . .'

'Of hunger?' the abbé cried, jumping up. 'Do you

say of hunger? Why, the vilest animals are not allowed to starve. The dogs wandering about the streets find a compassionate hand to throw them a piece of bread, and a man, a Christian, has died of hunger amidst men who also call themselves Christians! Is it possible? No, it cannot be!'

'It is as I have said,' replied Caderousse.

'But,' continued the priest, 'was the unhappy old man so completely forsaken by everyone that he died such a death?'

'It was not because Mercédès or Monsieur Morrel had forsaken him,' replied Caderousse. 'The poor old man took a strong dislike to this same Fernand whom Dantès named as one of his friends,' he added with an ironical smile.

'Was he not a friend then?' asked the abbé.

'Can a man be a friend to him whose wife he covets? Dantès was so large-hearted that he called them all his friends. Poor Edmond!'

'Do you know in what way Fernand wronged Dantès?'

'No one better than I.'

'Will you not tell me?'

'What good would it do?'

'Then you would prefer me to give these men who, you say, are false and faithless friends, a reward intended for faithful friendship?'

'You are right,' said Caderousse. 'Besides, what would poor Edmond's legacy be to them now? No more than a drop of water in the mighty ocean!'

'How so? Have they become rich and mighty?'

'Then you do not know their history?'

'No, tell it to me.'

Caderousse appeared to reflect for an instant. 'No,' he said. 'It would take too long.'

'You may please yourself, my friend,' said the abbé with an air of complete indifference. 'I respect your scruples and admire your sentiment. We will let the matter drop. I will sell the diamond.'

So saying he took the diamond out of his pocket and let the light play on it right in front of Caderousse.

'Oh, what a magnificent diamond!' exclaimed the latter in a voice almost hoarse with emotion. 'It must be worth at least fifty thousand francs.'

'Remember it is your wish that I divide the money amongst all four of you,' the abbé said calmly, replacing the diamond in the pocket of his cassock. 'Now, be kind enough to give me the addresses of Edmond's friends, so that I may carry out his last wishes.'

The perspiration stood out in big drops on Caderousse's forehead; he saw the abbé rise and go towards the door as if he wished to ascertain that his horse was all right; afterwards he returned and asked:

'Well, what have you decided to do?'

'To tell you everything,' was the innkeeper's reply.

'I really believe that is the best thing you can do,' replied the priest, 'not because I am anxious to know what you wish to conceal from me, but simply because it will be much better if you can help me to distribute the legacy as the testator would have desired. Begin; I am all attention.'

Caderousse went to the door and closed it, and, by way of greater precaution, shot the bolt. The priest chose a seat in a corner where he could listen at his ease and where he would have his back to the light while the narrator would have the light full on his face. There he sat, his head bent, his hands joined, or rather clenched, ready to listen with all attention. Caderousse took a stool and sat in front of him and began his story.

'It is a very sad story, monsieur,' said Caderousse shaking his head. 'I dare say you already know the beginning.'

'Yes, Edmond told me everything up to the moment of his arrest. He himself knew nothing except what touched him personally, for he never again set eyes on any of the five people I mentioned just now, nor did he ever hear their names mentioned.'

'Well, directly after Dantès' arrest in the middle of his betrothal feast Monsieur Morrel left to obtain further information. The news he brought us was very sad. The old father returned to the house alone, and, with tears streaming from his eyes, folded up his wedding clothes. He spent the whole night pacing up and down his room and did not go to bed at all, for my room was beneath his, and I heard him walking about the whole night long.

'The next day Mercédès went to Marseilles to implore Monsieur de Villefort's protection, but in vain. She paid the old man a visit at the same time. When she saw him so miserable and grief-stricken, she wanted to take him with her to her cottage to look after him, but the old man refused.

'"No," said he, "I will not leave the house. My poor son loves me more than anyone else, and, if he is let out of prison, he will come to see me first of all. What would he say if I were not there to welcome him?"

'The old man became more and more lonely with each succeeding day. Mercédès and Monsieur Morrel often came to see him, but they always found his door shut, and, though I knew he was at home, he never opened it to them. One day, contrary to custom, he received Mercédès, and when the poor girl, herself desperate and hopeless, tried to comfort him, he said:

'"Believe me, my daughter, he is dead. Instead of our waiting for him, it is he who awaits us. I am very glad that I am the elder, as I shall therefore be the first to see him again."

'However good and kind-hearted one may be, you can quite understand that one soon ceases to visit those that depress one, and thus it came about that poor old Dantès was left entirely alone. Now I only saw strangers go to his room from time to time, and these came out with suspicious-looking bundles: little by little he was selling all he possessed to eke out his miserable existence. At length he had nothing left but his few clothes.

'During the next three days I heard the old man pacing the floor as usual, but on the fourth day, there wasn't a sound to be heard. I ventured to go up to him. The door was locked, but I peeped through the keyhole and saw him so pale and haggard-looking that I felt sure he must be very ill. I sent word to Monsieur Morrel and myself ran for Mercédès. Neither of them wasted any time in coming. Monsieur Morrel brought with him a doctor, who diagnosed gastric enteritis and put his patient on a diet.

'Mercédès came again and saw such a change in the old man that, as before, she wanted to have him moved to her own cottage. Monsieur Morrel was also of the opinion that this would be best, and wanted to move him by force, but he protested so violently that they were afraid to do so. Mercédès remained at the bedside. Monsieur Morrel went away, making a sign to Mercédès that he had left a purse on the mantelshelf. Nevertheless, taking advantage of the doctor's instructions, the old man would eat nothing. Finally after nine days' despair and wasting, the old man died, cursing those who had caused all his misery. His last words to Mercédès were: "If you see my Edmond again, tell him I died blessing him."'

The abbé rose, and twice paced round the room, pressing his trembling hand to his parched throat.

'Who are the men who caused the son to die of despair and the father of hunger?' asked the priest at last.

'Two men who were jealous of him, the one through love and the other through ambition. Their names are Fernand and Danglars.'

'In what way did they show this jealousy?'

'They denounced Edmond as a Bonapartist agent.'

'Which of the two denounced him? Who was the real culprit?'

'Both were guilty. The letter was written on the day before the betrothal feast. It was Danglars who wrote it with his left hand, it was Fernand who posted it.'

'And yet you did not protest against such infamy?' said the abbé. 'Then you are their accomplice.'

'They both made me drink so excessively, monsieur, that I was no longer responsible for my actions.'

'But the next day you saw what consequences it had, yet you said nothing, though you were present when he was arrested.'

'Yes, monsieur, I was there and I tried to speak. I wanted to say all I knew, but Danglars prevented me. I will own that I stood in fear of the political state of things at that time, and I let myself be overruled. I kept silence. It was cowardly, I know, but it was not criminal.'

'I understand. You just let things take their course.'

'Yes, monsieur,' was Caderousse's rejoinder, 'and I regret it night and day.'

There followed a short silence; the abbé got up and paced the room in deep thought. At length he returned to his place and sat down, saying: 'You have mentioned a Monsieur Morrel two or three times. Who was he?'

'He was the owner of the *Pharaon*.'

'What part did he play in this sad affair?'

'The part of an honest, courageous, and affectionate man, monsieur. Twenty times did he intercede for Dantès. When the Emperor returned, he wrote, entreated, and threatened, with the result that during the second Restoration, he was persecuted as a Bonapartist. As I told you before, he came again and again to Dantès' father to persuade him to live with him in his house, and, as I also mentioned, the day before the old man's death, he left on the mantelshelf a purse which contained sufficient money to pay off his debts and to defray the expenses of the funeral. Thus the poor old man was enabled to die as he had lived, without doing wrong to anyone. I have still got the purse; it is a red silk one.'

'If Monsieur Morrel is still alive, he must be enjoying God's blessing: he must be rich and happy.'

Caderousse smiled bitterly. 'Yes, as happy as I am,' was the answer. 'He stands on the brink of poverty, and, what is more, of dishonour. After twenty-five years' work, after having gained the most honoured place in the business world of Marseilles, Monsieur Morrel is utterly ruined. He has lost five ships during the last two years, has had to bear the brunt of the bankruptcy of three large firms, and his only hope is now in the *Pharaon*, the very ship that poor Dantès commanded, which is expected from the Indies with a cargo of cochineal and indigo. If this ship goes down like the others, all is lost.'

'Has the unfortunate man a wife and children?'

'Yes, he has a wife who is behaving like a saint through all this trouble; he has a daughter who was to have married the man she loves, but his family will not allow him to marry the daughter of a bankrupt; and he has a son, a lieutenant in the army. But you may well understand that this only increases the wretched man's grief instead of alleviating it. If he were alone, he would blow out his brains and there would be an end to it.'

'It is terrible,' murmured the priest.

'It is thus that God rewards virtue, monsieur. Just look at me. I have never done a wrong action apart from the one I related to you a moment ago, yet I live in poverty, while Fernand and Danglars are rolling in wealth. Everything they have touched has turned into gold, whereas everything I have done has gone all wrong.'

'Danglars was the more guilty of the two, the instigator, was he not? What has become of him?'

'He left Marseilles and, upon the recommendation of Monsieur Morrel, who was unaware of his crime, he became cashier in a Spanish bank. During the war with Spain, he was employed in the commissariat of the French army and made a fortune. Then he speculated with his money and quadrupled his capital. He married his banker's daughter and was left a widower after a short time; then he married a widow, the daughter of the chamberlain who is in great favour at Court. He became a millionaire and was made a Baron. Thus he is now Baron Danglars, owns a large house in the Rue du Mont Blanc, has ten horses in his stable, six footmen in his antechamber, and I don't know how many millions in his coffers.'

'But how could Fernand, a poor fisherman, make a fortune? He had neither resources nor education. I must own this surpasses my comprehension.'

'It is beyond the comprehension of everyone. There must be some strange secret in his life of which we are all ignorant. It is all very mysterious. A few days before the Restoration, Fernand was enrolled in a fighting unit, reached the frontier, and took part in the battle of Ligny.

'The night following the battle, he was on sentry duty outside the door of a general who was in secret communication with the enemy and who intended going over to the English that very night. He suggested that Fernand should accompany him. To this Fernand agreed, and, deserting his post, followed the general.

'This would have meant a court-martial for Fernand if Napoleon had remained on the throne, but to the Bourbons it only served him as a recommendation. He returned to France with the epaulette of a sub-lieutenant and, as he still enjoyed the protection of the general, who stood in high favour, he was promoted captain during the Spanish war in 1823; that is to say, at the time when Danglars was first launching forth in speculation. Fernand was a Spaniard, so he was sent to Madrid to inquire into the feeling existing among his compatriots. While there he met Danglars, who became very friendly with him, promised his general support amongst the Royalists of the capital and the provinces, obtained promises for himself, and on his side made pledges. He led his regiment along paths known only to himself in gorges guarded by Royalists, and in short rendered such services during that short campaign that after the fall of Trocadero, he was promoted colonel and received the cross of an Officer of the Legion of Honour.'

'Fate! Fate!' murmured the abbé.

'Yes, but that is not all. Some time later it was stated that the Count of Morcerf, which was the name he now bore, had gone to Greece and entered the service of Ali Pasha with the rank of Instructor-General. Ali Pasha was killed, as you know, but before he died, he recompensed Fernand for his services by leaving him a considerable sum of money. Fernand returned to France, where his rank of lieutenant-general was confirmed, and today he owns a magnificent house in Paris in the Rue du Helder, number twenty-seven.'

The abbé opened his mouth as though to speak, hesitated for a moment, then, with a great effort, said: 'What about Mercédès? They tell me she has disappeared.'

'Disappeared?' said Caderousse. 'Yes, as the sun disappears only to rise with more splendour the next day.'

'Has she also made her fortune then?' asked the abbé with an ironical smile.

'Mercédès is at present one of the grandest ladies in Paris. At first she was utterly overcome by the blow which had robbed her of her Edmond. I have already told you how she importuned Villefort with entreaties, and have also touched upon her devoted care for Dantès' father. In the midst of her despair she was assailed by another trouble, the departure of Fernand, of whose crime she was unaware and whom she regarded as a brother.

'Mercédès was alone and uncared for. She spent three months weeping and sorrowing. No news of Edmond and none of Fernand, with nothing to distract her but an old man dying of despair.

'One evening after she had been sitting all day at the crossroads leading to Marseilles and the Catalans, as was her wont, she returned home more depressed than ever. Neither her lover nor her friend had returned along either of these two roads, neither had she any news of them.

'Suddenly she seemed to recognize a step behind her and turned round anxiously. The door opened, and Fernand entered in the uniform of a sub-lieutenant. It was only the half of what she was grieving for, but it was a portion of her past life restored to her. She seized Fernand's hands in an ecstasy of joy. This he took for love, whereas it was nothing more than joy at being no longer alone in the world, and at seeing a friend again after so many long hours of solitary sadness. Then you must remember she had never hated Fernand, she simply did not love him. Another one owned Mercédès' heart, and he was absent . . . he had disappeared . . . perhaps he was dead.

'The old man died. Had he lived, in all probability

Mercédès would never have become the wife of another; he would have been there to reproach her with her infidelity. Fernand realized that fact. As soon as he heard that the old man was dead, he returned. This time he was a lieutenant. He reminded her that he loved her. Mercédès asked for six months in which to await and bewail Edmond.'

'Well, that made eighteen months in all,' said the abbé with a bitter smile. 'What more could the most adored lover ask?' Then he murmured the words of the English poet: '"Frailty, thy name is woman!"'

'Six months later,' continued Caderousse, 'the wedding took place in the Church des Accoules.'

'The very church in which she was to have married Edmond,' murmured the abbé. 'The bridegroom was changed, that was all.' Aloud, he asked: 'Did you see Mercédès again?'

'Yes, during the Spanish war at Perpignan where Fernand had left her; she was attending to the education of her son.'

The abbé started. 'Her son, did you say?'

'Yes,' was Caderousse's reply, 'little Albert's education.'

'But I am sure Edmond told me she was the daughter of a simple fisherman and that, though she was beautiful, she was uneducated. Had she taken a course of instruction that she was able to teach her son?'

'Oh!' exclaimed Caderousse. 'Did he know his sweetheart so little? If crowns were bestowed upon beauty and intelligence, Mercédès would now be a queen. Her fortune was growing, and she grew with it. She learnt drawing, music, everything. Personally I think she did all this simply to distract her mind, to help her to forget; she crammed so much knowledge into her head to alleviate the weight in her heart. I must tell you everything as it is,' continued Caderousse. 'Her fortune and honours have no doubt afforded her some consolation; she is rich, she is a Countess, and yet . . .' Caderousse hesitated.

'Yet what?' asked the abbé.

'Yet I am sure she is not happy.'

'Do you know what has happened to Monsieur de Villefort and what part he played in Edmond's misfortune?'

'No, I only know that some time after he had him arrested he married Mademoiselle Renéede Saint-Méran and shortly afterwards left Marseilles. No doubt Dame Fortune has smiled upon him, too. No doubt like Danglars he is rich, and like Fernand covered with honours, while I alone, you understand, have remained poor, miserable, and forsaken by all.'

'You are mistaken, my friend,' said the abbé. 'There are times when God's justice tarries for a while and it appears to us that we are forgotten by Him, but the time always comes when we find it is not so, and here is the proof.'

With these words the abbé took the diamond from his pocket and handed it to Caderousse.

'Here, my friend,' he said. 'Take this, it is yours.'

'What! For me alone!' exclaimed Caderousse. 'Ah, monsieur, do not jest with me!'

'The diamond was to be divided amongst Edmond's friends. He had but one friend, therefore it cannot be divided. Take the diamond and sell it; it is worth fifty thousand francs, a sum which will, I trust, suffice to relieve you of your poverty.'

'Oh, monsieur, do not play with the happiness or despair of a man!' said Caderousse, putting out one hand timidly, while with the other he wiped away the perspiration that gathered in big drops on his forehead.

'I know what happiness means as I also know what despair means, and I should never play with either of these feelings. Take the diamond, but in exchange . . .'

Caderousse already had his hand on the diamond, but at these last words he hastily withdrew it.

The abbé smiled.

'In exchange,' continued he, 'give me the red silk purse Monsieur Morrel left on the mantelshelf in old Dantès' room.'

More and more astonished, Caderousse went to a large oak cupboard, opened it, and, taking out a long purse of faded red silk on two copper rings, once gilt, he handed it to the priest.

The abbé took it and gave the diamond in exchange.

'You are verily a man of God, monsieur!' exclaimed Caderousse.

The abbé rose and took his hat and gloves, unbarred the door, mounted his horse, and, saying goodbye to Caderousse, who was most effusive in his farewells, started off by the road he had come.

14

A few days later, the firm of Morrel and Son received a visitor, an Englishman, a representative from the bankers Thomson and French in Rome. Morrel and Son was vastly reduced from its busy, thriving state of some years before. Now only Coclès, an aged and loyal cashier, worked there, and a young clerk called Emmanuel Herbault, who stayed despite his family's protestations, because he was in love with Mademoiselle Julie Morrel.

To M. Morrel's dismay and consternation, the Englishman was holding bills which he had bought over the last few days from all Morrel's principal creditors. The sum was now owed in its entirety to Thomson and French. The Englishman leafed through the bills, adding them all up, and told Morrel the final figure.

What M. Morrel suffered during this enumeration is impossible to describe.

'Two hundred and eighty-seven thousand five hundred francs,' he repeated automatically.

'Yes, monsieur,' replied the Englishman. 'But,' he continued after a moment's silence, 'I will not conceal from you, Monsieur Morrel, that though I am fully aware of your blameless probity up to the present, public report is rife in Marseilles that you are not in a position to meet your obligations.'

At this almost brutal frankness Morrel turned pale.

'Up to the present, monsieur,' said he, 'and it is more than twenty-four years since I took over the directorship of the firm from my father, who had himself managed it for thirty-five years – until now not one bill signed by Morrel and Son has ever been presented for payment that has not been duly honoured.'

'I am fully aware of that,' replied the Englishman, 'but as one man of honour to another, tell me quite frankly, shall you pay these with the same exactitude?'

Morrel started and looked at this man who spoke to him with more assurance than he had hitherto shown.

'To questions put with such frankness,' said he, 'a straightforward answer must be given. Yes, monsieur, I shall pay if, as I hope, my ship arrives safely, for its arrival will restore to me the credit which one stroke of ill-fortune after another has deprived me of. But should, by some ill-chance, this, my last resource, the *Pharaon*, fail me, I fear, monsieur, I shall be compelled to suspend payment.'

'The *Pharaon* is your last hope, then?'

'Absolutely the last. And,' he continued, 'her delay is not natural. She left Calcutta on the 5th of February and should have been here more than a month ago.'

'What is that?' exclaimed the Englishman, listening intently. 'What is the meaning of this noise?'

'Oh, heavens!' cried Morrel, turning a ghastly colour. 'What fresh disaster is this?'

In truth, there was much noise on the staircase. People were running hither and thither, and now and then a cry of distress was heard. Morrel rose to open the door, but his strength failed him and he sank into his chair.

The two men sat facing each other: Morrel was trembling in every limb, while the stranger was looking at him with an expression of profound pity. The noise ceased, but, nevertheless, it was apparent that Morrel was simply awaiting events; the hubbub was not without reason and would naturally have its sequel.

The stranger thought he heard several people come up the stairs quietly and stop on the landing. A key was inserted in the lock of the first door, which creaked on its hinges. Julie entered, her cheeks bathed with tears. Supporting himself on the arm of his chair, Morrel rose unsteadily. He wanted to speak, but his voice failed him.

'Oh, Father! Father!' exclaimed the girl clasping her hands. 'Forgive your daughter for being the bearer of bad news. Father, be brave!'

Morrel turned deadly pale. 'So the *Pharaon* is lost?' he asked in a choked voice.

The girl made no answer, but she nodded her head and fell into his arms.

'And the crew?'

'Saved!' said the young girl. 'Saved by the Bordeaux vessel that has just entered the port.'

'Thank God!' said he. 'At least Thou strikest me alone!'

Scarcely had he uttered these words when Mme Morrel came in sobbing, followed by Emmanuel. Standing in the background were to be seen the stalwart forms of seven or eight half-naked sailors from the *Pharaon*. The Englishman started at sight of these men; he took a step towards them, but then restrained himself and withdrew to the farthest and darkest corner of the room.

Mme Morrel seated herself in a chair and took her husband's hand in hers, whilst Julie still lay with her head on her father's shoulder. Emmanuel remained in the middle of the room like a link between the Morrel family and the sailors at the door.

'How did it happen?' asked Morrel.

The sailors recounted a sad tale of storm and shipwreck, of heroism and rescue. When they had finished, Morrel told Coclès to pay the men what was owed them. Coclès and Emmanuel left with the sailors.

'Now,' said the shipowner to his wife and daughter, 'leave me awhile. I wish to speak with this gentleman.'

The two ladies looked at the stranger, whom they had entirely forgotten, and withdrew. When going out, however, the girl cast an entreating look on the Englishman, to which he responded with a smile, such as one would hardly expect to see on those stern features. The two men were left alone.

'Well, monsieur,' said Morrel, sinking into his chair. 'You have seen and heard all. I have nothing further to tell you.'

'Yes, monsieur, I have learnt that you are the victim of fresh misfortune, as unmerited as the rest. This has only confirmed my desire to render you a service. I am one of your principal creditors, am I not?'

'In any case, you are in possession of the bills that will fall due first.'

'Would you like the date of payment prolonged?'

'It would certainly save my honour and consequently my life.'

'How long do you ask?'

Morrel hesitated a moment and then he said: 'Three months. But do you think Messrs Thomson and French . . .'

'Do not worry about that. I will take all responsibility upon myself. Today is the 5th of June. Renew these bills up to the 5th of September, and at eleven o'clock' (at that moment the clock struck eleven) 'on the 5th of September, I shall present myself.'

'I shall await you, monsieur,' said Morrel, 'and you will be paid or else I shall be dead.'

These last words were said in such a low voice that the stranger did not hear them.

The bills were renewed and the old ones destroyed so that the unfortunate shipowner was given another three months in which to gather together his last resources.

The Englishman received his thanks with the coldness peculiar to his race and bade farewell to Morrel, who, calling down blessings on him, accompanied him to the door.

On the stairs he met Julie. She pretended to be going down, but in reality she was waiting for him.

'Oh, monsieur!' she exclaimed, clasping her hands.

'Mademoiselle,' said the stranger, 'one day you will receive a letter signed Sinbad the Sailor. Do exactly what the letter bids you to do, no matter how extraordinary the instructions may appear. Will you promise me to do this?'

'I promise.'

'Very good, then. Farewell, mademoiselle. Always remain as good and virtuous as you are now, and I am sure God will reward you by giving you Emmanuel as your husband.'

Julie uttered a faint exclamation and blushed like a rose, while the stranger nodded a farewell and went on his way.

The extension of time granted by Messrs Thomson and French's agent, at a time when Morrel least expected it, seemed to the poor shipowner like one of those returns to good fortune which announce to man that fate has at last become weary of spending her fury on him. The same day he related to his daughter, his wife, and Emmanuel all that had occurred, and a ray of hope, one might almost say of peace, once more entered their hearts.

Unfortunately, however, Morrel had other engagements than those with Thomson and French, who had shown themselves so considerate towards him, and, as has been said, one has correspondents only in business, and not friends. Any bill signed by Morrel was presented with the most scrupulous exactitude, and, thanks to the extension granted by the Englishman, each one was paid by Coclès on sight.

August rolled by in untiring and unsuccessful attempts on the part of Morrel to renew his old credit or to open up fresh ones. Then he remembered Danglars, who was now a millionaire and could save Morrel without taking a penny from his pocket by guaranteeing a loan; but there are times when one feels a repugnance one cannot master, and Morrel had delayed as long as possible before having recourse to this. His feeling of repugnance was justified, for he returned from Paris borne down by the humiliation of a refusal. Yet he uttered no complaint and spoke no harsh word. He embraced his weeping wife and daughter, shook hands with Emmanuel, and closeted himself in his office with Coclès.

When he appeared for dinner, he was outwardly quite calm. This apparent calmness, however, alarmed his wife and daughter more than the deepest dejection would have done. Emmanuel tried to reassure them, but his eloquence failed him. He was too well acquainted with the business of the firm not to realize that a terrible catastrophe was pending for the Morrel family.

Night came. The two women watched, hoping that when Morrel left his office he would rejoin them, but they heard him pass by their door, stepping very lightly, no doubt lest they should hear and call him. They heard him go to his room and lock the door.

Mme Morrel sent her daughter to bed, and an hour later, taking off her shoes, she crept down the landing and peeped through the keyhole to see what her husband was doing. She saw a retreating figure on the landing. It was Julie, who, being anxious, had anticipated her mother.

'He is writing,' she said to her mother. They understood each other without speaking. Mme Morrel stooped down to the keyhole. Morrel was indeed writing. The terrible idea flashed across her mind that he was making his will. It made her shudder, yet she had strength enough to say nothing.

Two days passed. On the morning of the 5th of September Morrel came down, calm as usual, but the agitation of the previous days had left its mark on his pale and careworn face. He was more affectionate towards his wife and daughter than he had ever been; he gazed fondly on the poor child and embraced her again and again. When he left the room Julie made as if to accompany him; but he pushed her back gently, saying:

'Stay with your mother.'

Julie tried to insist.

'I wish it!' said Morrel.

It was the first time Morrel had ever said 'I wish it' to his daughter, but he said it in a tone of such paternal fondness that Julie dared not advance a step. She remained rooted to the spot, and spoke never a word.

An instant later the door opened again. Julie felt two strong arms about her and a mouth pressing a kiss on her forehead. She looked up with an exclamation of joy: 'Maximilian! My brother!'

At these words Mme Morrel sprang up, and, running towards her son, threw herself in his arms.

'Mother, what has happened?' said the young man, looking alternately at Mme Morrel and her daughter. 'Your letter made me feel very anxious, so I hastened to you.'

'Julie, go and tell your father that Maximilian has come,' said Mme Morrel, making a sign to the young man.

The girl hastened to obey, but, on the first stair, she met a young man with a letter in his hand.

'Are you not Mademoiselle Julie Morrel?' he said with a very pronounced Italian acent.

'Yes, monsieur,' stammered Julie. 'What do you wish of me? I do not know you.'

'Read this letter,' said the man handing her a note.

The girl snatched the note from his hands, opened it hastily, and read:

Go this moment to number 15, Allées de Meilhan, ask the porter for the key to the room on the fifth floor. Enter the room, take a red silk purse that is on the corner of the mantelshelf and give it to your father. It is important that he should have it before eleven o'clock. You promised me blind obedience, and I now remind you of that promise.

SINBAD THE SAILOR

Julie uttered an exclamation of joy, yet even in her joy she felt a certain uneasiness. Was there nothing to fear? Was this not all a trap that had been laid for her? She hesitated and decided to ask advice, but a strange feeling urged her to apply to Emmanuel rather than to her brother or her mother. She told him all that had happened the day Thomson and French's agent came to see her father, repeated the promise she had made and showed him the letter.

'You must go, mademoiselle,' Emmanuel said, 'and I shall go with you.'

'Then it is your opinion, Emmanuel,' said the girl with some misgiving, 'that I should carry out these instructions?'

'Listen,' he said. 'Today is the 5th of September, and at eleven o'clock your father must pay out nearly three hundred thousand francs, whereas he does not possess fifteen thousand.'

'What will happen then?'

'If your father has not found someone to come to his aid by eleven o'clock, he will be obliged by twelve o'clock to declare himself bankrupt.'

'Come along then, come!' cried Julie, pulling Emmanuel after her.

In the meantime Mme Morrel had told her son everything. He knew that after his father's successive misfortunes all expenditure in the house had been rigidly cut down, but he was unaware that matters had come to such a pass. He was horror-struck.

Then he suddenly rushed out of the room and ran upstairs, expecting to find his father in the office, but he received no answer to his repeated knocks. As he was waiting at the door, however, his father came from his bedroom. He uttered a cry of surprise on seeing Maximilian; he did not know of his arrival. He stood where he was, pressing with his left hand something he was trying to conceal under his coat. Maximilian ran down the stairs quickly and threw himself round his father's neck. Suddenly he drew back, and stood there as pale as death.

'Father,' said he, 'why have you a brace of pistols under your coat?'

'Blood washes out dishonour!' said Morrel.

'Oh, Father, Father!' cried the young man. 'If only you could live!'

'I should be looked upon as a man who has broken his word and failed in his engagements. If I lived you would be ashamed of my name. When I am dead, you will raise your head and say, "I am the son of him who killed himself because, for the first time in his life, he was unable to keep his word." Now,' continued Morrel, 'leave me alone and keep your mother away. Once more farewell. Go, go, I need to be alone. You will find my will in the desk in my room.'

When his son had gone Morrel sank into his chair and looked up at the clock. He had only seven minutes left and the hand seemed to move round with incredible rapidity. The pistols were loaded; stretching out his hand, he seized one, murmuring his daughter's name. Putting the weapon down again, he took up his pen to write a few words. It occurred to him he might have been more affectionate in his farewell to his beloved daughter.

Then he turned to the clock again; he no longer counted by minutes, but by seconds. Taking the weapon once more, he opened his mouth with his eyes on the clock. The noise he made in cocking the pistol sent a shiver through him; a cold perspiration broke out on his forehead and he was seized by a mortal anguish.

He heard the outer door creak on its hinges. The inner door opened. The clock was about to strike eleven. Morrel did not turn round.

He put the pistol to his mouth . . . Suddenly he heard a cry . . . It was his daughter's voice. He turned round and saw Julie. The pistol dropped from his hands.

'Father!' cried the girl out of breath and overcome with joy. 'You are saved! You are saved!'

She threw herself into his arms, at the same time holding out to him a red silk purse.

'Saved, my child?' said he. 'What do you mean?'

'Yes, saved! See here!'

Morrel started at sight of the purse, for he had a faint recollection that it had once belonged to him. He took it in his hand. At one end it held the receipted bill for two hundred and eighty-seven thousand five hundred francs, at the other a diamond as big as a nut, with these two words written on a piece of parchment attached to it:

JULIE'S DOWRY

Morrel passed his hand across his brow: he thought he must be dreaming. At the same moment the clock struck eleven.

'Explain, my child,' said he. 'Where did you find this purse?'

'On the corner of the mantelshelf of a miserable little room on the fifth floor of number fifteen, Allées de Meilhan.'

'But this purse is not yours!'

Julie showed her father the letter she had received that morning.

Just then Emmanuel came rushing in full of excitement and joy.

'The *Pharaon*!' cried he. 'The *Pharaon*!'

'What? The *Pharaon*? Are you mad, Emmanuel? You know quite well she is lost.'

Then in came Maximilian. 'Father, how could you say the *Pharaon* was lost? The look-out has just signalled her, and she is putting into port.'

'If that is the case, my friends,' said his father, 'it must be a miracle. Let us go and see, but God have pity on us if it is a false report.'

They all went out and on the stairs met Mme Morrel, who had not dared to go into the office. They were soon on the Cannebière, where a large crowd was gathered. All made way for Morrel, and every voice was calling out: 'The *Pharaon*! The *Pharaon*!'

True enough, though wonderful to relate, there, in front of the Saint-Jean tower, was a ship with the words '*Pharaon* (Morrel and Son, Marseilles)' in white letters on her stern; she was the exact counterpart of the other *Pharaon*, and also carried a cargo of indigo and cochineal. She was casting her anchor with all sails brailed. On the deck Captain Gaumard was issuing orders.

As Morrel and his son were embracing each other on the quayside amid the applause of the onlookers, a man whose face was half hidden by a black beard and who had been watching the scene from behind a sentry-box, muttered to himself: 'Be happy, noble heart. May you be blessed for all the good you have done and will do hereafter!' And with a smile of joy he left his hiding-place without being observed, descended the steps to the water, and called out three times: 'Jacopo! Jacopo! Jacopo!'

A shallop came alongside, took him on board, and conveyed him to a beautifully rigged yacht. He jumped on deck with the nimbleness of a sailor, and from thence once more gazed on the happy scene on the quay.

'Now, farewell to kindness, humanity, gratitude,' said he. 'Farewell to all the sentiments which rejoice the heart. I have played the part of Providence in recompensing the good. May the god of vengeance now permit me to punish the wicked!'

Muttering these words, he made a sign, and the yacht immediately put out to sea.

15

Towards the beginning of the year 1838 two young men belonging to the best society of Paris were staying in Florence: one was Viscount Albert de Morcerf and the other Baron Franz d'Épinay. They had decided to spend the Carnival together at Rome, and Franz, who had lived in Italy for more than four years, was to be his friend's guide.

As it is no small matter to spend the Carnival at Rome, especially when you have no great desire to sleep in the Piazza del Popolo or the Campo Vaccino, they wrote to Signor Pastrini, the proprietor of the Hôtel de Londres, to ask him to reserve a comfortable suite for them.

On the Saturday evening before the Carnival they arrived in Rome. The suite reserved for them consisted of two small bedrooms and a sitting-room. The bedrooms overlooked the street, a fact which Pastrini commented upon as a priceless advantage. The remaining rooms on that floor were let to an immensely rich gentleman who was supposed to be either a Sicilian or a Maltese, the proprietor was not quite sure which.

'That is all very well, Pastrini,' said Franz, 'but we want some supper at once, and also a carriage for tomorrow and the following days.'

'You shall have supper instantly, signore, but as for the carriage . . . they have all been hired out for the Carnival. Still, I will see what I can do.'

The two young friends spent the next day sightseeing, and the day after that Franz had several letters to write and left Albert to his own devices. Albert made the most of his time; he took his letters of introduction to their addresses, and received invitations for every evening. He also achieved the great feat of seeing all Rome in one day, and spent the evening at the opera. Moreover, by the time he reached his hotel he had solved the carriage question. When the two friends were smoking their last cigar in their sitting-room before retiring for the night, Albert suddenly said:

'I have arranged a little surprise for you. You know how impossible it is to procure a carriage. Well, I have a wonderful idea.'

Franz looked at his friend as though he had no great confidence in his imagination.

'We cannot get a carriage and horses, but what about a wagon and a pair of oxen?'

Franz stared, and a smile of amused interest played about his lips.

'Yes, a wagon and a yoke of oxen. We will have the wagon decorated and we will dress ourselves up as Neapolitan harvesters, and represent a living picture after the magnificent painting by Leopold Robert.'

'Bravo!' exclaimed Franz. 'For once you have hit upon a capital idea. Have you told anyone about it?'

'I have told our host. When I came in, I sent for him and explained to him all that I should require. He assured me that it would be quite easy to obtain everything. I wanted to have the oxen's horns decorated, but he told me it would take three days to do it, so we must do without this superfluity.'

'Where is our host now?'

'Gone out in search of our things.'

As he spoke, the door opened, and their landlord put his head in.

'May I come in?' said he.

'Certainly,' Franz replied.

'Well, have you found the wagon and oxen for us?' said Albert.

'I have done better than that,' he replied in a very self-satisfied manner. 'Your Excellencies are aware that the Count of Monte Cristo is on the same floor as yourselves. Hearing of the dilemma in which you are placed, he offers you two seats in his carriage and two seats at his window in the Palazzo Ruspoli.'

Albert and Franz exchanged looks.

'But can we accept this offer from a stranger, a man we do not even know?' asked Albert.

'It seems to me,' said Franz to Albert, 'that if this man is as well-mannered as our host says he is, he would have conveyed his invitation to us in some other way, either in writing or –'

At this instant there was a knock at the door.

'Come in,' said Franz.

A servant wearing a very smart livery made his appearance.

'From the Count of Monte Cristo to Monsieur Franz d'Épinay and the Viscount Albert de Morcerf,' said he, handing two cards to the host, who gave them to the young men.

'The Count of Monte Cristo asks permission to call upon you tomorrow morning,' continued the servant. 'He will be honoured to know what hour is convenient to you.'

'Upon my word, there is nothing to find fault with here,' said Albert to Franz. 'Everything is as it should be.'

'Tell the Count that, on the contrary, we shall do ourselves the honour of calling upon him.'

The servant withdrew.

'That is what I should call assaulting us with politeness,' said Albert. 'Signor Pastrini, your Count of Monte Cristo is a very gentlemanly fellow.'

'You accept his offer then?'

'Of course we do,' replied Albert. 'Nevertheless, I must own that I regret the wagon and the harvesters, and if it were not for the window at the Palazzo Ruspoli to compensate us for our loss, I think I should revert to my first idea. What about you, Franz?'

'The window in the Palazzo Ruspoli is the deciding point with me, too.'

The next morning, they had only to cross the landing; the landlord preceded them and rang the bell. A servant opened the door.

'The French gentlemen,' said the landlord.

The servant bowed and invited them to enter.

They were conducted through two rooms, more luxuriously furnished than they had thought possible in Pastrini's hotel, and were then shown into a very elegant sitting-room. A Turkey carpet covered the parquet floor, and the most comfortably upholstered settees and chairs seemed to invite one to their soft, well-sprung seats and slanting backs. Magnificent paintings intermingled with glorious war trophies decorated the walls, while rich tapestried curtains hung before the door.

'If Your Excellencies will take a seat,' said the servant, 'I will let the Count know you are here.' And he disappeared through one of the doors.

Franz and Albert looked at one another and then at the furniture, pictures, and trophies. On closer inspection it all appeared to them even more magnificent than at first.

'Well, what do you think of it all?' Franz asked his friend.

'Upon my word, I think our neighbour must be some stockbroker who has speculated on the fall of Spanish funds; or else some prince travelling incognito.'

'Hush! That is what we are now going to find out, for here he comes.'

As he finished speaking the sound of a door turning on its hinges was heard, and almost immediately the tapestry was drawn aside to admit the owner of all these riches.

'Messieurs,' said the Count of Monte Cristo as he entered, 'pray accept my excuses for allowing myself to be forestalled, but I feared I might disturb you if I called on you at an early hour. Besides, you advised me you were coming, and I held myself at your disposal.'

'Franz and I owe you a thousand thanks, Count,' said Albert. 'You have truly extricated us from a great dilemma.'

'Indeed!' returned the Count, motioning the two young men to be seated on a settee. 'It is only that idiot Pastrini's fault that you were not relieved of your anxiety sooner. As soon as I learnt that I could be of use to you, I eagerly seized the opportunity of paying you my respects.'

The two young men bowed. They took their seats and spent a pleasant hour telling the Count about their experiences and acquaintances in Rome. Then there came a knock at the door.

'Excellency,' said the Count's steward Bertuccio, opening the door, 'a man in the habit of a friar wishes to speak with you.'

'Ah, yes, Bertuccio, I know what he wants,' said the Count. 'If you will go into the salon, you will find some excellent Havana cigars on the centre table. I will rejoin you in a minute.'

The two young men arose and went out by one door while the Count, after renewing his apologies, left by the other.

'Well, what do you think of the Count of Monte Cristo?' asked Franz of his friend.

'What do I think of him?' said Albert, obviously astonished that his companion should ask him such a question. 'I think he is a charming man who does the honours of his table to perfection; a man who has seen much, studied much, and thought much, and who possesses most excellent cigars,' he added appreciatively, sending out a whiff of smoke which rose to the ceiling in spirals.

'But did you notice how attentively he looked at you?' Franz asked.

'At me?'

'Yes.'

Albert thought for a moment.

'Ah, that is not surprising,' he said with a sigh. 'I have been away from Paris for nearly a year, and my clothes must have become old-fashioned. The Count probably thinks I come from the provinces; undeceive him, old man, and the first opportunity you have, tell him that this is not the case.'

Franz smiled, and an instant later the Count returned.

'Here I am, messieurs,' he said, 'and entirely at your service. I have given the necessary orders; the carriage will go to the Piazza del Popolo, and we shall go down the Corso if you really wish to. Take some of those cigars, Monsieur de Morcerf.'

'By Jove, I shall be delighted,' said Albert, 'for your Italian cigars are awful. When you come to Paris, I shall return all this hospitality.'

'I will not refuse; I hope to go there some day and, with your permission, I shall pay you a visit. Come along, messieurs, we have no time to lose; it is half-past twelve. Let us be off.'

By this time the Carnival had begun in real earnest. Picture the wide and beautiful Corso lined from end to end with tall palaces with their balconies tapestried and the windows draped, and at these windows and balconies three hundred thousand spectators, Romans, Italians, and strangers from every part of the world: aristocrats by birth side by side with aristocrats by wealth and genius; charming women who, succumbing to the influence of the spectacle, bent over the balconies or leaned out of the windows, showering confetti on the carriages and catching bouquets hurled up at them in return; the air thickened with sweetmeats thrown down and flowers thrown up; in the streets a gay, untiring, mad crowd in fantastic costumes: gigantic cabbages walking about, buffalo heads bellowing on human bodies, dogs walking on their hind legs. In the midst of all this a mask is raised revealing, as in Callot's dream of the temptation of St Anthony, a beautiful face that one follows only to be separated from it by these troops of demons such as one meets in one's dreams; picture all this to yourself, and you have a faint idea of the Carnival at Rome.

When they had driven round for the second time, the Count stopped the carriage and asked his companions' permission to quit them, leaving his carriage at their disposal.

'Messieurs,' said the Count, jumping out, 'when you are tired of being actors and wish to become spectators, you know you have seats at my window. In the meantime, my coachman, my window, and my servants are at your disposal.'

Franz thanked the Count for his kind offer; Albert, however, was busy coquetting with a carriageful of Roman peasants who had taken their stand near the Count's carriage, and was throwing bouquets at them.

Unfortunately for him the line of carriages drove on, and while he went towards the Piazza del Popolo, the carriage that had attracted his attention moved on toward the Palazzo di Venezia.

In spite of Albert's hopes, he could boast of no other adventure that day than that he had passed the carriage with the Roman peasants two or three times. Once, whether by accident or intentionally, his mask fell off. He took his remaining bouquets and threw them into the carriage.

One of the charming ladies whom Albert suspected to be disguised in the coquettish peasant's costume was doubtless touched by this gallantry, for, when the friends' carriage passed the next time, she threw him a bouquet of violets. Albert seized it and put in victoriously into his buttonhole, while the carriage continued its triumphant course.

'Well!' said Franz. 'Here is the beginning of an adventure.'

'Laugh as much as you like,' said Albert. 'I think you are right, though. Anyway, I shall not let this bouquet go!'

'I should think not indeed, it is a token of gratitude.'

The Count of Monte Cristo had given definite orders that his carriage should be at their disposal for the remaining days of the Carnival, and they were to make use of it without fear of trespassing too much on his kindness. The young men decided to take advantage of the Count's courtesy, and the next afternoon, having replaced their costume of the previous evening, which was somewhat the worse for the numerous combats they had engaged in, by a Roman peasant's attire, they gave orders for the horses to be harnessed. With a sentimental touch, Albert slipped the bouquet of faded violets in his buttonhole. They started forth and hastened towards the Corso by the Via Vittoria.

When they were going round the Corso for the second time, a bouquet of fresh violets was thrown into their carriage from one filled with pierrettes, from which it was quite clear to Albert that the peasants of the previous evening had changed their costumes.

Albert put the fresh flowers into his buttonhole, but kept the faded ones in his hand, and when he again met the carriage he put it amorously to his lips, which appeared to afford great amusement, not only to the one who had thrown it but also to her gay companions.

The day was no less animated than the previous evening; it is even probable that a keen observer would have noted more noise and gaiety. Once the two friends saw the Count at his window, but when they next passed he had disappeared. Needless to say, the flirtation between Albert and the pierrette with the violets lasted the whole day.

That evening, Franz noticed that Albert had something to ask him, but hesitated to formulate the request. He insisted upon it, however, declaring beforehand that he was willing to make any sacrifice for his pleasure. Albert's reluctance to tell his friend his secret lasted just as long as politeness demanded, and then he confessed to Franz that he would do him a great favour by permitting him to go in the carriage alone the next day.

Franz was not so selfish as to stand in Albert's way in the case of an adventure that promised to prove so agreeable to his curiosity and so flattering to his vanity. He felt assured that his friend would duly blurt out to him all that happened; and as a similar piece of good fortune had never fallen to his share during the three years that he had travelled in Italy, Franz was by no means sorry to learn what was the proper thing to do on such an occasion. He therefore promised Albert that he would be quite pleased to witness the Carnival on the morrow from the windows of the Ruspoli Palace.

The next morning he saw Albert pass and repass. He held an enormous bouquet, which he, doubtless, meant to make the bearer of his amorous epistle. This probability was changed into certainty when Franz saw the bouquet, a beautiful bunch of white camellias, in the hands of a charming pierrette dressed in rose-coloured satin.

The evening was no longer joy but ecstasy. Albert did not doubt that the fair unknown would reply in the same manner; nor was he mistaken, for the next evening saw him enter, triumphantly waving a folded paper he held by the corner.

'Well,' said he, 'what did I tell you?'

'She has answered you?' asked Franz.

'Read!'

Franz took the letter and read:

At seven o'clock on Tuesday evening, descend from your carriage opposite the Via dei Pontefici, and follow the Roman peasant who snatches your candle from you. When you arrive at the first step of the church of St Giacomo, be sure to fasten a knot of rose-coloured ribbons to the shoulder of your pierrot's costume so that you will be recognized. Until then you will not see me. Constancy and discretion.

'Well?' asked he, when Franz had finished reading. 'What do you think of that?'

'I think that the adventure is looking decidedly interesting,' said Franz, and on Tuesday evening he saw Albert off with a cheerful wave.

16

At eleven o'clock Albert had not come back. Franz put on his coat and went out, telling his host that he was spending the evening at the Duke of Bracciano's.

The Duke of Bracciano's house was at that time one of the most charming in Rome; his wife, who was one of the last descendants of the Colonnas, did the honours in the most perfect style, and the parties she gave attained European celebrity. Franz and Albert had brought letters of introduction to them, and the Duke's first question was as to what had become of Albert. Franz replied that he had left him when they were extinguishing the candles and had lost sight of him in the Via Macello.

'Do you know where he went to?' asked the Duke.

'Not exactly but I believe there was some question of a rendezvous.'

'Good heavens!' cried the Duke. 'It is a bad day, or rather night, to be out late. You know Rome better than he does and should not have let him go.'

Franz felt a shudder run down his back when he observed that the Duke was as uneasy in his mind as he himself was.

'I left word at the hotel that I had the honour of spending the evening with you, Duke,' he said, 'and that they were to inform me directly he returned.'

'Wait a moment; I believe one of my servants is looking for you.'

The Duke was not mistaken; on observing Franz, the servant came up to him.

'Excellency,' said he, 'the proprietor of the Hôtel de Londres has sent to inform you that a man is waiting for you there with a letter from Viscount de Morcerf.'

'A letter from the Viscount!' cried Franz. 'Where is the messenger?'

'He went away directly he saw me come into the ballroom to find you.'

Franz took his hat and hastened away. As he neared the hotel, he saw a man standing in the middle of the road and did not doubt he was Albert's messenger. He went up to him, and said:

'Have you not brought me a letter from Viscount de Morcerf?'

'What is Your Excellency's name?'

'Baron Franz d'Épinay.'

'Then the letter is addressed to Your Excellency.'

'Is there an answer?' asked Franz, taking the letter.

'Your friend hopes so!'

Franz went in and, as soon as his candle was lit, unfolded the paper. The letter was written in Albert's handwriting and signed by him. Franz read it twice before he could comprehend the contents, which were as follows:

DEAR FRANZ,

Directly you receive this, be good enough to take my letter of credit from my portfolio in the drawer of the writing-desk and add yours to it should it not be enough. Hasten to Torlonia's and draw out at once four thousand piastres, which give to bearer. It is urgent that this sum of money should be sent to me without delay.

I will say no more, for I count on you as you would count on me.

Yours ever,
ALBERT DE MORCERF

Beneath these lines the following words were written in a strange hand:

If the four thousand piastres are not in my hands by six in the morning Count Albert will have ceased to exist at seven o'clock.

LUIGI VAMPA

This second signature explained all to Franz. Albert had fallen into the hands of the famous bandit chief.

There was no time to lose. He hastened to the desk, opened it, found the portfolio in the drawer and in the portfolio the letter of credit: it was made out for six thousand piastres, but Albert had already spent three thousand. Franz had no letter of credit; as he lived at Florence and had come to Rome for but seven or eight days, he had only taken a hundred louis with him, and of these he had not more than fifty left.

Seven or eight hundred piastres were therefore lacking to make up the requisite sum. What could he do?

He was about to return to the Bracciano Palace without loss of time, when a bright idea occurred to him; he would appeal to the Count of Monte Cristo.

The Count was in a small room which was surrounded by divans which Franz had not yet seen.

'Well, what good wind blows you here at this hour?'

said he. 'Have you come to ask me to supper? That would indeed be very kind of you.'

'No, I have come to speak to you of a very serious matter. Are we alone?'

The Count went to the door and returned. 'Quite alone,' said he.

Franz gave him Albert's letter. 'Read that,' said he.

The Count read it.

'What do you say to that?' asked Franz.

'Have you the money he demands?'

'Yes, all but eight hundred piastres.'

The Count went to his desk, opened a drawer filled with gold and said:

'I hope you will not offend me by applying to anyone but me. It is not just the money, you see. It so happens that you have come to the right place. I know this Vampa, and he is in my debt. Perhaps one day I will tell you the story, but now is not the time.'

Franz was overjoyed. If there was any trace of his suspicions about the mysterious Count, he did not let them cloud his delight.

The Count knit his brows and remained silent a moment.

'If I were to seek Vampa, would you accompany me?' he asked.

'If my society would not be disagreeable.'

'Very well, then. It is a lovely night, and a drive in the outskirts of Rome will do us both good. Where is the man who brought this letter?'

'In the street.'

'We must learn where we are going to. I will call him in.'

The Count went to the window and whistled. The

man left the cover of the wall and advanced into the centre of the street.

'Come up here!' said the Count in the same tone in which he would have given an order to a servant. The messenger obeyed without the least hesitation, with alacrity rather, and, coming up the steps at a bound, entered the hotel; five seconds later he was at the door.

'Ah! It is you, Peppino,' said the Count.

Peppino glanced anxiously at Franz.

'Oh, you may speak before His Excellency,' said the Count. 'He is one of my friends. Permit me to give you this title,' continued the Count in French, 'it is necessary so as to give this man confidence.'

'Good,' returned Peppino, 'I am ready to answer any questions Your Excellency may address to me.'

'There is only one. Where has Vampa taken Viscount Albert?'

'To the catacombs of Saint Sebastian, sir.'

The Count turned to Franz.

'He is in a very picturesque spot. Do you know the catacombs of Saint Sebastian?'

'I have never been there, though I have often wanted to go.'

'Well, here is an opportunity ready to hand and it would be difficult to find a better one.'

The Count rang and a footman appeared.

'Order out the carriage,' he said, 'and remove the pistols which are in the holsters. You need not awaken the coachman. Ali will drive.'

In a very short time the noise of wheels was heard and the carriage stopped at the door. The Count took out his watch. 'Half-past twelve,' he said. 'If we started at five o'clock, we should be in time, but the delay might cause your friend an uneasy night, so we had better go with all speed to rescue him from the hands of the brigands. Are you still resolved to accompany me?'

'More determined than ever.'

'Well then, come along.'

Franz and the Count went downstairs accompanied by Peppino and found the carriage at the door with Ali on the box. Franz and the Count got in, Peppino placed himself beside Ali, and they set off at a rapid pace.

In due course they stopped, and Peppino opened the door.

'Excellency,' said Peppino, addressing the Count, 'have the goodness to follow me; the opening to the catacombs is only yards from here.'

'Very well,' said the Count, 'lead the way.'

And there behind a clump of bushes in the midst of several rocks an opening presented itself which was hardly large enough for a man to pass through. Peppino was the first to creep through the crack, but had not gone many steps before the subterranean passage suddenly widened. He stopped, lighted his torch, and looked round to ascertain whether the others were following him. Franz and the Count were still compelled to stoop, and there was only just sufficient width to allow them to walk two abreast. They had proceeded about fifty yards in this manner when the cry: 'Who goes there?' brought them to a standstill. At the same time, they saw the light of their torch reflected on the barrel of a carbine in the darkness beyond.

'A friend,' said Peppino, and, advancing alone, he

said a few words in an undertone to the sentry, who, like the first, saluted and signed to the nocturnal visitors to continue on their way.

Behind the sentry there were some twenty steps. Franz and the Count went down them and found themselves in front of the crossroads of a burial place. Five roads diverged like the rays of a star, and the sides of the walls, hollowed out into niches in the shape of coffins, indicated that they had at last come to the catacombs. In one of these cavities, of which it was impossible to discover the size, some rays of light were visible. The Count placed his hand on Franz's shoulder and said: 'Would you like to see a bandit camp at rest?'

'I should indeed,' was Franz's reply.

'Come with me, then. Peppino, put out the torch!'

Peppino obeyed, and they were in complete darkness. They proceeded in silence, the Count guiding Franz as if he possessed the peculiar faculty of seeing in the dark. Three arches confronted them, the centre one forming a door. On one side these arches opened on to the corridor in which Franz and the Count were standing, and on the other into a large square room entirely surrounded by niches similar to those already mentioned. In the centre of this room were four stones, which had formerly served as an altar, as was evident from the cross which still surmounted them. A lamp, placed at the base of a pillar, lighted with a pale and flickering flame the singular scene which presented itself to the eyes of the two visitors concealed in the shadow. A man was seated reading, with his elbow on the column and his back to the arches, through which the newcomers watched him. This was the chief of the band, Luigi Vampa. Around him, grouped according to fancy, could be seen some twenty brigands lying on their mantles or with their backs against one of the stone seats which ran all around the Columbarium; each one had his carbine within reach. Down below, silent, scarcely visible, and like a shadow, was a sentry, who was walking up and down before a kind of opening. When the Count thought Franz had gazed long enough on this picturesque tableau, he raised his finger to his lips to warn him to be quiet, and, ascending the three steps which lead from the corridor to the Columbarium, entered the room by the centre arch, and advanced towards Vampa, who was so intent on the book before him that he did not hear the sound of his footsteps.

'Who goes there?' cried the sentry, who was on the alert and saw by the light of the lamp a growing shadow approaching his chief.

At this cry Vampa rose quickly, at the same time taking a pistol from his belt. In a moment twenty bandits were on their feet with their carbines levelled at the Count.

'Well,' said he in a perfectly calm voice, and without moving a muscle, 'well, my dear Vampa, it appears to me that you receive your friends with a great deal of ceremony!'

'Ground arms!' shouted the chief with a commanding sweep of one hand, whilst with the other he respectfully took off his hat. Then, turning to the singular person who was watching this scene, he said: 'Excuse me, Count, but I was far from expecting the honour of a visit from you and did not recognize you.'

'It seems that your memory is equally short in everything, Vampa,' said the Count, 'and that, not only do you forget people's faces, but also the conditions you make with them.'

'What conditions have I forgotten, Count?' inquired the bandit with the air of a man who, having committed an error, is anxious to repair it.

'Was it not agreed,' asked the Count, 'that not only my person but that of my friends should be respected by you?'

'And how have I broken faith, Your Excellency?'

'You have this evening carried off and conveyed hither the Viscount Albert de Morcerf. Well,' continued the Count, in a tone which made Franz shudder, 'this young gentleman is one of my friends, this young gentleman is staying in the same hotel as myself, this young gentleman has done the Corso for a week in my carriage, and yet, I repeat to you, you have carried him off and conveyed him hither, and,' added the Count taking a letter from his pocket, 'you have set a ransom on him as if he were just anybody.'

'Why didn't some of you tell me all this?' inquired the brigand chief, turning towards his men, who all retreated before his look. 'Why have you allowed me to fail thus in my word towards a gentleman like the Count. By heavens! If I thought that one of you knew that the gentleman was a friend of His Excellency's, I would blow his brains out with my own hand!'

'You see,' said the Count, turning towards Franz, 'I told you there was some mistake.'

'Are you not alone?' asked Vampa with uneasiness.

'I am with the person to whom this letter was addressed, and to whom I desired to prove that Luigi Vampa was a man of his word. Come, Your Excellency, here is Luigi Vampa, who will himself express to you his regret at the mistake he has made.'

Franz approached; the chief advanced several steps toward him.

'Your Excellency is right welcome,' he said to him. 'You heard what the Count just said and also my reply; let me add that I would not have had such a thing happen, not even for the four thousand piastres at which I had fixed your friend's ransom.'

'But where is the Viscount?' said Franz, looking round anxiously.

'Nothing has happened to him, I hope?' asked the Count, with a frown.

'The prisoner is there,' replied Vampa, pointing to the recess in front of which the bandit sentry was on guard, 'and I will go myself and tell him he is free.'

The chief went towards the place he had pointed out as Albert's prison, and Franz and the Count followed. Vampa drew back a bolt and pushed open a door.

By the gleam of a lamp Albert was seen wrapped up in a cloak which one of the bandits had lent him, lying in a corner of the room in profound slumber.

'Well, I never!' said the Count, smiling in his own peculiar way. 'That is not so bad for a man who is to be shot at seven o'clock tomorrow morning!'

Vampa looked at Albert in admiration. 'You are right, Count,' he said, 'this must be one of your friends.'

Then, going up to Albert, he touched him on the shoulder, saying: 'Will Your Excellency please to awaken?'

Albert stretched out his arms, rubbed his eyes, and said: 'Ah, is that you, captain? Well, you might have let me sleep. I was having such a delightful dream. I was dancing the galop at the Duke's with the Countess G—'

Then he drew from his pocket his watch, which he had kept by him that he might see how the time sped.

'Half-past one only!' said he. 'Why the devil do you rouse me at this hour?'

'To tell you that you are free, Excellency! A gentleman to whom I can refuse nothing has come to demand your liberty.'

'Come here?'

'Yes, here.'

'Really, that's very kind of him!'

Albert looked round and perceived Franz.

'What? Is it you, Franz, who have been so friendly . . .?'

'No, not I, but our friend the Count of Monte Cristo.'

'You, Count?' said Albert gaily, the while arranging his neck-band and cuffs. 'You are really a most valuable friend, and I hope you will consider me as eternally obliged to you, in the first place for the carriage and now for this service!' And he put out his hand; the Count shuddered as he gave his own, but he gave it nevertheless.

The bandit gazed on this scene with amazement; he was evidently accustomed to see his prisoners grovel before him, yet here was one whose gay spirits never faltered, even for one moment. As for Franz, he was delighted at the way in which Albert had maintained the honour of his country, even in the presence of death.

*

On rising the next morning, Albert's first thought was to pay a visit to the Count. He had thanked him in the evening, it is true, but it seemed to him it was not too much to thank a man twice for a service such as the Count had rendered him.

The Count of Monte Cristo attracted Franz, yet filled him with terror, and he would not let Albert go alone. They were shown into the salon, where the Count joined them five minutes later.

Albert advanced towards him, saying: 'Permit me, Count, to say to you this morning what I expressed so badly yesterday evening. Never shall I forget the way in which you came to my assistance, nor the fact that I practically owe you my life. I have come to ask you whether I, my friends, or my acquaintances cannot serve you in any way. My father, the Count of Morcerf, who is of Spanish origin, holds a high position both in France and in Spain, and he and all who love me will be only too pleased to be of any service to you.'

'I will own that I expected your offer, Monsieur de Morcerf,' said the Count, 'and I accept it wholeheartedly. I had already decided to ask you a great favour. I have never yet been to Paris. I do not know it at all. I should probably have undertaken this indispensable journey long ago, had I known someone to introduce me into Paris society. Your offer has decided me. When I go to France, my dear Monsieur de Morcerf –' the Count accompanied these words with a peculiar smile – 'will you undertake to introduce me to the society of the capital, where I shall be as complete a stranger as though I came from Huron or Cochin China?'

'It would give me great pleasure to do so,' replied

Albert. 'You can depend on me and mine to do all in our power for you.'

'I accept your offer,' said the Count, 'for I assure you I have only been waiting for just such an opportunity to realize a hope I have had in view for some time past.'

'When do you propose going?'

'When shall you be there yourself?'

'Oh, I shall be there in a fortnight or three weeks at the latest.'

'Very well,' said the Count. 'I will wait three months. Today is the 21st of February. Will it suit you if I call on you on the 21st of May at half-past ten in the morning?'

'Splendid!' said Albert. 'Breakfast will be ready.'

'Where do you live?'

'Rue du Helder, number twenty-seven.'

'Very well,' said the Count. He took his notebook from his pocket and wrote: 'Rue du Helder, number twenty-seven, the 21st of May at ten-thirty a.m. And now,' said he, replacing his notebook, 'you may rely on me. The hand of your timepiece will not be more accurate than I shall be.'

'Shall I see you again before I leave?' Albert asked.

'That depends upon when you leave.'

'I leave at five o'clock tomorrow evening.'

'In that case I must bid you farewell. I have to go to Naples on business, and shall not be back until Saturday or Sunday. What about you, Baron?' the Count asked Franz. 'Are you leaving Rome too?'

'Yes, I am going to Venice. I intend staying in Italy for another year or two.'

'We shall not see you in Paris, then?'

'I regret that I shall not have that pleasure.'

'Well then, I wish you a safe journey, messieurs,' said the Count to the two friends, shaking hands with them both.

It was the first time Franz had touched this man's hand, and he felt a shudder go through him, for his hand was as cold as a corpse.

'It is quite understood then,' said Albert, 'that on your honour, you will visit me at number twenty-seven, Rue du Helder, at ten-thirty on the morning of the 21st of May, is it not?'

'At ten-thirty on the morning of the 21st of May,' repeated the Count.

Upon this the two young men took their leave of the Count and went to their own quarters.

'What is the matter with you?' Albert asked Franz. 'You have a somewhat worried look!'

'I must own,' said Franz, 'that the Count is a peculiar man, and I feel very uneasy about the appointment he has made with you in Paris.'

'Uneasy about our appointment! Really, my dear Franz, you must be mad!' exclaimed Albert.

'Whether I am mad or not, that's what I feel about it,' said Franz.

17

In the house in the Rue du Helder, to which Albert de Morcerf had invited the Count of Monte Cristo, great preparations were being made on the morning of the 21st of May to do honour to the guest.

Albert de Morcerf's house was at the corner of a large courtyard opposite another building set apart for the servants' quarters. Only two of the windows faced the street; three others overlooked the courtyard, and two at the back overlooked the garden. Between the court and the garden was the spacious and fashionable residence of the Count and Countess of Morcerf, built in the unsightly Imperial style. A high wall ran the whole length of the property facing the street, and was surmounted at intervals by vases, and divided in the middle by a large wrought-iron gate, with gilt scrollings, which served as a carriage entrance; while pedestrians passed in and out of the building through a small door next to the porter's lodge.

In the choice of a house for Albert it was easy to discern the delicate foresight of a mother, who, while not wishing to be separated from her son, realized that a young man of the Viscount's age needed entire liberty. On the other hand, the intelligent egotism of a young man enchanted with the free and easy life of an only son who had been thoroughly pampered could also be recognized.

The sound of the clock striking half-past ten had hardly died away when the door opened and the valet announced:

'His Excellency the Count of Monte Cristo!'

The Count appeared on the threshold dressed with the utmost simplicity, yet the most exacting dandy could not have found fault with his attire. He advanced smiling into the centre of the room and went straight up to Albert who shook his hand warmly.

'Punctuality is the politeness of kings,' said Monte Cristo, 'at any rate according to one of our sovereigns, but in spite of their goodwill, travellers cannot always achieve it. I trust, however, that you will accept my goodwill, Count, and pardon me the two or three seconds by which I have failed in keeping our appointment.'

'I was just announcing your visit to some of my friends whom I have invited to do honour to the promise you were good enough to make me, and whom I now have the pleasure of introducing to you. They are the Count of Château-Renaud; Monsieur Lucien Debray, private secretary to the Minister of the Interior; Monsieur Beauchamp, a formidable journalist and the terror of the French Government; and Monsieur Maximilian Morrel, Captain of Spahis.'

On hearing this latter name the Count, who had till now bowed courteously, but almost with the proverbial coldness and formality of the English, involuntarily took a step forward, and a slight tinge of red spread over his pale cheek.

'You wear the uniform of the new conquerors, monsieur,' he said. 'It is a handsome uniform.'

One could not have said what caused the Count's voice to vibrate so deeply or why his eye, usually so calm and limpid, now shone as though against his will.

'Have you never seen our Africans, Count?' Albert asked.

'Never!' replied the Count, who had gained complete possession over himself once more.

'Beneath this uniform beats one of the bravest and noblest hearts of the army.'

'Oh, Monsieur de Morcerf!' interrupted Morrel.

'Let me speak, Captain. We have just heard tell of such a heroic action on his part,' continued Albert, 'that though I see him today for the first time, I ask his permission to introduce him to you as my friend, since, as we have just heard, he saved the life of my friend Château-Renaud, just as you saved mine. I was in the middle of telling them the story of our Roman adventure when you arrived. But now, messieurs, breakfast is ready. Count, permit me to show you the way.'

They passed into the dining-room in silence.

The Count was, it soon became apparent, a most moderate eater and drinker. Albert remarked this and expressed his fear that at the outset Parisian life might be distasteful to the traveller in the most material, but at the same time the most essential, point.

'If you knew me better,' said the Count, smiling, 'you would not worry about such a matter in regard to a traveller like myself. Cooking does not enter into the calculations of a cosmopolitan like myself. I eat whatever is set before me, only I eat very little. Today, however, when you reproach me with moderation, I have a good appetite, for I have not eaten since yesterday morning.'

'Not since yesterday morning?' the guests exclaimed. 'You have not eaten for twenty-four hours?'

'No, I was compelled to deviate from my route to get some information at Nîmes, which made me a little late, so I would not wait for anything.'

'So you ate in your carriage?' said Morcerf.

'No, I slept as I always do when I am bored and have not the courage to amuse myself, or when I am hungry and have not the desire to eat.'

'Can you then command sleep at will?' asked Morrel.

'More or less. I have an infallible recipe.'

'But do you always carry this drug about with you?'

asked Beauchamp, who, being a journalist, was very incredulous.

'Always,' replied Monte Cristo.

'Would you mind if I asked to see one of these precious pills?' continued Beauchamp, hoping to take him at a disadvantage.

'Not at all,' replied the Count, and he took from his pocket a wonderful *bonbonnière* scooped out of a single emerald and closed by means of a gold screw, which, being turned, gave passage to a small round object of a greenish colour and about the size of a pea. The pill had an acrid and penetrating odour. There were four or five of them in the emerald, which was large enough to contain a dozen.

The *bonbonnière* passed from one guest to another, but it was to examine the wonderful emerald rather than to see the pills.

'It is a magnificent emerald, and the largest I have ever seen, though my mother has some remarkable family jewels,' said Château-Renaud.

'I had three like that one,' returned Monte Cristo. 'I gave one of them to the Grand Seigneur, who has had it mounted on his sword, and the second to His Holiness the Pope, who has had it set in his tiara opposite one that is very similar, but not quite so magnificent, which was given to his predecessor, Pius VII, by the Emperor Napoleon. I have kept the third one for myself and have had it hollowed out. This has certainly reduced its value by one-half, but has made it more adapted to the use I wished to make of it.'

Everyone looked at Monte Cristo in astonishment. He spoke so simply that it was evident he either was telling the truth or was mad.

'What did the two sovereigns give you in exchange for your magnificent gift?' asked Debray.

'The Grand Seigneur gave me a woman's freedom; His Holiness the life of a man.'

'You have no idea, Count, what pleasure it gives me to hear you talk thus,' said Morcerf. 'I had spoken of you to my friends as a fabulous man, a magician out of the *Arabian Nights*, a sorcerer of the Middle Ages, but Parisians are so subtle in paradoxes that they think the most incontestable truths are but flights of the imagination when such truths do not enter into their daily routine. For instance, they contest the existence of the bandits of the Roman Campagna or the Pontine Marshes. Pray tell them yourself, Count, that I was kidnapped by these bandits and that in all probability, without your generous intervention, I should today be awaiting the eternal resurrection in the Catacombs of Saint Sebastian instead of inviting them to breakfast in my humble little house in the Rue du Helder.'

'Tut, tut! You promised me never to speak of that trifle,' said Monte Cristo.

'If I relate all that I know,' said Morcerf, 'will you promise to tell what I do not know?'

'That is only fair,' replied Monte Cristo.

'Well, then, I will relate my story, though my pride must inevitably suffer thereby,' began Albert. 'For three days I thought I was the object of the attentions of a masked lady whom I took to be the descendant of Tullia or Poppaea, whereas I was but being lured on by the coquetry of a peasant. She enticed me to the depths of the Catacombs of Saint Sebastian. Here I was informed that if by six o'clock the next morning I had not produced a ransom of four thousand crowns, I should have ceased to exist by a quarter-past six. The letter is still to be seen and is in Franz's possession, signed by me and with a postscript by Luigi Vampa. That is all I know. What I do not know, Count, is how you contrived to instil such great respect into the Roman bandits, who have respect for so little. I will own that both Franz and I were lost in admiration.'

'I have known this famous Vampa for more than ten years,' said the Count. 'When he was quite young and still a shepherd, I once gave him a gold coin for showing me my way. To be under no obligation to me, he gave me a poniard carved by himself which you must have seen in my collection of arms. Later on, whether it was that he had forgotten this little exchange of presents which should have sealed our friendship, or whether it was that he did not recognize me, I know not, but he tried to kidnap me. I, however, captured him together with twelve of his men. I could have delivered him up to Roman justice, which is somewhat expeditious, but I did not do so. I set him and his men free.'

'On condition that he should sin no more!' said the journalist laughing. 'It delights me to see that they have kept their word so conscientiously.'

'No, Monsieur Beauchamp, on the simple condition that they should always respect me and mine. And,' continued the Count, 'I will appeal to these gentlemen, how could I have left my host in the hands of these terrible bandits, as you are pleased to call them? Besides, you know I had a motive in saving you. I thought you might be useful in introducing me into Parisian society when I visited France. No doubt you thought this but a vague plan on my part, but today you see you are faced with the stern reality and must submit to it under pain of breaking your word.'

'And I shall keep my word,' said Morcerf, 'but I fear you will be greatly disillusioned, accustomed as you are to mountains, picturesque surroundings, and fantastic horizons, whereas France is such a prosaic country and Paris such a civilized city. I can introduce you myself or get my friends to introduce you everywhere. You have really no need of anyone though. With your name, your fortune, and your talented mind –' Monte Cristo bowed with a somewhat ironical smile – 'you can present yourself everywhere and will be well received. I can, therefore, serve you in only one way. I can assist you in finding a suitable establishment. I will not offer to share my apartments with you, as I shared yours at Rome, for, except for myself, you would not see a shadow here, unless it were the shadow of a woman.'

'Ah, the reservation of a family man! May I congratulate you on your coming happiness?'

'It is nothing more than a project, Count.'

'And he who says project means accomplishment,' retorted Debray.

'Not at all!' said Morcerf. 'My father is anxious it should be so, and I hope soon to introduce to you, if not my wife, at least my future wife, Mademoiselle Eugénie Danglars.'

'Eugénie Danglars!' exclaimed Monte Cristo. 'One moment . . . Is not her father Baron Danglars?'

'Yes. Do you know him?'

'I do not know him,' said Monte Cristo, carelessly, 'but in all probability I shall not be long in making his acquaintance, since I have a credit opened with him through Richard and Blount of London, Arstein and Eskeles of Vienna, and Thomson and French of Rome.'

As he pronounced these last two names, Monte Cristo stole a glance at Maximilian Morrel, and if he expected to startle him, he was not disappointed. The young man started as though he had had an electric shock.

'Thomson and French?' said he. 'Do you know that firm?'

'They are my bankers in Rome,' said the Count calmly. 'Can I exert my influence with them on your behalf?'

'You might, perhaps, be able to help us in inquiries which have up to the present been ineffective. Some years back, these bankers rendered a great service to our firm, and for some reason have always denied having done so.'

'I am at your orders,' replied Monte Cristo.

'But in speaking of Monsieur Danglars, we have altogether strayed from the subject of our conversation,' said Maximilian. 'We were talking about a suitable house for the Count of Monte Cristo. I should like to offer him a suite in a charming little house in the Pompadour style which my sister has taken in the Rue Meslay.'

'You have a sister?' asked Monte Cristo.

'Yes, and an excellent one.'

'Married?'

'For the past nine years.'

'Happy?'

'As happy as it is permitted to a human creature to be,' replied Maximilian. 'She is married to a man she loves, who remained faithful to us in our bad fortune, Emmanuel Herbault. I live with them when I am on furlough,' continued Maximilian, 'and my brother-in-law Emmanuel and I will be only too pleased to place ourselves at your disposal, Count.'

'Thank you, Monsieur Morrel, thank you very much. I shall be most happy if you will introduce me to your brother-in-law and your sister, but I cannot accept your kind offer of a suite in your sister's house as my accommodation is already provided for.'

'What? Are you going to put up at a hotel?' exclaimed Morcerf. 'You will not be very comfortable.'

'I have decided to have my own house at Paris. I sent my valet on in advance, and he will have bought a house and furnished it ere this. He arrived here a week ago, and will have scoured the town with the instinct a sporting dog alone possesses. He knows all my whims, my likes, and my needs, and will have arranged everything to my liking. He knew I was to arrive at ten o'clock this morning, and was waiting for me at the Barrière de Fontainebleau from nine o'clock, and gave me this piece of paper. It is my new address. Number thirty, Champs-Élysées.'

The young men stared at one another. They did not know whether Monte Cristo was joking; there was such an air of simplicity about every word he uttered in spite of its originality, that it was impossible to believe he was not speaking the truth. Besides, why should he lie?

'We must content ourselves with doing the Count any little service within our power,' said Beauchamp. 'In my capacity of journalist, I will give him access to all the theatres of Paris.'

'Thank you, monsieur,' said the Count, smiling, 'I

have already instructed my steward to take a box for me at every theatre. You know my steward, Monsieur de Morcerf?'

'Is it by any chance the worthy Signor Bertuccio?'

'The very same; you saw him the day you honoured me by breakfasting with me. He is a very good man and has been a soldier and a smuggler, and in fact has tried his hand at everything possible. I would not even say that he has not been mixed up with the police for some trifling stabbing affair.'

'Then you have your household complete,' said Château-Renaud, 'you have a house in the Champs Élysées, servants and stewards. All you want now is a mistress.'

They had long since passed to dessert and cigars.

'My dear Albert, it is half-past twelve,' said Debray rising. 'Your guest is charming, but you know the best of friends must part, I must return to my office. Are you coming, Morrel?'

'As soon as I have handed the Count my card. He has promised to pay us a visit at fourteen, Rue Meslay.'

'Rest assured that I shall not forget,' said the Count with a bow.

Maximilian Morrel left with the Baron of Château-Renaud, leaving Monte Cristo alone with Morcerf.

18

Albert next showed his guest around his house. He found the Count to be a man of culture and taste who knew all the painters whose work hung on the walls, and who recognized at a glance the date and country of origin of his many antiques.

'And now that you have seen all my treasures, Count,' he said, 'will you accompany me to Monsieur de Morcerf, to whom I wrote from Rome giving an account of the service you rendered me and announcing your visit? I may say that both the Count and the Countess are anxious to tender you their thanks. Look upon this visit as an initiation into Paris life, a life of formalities, visits, and introductions.'

Monte Cristo bowed without replying. Albert called his valet and ordered him to announce to M. and Mme de Morcerf the arrival of the Count of Monte Cristo. On entering the salon they found themselves face to face with Monsieur de Morcerf himself.

He was a man of forty to forty-five years of age, but he appeared at least fifty, and his black moustache and eyebrows contrasted strangely with his almost white hair which was cut short in the military fashion. He was dressed in civilian clothes and wore in his buttonhole the ribbons indicating the different orders to which he belonged.

'Father,' said the young man, 'I have the honour to introduce to you the Count of Monte Cristo, the generous friend I had the good fortune to meet in the difficult circumstances with which you are acquainted.'

'You are welcome amongst us,' said the Count of Morcerf with a smile. 'In preserving the life of our only heir, you have rendered our house a service which solicits our eternal gratitude.'

So saying, the Count of Morcerf gave Monte Cristo

an armchair, while he seated himself opposite the window.

In taking the chair indicated to him, Monte Cristo arranged himself in such a manner as to be hidden in the shadow of the large velvet curtains whence he could read on the careworn features of the Count a whole history of secret griefs in each one of the wrinkles time had imprinted there.

'The Countess will join us here in ten minutes or so,' said Morcerf.

'It is a great honour for me,' said Monte Cristo, 'that on the very day of my arrival in Paris I should be brought into contact with a man whose merits equal his reputation, and on whom Dame Fortune, acting with equity for once, has never ceased to smile. But has she not on the Mitidja Plains or the Atlas Mountains still the baton of a marshal to offer you?'

'I have left the service, monsieur,' said Morcerf, turning somewhat red. 'I have hung up my sword and have flung myself into politics. I devote myself to industry and study the useful arts. I was anxious to do so during the twenty years I was in the army, but had not the time.'

'Such are the ideas that render your nation superior to all others,' replied Monte Cristo. 'A gentleman of high birth, in possession of a large fortune, you were content to gain your promotion as an obscure soldier. Then after becoming a general, a peer of France, a commander of the Legion of Honour, you are willing to go through another apprenticeship with no other prospects, no other reward than that one day you will serve your fellow creatures. Really, Count, this is most praiseworthy; it is even more than that, it is sublime.'

'If I were not afraid of wearying you, Count,' continued the General, obviously charmed with Monte Cristo's manners, 'I would have taken you to the Chamber with me; today's debate will be very interesting to such as do not know our modern senators.'

'I should be most grateful to you, Count, if you would renew this invitation another time. I have been flattered with the hope of an introduction to the Countess today, and I will wait for her.'

'Ah, here is my mother!' exclaimed Albert.

And in truth, as Monte Cristo turned round, he saw Mme de Morcerf, pale and motionless, on the threshold of the door. As Monte Cristo turned towards her, she let fall her arm which, for some reason, she had been resting against the gilt door-post. She had been standing there for some seconds, and had overheard the last words of the conversation.

Monte Cristo rose and bowed low to the Countess, who curtsied ceremoniously without saying a word.

'Whatever ails you, madam?' said the Count. 'Perhaps the heat of this room is too much for you?'

'Are you ill, Mother?' exclaimed the Viscount, rushing toward Mercédès.

She thanked them both with a smile. 'No,' said she. 'It has upset me a little to see for the first time him without whose intervention we should now be in tears and mourning. Monsieur, it is to you that I owe my son's life,' she continued, advancing with queenly majesty, 'and I bless you for this kindness. I am also grateful to you for giving me the opportunity of thanking you as I have blessed you, that is from the bottom of my heart.'

'Madame, the Count and yourself reward me too

generously for a very simple action. To save a man and thereby to spare a father's agony and a mother's feelings is not to do a noble deed, it is but an act of humanity.'

These words were uttered with the most exquisite softness and politeness.

'It is very fortunate for my son, Count, that he has found such a friend,' replied Madame de Morcerf, 'and I thank God that it is so.'

M. de Morcerf went up to her. 'Madame, I have already made my excuses to the Count,' said he. 'The session opened at two o'clock; it is now three, and I have to speak.'

'Go along, then, I will try to make up to the Count for your absence,' said the Countess in the same tone of deep feeling. 'Will you do us the honour, Count, of spending the rest of the day with us?' she continued, turning to Monte Cristo.

'Believe me, Countess, no one could appreciate your kind offer more than I do, but I stepped out of my travelling-carriage at your door this morning and know not yet where or how my residence is provided for. I know it is but a slight cause for uneasiness, yet it is quite appreciable.'

'Then we shall have this pleasure another time. Promise us that at least.'

Monte Cristo bowed without replying, but his gesture might well have been taken for assent.

'Then I will not detain you longer,' said the Countess. 'I would not have my gratitude become indiscreet or importunate.'

Monte Cristo bowed once more and took his leave. A carriage was waiting for him at the door.

When Albert returned to his mother he found her reclining in a deep velvet armchair in her boudoir.

'What is this name Monte Cristo?' asked the Countess when the servant had gone out. 'Is it a family name, the name of an estate, or simply a title?'

'I think it is nothing more than a title. The Count has bought an island in the Tuscan Archipelago. Otherwise he lays no claim to nobility and calls himself a "Count of Chance", though the general opinion in Rome is that he is a very great lord.'

The Countess was pensive for a moment, then after a short pause, she said: 'I am addressing a question to you, Albert, as your mother. You have seen Monsieur de Monte Cristo at home. You are perspicacious, know the ways of the world, and are more tactful than most men of your age. Do you think the Count is really what he appears to be?'

'I have seen so many strange traits in him,' replied Albert, 'that if you wish me to say what I think, I must say that I consider him as a man whom misfortune has branded; a derelict, as it were, of some old family, who, disinherited of his patrimony, has found one by dint of his own venturesome genius which places him above the rules of society. Monte Cristo is an island in the middle of the Mediterranean, without inhabitants or garrison, the resort of smugglers of every nationality and of pirates from every country. Who knows whether these worthy industrialists do not pay their lord for his protection?'

'Possibly,' said the Countess, deep in thought.

'What does it matter,' replied the young man, 'whether he be a smuggler or not? Now that you have seen him, Mother, you must agree that the Count of

Monte Cristo is a remarkable man who will create quite a sensation in Paris.'

'Has this man any friendship for you, Albert?' she asked with a nervous shudder.

'I believe so, Mother.'

There was a strange terror in the Countess's voice as she said:

'Albert, I have always put you on your guard against new acquaintances. Now you are a man and capable of giving me advice. Nevertheless, I repeat to you: be prudent, Albert.'

'Yet, if this advice is to be profitable, Mother, I must know in advance what I am to guard against. The Count does not gamble, he drinks nothing but water coloured with a little Spanish wine; he is said to be so rich that, without making himself a laughing-stock, he could not borrow money from me. What, then, have I to fear from him?'

The Countess did not answer. She was so deeply absorbed in her own thoughts that her eyes gradually closed. The young man stood before her, then, seeing her close her eyes, he listened for a moment to her peaceful breathing and tiptoed out of the room.

19

The next day, at five in the afternoon, the Count arrived at the residence of Baron Danglars, to keep an appointment. He was shown in to the Baron's presence.

'Have I the honour of addressing Monsieur de Monte Cristo?' inquired the Baron.

'And I of addressing Baron Danglars, Chevalier of the Legion of Honour and member of the Chamber of Deputies?' said the Count.

Monte Cristo repeated all the titles he had read on the Baron's card.

Danglars felt the thrust and bit his lip.

'I have received a letter of advice from Messrs Thomson and French,' he said.

'I am delighted to hear it, Baron. It will not be necessary to introduce myself, which is always embarrassing. You say you have received a letter of advice?'

'Yes, but I must confess I do not quite understand its meaning,' said Danglars. 'This letter . . . I have it with me I think . . .' He searched in his pocket. 'Yes, here it is. This letter opened credit on my bank to the Count of Monte Cristo for an unlimited sum.'

'Well, Baron, what is there incomprehensible in that?'

'Nothing, monsieur, but the word unlimited. The meaning of the word unlimited in connection with finances is so vague . . . And what is vague is doubtful, and in doubt, says the wise man, there is danger.'

'In other words,' replied Monte Cristo, 'if Thomson and French are inclined to commit a folly, Danglars' bank is not going to follow suit. No doubt Messrs Thomson and French do not need to consider figures in their operations, but Monsieur Danglars has a limit to his. As he said just now, he is a wise man.'

'No one has ever questioned my capital, monsieur,' replied the banker proudly.

'Then obviously I am the first one to do so.'

'How so?'

'The explanations you demand of me, monsieur, which certainly appear to imply hesitation . . .'

'Why, then, monsieur, I will try to make myself clear by asking you to name the amount for which you expect to draw on me,' continued Danglars after a moment's silence.

'But I have asked for unlimited credit because I am uncertain of the amount I shall require,' replied Monte Cristo, determined not to lose an inch of ground.

The banker thought the moment had come for him to take the upper hand; he flung himself back in the armchair and with a slow, arrogant smile on his lips, said: 'Do not fear to ask, monsieur; you will then be convinced that the resources of the firm of Danglars, limited though they may be, are sufficient to meet the highest demands, even though you asked for a million . . .'

'What did you say?'

'I said a million,' repeated Danglars with the audacity of stupidity.

'What should I do with a million?' said the Count. 'Good heavens! I should not have opened an account for such a trifling sum. Why, I always carry a million in my pocket-book or my suitcase.' And he took from his small card-case two Treasury bills of five hundred thousand francs each.

A man of Danglars' type requires to be overwhelmed, not merely pinpricked, and this blow had its effect. The banker was simply stunned. He stared at Monte Cristo in a stupefied manner, his eyes starting out of his head.

'Come, now, own that you mistrust Messrs Thomson and French. I expected this, and, though I am not very businesslike, I came forearmed. Here are two other letters of credit similar to the one addressed to you; one is from Arstein and Eskeles of Vienna on Baron Rothschild, the other is from Baring Bros. of London on Monsieur Lafitte. You have only to say the word, and I will relieve you of all anxiety by presenting my letter of credit to one or the other of these two firms.'

That was enough; Danglars was vanquished. Trembling visibly, he took the letters from London and Germany that the Count held out to him, opened them, verified the authenticity of the signatures with a care that would have been insulting to Monte Cristo had they not served to mislead the banker.

'Here are three signatures which are worth many millions,' said Danglars, rising as though to pay homage to the power of gold personified in the man before him. 'Three unlimited credits on our banking firms. Excuse me, Count, though I am no longer mistrustful, I cannot help being astonished.'

'But nothing can astonish a banking establishment like yours,' said Monte Cristo with a great show of politeness. 'You can send me some money, then, I suppose?'

'Speak, Count, I am at your service.'

'Well, since we understand each other and you no longer mistrust me . . . I am not presuming too much in saying this, am I? Let us fix on a general sum for the first year; six millions for example.'

'Very well, let it be six millions,' replied Danglars hoarsely.

'If I require more,' said Monte Cristo carelessly,

'we can add to it, but I do not expect to stay in Paris more than a year and I don't suppose I shall exceed that sum in a year. Anyway we shall see. To begin with, will you please send me tomorrow five hundred thousand francs, half in gold and half in notes? I shall be at home until noon, but should I have to go out, I will leave the receipt with my steward.'

'You shall have the money at ten o'clock in the morning, Count.'

The Count rose.

'I must confess to you, Count,' said Danglars, 'I thought I was well informed on all the large fortunes of Europe, and yet I must own that though yours appears to be very considerable I had no knowledge of it. Is it of recent date?'

'No, monsieur; on the contrary, it is of very long standing,' replied Monte Cristo. 'It is a kind of family treasure which it was forbidden to touch. The interest has gone on accumulating and has trebled the capital. The period fixed by the testator expired only a few years ago, so your ignorance of the matter was quite natural. You will know more about it, though, in a short time.'

The Count accompanied his words with one of those pale smiles that struck such terror into the heart of Franz d'Épinay.

'If you would allow me, Count, I should like to introduce you to Baroness Danglars. Excuse my haste, but a client like you almost forms part of the family.'

Monte Cristo bowed as a sign that he accepted the proffered honour. The financier rang the bell, and a footman in a brilliant livery appeared.

'Is the Baroness at home?' asked Danglars.

'Yes, Monsieur le Baron,' replied the footman.

'Is she alone?'

'No, Monsieur le Baron, Monsieur Debray is with her.'

Danglars nodded his head, then turning to the Count, he said: 'Monsieur Debray is an old friend of ours and private secretary to the Minister of the Interior. As for my wife, she belongs to an ancient family and lowered herself in marrying me. She was Mademoiselle de Sevières, and when I married her she was a widow after the death of her first husband, Colonel the Marquis de Nargonne.'

'I have not the honour of knowing Madame Danglars, but I have already met Monsieur Lucien Debray.'

'Really? Where?'

'At the house of Monsieur de Morcerf.'

'Ah, you know the little Viscount then?'

'We were together at Rome during the Carnival.'

'It is true,' said Danglars. 'Have I not heard something about a strange adventure with bandits in the ruins? He had a most miraculous escape! I believe he told my daughter and wife something about it when he returned from Italy.'

'The Baroness awaits your pleasure, messieurs!' said the footman, who had been to inquire of his mistress whether she would receive visitors.

'I will go on in front to show you the way,' said Danglars, bowing.

'And I will follow you!'

Later, through his young friends Albert de Morcerf, Maximilian Morrel and Lucien Debray, the Count learned that the Baron made a great deal of his money through speculating on the prices of stocks and shares. The young men fell to talking idly and jokingly about how a rumour started by someone as influential as Debray could influence the rise or fall of the price of stocks and shares, so that a banker such as Danglars could win or lose a small fortune in the space of a few hours. The Count could not help but notice that when this topic of conversation arose, Debray felt most uncomfortable and left within a few minutes.

But the Count did not restrict his company to his new young friends. His entry into Parisian high society was perfectly executed. Within a few days he had charmed Baroness Danglars and her friend Madame de Villefort, and had become a topic of conversation in every cultured salon. On a visit to Madame de Villefort, her wilful young son Edward had fainted in the heat, and the Count had been able to revive him with a medicine. During the ensuing conversation about medicines, the Count perceived her intense interest in the subject, and he had been able to oblige her with the gift of a tincture of his own devising, one drop of which acted as a powerful restorative, while five or six drops, dissolved imperceptibly in a glass of wine, would certainly kill whoever drank it.

After he had been in Paris about a week, the Count took up Morrel's invitation to visit. Coclès opened the door, and the Count's servant Baptistin, springing from the box, asked if M. and Mme Herbault and M. Maximilian Morrel were at home to the Count of Monte Cristo.

'To the Count of Monte Cristo!' cried Maximilian,

throwing away his cigar and hastening towards his visitor. 'I should think we are at home to him! A thousand thanks, Count, for having kept your promise.'

The young officer shook the Count's hand so cordially that there could be no doubt as to the sincerity of his feelings.

'Come along,' said Maximilian, 'I will announce you myself.'

Julie and Emmanuel Herbault were in the salon, waiting to receive the Count.

The birds could be heard chirping in a neighbouring aviary; the laburnum and acacia trees spread their branches so close to the window that the clusters of bloom almost formed a border to the blue velvet curtains. Everything in this little retreat breathed peaceful tranquillity, from the song of the birds to the smiles of its owners. From the moment the Count entered, he sensed the atmosphere of happiness; he stood silent and pensive, forgetting that the others were waiting for him to continue the conversation which had been interrupted during the exchange of salutations.

He suddenly became aware of this almost embarrassing silence and, tearing himself away from his dreams with a great effort, he said:

'Pray excuse my emotion, madame. It must astonish you who are accustomed to the peace and happiness I find here, but it is so unusual for me to find contentment expressed on a human face, that I cannot grow weary of looking at you and your husband.'

'We are very happy, monsieur,' replied Julie, 'but we have gone through long and bitter suffering, and there are few people who have bought their happiness at such a high price.'

The Count's face manifested great curiosity.

'It is a family history, Count,' said Maximilian. 'The humble little picture would have no interest for you who are accustomed to the misfortunes of the illustrious and the joys of the rich. We have known bitter suffering.'

'And did God send you consolation in your sorrow as He does to all?' asked Monte Cristo.

'Yes, Count, we can truly say that He did,' replied Julie. 'He did for us what He only does for His elect: He sent us one of His angels.'

Monte Cristo got up and, without replying, for he feared the tremulousness of his voice would betray his emotion, began to pace round the room.

'Our magnificence makes you smile!' said Maximilian, who was watching Monte Cristo.

'Not at all,' replied Monte Cristo, deathly pale and pressing one hand to his heart to still its throbbings, while with the other he pointed to a glass case under which lay a silk purse carefully placed on a black velvet cushion. 'I was only wondering what could be the use of this purse containing what looks like a piece of paper at one end and a fairly valuable diamond at the other.'

'That is the most precious of our family treasures, Count.'

'The diamond is, indeed, quite a good one.'

'My brother was not alluding to the value of the stone, though it has been estimated at a hundred thousand francs; what he meant was that the articles contained in that purse are the relics of the angel I mentioned just now. We leave it out in the open, so that our benefactor may be compelled to betray his presence by his emotion.'

'Really!' said Monte Cristo in a stifled voice.

'This has touched the hand of a man who saved my father from death, all of us from ruin, and our name from dishonour,' said Maximilian, raising the glass case and devoutly kissing the silk purse. 'It has touched the hand of one whose merit it is that, though we were doomed to misery and mourning, others now express their wonder at our happiness. This letter,' continued Maximilian, taking the piece of paper from the purse and handing it to the Count, 'this letter was written by him on a day when my father had taken a desperate resolution, and the diamond was given by our unknown benefactor, an Englishman, to my sister as her dowry.'

Monte Cristo opened the letter and read it with an indescribably happy expression. As our readers will know, it was the note addressed to Julie and signed 'Sinbad the Sailor'.

'An Englishman?' he asked, deep in thought and feeling most uneasy every time Julie looked at him. 'An Englishman, did you say?'

'Yes,' replied Morrel, 'an Englishman who introduced himself to us as the representative of Messrs Thomson and French of Rome. That is why you saw me start the other day when you mentioned that they were your bankers. However, my father always said it was not an Englishman who had done us this good turn.'

Monte Cristo started. 'What did your father tell you?' he asked.

'My father regarded the deed as a miracle. He believed that a benefactor had come from his tomb to help us. It was a touching superstition, Count, and, though I could not credit it myself, I would not destroy his faith in it. How often in his dreams did he not mutter the name of a dear friend who was lost to him for ever! On his deathbed, when his mind had been given that lucidity that the near approach of death brings with it, this thought which had till then only been a superstition, became a conviction. The last words he spoke were: "Maximilian, it was Edmond Dantès!"'

At these words, the Count, who had been gradually changing colour, became alarmingly pale. The blood rushed from his head, and he could not speak for a few seconds. He took out his watch as though he had forgotten the time, picked up his hat, took a hurried and embarrassed leave of Mme Herbault and, pressing the hands of Emmanuel and Maximilian, said: 'Permit me to renew my visit from time to time, madame. I have spent a happy hour with you and am very grateful for the kind way in which you have received me. This is the first time for many years that I have given way to my feelings. But now I have an engagement which I cannot avoid. I have promised to take to the Opera a Grecian princess of my acquaintance who has never yet seen Grand Opera and is relying on me to escort her.' With that he strode rapidly out of the room.

'What a peculiar man this Count of Monte Cristo is,' said Emmanuel.

'He certainly is,' replied Maximilian, 'but I believe he is very noble-hearted, and I am sure he likes us.'

'As for me,' said Julie, 'his voice went to my heart, and two or three times it occurred to me that I had heard it before.'

20

M. Noirtier de Villefort, aged and paralysed, lived in the same house as his son. The only person in the whole household he truly loved, and perhaps the only person who truly loved him, was young Valentine, the daughter of Gérard de Villefort's first marriage. Indeed, it was one of the reasons why the present Madame de Villefort was jealous of Valentine: not only was she rich in her own right, from her mother's money, but she would undoubtedly inherit from M. Noirtier too, while her beloved – and rather spoiled – son Edward would not see any of this money. Once Valentine had expressed a desire to enter a convent, and Mme de Villefort had been most encouraging – knowing that she would thereby forfeit her claim to any money.

But all this was months ago. Today, a few weeks after the Count's arrival in Paris, M. de Villefort entered his father's room followed by Mme de Villefort. After greeting the old man and dismissing Barrois, his old servant, they seated themselves on either side of the old gentleman.

M. Noirtier was sitting in his wheelchair, to which he was carried every morning and left there until the evening. Sight and hearing were the only two senses that, like two solitary sparks, animated this poor human body that was so near the grave. His hair was white and long, reaching down to his shoulders, while his eyes were black, overshadowed by black eyebrows, and, as is generally the case when one organ is used to the exclusion of the others, in these eyes were concentrated all the activity, skill, strength, and intelligence which had formerly characterized his whole body and mind. It is true that the gesture of the arm, the sound of the voice, the attitude of the body were now lacking, but his masterful eye supplied their place. He commanded with his eyes and thanked with his eyes; he was a corpse with living eyes, and nothing was more terrifying than when, in this face of marble, they were lit up in fiery anger or sparkled with joy.

'Do not be astonished, monsieur,' Villefort began, 'that Valentine is not with us or that I have dismissed Barrois, for our interview is one which could not take place before a young girl or a servant. Madame de Villefort and I have a communication to make which we feel sure will be agreeable to you. We are going to marry Valentine.'

A wax figure could not have evinced more indifference on hearing this intelligence than did M. Noirtier.

'The marriage will take place within three months,' continued Villefort.

The old man's eyes were still expressionless.

Mme de Villefort then took her part in the conversation, and added: 'We thought this news would be of interest to you, monsieur, for Valentine has always appeared to be the object of your affection. It now only remains for us to tell you the name of the young man for whom she is destined. It is one of the most desirable connections Valentine could aspire to; he has a fortune, a good name, and her future happiness is guaranteed by the good qualities and tastes of him for whom we have destined her. His name is not unknown to you, for the young man in question is Monsieur Franz de Quesnel, Baron d'Épinay.'

During his wife's discourse, Villefort fixed his eyes upon the old man with greater attention than ever. When the name of Franz d'Épinay was uttered Noirtier's eyes, whose every expression was comprehensible to his son, quivered like lips trying to speak, and sent forth a lightning dart. The Procureur du Roi was well aware of the reports formerly current of public enmity between his own father and Franz's father, and he understood Noirtier's agitation and anger. Feigning not to perceive either, however, he resumed the conversation where his wife had left off.

'It is important, monsieur,' he said, 'that Valentine, who is about to enter upon her nineteenth year, should finally be settled in life. Nevertheless, we have not forgotten you in our discussions on the matter and have ascertained that the future husband of Valentine will consent, not to live with you, as that might be embarrassing for a young couple, but that you live with them. In this way you and Valentine, who are so greatly attached to one another, will not be separated, and you will not need to make any change in your mode of living. The only difference will be that you will have two children to take care of you instead of one.'

Noirtier's look was one of fury. It was evident that something desperate was passing through the old man's mind and that there rose to his throat a cry of anger and grief which, being unable to find vent in utterance, was choking him, for his face became purple and his lips blue.

'This marriage,' continued Mme de Villefort, 'is acceptable to Monsieur d'Épinay and his family, which, by the way, only consists of an uncle and aunt. His mother died in giving him birth, and his father was assassinated in 1815, that is to say, when the child was barely two years of age. He has, therefore, only his own wishes to consult.'

'That assassination was most mysterious,' continued Villefort, 'and the perpetrators are still unknown, although suspicion has fallen on many.'

Noirtier made such an effort to speak that his lips expanded into a weird kind of smile.

'Now the real criminals,' continued Villefort, 'those who are conscious of having committed the crime and upon whose heads the justice of man may fall during their lifetime and the justice of God after their death, would be only too happy if they had, like us, a daughter to offer to Monsieur Franz d'Épinay to allay all appearances of suspicion.'

Noirtier composed his feelings with a mastery one would not have supposed existed in that shattered frame.

'I understand,' his look said to Villefort, and this look expressed at once a feeling of profound contempt and intelligent anger. Villefort read in it all that it contained, but merely shrugged his shoulders in reply, and made a sign to his wife to take her leave.

'I will leave you now,' she said. 'May I send Edward to pay his respects to you?'

It had been arranged that the old man should express assent by closing his eyes, refusal by blinking several times, a desire for something by casting a look heavenward. If he wanted Valentine, he only closed his right eye, if Barrois the left.

At Mme de Villefort's proposal he blinked vigorously. Vexed at this refusal, Mme de Villefort bit her lip as she said: 'Would you like me to send Valentine then?'

'Yes,' signed the old man, shutting his right eye tightly.

M. and Mme de Villefort bowed and left the room, giving orders for Valentine to be summoned. She had, however, already been warned that her presence would be required in her grandfather's room during the day. Still flushed with emotion, she entered as soon as her parents had left. One glance at her grandfather told her how much he was suffering, and that he had a great deal to communicate to her.

'Grandpapa dear, what has happened?' she exclaimed. 'Have they vexed you? Are you angry?'

'Yes,' said he closing his eyes.

'With whom are you angry? Is it with my father? No. With Madame de Villefort? No. With me?'

The old man made a sign of assent.

'With me?' repeated Valentine astonished. 'What have I done, dear Grandpapa? I have not seen you the whole day. Has anyone been speaking against me?'

'Yes,' said the old man, closing his eyes with emphasis.

'Let me think. I assure you, Grandpapa . . . Ah! Monsieur and Madame de Villefort have been here. They must have said something to annoy you? What is it? How you frighten me! Oh, dear, what can they have said?' She thought for a moment. 'I have it,' she said, lowering her voice and drawing closer to the old man. 'Did they perhaps speak of my marriage?'

'Yes,' replied the angry look.

'Did they tell you that Monsieur d'Épinay agrees that we shall all live together?'

'Yes.'

'Then why are you angry?'

The old man's eyes beamed with an expression of gentle affection.

'I understand,' said Valentine. 'It is because you love me.'

The old man made a sign of assent.

'Are you afraid I shall be unhappy?'

'Yes.'

'Do you not like Franz?'

His eyes repeated three or four times: 'No, no, no.'

'Then you are very grieved?'

'Yes.'

'Well, listen,' said Valentine, throwing herself on her knees and putting her arms round his neck. 'I am grieved, too, for I do not love Monsieur Franz d'Épinay. If only you could help me! If only we could frustrate their plans! But you are powerless against them, though your mind is so active and your will so firm.'

As she said these words, there was such a look of deep cunning in Noirtier's eyes, that the girl thought she read these words therein: 'You are mistaken, I can still do much for you.'

Noirtier raised his eyes heavenward. It was the sign agreed upon between Valentine and himself whenever he wanted anything.

'What do you wish, Grandpapa?' She then recited all the letters of the alphabet until she came to N, all the while watching his eyes with a smile on her face. When she came to N he signalled assent.

'Then what you desire begins with the letter N.

Now, let me see what you can want that begins with the letter N. Na . . . ne . . . ni . . . no . . .'

'Yes, yes, yes,' said the old man's eyes.

Valentine fetched a dictionary, which she placed on a desk before Noirtier. She opened it, and, as soon as she saw that his eyes were fixed on its pages, she ran her fingers quickly up and down the columns. All the practice she had had during the six years since M. Noirtier first fell into this pitiable state had made her expert at detecting his wishes in this manner, and she guessed his thoughts as quickly as though he himself had been able to seek for what he wanted.

At the word 'Notary' the old man made a sign for her to stop.

'You wish me to send for a notary?' asked Valentine.

'Yes.'

'Then he shall be sent for immediately.'

Valentine rang the bell, and told the servant to request M. and Mme de Villefort to come to M. Noirtier.

And when the notary arrived, old M. Noirtier made a will. His beloved granddaughter Valentine would not receive a sou if she married M. Franz d'Épinay. Instead, he would leave all his fortune of nine hundred thousand francs to charity.

On returning to their own apartments, M. and Mme de Villefort learned that the Count of Monte Cristo, who had come to pay them a visit, had, during their absence, been shown into the salon where he was awaiting them. Mme de Villefort was too agitated to see him at once and retired to her bedroom, while her husband, being more self-possessed, went straight into the salon.

But though he was able to master his feelings and compose his features, he could not dispel the cloud that shadowed his brow, and the Count, who received him with a radiant smile, noticed his gloomy and preoccupied manner.

'What on earth is the matter, Monsieur de Villefort?' said Monte Cristo after the first compliments were exchanged. 'Have you just been drawing up some capital indictment?'

'No, Count,' said he, trying to smile, 'this time I am the victim. It is I who have lost my case, and fate, obstinacy, and madness have been the counsel for the prosecution.'

'What do you mean?' asked the Count, with well-feigned interest. 'Have you really met with some serious misfortune?'

'Oh, it is not worth mentioning,' said he, with a calmness that betokened bitterness. 'It is nothing, only a loss of money.'

'Loss of money is, indeed, somewhat insignificant to a man with a fortune such as you possess, and to a mind as elevated and philosophical as yours is.'

'It is, however, not the loss of the money that grieves me, though after all nine hundred thousand francs is worthy of regret, and annoyance at its loss is quite comprehensible. What hurts me is the ill-will manifested by fate, chance, or whatever the designation of the power may be that has dealt this blow. My hopes of a fortune are dashed to the ground, and perhaps even my daughter's future blasted by the whims of an old man who has sunk into second childhood.'

'Nine hundred thousand francs, did you say?'

claimed the Count. 'That is certainly a sum of money that even a philosopher might regret. Who has caused you this annoyance?'

'My father, of whom I spoke to you.'

'My dear,' said Mme de Villefort, who had just entered the room, 'perhaps you are exaggerating the evil.'

'Madame,' said the Count, bowing.

Mme de Villefort acknowledged the salutation with one of her most gracious smiles.

'What is this Monsieur de Villefort has just been telling me?' asked Monto Cristo. 'What an incomprehensible misfortune!'

'Incomprehensible! That is the very word,' exclaimed Villefort, shrugging his shoulders. 'A whim born of old age!'

'Is there no means of making him revoke his decision?'

'There is,' was Mme de Villefort's reply. 'It is even in my husband's power to have the will changed in Valentine's favour instead of its being to her prejudice.'

'My dear,' said Villefort in answer to his wife, 'it is distasteful to me to play the patriarch in my own house; I have never believed that the fate of the universe depended upon a word from my lips. Nevertheless, my opinions must be respected in my family, and the insanity of an old man and the caprices of a child shall not be allowed to frustrate a project I have entertained for so many years. The Baron d'Épinay was my friend, as you know, and an alliance with his son is most desirable and appropriate.'

'But it seems to me,' said Monte Cristo after a

moment's silence, 'and I crave your pardon for what I am about to say, it seems to me that if Monsieur Noirtier disinherits Mademoiselle de Villefort because she wishes to marry a young man whose father he detested, he cannot have the same cause for complaint against this dear child Edward.'

'You are right, Count. Is it not atrociously unjust?' cried Mme de Villefort in tones impossible to describe. 'Poor Edward is just as much Monsieur Noirtier's grandchild as Valentine is, and yet if she were not going to marry Monsieur Franz she would inherit all his riches. Edward bears the family name, yet, even though she be disinherited by her grandfather, she will be three times as rich as he!'

Having thrust his dart, the Count rose to depart.

'Are you leaving us, Count?' said Mme de Villefort.

'I am obliged to, madame. I am going, merely as a looker-on, you understand, to see something that has given me food for many long hours' thought.'

'What is that?'

'The telegraph. There, my secret is out!'

'The telegraph!' repeated Mme de Villefort.

'Yes, indeed. On a hillock at the end of the road I have sometimes seen these black, accommodating arms shining in the sun like so many spiders' legs, and I assure you they have always filled me with deep emotion, for I thought of the strange signs cleaving the air with such precision, conveying the unknown thoughts of one man seated at his table three hundred leagues distant to another man at another table at the other end of the line; that these signs sped through the grey clouds or blue sky solely at the will of the all-powerful operator. I was seized with a strange desire to see this living chrysalis at close quarters, and to be present at the little comedy he plays for the benefit of his fellow chrysalis by pulling one piece of tape after another. I will tell you my impressions on Saturday.'

The Count of Monte Cristo hereupon took his departure. That same evening the following telegram was read in the *Messager*:

King Don Carlos has escaped the vigilance exercised over him at Burgos and has returned to Spain across the Catalonian frontier. Barcelona has risen in his favour.

All that evening nothing was talked about but Danglars' foresight in selling his shares, and his luck as a speculator in having lost but five hundred thousand francs by the deal.

The next day the following paragraph was read in the *Moniteur*:

The report published in yesterday's *Messager* of the flight of Don Carlos and the revolt of Barcelona is devoid of all foundation. King Don Carlos has not left Burgos, and perfect peace reigns in the Peninsula. A telegraphic sign improperly interpreted owing to the fog gave rise to this error.

Shares rose to double the price to which they had fallen, so that, with what he had actually lost and what he had failed to gain, it meant a difference of a million francs to Danglars.

21

One evening, a day or two later, Lucien Debray was with Mme Danglars, talking of this and that, when suddenly the door opened and M. Danglars entered. 'Good evening, madame,' said he. 'Good evening, Monsieur Debray!'

The Baroness no doubt thought that this unexpected visit signified a desire to repair some sharp words he had uttered during the day. Assuming a dignified air, she turned to Lucien and, without answering her husband, said: 'Read something to me, Monsieur Debray.'

'Excuse me,' said the Baron. 'You will tire yourself if you stay up so late, Baroness; it is eleven o'clock and Monsieur has far to go.'

Debray was dumbfounded, for, though Danglars' tone was perfectly calm and polite, he seemed to detect in it a certain determination to do his own will that evening and not his wife's. The Baroness was equally surprised and showed it by a look which would no doubt have given her husband food for thought if he had not been busy reading the closing prices of shares in the paper. The haughty look was entirely lost on him.

'Monsieur Lucien,' said the Baroness, 'I assure you I have not the least inclination for sleep. I have much to tell you this evening, and you shall listen to me though you go to sleep standing.'

'At your service, madame,' replied Lucien phlegmatically.

'My dear Monsieur Debray, don't ruin a good night's rest by staying here and listening to Madame Danglars' follies tonight,' said M. Danglars; 'you can hear them just as well tomorrow. Besides, I claim tonight for myself, and, with your permission I propose to talk over some important business matters with my wife.'

This time the blow was struck with such directness that Lucien and the Baroness were staggered. They exchanged looks as though each were asking the other for help in the face of such intrusion, but the irresistible power of the master of the house prevailed and he gained the ascendancy.

Debray stammered out a few words, bowed and left the room.

'Do you know monsieur,' said the Baroness when Lucien had gone, 'you are really making progress? As a rule you are merely churlish, tonight you are brutal.'

'That is because I am in a worse temper tonight than usual,' replied Danglars.

'What is your bad temper to me?' replied the Baroness, irritated at her husband's impassiveness. 'What have I to do with it?'

'I have just lost seven hundred thousand francs in the Spanish loan.'

'And do you wish to make me responsible for your losses?' asked the Baroness with a sneer. 'Is it my fault that you have lost seven hundred thousand francs?'

'In any case it is not mine.'

'Once and for all, monsieur, I will not have you talk money with me,' returned the Baroness sharply. 'It is a language I learnt neither with my parents nor in my first husband's house. The jingling of crowns being counted and re-counted is odious to me, and there is nothing but the sound of your voice that I dislike more.'

'That is really strange!' replied Danglars. 'I always thought you took the greatest interest in my affairs!'

'I should like you to show me on what occasion.'

'Oh, that's easily done. Last February you were the first to tell me of the Hayti bonds. You dreamt that a ship had entered the harbour at Havre, bringing the news that a payment which had been looked on as lost was about to be effected. I know how clear-sighted your dreams are. On the quiet I bought up all the bonds of the Hayti debt I could lay my hands on, and made four hundred thousand francs, of which I conscientiously paid you one hundred thousand. You spent it as you wished, but that was your affair.

'In March there was talk of a railway concession. Three companies presented themselves, each offering equal securities. You told me that your instinct suggested that the privilege would be given to a so-called Southern Company. I instantly subscribed two thirds of the company's shares and made a million out of the deal. I gave you two hundred and fifty thousand francs for pin-money. What have you done with it?'

'But what are you driving at, monsieur?' cried the Baroness, trembling with anger and impatience.

'Have patience, madame, I am coming to it. In April you dined with the Minister. The conversation turned upon Spain and you heard some secret information. There was talk of the expulsion of Don Carlos. I bought some Spanish bonds. Your information was correct, and I made six hundred thousand francs the day Charles V crossed the Bidassoa. Of these six hundred thousand francs you had fifty thousand crowns. They were yours, and you disposed of them according to your fancy. I do not ask you to account for the money, but it is none the less true that you have received five hundred thousand francs this year.

'Then three days ago you talked politics with Monsieur Debray, and you gathered from his words that Don Carlos had returned to Spain. I sold out, the news was spread, and a panic ensued. I did not sell the bonds, I gave them away. The next day it transpired that the news was false, but it cost me seven hundred thousand francs.'

'Well?'

'Well, since I give you a quarter of my profits, it is only right you should give me a quarter of what I lose. The quarter of seven hundred thousand francs is one hundred and seventy-five thousand francs!'

'That is ridiculous, and really I do not see why you should bring Debray's name into this affair.'

'No gesticulations, screams, or modern drama, if you please, madame, otherwise I shall be compelled to tell you that I can see Monsieur Debray having the laugh of you over the five hundred thousand francs you have handed to him this year, and priding himself on the fact that he has finally found that which the most skilful gamblers have never discovered, that is a game in which he wins without risking a stake and is no loser when he loses.'

The Baroness was boiling with rage.

'You wretch!' said she. 'You are worse than despicable!'

'But I note with pleasure, madame, that you are not far behind me in that respect.'

Mme Danglars was simply overwhelmed, but she made a supreme effort to reply to this last attack. She sank into a chair. Danglars did not even look at her, though she did her best to faint. Without saying another word, he opened the door and went into his room; when Mme Danglars recovered from her semi-faint she thought she must have had a bad dream.

The day following this scene, M. Debray's carriage did not make its appearance at the customary hour to pay a little visit to Mme Danglars on his way to the office. She, therefore, ordered her carriage to be brought round and went out. This was only what Danglars expected.

From midday until two o'clock Danglars stayed in his office deciphering telegrams and heaping figure upon figure until he became increasingly depressed. He entered his carriage and told the coachman to drive him to number thirty, Avenue des Champs-Élysées.

Monte Cristo was at home, but he was engaged with someone and asked Danglars to wait a moment in the salon. While the banker was waiting, the door opened, and a man in priest's garb entered. He was evidently more familiar with the house than the Baron, for, instead of waiting, he merely bowed and passing into the other room disappeared. A minute later the door through which the priest had entered reopened, and Monte Cristo made his appearance.

'Pray, excuse me, Baron,' said he, 'but one of my good friends, Abbé Busoni, whom you may have seen pass by, has just arrived in Paris. It is a long time since we saw each other, and I could not make up my mind to leave him at once. I trust you will find the motive good enough to forgive my keeping you waiting. But what ails you, Baron? You look quite careworn; really, you alarm me. A careworn capitalist is like a comet, he presages some great misfortune to the world.'

'Ill-luck has been dogging my steps for the last few days,' said Danglars, 'and I receive nothing but bad news.'

Monte Cristo made polite inquiries about the Baron's business affairs, but gradually the conversation came round to mutual acquaintances, and especially the proposed marriage between Danglars' daughter Eugénie and Albert de Morcerf.

'The Morcerfs,' said the Baron. 'See here, Count, you are a gentleman, are you not?'

'I hope so.'

'And you understand something about heraldry?'

'A little.'

'Well, look at my coat-of-arms; it is worth more than Morcerf's, for, though I may not be a Baron by birth, I do at least keep to my own name, whereas Morcerf is not his name at all.'

'Do you really mean that?'

'I have been made a Baron, so I actually am one; he has given himself the title of Count, therefore he is not one at all.'

'Impossible!'

'Monsieur de Morcerf and I have been friends, or rather acquaintances, for the last thirty years. As you know, I make good use of my coat-of-arms, and I do so for the simple reason that I never forget whence I sprang.'

'Which shows either great pride or great humility,' said Monte Cristo.

'When I was a clerk, Morcerf was but a simple fisherman.'

'What was his name?'

'Fernand Mondego.'

'Are you sure of that?'

'Good gracious, he has sold me enough fish for me to know his name.'

'Then why are you letting his son marry your daughter?'

'Because as Fernand and Danglars are both upstarts, have both been given a title of nobility and become rich, there is a great similarity between them – except for one thing that has been said about him which has never been said about me.'

'What is that?'

'Nothing.'

'I understand! What you have just told me has brought back to my mind that I have heard his name in Greece.'

'In connexion with the Ali Pasha affair?'

'Just so.'

'That is a mystery I would give much to discover,' replied Danglars.

'It would not be difficult. No doubt you have correspondents in Greece, perhaps at Janina?'

'I have them everywhere.'

'Why not write to your correspondent at Janina and ask him what part a certain Frenchman named Fernand played in the Ali Tebelin affair?'

'You are right!' exclaimed Danglars, rising quickly. 'I will write this very day.'

'And if you receive any scandalous news . . .'

'I will let you know.'

'I should be much obliged.'

Danglars rushed out of the room and leapt into his carriage.

22

Scarcely had M. Danglars left the Count of Monte Cristo to write in all haste to his correspondent at Janina when Albert de Morcerf was announced. The Count received him with his habitual smile.

'Listen,' Albert said breathlessly, 'my mother . . . no not my mother, my father is thinking of giving a ball.'

'At this time of the year?'

'Summer balls are fashionable. You see, those who remain in Paris in the month of July are the real Parisians.'

'Well,' said the Count with a smile, 'I do not know whether I shall go to your ball myself.'

'Why not?'

'In the first place because you have not yet invited me.'

'I have come for that express purpose.'

'That is very kind of you. I may, however, still be compelled to refuse.'

'When I tell you that my mother especially asks you to come, I am sure you will brush aside all obstacles.'

'The Countess of Morcerf asks me?' inquired Monte Cristo with a start.

'I can assure you, Count, Madame de Morcerf speaks freely to me, and if you have not been stirred by a sympathetic impulse during the last four days, it must be that you have no response in you, for we have talked incessantly of you. May we expect you on Saturday?'

'You may, since Madame de Morcerf expressly invites me.'

'You are very kind.'

'Will Monsieur Danglars be there?'

'Oh, yes, he has been invited. My father has seen to that. We shall also try to persuade Monsieur de Villefort to come, but have not much hope of success. Do you dance, Count?'

'No, I do not, but I enjoy watching others. Does your mother dance?'

'No, never. You can entertain her. She is very anxious to have a talk with you.'

'Really?'

'On my word of honour. Do you know, you are the first person in whom my mother has manifested such curiosity.'

Albert rose and took his hat; the Count accompanied him to the door.

'By the way,' asked the Count, 'when does Monsieur d'Épinay arrive?'

'In five or six days at the latest.'

'And when is he to be married?'

'As soon as Monsieur and Madame de Saint-Méran arrive.'

'Bring him to see me when he comes. Though you always say I do not like him, I shall be very glad to see him.'

'Your orders shall be obeyed, Count.'

'Goodbye!'

'Until Saturday. That is quite certain?'

'I have given you my promise.'

It was in the warmest days of June when, in due course of time, the Saturday arrived on which M. de Morcerf's ball was to take place. It was ten o'clock in the evening. From the rooms on the ground floor might be heard the sounds of music and the whirl of the waltz and galop, while brilliant light streamed through the interstices of the venetian blinds. At that moment the garden was occupied only by some ten servants, who were preparing the supper-tables. The paths had already been illuminated by brilliant coloured lanterns, and a mass of choice flowers and numberless candles helped to decorate the sumptuous supper-tables.

No sooner had the Countess returned to the salon after giving her final orders than the guests began to arrive, drawn thither by the charming hospitality of the Countess more than by the distinguished position of the Count. Mme Danglars came, not only beautiful in person but radiantly splendid. Albert went up to her and, paying her well-merited compliments on her toilette, offered her his arm and conducted her to a seat.

'Now, tell me . . .' the Baroness began.

'What do you wish to know, madame?'

'Is the Count of Monte Cristo not coming this evening?'

'Seventeen!' said Albert.

'What do you mean?'

'Only that you are the seventeenth person who has

put that same question to me,' replied Albert laughing. 'He is doing well . . . I congratulate him.'

'Were you at the Opera yesterday? He was there.'

'No, I did not go. Did the eccentric man do anything original?'

'Does he ever do anything else? Elssler was dancing in *Le Diable Boiteux*, and the Greek princess whom he always takes to the theatre was in raptures. After the *cachucha*, he threw the dancer a bouquet in between the flowers of which there was a magnificent ring; when she appeared again in the third act, she did honour to the gift by wearing it on her little finger. But leave me here now and go and pay your respects to Madame de Villefort. I can see she is longing to have a talk with you.'

Albert bowed and went toward Mme de Villefort, who was about to say something when Albert interrupted her.

'I am sure I know what you are going to ask me,' he said.

'What is it?'

'Whether the Count of Monte Cristo is coming.'

'Not at all. I was not even thinking of him just then. I wanted to ask you whether you had received news of Franz.'

'I had a letter from him yesterday. He was then leaving for Paris.'

'That's good. Now what about the Count?'

'The Count is coming right enough.'

Just then a handsome young man with keen eyes, black hair, and a glossy moustache bowed respectfully to Mme de Villefort. Albert held out his hand to him.

'Madame, I have the honour of presenting to you

Monsieur Maximilian Morrel, Captain of Spahis, one of our best and bravest officers.'

'I had the pleasure of meeting this gentleman at Auteuil, at the Count of Monte Cristo's,' replied Mme de Villefort, turning away with marked coldness.

This remark, and above all the tone in which it was said, chilled the heart of poor Morrel. There was a recompense in store for him, however. Turning round, he perceived near the door a beautiful figure all in white, whose large blue eyes were fixed on him without any apparent expression, whilst the bouquet of myosotis slowly rose to her lips.

Morrel understood the salutation so well that, with the same expressionless look in his eyes, he raised his handkerchief to his mouth. These two living statues, whose hearts beat so violently under their apparently marble-like forms yet were separated from each other by the whole length of the room, forgot themselves for a moment, or rather for a moment forgot everybody and everything in their mute contemplation of one another. They might have remained lost in each other much longer without anyone noticing their obliviousness to all things around them had not the Count of Monte Cristo just entered. The Count seemed to exercise a fascination, whether artificial or natural, which attracted general attention wherever he went.

He advanced, exchanging bows on his way, to where Mme de Morcerf was standing before a flower-laden mantelshelf. She had seen his entrance in a mirror placed opposite the door and was prepared to receive him. She turned towards him with a serene smile just as he was bowing to her. No doubt she thought the Count would speak to her, while he on the other hand thought she was about to address him. They both remained silent, therefore, apparently feeling that banalities were out of place between them, so after exchanging salutations, Monte Cristo went in search of Albert.

'Have you seen my mother?' was Albert's first remark.

'I have just had the pleasure,' said the Count, 'but I have not yet seen your father.'

'He is talking politics with a small group of great celebrities.'

Just then the Count felt his arm pressed; he turned round to find himself face to face with Danglars.

'Ah, it is you, Baron,' said he.

'Why do you call me Baron?' returned Danglars. 'You know quite well I care nothing for my title. I am not like you in that respect Viscount; you lay great value on your title, do you not?'

'Certainly I do,' replied Albert, 'for if I were not a viscount, I should be nothing at all, whereas, while sacrificing your title of Baron, you would still be a millionaire.'

'Which appears to me the finest title in existence,' replied Danglars.

'Unfortunately,' said Monte Cristo, 'the title of millionaire does not always last one's lifetime as does that of Baron, Peer of France, or Academician. As a proof you have only to consider the case of the millionaires Francke and Poulmann, of Frankfurt, who have just become bankrupt.'

'Is that really the case?' asked Danglars, turning pale.

'Indeed it is. I received the news this evening by

courier. I had about a million deposited with them, but, having been warned in time, I demanded its withdrawal some four weeks ago.'

'Good heavens! They have drawn on me for two hundred thousand francs!'

'Well, you are warned.'

'But the warning has come too late,' said Danglars. 'I have honoured their signature.'

'Ah, well,' said the Count, 'that's another two hundred thousand francs gone to join . . .'

'Hush, do not mention such things in public,' said the banker.

In the meantime the heat in the room had become excessive. Footmen went round with trays laden with fruit and ices. Monte Cristo wiped with his handkerchief the perspiration that had gathered on his forehead. Nevertheless he stepped back when the tray passed before him and would not take refreshment.

Mme de Morcerf did not lose sight of Monte Cristo. She saw him refuse to take anything from the tray and even noticed his movement as he withdrew from it.

'Albert,' said she, 'have you noticed that the Count will not accept an invitation to dine with your father?'

'But he breakfasted with me,' said Albert. 'In fact it was at that breakfast that he was first introduced into our society.'

'That is not your father's house. I have been watching him tonight, he has not taken anything. Perhaps it is the heat.'

She left the room, and an instant later the venetian blinds were opened, permitting a view, through the jasmine and clematis that overhung the windows, of the lantern-illuminated garden. Dancers, players, and talkers all uttered an exclamation of joy; everybody inhaled with delight the air that flowed in.

At the same moment Mercédès returned, even paler than before, but with a determined look on her face which was characteristic of her in certain circumstances. She went straight up to the group of gentlemen round her husband, and said: 'Do not detain these gentlemen here; if they are not playing I have no doubt they would prefer to take the fresh air in the garden rather than stay in this suffocating room.'

'But, madame, we will not go into the garden alone!' said a gallant old general.

'Very well, I will set the example,' said Mercédès, and turning to Monte Cristo, she added: 'Will you give me your arm, Count!'

The Count was staggered at these simple words; he looked at Mercédès. It was but a momentary glance, but the Count put so many thoughts into that one look that it seemed to Mercédès it lasted a century. He offered the Countess his arm; she laid her delicate hand gently on it, and together they went into the garden, followed by some twenty of the guests. With her companion, Mme de Morcerf passed under an archway of lime-trees leading to a conservatory.

'Did you not find it too hot in the room?' said she.

'Yes, madame, but it was an excellent idea of yours to open the windows and venetian blinds.'

She led him to the conservatory and offered him various fruits, but all were refused.

'There is a touching Arabian custom, Count,' Mercédès said at last, looking at Monte Cristo supplicatingly, 'which makes eternal friends of those who share bread and salt under the same roof.'

'I know it, madame, but we are in France and not in Arabia, and in France eternal friendships are as rare as the beautiful custom you just mentioned.'

'But we are friends, are we not?' said the Countess breathlessly, with her eyes fixed on Monte Cristo, whose arm she convulsively clasped between her two hands.

'Certainly we are friends, madame,' he replied. 'In any case, why should we not be?'

His tone was so different from what Mercédès desired that she turned away to give vent to a sigh resembling a groan.

'Thank you!' was all she said; she began to walk on, and they went all round the garden without uttering another word. After about ten minutes' silence, she suddenly said: 'Is it true that you have seen much, travelled far, and suffered deeply?'

'I have suffered deeply, madame,' answered Monte Cristo.

'Are you not married?' asked the Countess.

'I, married!' exclaimed Monte Cristo shuddering. 'Who could have told you that?'

'No one told me you were, but you have frequently been seen at the Opera with a young and lovely person.'

'She is a slave whom I bought in Constantinople, madame, the daughter of a prince. Having no one else to love in the world, I have adopted her as my daughter.'

'You live alone, then?'

'I do.'

'You have no sister, no son, no father?'

'I have no one.'

'How can you live thus, with no one to attach you to life?'

'It is not my fault, madame. At Malta, I loved a young girl, and was on the point of marrying her when war came and carried me away, as in a whirlpool. I thought she loved me well enough to wait for me, even to remain faithful to my memory. When I returned she was married. Most men who have passed thirty have the same tale to tell, but perhaps my heart was weaker than that of others, and in consequence I suffered more than they would have done in my place. That's all.'

The Countess stopped for a moment, as if gasping for breath. 'Yes,' she said, 'and you have still preserved this love in your heart – one can only love once. And have you forgiven her for all she has made you suffer?'

'Yes, I have forgiven her.'

'But only her. Do you still hate those who separated you?'

At this moment Albert ran up to them.

'Oh, Mother!' he exclaimed. 'Such a misfortune has happened!'

'What has happened?' asked the Countess, as though awaking from a dream to the realities of life. 'A misfortune, did you say? Indeed, it is little more than I should expect!'

'Monsieur de Villefort has come to fetch his wife and daughter.'

'Why?'

'Madame de Saint-Méran has just arrived in Paris, bringing the news of Monsieur de Saint-Méran's death, which occurred at the first stage after he left Marseilles. Madame de Villefort was in very good spirits when her husband came, and could neither understand nor believe in such misfortune. At the first words, however, Mademoiselle Valentine guessed the whole truth, notwithstanding all her father's precautions; the blow struck her like a thunderbolt, and she fell down senseless.'

'How was Monsieur de Saint-Méran related to Mademoiselle Valentine?' asked the Count.

'He was her maternal grandfather. He was coming here to hasten her marriage with Franz.'

'Indeed!'

'Franz is reprieved then! Why is Monsieur de Saint-Méran not grandfather to Mademoiselle Danglars too?'

'Albert! Albert!' said Mme de Morcerf, in a tone of mild reproof. 'What are you saying? Ah! Count, he esteems you so highly. Tell him he has spoken amiss.'

So saying she took two or three steps forward. Monte Cristo glanced after her with such a pensive expression, at the same time so full of affectionate admiration, that she retraced her steps. Taking his hand and that of her son, she joined them together, saying: 'We are friends, are we not?'

'Oh, madame, I do not presume to call myself your friend, but at all times I am your most respectful servant.'

23

Valentine found her grandmother in bed; silent caresses, heart-rending sobs, broken sighs, and burning tears were the sole recountable details of the distressing interview, at which Mme de Villefort was present, leaning on her husband's arm, and manifesting, outwardly at least, great sympathy for the poor widow.

After a few moments she whispered to her husband: 'I think it would be better for me to retire, for the sight of me still appears to distress your mother-in-law.'

Mme de Saint-Méran heard her and whispered to Valentine: 'Yes, yes, let her go, but you stay with me.'

Mme de Villefort went out and Valentine remained alone with her grandmother, for the Procureur du Roi, dismayed at the sudden death, had followed his wife.

At last, worn out with grief, Mme de Saint-Méran succumbed to her fatigue and fell into a feverish sleep. Valentine placed a small table within her reach and on it a decanter of orangeade, her usual beverage, and, leaving her bedside went to see old Noirtier. She went up to the old man and kissed him. He looked at her with such tenderness that she again burst into tears.

'Yes, yes, I understand,' she said. 'You wish to convey to me that I have still a good grandfather, do you not?'

He intimated that such was his meaning.

'Happily I have,' returned Valentine. 'Otherwise what would become of me?'

It was one o'clock in the morning. Barrois, who wished to go to bed himself, remarked that after such a distressing evening everyone had need of rest. M. Noirtier would have liked to say that all the repose he needed was to be found in his granddaughter's presence, but he bade her good-night, for grief and fatigue had made her look quite ill.

When Valentine went to see her grandmother the next day she found her still in bed. The fever had not abated; on the contrary, the old Marquise's eyes were lit up with a dull fire and she was prone to great nervous irritability.

'Oh, Grandmama, are you feeling worse?' exclaimed Valentine on perceiving all these symptoms.

'No, child, but I was impatiently waiting for you to fetch your father to me.'

'My father?' inquired Valentine uneasily.

'Yes, I wish to speak to him.'

Valentine did not dare oppose her grandmother's wish, and an instant later Villefort entered.

'You wrote me, monsieur, concerning this child's marriage,' said Mme de Saint-Méran, coming straight to the point as though afraid she had not much time left.

'Yes, madame,' replied Villefort. 'The matter has already been settled.'

'Is not the name of your future son-in-law Monsieur Franz d'Épinay?'

'Yes, madame.'

'Is he the son of General d'Épinay, who belonged to our party and was assassinated a few days before the usurper returned from Elba?'

'The very same.'

'Is he not opposed to this alliance with the granddaughter of a Jacobin?'

'Our civil dissensions are now happily dispelled,' said Villefort. 'Monsieur d'Épinay was little more than a child when his father died. He hardly knows Monsieur Noirtier and will greet him, if not with pleasure, at least with unconcern.'

'Is it a desirable match?'

'In every respect. He is one of the most gentlemanly young men I know.'

Valentine remained silent throughout this conversation.

'Then, monsieur, you must hasten on the marriage, for I have not much longer to live,' said Mme de Saint-Méran after a few seconds' reflection.

'You, madame?' 'You, Grandmama?' cried Monsieur de Villefort and Valentine simultaneously.

'I know what I am saying,' returned the Marquise. 'You must hasten on the arrangements so that the poor motherless child may at least have a grandmother to bless her marriage. I am all that is left to her of dear Renée, whom you appear so soon to have forgotten.'

'But, Grandmama, consider decorum – our recent mourning. Would you have me begin my married life under such sad auspices?'

'Nay, I tell you I am going to die, and before dying I wish to see your husband. I wish to bid him make my child happy, to read in his eyes whether he intends to obey me. In short, I must know him,' continued the grandmother with a terrifying expression in her eyes, 'so that I may arise from the depths of my grave to seek him out if he is not all he should be.'

'Madame, you must dispel such feverish ideas that are almost akin to madness,' said Villefort. 'When once the dead are laid in their graves, they remain there never to rise again.'

'And I tell you, monsieur, it is not as you think. Last night my sleep was sorely troubled. It seemed as though my soul were already hovering over my body; my eyes, which I tried to open, closed against my will;

and, what will appear impossible, above all to you, monsieur, with my eyes shut I saw in yonder dark corner, where there is a door leading to Madame de Villefort's dressing-room, I tell you I saw a white figure enter noiselessly.'

Valentine screamed.

'It was the fever acting on you, madame,' said Villefort.

'Doubt my word if it pleases you, but I am sure of what I say. I saw a white figure, and, as if God feared I should discredit the testimony of my senses, I heard my tumbler move – the same one that is now on the table.'

'But it was a dream, Grandmama!'

'So far was it from being a dream that I stretched out my hand towards the bell, but as I did so the shadow disappeared and my maid entered with a light. Phantoms are visible only to those who are intended to see them. It was my husband's spirit. If my husband's spirit can come to me, why should not mine appear to guard my granddaughter? It seems to me there is an even stronger tie between us.'

'Madame, do not give way to such gloomy thoughts,' said Villefort, deeply affected in spite of himself. 'You will live long with us, happy, loved, and honoured, and we will help you to forget . . .'

'Never, never, never!' said the Marquise. 'When does Monsieur d'Épinay return?'

'We expect him any moment.'

'It is well; as soon as he arrives, let me know. We must lose no time. Then I also wish to see a notary that I may be assured that all our property reverts to Valentine.'

'Ah, Grandmother,' murmured Valentine pressing her lips to her grandmother's burning brow, 'do you wish to kill me? Oh, how feverish you are! It is a doctor we must send for, not a notary.'

'A doctor?' she said, shrugging her shoulders. 'I am not ill; I am thirsty – nothing more.'

'What are you drinking, Grandmama?'

'The same as usual, my dear, orangeade. Give me my glass, Valentine.'

Valentine poured the orangeade into a glass and gave it to her grandmother, though not without a feeling of dread, for it was the same glass she declared the shadow had touched. The Marquise drained the glass at a single draught, and then, turning over on her pillow, repeated: 'The notary! The notary!'

M. de Villefort left the room, and Valentine seated herself at her grandmother's bedside.

Two hours passed thus, during which Mme de Saint-Méran was in a restless, feverish sleep. At last the notary arrived. He was announced in a very low voice; nevertheless Mme de Saint-Méran heard and raised herself on her pillows.

'Go, Valentine, go,' she said, 'and leave me alone with this gentleman.'

Valentine kissed her grandmother and left the room with her handkerchief to her eyes. At the door she met the valet who told her the doctor was waiting in the salon. She instantly went down.

'Dear Monsieur d'Avrigny, we have been waiting for you with such impatience.'

'Who is ill, dear child?' said he. 'Not your father or Madame de Villefort?'

'It is my grandmother who needs your services. You know the calamity that has befallen us?'

'I know nothing,' said M. d'Avrigny.

'Alas!' said Valentine, choking back her tears. 'My grandfather is dead.'

'Monsieur de Saint-Méran?'

'Yes.'

'Suddenly?'

'From an apoplectic stroke.'

'An apoplectic stroke?' repeated the doctor.

'Yes! And my poor grandmother fancies that her husband, whom she never left, is calling her, and that she must go and join him. Oh! Monsieur d'Avrigny, I beseech you, do something for her!'

'Where is she?'

'In her room with the notary.'

The doctor pressed Valentine's hand, and, while he visited her grandmother, she went into the garden. After remaining for a short time in the flower garden surrounding the house, and gathering a rose to place in her waist or hair, she turned into the dark avenue which led to the bench, from thence to the gate. As she advanced she fancied she heard a voice pronounce her name. She stopped astonished, then the voice reached her ear more distinctly, and she recognized it as the voice of Maximilian.

It was indeed Maximilian Morrel. He had been in despair since the previous day. With the instinct of a lover he had divined that with the arrival of Mme de Saint-Méran and the death of the Marquis some change would take place in the Villefort household which would touch his love for Valentine.

Valentine had not expected to see Morrel, for it was not his usual hour, and it was only pure chance or, better still, a happy sympathy that took her into the garden. When she appeared, Morrel called her, and she ran to the gate.

'You here, at this hour!' she said.

'Yes, my poor dear,' replied Morrel. 'I have come to bring and to hear bad tidings.'

'This is indeed a house of mourning,' said Valentine. 'Speak, Maximilian, yet in truth my cup of sorrow seems full to overflowing.'

'Dear Valentine, listen, I entreat you,' said Morrel endeavouring to conceal his emotion. 'I have something grave to tell you. When are you to be married?'

'I will conceal nothing from you, Maximilian,' said Valentine. 'This morning the subject was introduced and my grandmother, in whom I had hoped to find a sure support, not only declares herself favourable to the marriage, but is so anxious for it that the day after Monsieur d'Épinay arrives the contract will be signed.'

A sob of anguish was wrung from the young man's breast, and he looked long and mournfully at his beloved.

'Alas!' he whispered. 'It is terrible thus to hear the woman you love calmly say: "The time of your execution is fixed, and will take place in a few hours; it had to be, and I will do nothing to prevent it!" Monsieur d'Épinay arrived this morning!'

Valentine uttered a cry.

'And now, Valentine, answer me, and remember that my life or death depends on your answer. What do you intend doing? Are you prepared to fight against our ill-fortune, Valentine? Tell me, for this is what I have come to ask you.'

Valentine trembled visibly, and stared at Maximilian with wide-open eyes. The idea of opposing her grandmother, her father, in short her whole family, had never occurred to her.

'What is this you bid me do, Maximilian?' asked Valentine. 'How could I oppose my father's orders and my dying grandmother's wish! It is impossible!'

Morrel started.

'You are too noble-hearted not to understand me, and your very silence is proof that you do. I fight! God preserve me from it! No, I need all my strength to hold back my tears. Never could I grieve my father or disturb the last moments of my grandmother!'

'You are right,' said Morrel phlegmatically. 'This is what I shall do: I shall wait until you are actually married, for I will not lose the smallest of one of those unexpected chances fate sometimes holds in store for us. After all, Monsieur Franz might die, a thunderbolt might fall on the altar as you approach it; everything appears possible to the condemned man, to whom a miracle becomes an everyday occurrence when it is a question of saving his life. I shall therefore wait until the very last moment, and when my fate is sealed, and my misery beyond all hope and remedy, I shall write a confidential letter to my brother-in-law, another one to the prefect of police, to notify him of my design; then, in a corner of some wood, in a ditch, or on the bank of some river, I shall blow out my brains, as certainly as I am the son of the most honest man who ever breathed in France.'

A convulsive trembling shook Valentine in every limb; she relaxed her hold of the gate, her arms fell to her sides, and two large tears rolled down her cheeks.

The young man stood before her, gloomy and resolute.

Valentine fell on her knees, pressing her hand to her breaking heart.

'Maximilian, my friend, my brother on earth, my real husband before Heaven,' she cried, 'I entreat you, do as I am going to do – live in suffering; one day, perhaps, we shall be united.'

'Farewell!' repeated Morrel.

'My God,' said Valentine, raising her two hands to Heaven with a sublime expression on her face. 'Thou seest I have done my utmost to remain a dutiful daughter. I have begged, entreated, implored. He has heeded neither my entreaties, nor my supplications, nor my tears . . . I would rather die of shame than of remorse,' she continued, wiping away her tears and resuming her air of determination. 'You shall live, Maximilian, and I shall belong to no other than you! When shall it be? At once? Speak, command, I will obey.'

Morrel had already gone several steps; he returned on hearing these words, and pale with joy, his heart beating tumultuously, he held his two hands through the gate to Valentine, and said:

'Valentine, my beloved, you must not speak to me thus; better let me die. Why should I win you by force if you love me as I love you? Is it for pity that you compel me to live? Then I would rather die!'

''Tis too true!' murmured Valentine to herself. 'Who but he loves me? Who but he has consoled me in all my sorrow? In whom but in him do my hopes lie, and to whom but to him can I fly when in trouble? He is my all! Yes, you are right, Maximilian, I will follow you. I will leave my father's home, leave all! Ungrateful girl that I am!' she cried, sobbing. 'Yes, I will leave all, even my grandfather whom I had nearly forgotten!'

'No, you shall not leave him,' said Maximilian. 'You say that your grandfather likes me. Very well, then, before you flee, tell him all; his consent will be your justification before God. As soon as we are married, he shall come to us: instead of one child, he will have two children. Oh, Valentine, instead of our present hopelessness, nought but happiness is in store for you and me. But if they disregard your entreaties, Valentine,' he continued, 'if your father and Madame de Saint-Méran insist on sending for Monsieur d'Épinay tomorrow to sign the contract . . .'

'You have my word, Maximilian.'

'Instead of signing . . .'

'I shall flee with you, but until then, Morrel, let us not tempt Providence. We will see each other no more: it is a marvel, almost a miracle one might say, that we have not been discovered before. If it were found out, and if they learned how we see each other, our last resource would be gone. In the meantime I will write to you. I hate this marriage, Maximilian, as much as you do.'

'Thank you, my beloved Valentine,' Morrel replied. 'Then all is settled. As soon as I know the time, I will hasten here. You will climb the wall with my help and then all will be easy. A carriage will be awaiting us at the gate which will take us to my sister's.'

'So be it! Goodbye!' said Valentine, tearing herself away. '*Au revoir!*'

'You will be sure to write to me?'

'Yes.'

'Thank you, my beloved wife. *Au revoir!*'

Morrel stayed, listening, till the sound of her footsteps on the gravel had died away, then he raised his eyes heavenward with an ineffable smile of gratitude that such supreme love should be given him.

The young man returned home and waited the whole of that evening and the next day without receiving any news. Towards ten o'clock of the third day, however, he received by post a note which he knew was from Valentine, although he had never before seen her handwriting. The note read as follows:

Tears, supplications, entreaties have been of no avail. I went to the church of St Philip du Roule yesterday and for two hours prayed most fervently. But God appears as unfeeling as man is and the signing of the contract is fixed for this evening at nine o'clock. I have but one heart and can give my hand to one person only: both my hand and my heart are yours, Maximilian.

I shall see you this evening at the gate at a quarter to nine.

Your wife,

VALENTINE DE VILLEFORT

P.S. – I think they are keeping it a secret from Grandpapa Noirtier that the contract is to be signed tomorrow.

Not satisfied with the information Valentine had given him, Morrel went in search of the notary, who confirmed the fact that the signing of the contract had been fixed for nine o'clock that evening.

Maximilian had made all arrangements for the elopement. Two ladders were hidden in the clover near the garden; a cabriolet, which was to take Maximilian to the gate, was in readiness. No servants would accompany him, and the lanterns would not be lit till they reached the first bend of the road.

From time to time a shudder passed through Morrel's whole frame as he thought of the moment when he would assist Valentine in her descent from the top of the wall, and when he would clasp in his arms the trembling form of her whose fingertips he had as yet hardly ventured to kiss.

In the afternoon, when the hour drew near, Morrel felt the necessity of being alone. He shut himself up in his room and attempted to read, but his eyes passed over the pages without understanding what he was reading, and in the end he flung the book from him. At last the hour arrived. The horse and cabriolet were concealed behind some ruins where Maximilian was accustomed to hide.

The day gradually drew to its close, and the bushes in the garden became nothing but indistinct masses. Morrel came out of his hiding-place, and, with beating heart, looked through the hole in the paling. There was no one to be seen. The clock struck nine . . . half-past nine . . . ten! In the darkness he searched in vain for the white dress, in the stillness he waited in vain for the sound of footsteps. Then one idea took possession of his mind: she had been coming to him, but her strength had failed her and she had fallen in a faint on one of the garden paths. He ventured to call her name, and he seemed to hear an inarticulate moan in response. He scaled the wall and jumped down on the other side. Distracted and half mad with anxiety, he decided to risk everything and anything in order to ascertain if and what misfortune had befallen Valentine. He reached the outskirts of the clump of trees and was just about to cross the open flower-garden with all possible speed when a distant voice, borne upon the wind, reached his ear.

He retreated a step and stood motionless, concealed, hidden among the trees. He made up his mind that if Valentine was alone, he would warn her of his presence; if she was accompanied, he would at least see her and know whether she was safe and well.

Just then the moon escaped from behind a cloud and by its light Morrel saw Villefort on the steps followed by a man in black garb. They descended the steps and approached the clump of trees where Morrel was hiding, and he soon recognized the other gentleman as Doctor d'Avrigny. After a short time, their footsteps ceased to crunch the gravel, and the following conversation reached his ears:

'Oh, Doctor, the hand of God is heavy upon us! What a terrible death! What a blow! Seek not to console me, for alas, the wound is too deep and too fresh. Dead! Dead!'

A cold perspiration broke out on Maximilian's forehead, and his teeth chattered. Who was dead in that house that Villefort himself called accursed?

'I have not brought you here to console you. Quite the contrary,' said the doctor, in a voice that added to the young man's terror.

'What do you mean?' asked the Procureur du Roi in alarm.

'What I mean is, that behind the misfortune that has just befallen you, there is perhaps a much greater one. Are we quite alone?'

'Yes, quite alone. But why such precautions?'

'I have a terrible secret to confide in you,' said the doctor.

'Let us sit down.'

Villefort sank on to a bench. The doctor stood in front of him, one hand on his shoulder. Petrified with fear, Morrel put one hand to his head, and pressed the other to his heart to stop the beatings lest they should be heard.

'Speak, Doctor, I am listening,' said Villefort. 'Strike your blow. I am prepared for all.'

'Madame de Saint-Méran had attained a great age, it is true, but she was in excellent health.'

Morrel began to breathe freely again.

'Grief has killed her,' said Villefort. 'Yes, Doctor, grief! After living with the Marquis for more than forty years!'

'It is not grief, my dear Villefort,' said the doctor. 'Grief does kill, though very rarely, but not in a day not in an hour, nor yet in ten minutes. She was poisoned!'

'Oh, Doctor! Doctor!'

'All the symptoms were there; sleep disturbed by nervous tremors, excitement of the brain followed by torpor. Madame de Saint-Méran has succumbed to a large dose of brucine or strychnine, which has doubtless been administered to her by mistake.'

Villefort seized the doctor's hands.

'It is impossible!' he said. 'Am I dreaming? Surely I must be. It is terrible to hear such things from a man like you! For pity's sake, Doctor, tell me you have been mistaken!'

'Did anyone see Madame de Saint-Méran besides myself?'

'No one.'

'Has any prescription been made up at the chemist's that has not been shown me?'

'None.'

'Had Madame de Saint-Méran any enemies?'

'I do not know of any.'

'Would her death be to anyone's interest?'

'No, no, surely not! My daughter is her sole heiress, Valentine alone . . . Oh, if such a thought came into my heart, I should stab that heart to punish it for having harboured such a thought if only for one moment.'

'God forbid that I should accuse anyone,' exclaimed M. d'Avrigny. 'I speak of an accident, a mistake, you understand. But whether accident or mistake, the fact remains and is appealing to my conscience, which compels me to speak to you. Make inquiries.'

'Of whom? How? About what?'

'Is it not possible that Barrois, the old servant, has made a mistake and given Madame de Saint-Méran a potion prepared for his master?'

'But how could a potion prepared for my father kill Madame de Saint-Méran?'

'Nothing more simple. You know that in the case of certain diseases poison becomes a remedy. Paralysis is one of these cases. I have been giving Monsieur Noirtier brucine for the past three months, and in his last prescription I ordered six grains, a quantity that would be perfectly safe for one whose paralysed organs have gradually become accustomed to it, whereas it would be sufficient to kill anyone else.'

'But there is no communication between Monsieur Noirtier's room and that of Madame de Saint-Méran, and Barrois never went near my mother-in-law.'

'It is through carelessness that this has happened; watch your servants. If it is the work of hatred, watch your enemies. In the meantime let us bury this terrible secret in the depths of our hearts. Keep constant watch, for it may be that it will not end here. Make active investigations and seek out the culprit, and if you should find him, I shall say to you: "You are a magistrate, do as you will."'

'Oh, thank you, Doctor, thank you!' said Villefort with indescribable joy. 'Never have I had better friend than you.'

Fearing lest d'Avrigny might think better of his decision, he rose and ran into the house. The doctor also went away.

As though he had need of air, Morrel immediately put his head out of the bushes, and the moon shining on his face gave him the appearance of a ghost.

'I have been protected in a wonderful yet terrible way,' said he. 'Valentine, my poor Valentine! How will she bear so much sorrow?'

As though in answer, he seemed to hear a sob coming from one of the open windows of the house, and he thought he heard his name called by a shadow at the window. He rushed out of his hiding-place, and, at the risk of being seen and of frightening Valentine, and thus causing some exclamation to escape her lips which would lead to discovery, he crossed the flower-garden, which looked like a large white lake in the moonlight, reached the steps, ran up them quickly, and pushed open the door, which offered no resistance. The description of the house Valentine had given him now stood him in good stead, and the thick carpets deadened his tread. He reached the top of the stairs without any accident; a half-open door, from which issued a stream of light, and the sound of a sob indicated to him which direction to take. Pushing open the door, he entered the room.

In an alcove, under a white sheet, lay the corpse, more terrifying than ever to Morrel since chance had revealed to him the secret concerning the dead woman. Beside the bed knelt Valentine, her hands stretched out in front of her and her whole frame shaking with sobs. The moon shining through the open blinds made pale the light of the lamp, and cast a sepulchral hue over this picture of desolation. Morrel was not of a pious or impressionable nature, but to see Valentine suffering and weeping was almost more than he could endure in silence. With a deep sigh he murmured her name, and the tear-stained face buried in the velvet of the armchair was slowly raised and turned towards him. Valentine manifested no astonishment at seeing him.

'How came you here?' she asked. 'Alas! I should say you are welcome, but that Death has opened the doors of this house to you!'

'Valentine, I have been waiting there since half-past eight,' said Morrel in a trembling voice. 'Such anxiety was tearing at my heart when you did not come that I scaled the wall and . . .'

'But we shall be lost if you are found here!' said Valentine in a voice devoid of all fear or anger.

'Forgive me,' replied Morrel in the same tone. 'I will go at once.'

'No, you cannot go out either by the front door or the garden gate. There is only one safe way open to you and that is through my grandfather's room. Follow me!'

'Have you thought what that means?'

'I have thought long since. He is the only friend I have in the world and we both have need of him. Come!'

Valentine crossed the corridor and went down a small staircase which led to Noirtier's room. She entered; Morrel followed her on tiptoe.

Still in his chair, Noirtier was listening for the least sound. He had been informed by his old servant of all that had happened and was now watching the door with eager eyes. He saw Valentine, and his eyes brightened. There was something grave and solemn about the girl's whole attitude which struck the old man, and his eyes looked on her questioningly.

'Dear Grandpapa,' she said, 'you know that Grandmama Saint-Méran died an hour ago, and now I have no one but you in the whole world to love me.'

An expression of infinite tenderness shone in the old man's eyes.

'Thus to you alone can I confide all my sorrows and hopes.'

The old man made a sign of assent.

Valentine took Maximilian by the hand. 'Then look well at this gentleman,' said she.

Somewhat astonished, the paralytic fixed his scrutinizing gaze on Morrel.

'This is Maximilian Morrel,' said she, 'the son of an honest merchant of Marseilles, of whom you have doubtless heard.'

'Yes,' was the answer.

'It is an irreproachable name, and Maximilian is in a fair way to making it a glorious one, for, though but thirty years of age, he is Captain of Spahis and an Officer of the Legion of Honour.'

The old man made a sign that he recollected him.

Valentine threw herself on her knees before the old man saying: 'Grandpapa, I love him and will belong to no other. If they force me to marry another, I shall die or kill myself.'

The paralytic's eyes expressed a wealth of tumultuous thoughts.

'You like Monsieur Maximilian Morrel, do you not, Grandfather?' asked Valentine.

'Yes,' was the old man's motionless reply.

'Will you protect us, then, who are your children, against my father's will?'

Noirtier fixed his intelligent gaze on Morrel as though to say: 'That depends.'

Maximilian understood him.

'Mademoiselle, you have a sacred duty to fulfil in your grandmother's room. Will you permit me to have a few minutes' conversation with Monsieur Noirtier?'

'Yes, yes, that is right,' said the old man's eyes. Then he looked at Valentine with an expression of anxiety.

'You wonder how he will understand you, Grandpapa? Have no fear; we have spoken of you so often that he knows quite well how I converse with you.' Then turning to Maximilian with a smile that was adorable, though overshadowed by great sadness, she said: 'He knows all that I know.'

Valentine rose and kissed her grandfather tenderly, and, taking leave of Morrel, sorrowfully left the two men together.

Then, to show that he was in Valentine's confidence and knew all their secrets, Morrel took the dictionary, a pen and some paper and placed them on the table near the lamp.

'First of all, monsieur,' said he, 'permit me to tell you who I am, how deeply I love Valentine, and what plans I entertain in regard to her.'

'I am listening,' said Noirtier's eyes.

Morrel related how he had become acquainted with Valentine, how he had learned to love her, and how in her unhappiness and solitude Valentine had welcomed his offer of devotion; he gave full information regarding his birth and position, and more than once when he questioned the paralytic's eye, it said to him: 'That is well! Continue!'

Then Morrel related to him how they had intended to flee together that very night. When he had finished speaking, Noirtier closed and opened his eyes several times which, as we know, was his manner of expressing negation.

'No?' said Morrel. 'You disapprove of my plan?'

'Yes, I do disapprove of it.'

'But then, what am I to do?' asked Morrel. 'Madame de Saint-Méran's last words were to the effect that her grandchild's marriage should not be delayed. Am I to allow it to take place?'

Noirtier remained motionless.

'I understand you,' said Morrel. 'I am to wait. But we shall be lost if we delay. Alone Valentine is powerless, and she will be compelled to submit like a child. It was little short of miraculous the way I gained admittance to this house to learn what was happening, and was permitted to enter your room; but I cannot reasonably expect the fates to be so kind to me again. Believe me, there is no other course for me to take. Do you give Mademoiselle Valentine permission to entrust herself to my honour?'

'No!' looked the old man.

'Whence will help come to us then; are we to seek it in chance?'

'No.'

'In you?'

'Yes.'

'Do you fully comprehend what I ask, monsieur? Forgive my importunity, but my life depends upon your answer. Is our salvation to come from you?'

'Yes.'

'But the contract?'

Again the same smile.

'Do you mean to say that it will not be signed?'

'I do,' said Noirtier.

'The contract will not be signed!' exclaimed Morrel. 'Forgive me, but I cannot help doubting such happiness. Will the contract really not be signed?'

'No,' said the paralytic.

Whether it was that Noirtier understood the young man's decision, or whether he had not complete confidence in his docility, he looked steadily at him.

'What do you wish, monsieur?' asked Morrel. 'Do you wish me to renew my promise to do nothing?'

'Yes,' motioned the old man with great solemnity.

Morrel understood that the old man attached great importance to an oath. He held up his hand: 'On my honour,' said he, 'I swear to await your decision before acting in any way against Monsieur d'Épinay.'

'That is right,' said the old man with his eyes.

'Do you wish me to retire now, monsieur?' asked Morrel.

'Yes.'

'Without seeing Mademoiselle Valentine again?'

'Yes.'

Morrel made a sign that he was ready to obey. 'Now, monsieur, will you permit your grandson to embrace you as your granddaughter did just now?'

There was no mistaking the expression in Noirtier's eyes.

The young man pressed his lips to the old man's forehead, on the same spot where the girl had imprinted her kiss. Then he bowed again and retired.

He found the old servant waiting for him on the landing. Valentine had given him all instructions. He took Morrel along a dark corridor which led to a small door opening on to the garden. Once in the garden, Morrel soon scaled the wall, and by means of his ladder reached the field where his cabriolet was waiting for him. He jumped in, and worn out by so many emotions, though feeling more at peace, he reached his home toward midnight, threw himself on his bed, and fell into a deep, dreamless sleep.

24

No sooner were the Marquis and Marquise laid to rest together in the family vault than M. de Villefort thought about putting into execution the Marquise's last wishes. He sent a message to Valentine to request her to be in the salon in half an hour, as he was expecting M. d'Épinay, his two witnesses, and the notary.

This unexpected news created a great stir throughout the house. Mme de Villefort could scarcely believe it, and Valentine was thunderstruck. She looked round her, as though seeking for help, and would have gone to her grandfather, but on the stairs she met M. de Villefort, who, taking her arm, conducted her to the salon. In the hall she met Barrois, and threw him a despairing look. A moment later Mme de Villefort, with her son Edward, joined them. It was evident the young woman shared the family grief, for she was pallid, and looked terribly fatigued.

She sat down with Edward on her knees, and from time to time convulsively caught him to her breast. Soon the rumbling of two carriages was heard. The notary alighted from one, and Franz and his friends from the other.

Everyone was now united in the salon. Valentine was so pale that one could trace the blue veins round her eyes and down her cheeks.

After arranging his papers on the table in true lawyer-like fashion, the notary seated himself in an armchair and, taking off his eyeglasses, turned to Franz. 'Are you Monsieur Franz de Quesnel, Baron d'Épinay?' he asked, though he knew perfectly well that he was.

'Yes, monsieur,' replied Franz.

The notary bowed. 'I must warn you, monsieur,' he continued, 'on Monsieur de Villefort's behalf, that your projected marriage with mademoiselle has effected a change in Monsieur Noirtier's designs toward his granddaughter, and that he has disinherited her entirely. I will add, however, that the testator has no right to will away the whole of his fortune. In doing so he has made the will contestable and liable to be declared null and void.'

'That is right,' said Villefort, 'but I should like to

warn Monsieur d'Épinay that never in my lifetime shall the will be contested, for my position does not permit of the slightest scandal.'

'I greatly regret that this point should have been raised in Mademoiselle Valentine's presence,' said Franz. 'I have never asked the amount of her fortune, which, reduced though it may be, is still considerably larger than mine. What my family seeks in this alliance with Mademoiselle de Villefort is prestige, what I seek is happiness.'

Valentine made a slight movement in acknowledgment, while two large tears rolled down her cheeks

At that moment, the door opened and Barrois appeared.

'Messieurs,' said he, in a voice strangely firm for a servant speaking to his masters on such a solemn occasion, 'messieurs, Monsieur Noirtier de Villefort desires to have speech with Monsieur Franz de Quesnel, Baron d'Épinay, immediately.'

That there might be no mistake made in the person, he also, like the notary, gave Franz his full title.

Valentine instinctively raised her eyes to the ceiling to thank her God in Heaven.

'Valentine, please go and see what this new whim of your grandfather's is,' said Villefort.

Valentine jumped up to obey, but M. de Villefort changed his mind.

'Wait,' said he, 'I will accompany you.'

'Excuse me, monsieur,' spoke Franz, 'it seems to me that since Monsieur Noirtier has sent for me it is only right that I should do as he desires; besides, I shall be happy to pay him my respects, as I have not yet had the opportunity of doing so.'

'I beg you, monsieur, do not give yourself so much trouble,' said Villefort with visible uneasiness.

'Pardon me, monsieur,' said Franz in a determined tone, 'I will not miss this opportunity of showing Monsieur Noirtier that he does wrong to harbour bad feeling towards me, and that I am decided to overcome it by my devotedness.'

With these words he rose and followed Valentine, who was running downstairs with the joy of a ship-wrecked mariner who has touched a rock. M. de Ville-fort followed them.

Noirtier was waiting, dressed in black, and seated in his chair. When the three persons he expected to see had entered his room, he looked at the door, and his valet immediately closed it.

Villefort went up to Noirtier.

'Here is Monsieur Franz d'Épinay,' said he. 'You sent for him; he has granted your wish. We have long desired this interview, and I hope it will prove to you that your opposition to this marriage is ill-founded.'

Noirtier's sole answer was a look which made the blood run cold in Villefort's veins. He made a sign to Valentine to approach.

With her usual alertness in conversing with her grandfather, she very quickly understood him to sig-nify the word 'Key'. Then she consulted the paralytic's eyes, which were fixed on the drawer of a little chest placed between the windows. She opened it, and, found therein a key.

The paralytic made a sign that that was what he wanted, and then his eyes rested on a writing-desk which had been forgotten for years and which was believed to contain nothing but useless papers.

'Do you wish me to open the desk?' asked Valentine.

'Yes,' signalled the old man.

'Do you wish me to open the drawers?'

'Yes.'

'The middle one?'

'Yes.'

Valentine opened it and took out a bundle of papers.

'Is this what you want, Grandpapa?' said she.

'No.'

She took out all the papers, one after the other, till there were no more left in the drawer.

'The drawer is empty now,' said she.

Noirtier's eyes were fixed on the dictionary.

'Very well,' said Valentine, 'I understand you,' and she repeated the letters of the alphabet; at S Noirtier stopped her. She opened the dictionary and found the word 'Secret'. Noirtier looked at the door by which his servant had gone out.

'Do you wish me to call Barrois?' Valentine said.

'Yes.'

She did as he bade her.

Villefort was becoming more and more impatient during this conversation, and Franz was stupefied with amazement.

The old servant entered.

'Barrois,' began Valentine, 'my grandfather desired me to take a key from this chest and open his desk. There is a secret drawer which you apparently understand; open it.'

Barrois looked at his master.

'Obey!' said Noirtier's intelligent eyes.

Barrois obeyed and took out the false bottom, revealing a bundle of papers tied together with a black ribbon.

'Is this what you wish, monsieur?' asked Barrois.

'Yes.'

'Shall I give the papers to Monsieur de Villefort?'

'No.'

'To Monsieur Franz d'Épinay?'

'Yes.'

Amazed, Franz advanced a step and took the papers from Barrois.

'And what do you wish me to do with this paper, monsieur?' he asked.

'He doubtless wishes you to keep it, sealed as it is,' said the Procureur du Roi.

'No, no!' replied Noirtier vigorously.

'Perhaps you wish Monsieur Franz to read it?' said Valentine.

'Yes,' was the reply.

'Then let us be seated,' said Villefort impatiently, 'for it will take some time.'

Villefort sat down, but Valentine remained standing beside her grandfather, leaning against his chair, while Franz stood before him. He held the mysterious document in his hand; he unsealed the envelope, and complete silence reigned in the room as he read.

The document contained full details of the death of Franz's father, General de Quesnel. In 1815, the Bonapartist club in Paris had tried to recruit him, but he had refused, insisting on his loyalty to the king. He had taken an oath of silence, however, since he now knew the faces of several members of the club. As the President of the club was escorting the General home in his carriage, the General insulted the President by implying that he was brave only when surrounded by the other members of the club. This was a matter of honour. The President stopped the carriage and a duel was fought. Although the President was twice wounded in the arm, he killed his opponent, the General.

When Franz had finished reading this report, truly a terrible ordeal for a son – when Valentine, pale with emotion, had wiped away her tears, and Villefort, trembling in a corner, had attempted to calm the storm by sending appealing looks at the implacable old man, he turned to Noirtier with the following words:

'Since you know this terrible story in all its details, monsieur, and have had it witnessed by honourable signatures; since you seem to take some interest in me, although, until now, that interest has brought me nothing but grief, do not refuse me the satisfaction of making known to me the name of the President of the club, so that I may at least learn who killed my poor father.'

Dazed and bewildered, Villefort reached for the door handle. Valentine knew what her grandfather's answer must be, for she had often seen the scars of two sword wounds on his arm, and she drew back a few steps.

'I pray you, do not prolong this horrible scene,' said Villefort. 'The names have been concealed intentionally. My father does not know the President, and, even if he did, he would not know how to communicate his name to you; proper names are not to be found in the dictionary.'

'Woe is me!' cried Franz. 'The only hope that sustained me throughout this report, and gave me the strength to finish reading it, was that I should at least learn the name of him who killed my father.' Then turning to Noirtier: 'Oh! I entreat you, in the name of all that is holy, do what you can to indicate to me, to make me understand.'

'Yes,' was Noirtier's reply.

Noirtier looked at the dictionary. Franz took it, trembling nervously, and repeated the letters of the alphabet till he came to M, when the old man made a sign for him to stop.

The young man's finger glided over the words, but at each one Noirtier made a sign in the negative.

Finally he came to the word 'Myself'.

'Yes,' motioned the old man.

'You?' cried Franz, his hair standing on end. 'You, Monsieur Noirtier? It was you who killed my father?'

'Yes,' replied Noirtier, with a majestic look at the young man.

Franz sank lifeless into a chair.

Villefort opened the door and fled, for he was seized with the impulse to choke out of the old man the little life that remained to him.

25

The following morning a note was delivered to the Count of Monte Cristo's residence. It was signed by Baron Danglars, and it read simply: 'I have received news from Greece.'

While the Count was wondering what to make of this message, Albert de Morcerf himself arrived and was shown in by Baptistin. He had come fresh from the Baron's, where he had been treated with indifference by Mlle Danglars.

'Not that I care, you understand,' he protested, 'but no young man likes to be spurned by a beautiful woman . . . Ah, but what is that I hear!' he added, bending his ear towards a door through which sounds were issuing similar to those of a guitar.

'That is the sound of my slave Haydee's guzla.'

'Haydee! What a charming name! But why do you call her your slave? There are no slaves now!'

'Since Haydee is my slave there must be.'

'Really, Count, you have nothing and do nothing like other people. Monte Cristo's slave! What a position in France! To judge from the lavish way in which you spend your money, it must be worth a hundred thousand crowns a year.'

'A hundred thousand crowns! The poor child possesses a great deal more than that. She came into the world to a cradle lined with treasure compared with which those in *A Thousand and One Nights* are as nought.'

'Is she a real princess then?'

'She is; one of the greatest in her country.'

'I thought as much. But tell me, how did such a princess become your slave?'

'You are one of my friends and will not chatter. Do you promise to keep a secret?'

'On my word of honour.'

'Do you know the history of the Pasha of Janina?'

'Of Ali Tebelin? Surely, since my father made his fortune in his service.'

'True, I had forgotten that.'

'Well, what has Haydee to do with Ali Tebelin?'

'She is merely his daughter!'

'What! The daughter of Ali Pasha your slave!'

'Oh, dear me, yes.'

'But how?'

'Simply that I was passing through the market in Constantinople one fine day and bought her.'

'Wonderful! With you, Count, life becomes a dream. Now, listen, I am going to ask you something very indiscreet.'

'Say on.'

'Since you go out with her and take her to the Opera . . .'

'Well?'

'Will you introduce me to your princess?'

'With pleasure, but on two conditions.'

'I accept them in advance.'

'The first is that you never tell anyone of this introduction; the second is that you do not tell her that your father served under her father.'

'Very well.' Morcerf held up his hand. 'I swear I will not.'

The Count again struck the gong, whereupon Ali appeared and Monte Cristo said to him: 'Inform your mistress that I am coming to take my coffee with her, and give her to understand that I ask permission to introduce one of my friends to her.'

Ali bowed and retired.

'Then it is understood that you will not ask her any direct questions. If you wish to know anything, tell me and I will ask her.'

'Agreed!'

Ali reappeared for the third time and held up the door curtain as an indication to his master and Albert that they were welcome.

'Let us go,' said Monte Cristo.

Haydee was awaiting them in her salon, her eyes wide open with surprise. This was the first time that any other man than Monte Cristo had found his way to her room. She was seated in a corner of a sofa with her legs crossed under her, thus making, as it were, a nest of the richly embroidered striped Eastern material that fell in soft folds around her. Beside her was the instrument whose sounds had revealed her presence. Altogether she made a charming picture.

'Whom do you bring me?' the girl asked of Monte Cristo in Romaic. 'A brother, a friend, a simple acquaintance, or an enemy?'

'A friend,' replied Monte Cristo in the same language.

'His name?'

'Count Albert. It is he whom I delivered from the hands of the bandits in Rome.'

'In what tongue do you wish me to speak to him?'

Monte Cristo thought for a moment. 'You will speak in Italian,' said he at last. Then turning towards Albert: 'It is a pity you do not speak either modern or ancient Greek. Haydee speaks both to perfection, and the poor girl may give you a wrong impression of herself by being forced to speak in Italian.'

He made a sign to Haydee.

'Welcome, my friend, who have come hither with my lord and master,' said the girl in excellent Italian. 'Ali, bring coffee and pipes,' she then added.

Ali went to execute his young mistress's order, while Monte Cristo and Albert drew their seats up to a table which contained a narghile as its centrepiece, and on which were arranged flowers, drawings, and music albums. When they were settled, Albert turned towards Haydee and said: 'At what age did you leave Greece, signora?'

'When I was five years old,' responded Haydee.

'Count,' said Morcerf to Monte Cristo, 'you should let the signora tell us something of her sad history. You have forbidden me to mention my father to her, but perhaps she may speak of him herself, and you have no idea what happiness it would give me to hear his name pronounced by those beautiful lips.'

Monte Cristo turned towards Haydee and, making a sign to her to pay great attention to the injunction he was about to impose on her, said in Greek: 'Tell us your father's fate, but mention not the treason nor the name of the traitor.'

Haydee sighed deeply, and a dark cloud passed over her beautiful brow.

'Nothing makes such a deep impression on our minds as our earliest memories,' she said, 'and all those of my childhood are mingled with sadness. Do you really wish me to relate them?'

'I implore you to tell them!' said Albert.

'Well, I was four years old when I was awakened one evening by my mother. We were at the palace at Janina. She snatched me up with the cushions on which I was lying, and when I opened my eyes I perceived that hers were filled with big tears. She carried me away without a word. On seeing her weeping, I began to cry too. "Be quiet, child!" she said.

'At any other time, no matter what my mother might do to console me, or what threats she held out to me, I should have continued to cry, but this time there was such a note of terror in her voice that I stopped instantly. She bore me rapidly away. Then I perceived that we were going down a wide staircase and rushing on in front of us were my mother's women, carrying trunks, bags, clothing, jewellery, and purses filled with gold. Behind the women came a guard of twenty men armed with long rifles and pistols.

'"Quickly, quickly!" said a voice from the end of the gallery, and every one bent forward like a field of corn bowed down by the passing wind. It was my father's voice. He marched in the rearmost, clad in his most splendid robes and holding in his hand the carbine your Emperor gave him. Leaning on his favourite, Selim, he drove us on before him as a shepherd drives his straggling flock. My father,' continued Haydee, raising her head, 'was an illustrious man known in Europe under the name of Ali Tebelin, Pasha of Janina, before whom all Turkey trembled.'

Without any apparent reason, Albert shuddered on hearing these words uttered with such unspeakable pride and dignity. There seemed to be something terrifying and sombre lurking in the maiden's eyes.

'Soon we came to a halt; we had reached the bottom of the staircase and were on the borders of a lake. My mother pressed me to her heaving bosom, and two paces from us I saw my father looking anxiously round him. Before us were four marble steps, at the bottom of which was a small boat. In the middle of the lake a black object was discernible; it was the kiosk to which we were going. It looked to me to be very far away, but that was probably owing to the darkness of the night.

'We stepped into the boat. I remember noticing that there was no sound as the oars skimmed the water, and

I leaned over to look for the cause: they were muffled with the sashes of our Palikars. Besides the oarsmen there was no one in the boat but some women, my father, my mother, Selim, and myself. The Palikars had remained on the edge of the lake to protect us in case of pursuit. Our bark sped like the wind.

'"Why is our boat going so fast?" I asked my mother.

'"Hush, child, hush!" she said. "It is because we are fleeing."

'I did not understand. Why should my father, the all-powerful one, flee? He before whom others were accustomed to flee? He who had taken as his device: "They hate me, therefore they fear me."

'My father was indeed fleeing across the lake. He told me later that the garrison of the Janina Castle, tired of long service . . .'

Here Haydee cast a questioning look at Monte Cristo, who had never taken his eyes off her. She then continued slowly as though inventing or suppressing some part of her narrative.

'You were saying, signora,' returned Albert, who was paying the utmost attention to the recital, 'that the garrison of Janina, tired of long service . . .'

'Had treated with the Seraskier Kourschid sent by the Sultan to seize my father. Upon learning this Ali Tebelin sent to the Sultan a French officer in whom he placed entire confidence, and then resolved to retire to the place of retreat he had since long prepared for himself.'

'Do you recollect the officer's name, signora?' Albert asked.

Monte Cristo exchanged a lightning-like glance with the girl which was unobserved by Morcerf.

'No, I do not recollect his name,' she said, 'but it may come to my mind later on.'

Albert was about to mention his father's name when Monte Cristo quietly held up his finger enjoining silence, and, remembering his oath, the young man obeyed.

'It was towards this kiosk that we were making our way. From the outside the kiosk appeared to consist of nothing more than a ground floor ornamented with arabesques with a terrace leading down to the water, and another storey overlooking the lake. Under the ground floor, however, was a vast subterranean cave extending the whole length of the island, whither my mother and myself together with our womenfolk were taken, and where sixty thousand bags and two hundred casks were piled up in a heap. The bags contained twenty-five millions in gold, and the casks were filled with thirty thousand pounds of powder.

'Near these casks stood Selim, my father's favourite slave, whom I mentioned just now. Night and day he stood on guard, holding a lance at the tip of which was a lighted match. His orders were that directly my father gave him the signal, he was to blow up everything, kiosk, guards, women, gold, and the Pasha himself. I still see before me the pale-faced, black-eyed young soldier, and when the angel of Death comes to fetch me I am sure I shall recognize Selim.

'I cannot tell you how long we remained thus, for at that period I was ignorant of the meaning of time. One morning my father sent for us; we found him quite calm but paler than usual.

'"Have courage, Vasiliki," he said to my mother. "Today my lord's decree arrives, and my fate will be decided. If I am pardoned, we shall return to Janina in triumph, but if the news is bad, we shall flee tonight."

'"But what if they do not let us flee?"

'"Set your mind at rest on that score," replied Ali with a smile. "Selim and his fiery lance will settle them. They want my death, but they will not want to die with me."

'All of a sudden, he started up abruptly. Without taking his eyes from the object which was attracting his attention, he asked for his telescope, and my mother, whiter than the stucco against which she was leaning, gave it to him. I saw my father's hands trembling.

'"A ship . . .! two . . .! three . . .! four!" he murmured.

'With that he rose, and as I sit here I can still see him priming his pistols.

'"Vasiliki," he said to my mother, visibly trembling, "the time has now come when our fate will be decided, for in half an hour we shall learn the Sublime Sultan's answer. Go to the cave with Haydee."

"I will not leave you," said Vasiliki. "If you die, my master, I will die with you."

'"Go and stay with Selim!" cried my father.

'"Farewell, my lord!" murmured my mother, obedient to the end and bowed down by the near approach of death.

'"Take Vasiliki away," he said to one of the Palikars.

'But I, whom they had forgotten, ran up to him and held out my arms to him. He saw me, and, bending down, pressed his lips to my forehead.

'All this time twenty Palikars, hidden by the carved woodwork, were seated at my father's feet watching with bloodshot eyes the arrival of the boats. Their long guns, inlaid with mother-of-pearl and silver, were ready to hand and a large number of cartridges were strewn about the floor. My father looked at his watch and began pacing up and down with a look of anguish on his face. This was the scene which impressed itself on my mind when I left my father after he had given me that last kiss.'

These sad reminiscences appeared for a single instant to have deprived Haydee of the power of speech.

Monte Cristo looked at her with an indefinable expression of interest and pity.

'Continue, my child,' he said to her in Romaic.

Haydee raised her head as though the sonorous words uttered by Monte Cristo had awakened her from a dream, and she resumed her narrative.

'It was four o'clock in the afternoon, but whereas the day was brilliant and bright outside, we in the cave were plunged in darkness. One single light shone in our cave like a solitary star twinkling in a dark and cloud-covered sky; it was Selim's match.

'From time to time Selim repeated the sacred words: "Allah is great!" My mother was a Christian, and she prayed incessantly, but she still had a ray of hope. When she was leaving the terrace she had thought she recognized the Frenchman who had been sent to Constantinople and in whom my father placed implicit confidence, for he well knew that the soldiers of the French King are generally noble and generous. She advanced towards the staircase and listened. "They are drawing near," she said. "If only they bring life and peace to us!"

'"What do you fear, Vasiliki?" replied Selim in a

voice so gentle and at the same time so proud. "If they do not bring peace, we will give them death." And he revived the flame of his lance.

'But I, who was only an unsophisticated child, was frightened by this courage, which appeared to me both ferocious and insensate, and I was filled with alarm by the atmosphere of death I seemed to feel all round me and to see in Selim's flame. My mother must have had the same impression, for I felt her shudder.

'"Oh, Mama, Mama!" I cried. "Are we going to die?"

'"May God preserve you, my child, from ever desiring the death you fear today!" said my mother. Then in a low, voice to Selim: "What are my master's orders?"

'"If he sends me his poniard, it signifies that the Sultan has refused his pardon, and I am to apply the match; if he sends me his ring, it means that the Sultan pardons him and I am to hand over the powder."

'"Friend," said my mother, "when the master's order arrives and if it be the poniard he sends, we will both bare out throats to you and do you kill us with the same poniard instead of dispatching us by that terrible death we both fear."

'"I will, Vasiliki," was Selim's calm reply.

'All of a sudden we heard loud shouts. We listened. They were shouts of joy. The name of the French officer who had been sent to Constantinople burst from the throats of the Palikars on all sides. It was evident he had brought the Sultan's answer and that the answer was a favourable one.'

'Do you not recollect the name?' said Morcerf, ready to aid the narrator's memory.

Monte Cristo made a sign to her.

'I do not remember it,' responded Haydee. 'The noise increased; there was the sound of approaching footsteps; they were descending the steps to the cave. Selim made ready his lance. Soon a figure appeared in the grey twilight created by the rays of day which penetrated to the entrance of the cave.

'"Who goes there?" cried Selim. "Whosoever it may be, advance no farther!"

'"Glory be to the Sultan!" said the figure. "He has granted full pardon to the Vizier Ali and not only grants him his life, but restores to him his fortune and all his possessions."'

Haydee wiped her eyes and forehead and continued:

'By this time our eyes had become accustomed to the darkness and we recognized the Pasha's envoy: he was a friend. Selim too recognized him, but the brave young man had one duty to fulfil – that was, to obey.

'"In whose name do you come?" said he.

'"I come in the name of our master, Ali Tebelin."

'"If you come in the name of Ali, do you know what you have to hand me?"

'"Yes," said the messenger. "I bring the ring."

'So saying he held his hand above his head, but from where we were it was too dark and he too far away for Selim to distinguish and recognize the object he held up.

'"I see not what you have there," said Selim.

'"Come nearer, or if you so wish, I will come nearer to you," replied the messenger.

'"Neither the one nor the other," replied the young soldier. "On the spot where you now stand, so that the rays of this light may fall on it, set down the object you wish to show me and retire till I have seen it."

'"It shall be done," answered the messenger. Placing the symbol on the spot indicated, he withdrew.

'Our hearts beat fast, for the object was actually a ring, but was it my father's ring? Still holding in his hand the lighted match, Selim went to the entrance, bent down and picked up the token. "The master's ring!" he exclaimed, kissing it. "All is well!" Throwing the match on the ground, he trampled on it till it was extinguished.

'The messenger uttered a cry of joy and clapped his hands. At this signal, four of the Seraskier Kourschid's soldiers rushed in, and Selim fell pierced by the dagger of each of the men. Intoxicated by their crime, though still pale with fear, they then rushed into the cave and made for the bags of gold.

'By this time my mother had seized me in her arms and, running nimbly along windings known only to ourselves, reached some secret stairs, where reigned a frightful tumult and confusion. The lower halls were filled with the armed ruffians of Kourschid, our enemies. My mother glued her eyes to a chink in the boards; there happened to be an aperture in front of me, and I looked through it.

'"What do you want?" we heard my father saying to some men who held in their hands a piece of paper inscribed with letters of gold.

'"We wish to communicate to you the will of His Highness. Do you see this decree?"

'"I do," was my father's reply.

'"Well, read it. It demands your head."

'My father burst into laughter, more terrible to hear than the wildest threats, and he had not ceased when two pistol shots rang out and the two men were dead.

'The Palikars, who were lying face down all round my father, rose and began firing. The room became filled with noise, flames, and smoke. At the same time firing started on the other side of the hall, and the boards all around us were soon riddled with shot.

'Oh, how handsome, how noble was the Vizier Ali Tebelin, my father, as he stood there in the midst of the shot, his scimitar in his hand, his face black with powder! How his enemies fled before him!

'"Selim! Selim!" cried he. "Guardian of the fire, do your duty!"

'"Selim is dead," replied a voice which seemed to come from the depths of the kiosk, "and you, my lord Ali, are lost!" At the same moment a dull report was heard, and the flooring was shattered to atoms all around my father.

'Twenty shots were fired from underneath through the gap thus created, and flames rushed up as from the crater of a volcano and, gaining the hangings, quickly devoured them.

'In the midst of this frightful tumult two reports more distinct than the others, and two cries more heart-rending than all the rest, petrified me with terror. These two shots had mortally wounded my father, and it was he who had uttered the two cries. He fell on one knee; instantly twenty hands were stretched out and twenty blows were dealt simultaneously at one man. My father disappeared in a blaze of fire stirred by these roaring demons as though hell had opened under his feet. I felt myself roll to the ground; my mother had fainted.'

Haydee's arms fell to her side, and, uttering a groan, she looked at the Count as though to ask him whether he was satisfied with her obedience. Monte Cristo went up to her and, taking her hand, said to her in Romaic: 'Calm yourself, dear child, and console yourself in the thought that there is a God who punishes traitors.'

'When my mother recovered consciousness we were before the Seraskier. "Kill me," she said to him, "but preserve the honour of Ali's widow."

'"It is not to me that you have to address yourself," Kourschid said.

'"Then to whom?"

'"To your new master."

'"Who is my new master?"

'"Here he is," said Kourschid, pointing to one of those who had most contributed to my father's death.'

'Then you became that man's property?' asked Albert.

'No,' responded Haydee. 'He did not dare keep us; he sold us to some slave merchants who were going to Constantinople. We crossed over Greece and arrived at the imperial gates in a dying condition, surrounded by a curious crowd who made way for us to pass. My mother followed the direction of their eyes and with a cry suddenly fell to the ground, pointing to a head on a spike of the gate. Above this head were written the words:

THIS IS THE HEAD OF ALI TEBELIN, PASHA OF JANINA.

'Weeping, I tried to raise my mother. She was dead!

'I was taken to the bazaar; a rich American bought

me, had me educated, and, when I was thirteen years of age, he sold me to the Sultan Mahommed.'

'From whom I bought her, as I told you, Albert, for an emerald similar to the one in which I keep my hashish pills,' said the Count.

'You are good, you are great, my lord,' said Haydee, kissing Monte Cristo's hand. 'I am very happy to belong to you.'

Albert was quite bewildered by all he had heard.

'Finish your coffee,' said the Count. 'The story is ended.'

26

Franz left Noirtier's room so distraught that even Valentine felt pity for him. Villefort only muttered some incoherent words and took refuge in his study. Two hours later he received the following letter:

After all that has been disclosed this morning, Monsieur Noirtier de Villefort will appreciate the impossibility of an alliance between his family and that of Monsieur Franz d'Épinay. Monsieur Franz d'Épinay is sorry to think that Monsieur de Villefort, who appeared to be cognizant of the incidents related, should not have anticipated him in the expression of this view.

This outspoken letter from a young man who had always shown so much respect towards him was a deadly blow to the pride of a man like Villefort.

In the meantime Valentine, happy though at the same time terrified at all she had heard, embraced the feeble old man in loving gratitude for having broken a tie she had considered indissoluble, and asked his permission to go to her room for a while to recover her composure. Instead of going to her room, however, Valentine went into the garden. Maximilian was waiting in his customary place ready for any emergency, and convinced that Valentine would run to him the first moment she was free to do so.

He was not mistaken. With his eyes glued to the cracks in the palings he saw her running towards him and throwing her usual precaution to the winds. The first word she uttered filled his heart with joy.

'Saved!' she cried.

'Saved?' repeated Morrel, unable to believe such happiness. 'Who has saved us?'

'My grandfather. You should really love him, Morrel!'

Morrel swore to love him with his whole heart; the oath cost him nothing, for at that moment he felt it was not sufficient to love him as a father or a friend; he almost adored him as a god.

'How did he manage it?' he asked. 'What means did he use?'

Valentine was about to recount everything when she remembered that at the root of all was a secret which did not belong wholly to her grandfather.

'I will tell you all about it later,' she said.

'When?'

'When I am your wife.'

The turn the conversation was taking was so pleasing to Morrel that he was quite content to leave the matter at that and be satisfied with the one all-important piece of news for that day. He would not leave her, however, till she had given her promise that she would see him the next evening. This Valentine was ready to do. Her outlook had undergone a complete change and it was certainly less difficult for her now to believe that she would marry Maximilian than it was for her to believe an hour back that she would not marry Franz.

In the meantime Mme de Villefort went up to Noirtier's room, where she was received with the habitual cold and forbidding look.

'Now that this marriage, which I know did not meet with your approval, has been stopped, I have come to speak to you of something which neither Monsieur de Villefort nor Valentine could mention,' she said.

Noirtier's eyes bade her proceed.

'As the only one disinterested and therefore the only one who has the right to speak on the matter,' she continued, 'I come to ask you to restore, not your love, for that she has always had, but your fortune to your grandchild.'

For an instant Noirtier's eyes hesitated; evidently he was trying to find a motive for this request, but was unable to do so.

'May I hope, monsieur,' said Mme de Villefort, 'that your intentions coincide with my request?'

'Yes,' signalled Noirtier.

'In that case, I leave you a grateful and happy woman, monsieur,' she said, and, bowing to Noirtier, she withdrew.

True to his word, M. Noirtier sent for the notary the next day: the first will was torn up and a new one made in which he left the whole of his fortune to Valentine on condition that she should not separate herself from him.

While the events recorded above were taking place in the house of Monsieur de Villefort, the Count of Morcerf had ordered his carriage and driven to the Rue de la Chausée d'Antin. Danglars was making his monthly balance, and it was certainly not the best time to find him in a good humour; as a matter of fact, it had not been so for the past few months.

On seeing his old friend, he assumed his most commanding air and seated himself squarely in his chair. Morcerf, on the other hand, laid aside his habitual stiffness of manner and was almost jovial and affable. Feeling sure that his overtures would be well received, he lost no time in coming to the point.

'Well, here I am, Baron. We have made no headway in our plans since our former conversation.'

'What plans, Count?' Danglars asked as though vainly trying to discover some explanation of the General's words.

'Since you are such a stickler, my dear Baron, and since you desire to remind me that the ceremony is to be carried out in all due form, I will comply with your wishes.' With a forced smile he rose, made a deep bow to Danglars, and said: 'I have the honour, Baron, to ask the hand of Mademoiselle Eugénie Danglars, your daughter, for my son the Viscount Albert de Morcerf.'

But instead of welcoming these words as Morcerf had every right to expect, Danglars knit his brows and, without even inviting the Count to take a seat, replied:

'Before giving you an answer, Count, I must think the matter over.'

'What do you mean?' asked Morcerf. 'I do not understand you.'

'What I mean is that during the last fortnight unforeseen circumstances . . .'

'Excuse me, but is this a play we are acting?'

'A play?'

'Yes. Pray let us be more explicit.'

Danglars made no reply.

'Have you changed your mind so soon?' continued Morcerf. 'Or have you but egged me on to make this proposal in order to see me humiliated?'

Danglars understood that if he continued the conversation in the same strain as that in which he had begun it, he might be taken at a disadvantage, so he said: 'I quite comprehend that you are amazed at my reserve, Count. Believe me, I am the first one to regret that painful circumstances compel me to act thus.'

'These are but so many empty words,' replied the Count. 'They might perhaps satisfy an ordinary man, but not the Count of Morcerf. When a man of his position comes to another man to remind him of his plighted word, and that man breaks his word, he is at least justified in demanding from him a good reason for his conduct.'

Danglars was a coward but did not wish to appear one; besides he was annoyed at the tone Morcerf had adopted.

'I do not break my word without good reason,' he retorted.

'What do you mean by that?'

'That my reason is good enough, but it is not an

easy one to tell. You may be thankful I do not give a more detailed explanation.'

A nervous trembling caused by repressed anger shook Morcerf's whole frame, but pulling himself together with a violent effort, he said: 'I have the right to insist on an explanation. Have you anything against my son? Against Madame de Morcerf? Is my fortune too small for you? Is it because my opinions differ from yours?'

'Nothing of the kind, monsieur,' said Danglars. 'Seek no more for a reason, I pray. I am really quite ashamed to see you indulging in such self-examination.'

'Enough, monsieur, we will drop the subject,' said Morcerf, as, crumpling his gloves up in his rage, he left the room.

Danglars noticed that not once had Morcerf dared to ask whether it was on his own account that he, Danglars, had broken his word.

As soon as he awoke the next morning, Danglars asked for the newspapers. He flung three or four on one side till he came to the *Impartial*, of which Beauchamp was the chief editor. He hastily tore off the wrapper and opened it nervously. Disdainfully passing over the leading article, he came to the miscellaneous news column, and, with a malicious smile, stopped at a paragraph which read as follows:

A correspondent at Janina writes: A fact hitherto unknown, or at any rate unpublished, has just come to my knowledge. The castles defending this town were given up to the Turks by a French officer in whom the Vizier Ali Tebelin had placed entire confidence. This French officer who was in the service of Ali, Pasha of Janina, and who not only surrendered the Castle of Janina, but also sold his benefactor to the Turks, at that time was called Fernand, but he has since added to his Christian name a title of nobility and a family name. He is now styled the Count of Morcerf and ranks among the peers.

'Good!' Danglars observed after having read the paragraph. 'Here is a nice little article on Colonel Fernand which will, methinks, relieve me of the necessity of giving any explanation to the Count of Morcerf.'

27

Morrel was, indeed, very happy. M. Noirtier had sent for him, and he was in such haste to learn the reason that, trusting to his own two legs more than to the four legs of a cab-horse, he started off from the Rue Meslay at a rapid pace and ran all the way to the Faubourg Saint-Honoré, while Barrois followed as well he might. Morrel was thirty-one years of age and was urged on by love; Barrois was sixty and parched with the heat. On arriving at the house, Morrel was not even out of breath, for love lends wings; but Barrois had not been in love for many long years and was bathed in perspiration.

The old servant let Morrel in by a private door, and before long the rustling of a dress on the parquet floor announced the arrival of Valentine. She looked adorable in her mourning, in fact so charming that Morrel could almost have dispensed with his interview with Noirtier; but the old man's chair was soon heard being wheeled along to the room in which they were awaiting him.

Noirtier acknowledged with a kind look Morrel's effusive thanks for his marvellous intervention which had saved Valentine and himself from despair. Then, in view of the new favour accorded him, Maximilian sought Valentine's eyes; she was sitting in the far corner timidly waiting till she was forced to speak. Noirtier fixed his eyes on her.

'Am I to say what you told me?' she asked.

'Yes,' was Noirtier's reply.

'Grandpapa Noirtier had a great many things to say to you, Monsieur Morrel,' said Valentine to the young man, who was devouring her with his eyes. 'These he told me three days ago, and he has sent for you today that I may repeat them all to you. Since he has chosen me as his interpreter, I will repeat everything in the light of his intentions.'

'I am listening with the greatest impatience,' replied the young man. 'Pray speak, mademoiselle.'

'My grandfather wishes to leave this house,' she continued. 'Barrois is now looking for a suitable flat for him.'

'But what will become of you, mademoiselle, who are so dear and so necessary to Monsieur Noirtier?'

'Me?' replied Valentine. 'It is quite agreed that I shall not leave my grandfather. I shall live with him. Then I shall be free and have an independent income, and with my grandfather's consent I shall keep the promise I made you.'

Valentine said these last words in such a low voice that nothing but Morrel's great interest in them made them audible to him.

'When I am with my grandfather,' continued Valentine, 'Monsieur Morrel can come and see me in the presence of my good and worthy protector, and if we still feel that our future happiness lies in a union with each other, he can come and claim me. I shall be waiting for him.'

'Oh!' cried Morrel. 'What have I done to deserve such happiness?'

Noirtier looked at the lovers with ineffable tenderness. Barrois, before whom there were no secrets, had remained at the far end of the room and smiled happily as he wiped away the last drops of perspiration that were rolling down his bald forehead.

'How hot poor old Barrois is!' said Valentine.

'That is because I have been running fast, mademoiselle, but I must give Monsieur Morrel the credit for running still faster.'

Noirtier indicated by a look a tray on which were standing a decanter of lemonade and a tumbler. Noirtier himself had drunk some of the lemonade half an hour before.

'Have some of this lemonade, Barrois,' the girl said. 'I can see you are looking at it with envious eyes.'

'The fact is, mademoiselle, I am dying of thirst, and I shall be only too glad to drink your health in a glass of lemonade.'

Barrois took the tray and was hardly outside the door, which he had forgotten to close, when they saw him throw back his head to empty the tumbler Valentine had filled for him. Valentine and Morrel were bidding each other goodbye; they heard a bell ringing on Villefort's staircase. It was the signal that a visitor had called. Valentine looked at the clock.

'It is noon,' said she, 'and as it is Saturday, it is doubtless the doctor. He will come here, so Monsieur Morrel had better go, do you not think so, Grandpapa?'

'Yes,' replied the old man.

'Barrois!' called Valentine, 'Barrois, come!'

The voice of the old servant was heard to reply: 'I am coming, mademoiselle.'

'Barrois will conduct you to the door,' Valentine said to Morrel. 'And now, remember, Monsieur l'Officier, Grandpapa does not wish us to risk anything that might compromise our happiness.'

'I have promised to wait, and wait I shall,' said Morrel.

At that moment Barrois entered.

'Who rang?' asked Valentine.

'Doctor d'Avrigny,' said Barrois, staggering.

'What is the matter, Barrois?' Valentine asked him.

The servant did not answer; he looked at his master with wildly staring eyes, while his cramped hand groped for some support to prevent himself from falling.

'He is going to fall!' cried Morrel.

In fact, the trembling fit which had come over Barrois gradually increased, and the twitching of his facial muscles announced a very grave nervous attack. Seeing his old servant in this state, Noirtier looked at him affectionately, and in those intelligent eyes was expressed every emotion that moves the human heart.

Barrois went a few steps toward his master.

'Oh, my God! My God! Lord have pity on me!' he cried. 'What is the matter with me? I am ill. I cannot see. A thousand darts of fire are piercing my brain. Oh, don't touch me! Don't touch me!'

His haggard eyes started out of their sockets, his head fell back, and the rest of his body stiffened. Valentine uttered a cry of horror, and Morrel took her in his arms as though to defend her against some unknown danger.

'Monsieur d'Avrigny! Monsieur d'Avrigny!' the girl called out in a choking voice. 'Help! Help!'

Barrois turned round, walked a few steps, stumbled and fell at his master's feet with his hand on his knee, and cried out: 'My master! My good master!'

Attracted by the screams, Villefort rushed into the room. Morrel instantly relaxed his hold of Valentine, who was now in a half-fainting condition, and going to a far corner of the room, hid behind a curtain. As pale as if he had seen a snake start up to attack him, he gazed in horror on the agonized sufferer. Noirtier was burning with impatience and terror, his soul went out to help the poor old man who was his friend rather than his servant. The terrible struggle between life and death that was going on within him made his veins stand out and the few remaining live muscles round his eyes contract.

With convulsed features, bloodshot eyes, and head thrown back, Barrois lay beating the floor with his hands, whilst his legs had become so stiff that they looked more ready to break than to bend. He was foaming at the mouth and his breathing was laboured. Stupefied, Villefort stood still for an instant, gazing on the spectacle which had met his eyes directly he entered the room. He had not seen Morrel. After a second's dumb contemplation of the scene, during which his face had turned deathly pale and his hair appeared to stand on end, he rushed to the door crying out: 'Doctor! Doctor! Come! Come!'

'Madame de Villefort, come! Oh, come quickly, and bring your smelling-salts!' Valentine called, running up the stairs.

'What is the matter?' Mme de Villefort asked in a metallic and constrained voice.

'Oh, come quickly.'

'But where is the doctor?' cried Villefort. 'Where can he have gone?'

The stairs were heard to creak as Mme de Villefort slowly came down them, holding in one hand a handkerchief, with which she was wiping her face, and in the other a bottle of smelling-salts. When she entered the room, her first glance was for Noirtier, who save for the emotion he naturally felt in the circumstances, appeared to be in his usual state of health; then her eyes fell on the dying man. She turned pale as she saw him, and her eyes, as it were, leapt from the servant to his master.

'For pity's sake, where is the doctor, madame?' exclaimed Valentine. 'He went into your room. Barrois has an attack of apoplexy, as you see, and he may be saved if he is bled.'

'Has he eaten anything lately?' asked Mme de Villefort, evading the question.

'He has not yet had his breakfast,' replied Valentine, 'but he was running very fast this morning on an errand for my grandfather, and when he came back he drank a glass of lemonade.'

'Why did he not have some wine? Lemonade is very bad.'

'The lemonade was near at hand in Grandpapa's decanter. Poor Barrois was thirsty, and he drank what he could get.'

Mme de Villefort started; M. Noirtier watched her with the closest scrutiny.

'I ask you once more, madame, where is the doctor?' said Villefort. 'For heaven's sake, answer!'

'He is with Edward, who is poorly,' replied Mme de Villefort, seeing she could no longer evade the question.

Villefort rushed up the stairs to fetch him.

'Here,' said the young woman, giving the smelling salts to Valentine. 'The doctor will doubtless bleed him, so I will return to my room. I cannot bear the sight of blood.'

With which she followed her husband.

Morrel emerged from his dark corner where he had remained unseen throughout the general consternation.

'Go quickly, Maximilian, and wait till I call you,' said Valentine to him.

Morrel cast a questioning glance at Noirtier, and the old man, who had not lost his composure, made a sign of approval. The young man pressed Valentine's hand to his heart, and left by the deserted landing just as Villefort and the doctor came in together by the opposite door.

Barrois was returning to consciousness; the attack had passed. He began to groan and raised himself on one knee. D'Avrigny and Villefort carried him on to a sofa.

'What do you prescribe, Doctor?' asked Villefort.

'Get me some water and ether, and send for some oil of turpentine and tartaric acid. And now let every one retire.'

'Must I go too?' Valentine asked timidly.

'Yes, mademoiselle, you particularly,' said the doctor abruptly.

Valentine looked at d'Avrigny in astonishment, but, after kissing her grandfather, left the room. The doctor shut the door behind her with a look of grim determination.

'See, Doctor, he is coming round. It was only a slight attack after all.'

M. d'Avrigny smiled grimly.

'How do you feel?' he asked Barrois.

'A little better, Doctor.'

'Can you drink this glass of ether and water?'

'I will try, but do not touch me.'

'Why not?'

'I feel that if you touch me, if only with the tip of your fingers, the attack will return.'

Barrois took the glass, put it to his lips, and drank about half of its contents.

'Where have you pain?' the doctor asked.

'Everywhere. It is as though I had frightful cramp everywhere.'

'What have you eaten today?'

'Nothing at all. All I have taken is a glass of my master's lemonade,' Barrois replied, making a sign with his head towards Noirtier, who was sitting motionless in his chair, contemplating this dreadful scene without letting a movement or a word escape him.

'Where is the lemonade?' asked the doctor eagerly.

'In the decanter in the kitchen.'

'Shall I fetch it, Doctor?' Villefort asked.

'No, stay here and try to make the patient drink the rest of this ether and water.'

'But the lemonade . . .'

'I will fetch it myself.'

D'Avrigny bounded towards the door, and, rushing down the servants' staircase, nearly knocked over Mme de Villefort, who was also going into the kitchen. She screamed, but the doctor did not even take any notice of her. Obsessed with the one idea, he jumped down the last three or four stairs and flew into the kitchen. Seeing the decanter three parts empty, he pounced upon it like an eagle upon its prey, and with it returned to the sick-room out of breath. Mme de Villefort was slowly going up the stairs leading to her room.

'Is this the decanter?' Monsieur d'Avrigny asked Barrois.

'Yes, Doctor.'

'Is this some of the same lemonade you drank?'

'I believe so.'

'What did it taste like?'

'It had a bitter taste.'

The doctor poured several drops of the lemonade into the palm of his hand, sucked it up with his lips, and, after rinsing his mouth with it as one does when tasting wine, he spat it out into the fireplace.

'It is the same right enough,' he said. 'Did you drink some too, Noirtier?'

'Yes,' looked the old man.

'Did you notice the bitter taste?'

'Yes.'

'Oh, Doctor, the fit is coming on again! Oh, God, have pity on me!'

The doctor ran to his patient.

'The tartar emetic, Villefort, see if it has come!'

Villefort rushed out shouting: 'The emetic! Has it not been brought yet?'

'If I had some means of injecting air into his lungs,' said d'Avrigny, looking around him, 'I might possibly be able to prevent asphyxiation. But there is nothing, nothing!'

'Are you going to let me die without help, Doctor? Oh, I am dying! Have pity on me, I am dying!'

Barrois was seized with a nervous attack which was more acute than the first one. He had slipped from the sofa on to the floor and lay stretched stiff and rolling in pain. The doctor left him, for he could do nothing to help him. Going over to Noirtier, he asked him in a low voice:

'How, do you feel? Well?'

'Yes.'

'Does, your stomach feel light or heavy? Light?'

'Yes.'

'The same as when you have taken the pills I ordered you to take every Sunday?'

'Yes.'

'Did Barrois make the lemonade?'

'Yes.'

'Did you invite him to drink it?'

'No.'

'Monsieur de Villefort?'

'No.'

'Madame de Villefort?'

'No.'

'It was Valentine, then?'

'Yes.'

A sigh from Barrois, and a yawn which made his jaw-bones crack, attracted the attention of d'Avrigny, who hastened to his side.

'Can you speak, Barrois?'

Barrois uttered a few inaudible words.

'Make an effort, my friend.'

Barrois opened his bloodshot eyes.

'Who made the lemonade?'

'I did.'

'Did you take it to your master as soon as it was made?'

'No.'

'Did you leave it somewhere, then?'

'In the pantry, because I was called away.'

'Who brought it into this room?'

'Mademoiselle Valentine.'

'Oh, again!' exclaimed d'Avrigny, striking his forehead.

'Doctor! Doctor!' cried Barrois, who felt a third attack approaching.

'Are they never going to bring the emetic?' cried the doctor.

'Here is a glass with one already prepared by the chemist himself, who has come back with me,' said Villefort.

'Drink!' said the doctor to Barrois.

'Impossible, Doctor. It is too late. My throat is closing up. I am suffocating. Oh, my heart! My head! Oh, what agony! Am I going to suffer like this for long?'

'No, no, my friend,' said the doctor. 'You will soon be suffering no more.'

'Oh, I understand,' said the poor wretch. 'My God, have pity on me.' With a cry he fell back as though struck by lightning. D'Avrigny placed his hand to his heart and put a mirror to his mouth.

'Well?' said Villefort.

'Go to the kitchen quickly and ask for some syrup of violets.' Villefort went immediately.

'Do not be alarmed, Monsieur Noirtier,' said the doctor. 'I am taking my patient into another room to bleed him; such an attack is truly ghastly to behold.'

Taking Barrois under the arms, he dragged him into an adjoining room, but returned at once for the remainder of the lemonade.

Noirtier closed his right eye.

'You want Valentine? I will have her sent to you.'

Villefort came back with the syrup of violets and met d'Avrigny on the landing.

'Come with me,' said the doctor, taking him into the room where the dead man lay.

'Is he still unconscious?' asked Villefort.

'He is dead.'

Villefort started back, clasped his hands to his head, and looking at the dead man, exclaimed in tones of infinite pity, 'Dead so soon!'

'Yes, it was very quick, was it not?' said d'Avrigny, 'but that should not astonish you. Monsieur and Madame de Saint-Méran died just as suddenly. Death makes a very sudden appearance in your house, Monsieur de Villefort.'

'What?' cried the magistrate in a tone of horror and consternation. 'Are you still harping on that terrible idea?'

'I am, monsieur, and the thought has not left me for one instant,' said d'Avrigny solemnly. 'Furthermore, that you may be convinced that I have made no mistake this time, listen to what I have to say.'

Villefort trembled convulsively.

'There is a poison which destroys life without leaving any traces after it. I know the poison well. I have made a deep study of it. I recognize the presence of this poison in poor Barrois just as I did in Madame de Saint-Méran. There is one means of detecting its presence. It restores the blue colour of litmus paper which has been dyed red by an acid, and it turns syrup of violets green. We have no litmus paper, but we have syrup of violets. If the lemonade is pure and inoffensive, the syrup will retain its colour; on the other hand, if it contains poison, the syrup will turn green. Watch closely!'

The doctor slowly poured a few drops of lemonade into the cup, and a cloudy sediment was immediately formed at the bottom. First of all this sediment took on a blue hue, then it changed from sapphire to the colour of opal, and again to emerald – to change no more. The experiment left no room for doubt.

'The unfortunate Barrois has been poisoned,' said d'Avrigny, 'and I am ready to answer for this statement before God and man.'

Villefort made no reply; he raised his arms heavenward, opened wide his haggard eyes and sank back into a chair horror-stricken.

M. d'Avrigny soon brought the magistrate round, though he still looked like another corpse in this chamber of death.

'Death is in my house!' he exclaimed.

'Say rather crime,' replied the doctor, 'for the time has now come when we must act. We must put an end to these incessant deaths. So far as I am concerned, I feel I can no longer conscientiously hold such secrets unless I have the hope of soon seeing the victims, and through them society, avenged.'

Villefort wrung his hands and cast a pleading look on the doctor, but the latter continued pitilessly:

'An axiom of jurisprudence says: 'Seek whom the crime would profit!'

'Alas! Doctor, how many times has not justice been deceived by those fatal words!' exclaimed Villefort. 'I know why, but I think this crime . . .'

'Ah, you admit at last that it is a crime?'

'Yes, I acknowledge it. What else can I do? But let me continue. It seems to me this crime is directed against me alone and not against the victims. I sense some calamity for myself at the root of all these strange disasters.'

'Oh, Man,' muttered d'Avrigny. 'The most selfish of all creatures, who believes that the earth turns, the sun shines, and the scythe of death reaps for him alone. And have those who have lost their lives lost nothing? Monsieur de Saint-Méran, Madame de Saint-Méran, Monsieur Noirtier . . .'

'Monsieur Noirtier?'

'Certainly. Do you think it was the unfortunate servant's life they wanted? No, Noirtier was intended to drink the lemonade; the other one only drank it by accident.'

'How was it my father did not succumb?'

'As I told you one evening in the garden after the death of Madame de Saint-Méran, his system has become accustomed to this very poison; no one, not even the murderer himself, knows that for the past year I have been treating Monsieur Noirtier with brucine for his paralysis, whereas the murderer knows, and has proved by experience, that brucine is a virulent poison.'

'Stop! For heaven's sake, have pity on me!' cried Villefort, wringing his hands.

'Let us follow the criminal's course. He kills Monsieur de Saint-Méran, then Madame de Saint-Méran; a double inheritance to look forward to.'

Villefort wiped away the perspiration that was streaming down his forehead.

'Listen! Monsieur Noirtier willed his fortune away

from you and your family,' continued M. d'Avrigny pitilessly, 'so he is spared. But he has no sooner destroyed his first will and made a second one than he becomes the victim, no doubt lest he should make a third will. This will was made the day before yesterday, I believe. You see there was no time lost.'

'Have mercy, Doctor. Have mercy on my daughter!' murmured Villefort.

'You see it is you yourself who have named her, you, her father! Mademoiselle de Villefort herself packed the medicines that were sent to Monsieur de Saint-Méran, and he is dead. She prepared the cooling draughts for Madame de Saint-Méran, and she is dead. Mademoiselle de Villefort took from Barrois, who was sent out, the decanter with the lemonade her grandfather generally drinks in the morning, and he escapes but by a miracle. Mademoiselle de Villefort is the guilty one! She is the poisoner, and I denounce her as such. Now, do your duty, Monsieur le Procureur du Roi!'

'Doctor, I can hold out no longer. I no longer defend myself. I believe you. But for pity's sake, spare my life, my honour! And what if you are wrong and my daughter is innocent?'

'Very well,' said the doctor after a moment's silence. 'I will wait.'

Villefort looked at him as though he still doubted his words.

'But remember this,' continued M. d'Avrigny solemnly and slowly. 'If someone falls ill in your house, if you yourself are stricken, do not send for me – I shall not come. I will share this terrible secret with you, but I will not let shame and remorse eat into my conscience like a worm, just as misfortune and crime will undermine the foundations of your house. And so, goodbye.'

28

The paragraph which appeared in the papers regarding the part Morcerf had played in the surrender of Janina caused great excitement in the Chamber of Peers among the usually calm groups of that high assembly. That day almost every member had arrived before the usual hour to discuss with his compeers the sinister event that was to fix public attention on one of the best-known names in that illustrious body.

The Count of Morcerf alone was ignorant of the news. He did not receive the newspaper containing the defamatory information and had spent the morning writing letters and trying a new horse. He arrived at the Chamber at his usual hour, and with proud step and haughty mien alighted from his carriage and passed along the corridors into the hall without remarking the hesitation of the doorkeepers, or the coldness of his colleagues. The sitting had been in progress about half an hour when he entered.

Everyone had the accusing paper before him, and it was evident that all were aching to start the debate, but, as is generally the case, no one wished to take upon himself the responsibility of opening the attack. At length, one of the peers, an open enemy of Morcerf's, ascended the tribune with such solemnity that all felt that the desired moment had arrived.

There was an awe-inspiring silence. Morcerf alone was ignorant of the cause of the deep attention given to an orator they were accustomed to hear with indifference. The Count paid little heed to the preamble, but when Janina and Colonel Fernand were mentioned, the Count of Morcerf turned so horribly pale that a shudder went through the whole assembly and all eyes were turned towards him.

The article was read during this painful silence, and then the speaker declared his reluctance to open the subject, and the difficulty of his task, but it was the honour of M. de Morcerf and of the whole Chamber he proposed to defend by introducing a debate on these personal and ever-pressing questions. He concluded by demanding a speedy inquiry into the matter before the calumny had time to spread, so that M. de Morcerf might be reinstated in the position in public opinion he had so long held.

Morcerf was so completely overwhelmed by this enormous and unexpected attack that it was almost more than he could do to stammer a few words in reply, staring the while at his colleagues with wide-open eyes. This nervousness, which might have been due to the astonishment of innocence as much as to shame of guilt, evoked some sympathy in his favour. An inquiry was voted for, and the Count was asked what time he required to prepare his defence. On realizing that this terrible blow had still left him alive, Morcerf's courage returned to him.

'My brother peers,' he replied, 'it is not with time that one repulses an attack of this kind that has been made on me by some unknown enemies. I therefore request that the inquiry be instituted as soon as possible, and I undertake to furnish the Chamber with all the necessary evidence.'

'Is the Chamber of the opinion that the inquiry should take place this very day?' asked the President.

'Yes!' was the unanimous reply.

A Committee of twelve members was appointed to examine the evidence supplied by Morcerf, and the first session was fixed for eight o'clock that evening in the committee room. This decision arrived at, Morcerf asked permission to retire; he had to collect the evidence he had long since prepared against such a storm, which his cunning and indomitable character had foreseen.

Everyone arrived punctually at eight o'clock. M. de Morcerf entered the hall at the last stroke of the clock. In his hand he carried some papers. He was carefully but simply dressed, and, according to the ancient military custom, wore his coat buttoned up to the chin. Outwardly he was calm, and, contrary to habit, walked with an unaffected gait.

His presence produced a most favourable effect, and the Committee was far from being ill-disposed towards him. Several of the members went forward to shake hands with him. One of the doorkeepers handed a letter to the President.

'You are now at liberty to speak,' said the President, unsealing his letter.

The Count commenced his defence in a most eloquent and skilful manner. He produced evidence to show that the Vizier of Janina had honoured him with entire confidence up to his last hour, the best proof being that he had entrusted him with a mission to the Sultan himself, the result of which meant life or death to him. He showed the ring with which Ali Pasha generally sealed his letters, and which he had given him as a token of authority so that upon his return he might gain access to him at any hour of the day or night. He said his mission had unfortunately failed, and, when he returned to defend his benefactor, he found him dead. So great was Ali Pasha's confidence in him, however, that before he died he had entrusted his favourite wife and his daughter to his care.

In the meantime, the President carelessly glanced at the letter that had been given him, but the very first lines aroused his attention; he read the missive again and again, then, fixing his eyes on Morcerf, said:

'You say, Count, that the Vizier of Janina confided his wife and daughter to your care.'

'Yes, Monsieur le Président,' replied Morcerf. 'But in that, as in all else, misfortune dogged my steps. Upon my return, Vasiliki and her daughter Haydee had disappeared.'

'Do you know them?'

'Thanks to my intimacy with the Pasha and his great confidence in me, I saw them more than twenty times.'

'Have you any idea what has become of them?'

'I have been told that they succumbed to their grief, and maybe to their privation. I was not rich, my life was in constant danger, and, much to my regret, I could not go in search of them.'

The President frowned almost imperceptibly as he said: 'Messieurs, you have heard Monsieur de Morcerf's defence. Now, Count, can you produce any witnesses to support the truth of what you say?'

'Alas, I cannot,' replied the Count. 'All those who were at the Pasha's Court and who knew me there are either scattered or dead. The most convincing evidence I can put forward is the complete absence of testimony against my honour, and the clean record of my military career.'

A murmur of approbation went through the assembly, and at this moment, M. Morcerf's cause was gained; it only needed to be put to the vote when the President rose and said: 'Messieurs, you and the Count will, I presume, not be averse to hearing a witness who claims to hold important evidence and has come forward of his own accord. He is doubtless come to prove the perfect innocence of our colleague. Here is the letter I have just received on the matter.' The President read as follows:

'Monsieur le Président,

'I can furnish the Committee of Inquiry appointed to examine the conduct in Epirus and Macedonia of a certain Lieutenant-General the Count of Morcerf with important facts.'

The President made a short pause. The Count of Morcerf turned deathly pale, and the tightly clenched papers that he held in his hand audibly crackled.

The President resumed:

'I was present at Ali Pasha's death and know what became of Vasiliki and Haydee. I hold myself at the disposal of the Committee, and even claim the honour of being heard. I shall be waiting in the corridor when this note is handed to you.'

'Who is this witness, or rather enemy?' said the Count, in a very changed voice.

'We shall learn in a moment, monsieur. Is the Committee agreed to hear this witness?'

'Yes, yes,' was the unanimous reply.

The President called the doorkeeper, and inquired of him whether anyone was waiting in the corridors.

'A woman, accompanied by her attendant,' said the doorkeeper.

The members looked at each other in amazement.

'Let this woman enter,' said the President.

All eyes were turned towards the door, and five minutes later the doorkeeper reappeared. Behind him came a woman enveloped in a large veil which completely covered her, but the form outlined, and the perfume which exhaled from her, denoted that she was a young and elegant woman. The President requested her to lay aside her veil, and it was seen that she was dressed in Grecian attire and was a remarkably beautiful woman.

'Madame,' began the President. 'You state in your letter to the Committee that you have important information on the Janina affair, and that you were an eyewitness of the events. Permit me to remark that you must have been very young then.'

'I was four years old, but as the events so peculiarly concerned me not a detail has escaped my memory.'

'How did these events so concern you? Who are you that this tragedy should have made so deep an impression on you?'

'My name is Haydee,' replied the young woman. 'I am the daughter of Ali Tebelin, Pasha of Janina, and of Vasiliki, his much-beloved wife.'

The modest and at the same time proud blush that suffused the young woman's cheeks, the fire in her eye and the majestic way in which she revealed her identity made an indescribable impression on the assembly. The Count, on the other hand, could not have been more abashed if a thunderbolt had fallen and opened a chasm at his feet.

'Madame,' resumed the President, making a respectful bow, 'permit me a simple question. Can you prove the authenticity of what you say?'

'I can, monsieur,' said Haydee, taking a perfumed satin bag from under her veil. 'Here is my birth certificate, drawn up by my father and signed by his principal officers, also my certificate of baptism, my father having allowed me to be brought up in my mother's religion. This latter bears the seal of the Grand Primate of Macedonia and Epirus. Lastly, and this is perhaps the most important, I have the document pertaining to the sale of my person and that of my mother to an Armenian merchant, named El Kobbir, effected by the French officer who, in his infamous treaty with the Porte, had reserved for his share of the booty the wife and daughter of his benefactor. These he sold for the sum of four hundred thousand francs.'

A ghastly pallor spread over the Count's cheeks and his eyes became bloodshot when he heard these terrible imputations, which were received by the assembly in grim silence.

Haydee, still calm, but more dangerous in her very calmness than another would have been in anger, handed to the President the record of her sale, drawn up in the Arab tongue.

As it was thought likely that a testimony might be

forthcoming in the Arabic, Romaic, or Turkish language, the interpreter of the Chamber had been advised that his presence might be needed, and he was now summoned. One of the peers to whom the Arabic tongue was familiar, followed closely the original text as the translator read:

'I, El Kobbir, slave merchant and purveyor to the harem of His Highness, acknowledge having received for transmission to the Sublime Sultan from the Count of Monte Cristo an emerald valued at eight hundred thousand francs as purchase money for a young Christian slave, aged eleven years, of the name of Haydee, a recognized daughter of the late Ali Tebelin, Pasha of Janina, and of Vasiliki, his favourite, she having been sold to me seven years ago together with her mother, who died on her arrival at Constantinople, by a French Colonel in the service of the Vizier Ali Tebelin of the name of Fernand Mondego.

'The aforesaid purchase was made on behalf of His Highness, whose mandate I had, for the sum of four hundred thousand francs.

'Given at Constantinople with the authorization of His Highness in the year 1247 of the Hegira.

'Signed: EL KOBBIR

'In order to give this document due credence and authority, it will be vested with the imperial seal, which the vendor consents to have affixed.'

Besides the merchant's signature was the seal of the Sublime Sultan.

A dreadful silence followed. The Count was speechless; his eyes instinctively sought Haydee, and he fixed her with a frenzied stare.

'Is it permitted, madame, to interrogate the Count

of Monte Cristo, who, I believe, is staying in Paris just now?' asked the President.

'The Count of Monte Cristo, my second father, has been in Normandy for the past three days, monsieur.'

'Then who advised you to take this step, for which this Committee is indebted to you, and which was the natural proceeding in view of your birth and misfortunes?'

'This step was urged upon me by my grief and respect. May God forgive me! Though I am a Christian, my one thought has always been to avenge my illustrious father's death. Therefore, as soon as I set foot in France and learned that the traitor lived in Paris, I have ever watched for this opportunity. I live a retired life in my noble protector's house; I wish it so because I like retirement and silence, so that I may live in the thoughts and memories of the past. The Count of Monte Cristo surrounds me with every paternal care, and in the silence of my apartments I receive each day all newspapers and periodicals. From them I glean all information concerning what is going on in the world; from them I learned what transpired in the Chamber this morning and what was to take place this evening.'

'Then the Count of Monte Cristo knows nothing of this action on your part?' asked the President.

'He is in absolute ignorance of it, monsieur, and my only fear is that he may disapprove of what I have done. Nevertheless, this is a glorious day for me,' continued the young woman, raising her eager eyes heavenward, 'the day when I at last have the opportunity of avenging my father.'

During all this time the Count had not uttered a

single word; his colleagues looked at him, no doubt commiserating with him on this calamity which had been wrought on him by a woman. The ever-increasing lines and wrinkles on his face betrayed his misery.

'Monsieur de Morcerf, do you recognize this lady as the daughter of Ali Tebelin, Pasha of Janina?'

'No,' said Morcerf, making an effort to rise. 'This is nothing but a plot woven against me by my enemies.'

Haydee was looking at the door as though she expected someone, and at these words she turned round sharply, and seeing the Count standing there, uttered a fearful cry.

'You do not recognize me!' she cried. 'Fortunately I recognize you! You are Fernand Mondego, the French officer who instructed my father's troops. It was you who surrendered the castle of Janina! It was you who, having been sent to Constantinople by my father to treat directly with the Sultan for the life or death of your benefactor, brought back a falsified decree granting full pardon! It was you who obtained with this same decree the Pasha's ring which would secure for you the obedience of Selim, the guardian of the fire! It was you who stabbed Selim! It was you who sold my mother and myself to El Kobbir! Murderer! Murderer! Your master's blood is still on your brow! Look at him, all of you!'

These words were spoken with such vehemence and with such force of truth that everyone looked at the Count's forehead, and he himself put his hand up as though he felt Ali's blood still warm upon his forehead.

'You positively recognize Monsieur de Morcerf as this same officer, Fernand Mondego?'

'Do I recognize him?' cried Haydee. 'Oh, Mother! You said to me: "You are free. You had a father whom you loved; you were destined to be almost a queen. Look well at this man who has made you a slave; it is he who has placed your father's head on the pike, it is he who has sold us, it is he who has betrayed us! Look at his right hand with its large scar. If you forget his face, you will recognize this hand into which El Kobbir's gold fell, piece by piece!" Oh, yes, I know him! Let him tell you himself whether he does not recognize me now!'

Each word cut Morcerf like a knife, and broke down his determination. At the last words he instinctively hid his hand in his bosom, for as a matter of fact it bore the mark of a wound, and once more he sank back into his chair.

This scene had set the opinions of the assembly in a veritable turmoil, like leaves torn from their branches by the violence of a north wind.

'Do not lose courage, Count,' said the President. 'The justice of this court, like that of God, is supreme and equal to all; it will not permit you to be crushed by your enemies without giving you the means of defending yourself. Do you wish to have further investigations made? Do you wish me to send two members of the Chamber to Janina? Speak!'

Morcerf made no reply.

All the members of the Committee looked at one another in horror.

'What have you decided?' the President asked.

'Nothing,' said the Count, in a toneless voice.

'Then Ali Tebelin's daughter has spoken the truth? She is indeed the dreaded witness in the face of whose evidence the guilty one dares not answer: "Not guilty?" You have actually committed the crimes of which she accuses you?'

The Count cast around him a look of despair such as would have elicited mercy from a tiger, but it could not disarm his judges; then he raised his eyes towards the roof but instantly turned them away again, as though fearful lest it should open and he should find himself before that other tribunal they call Heaven, and face to face with that other judge whom they call God. He tore at the buttons that fastened the coat which was choking him and walked out of the room like one demented. For an instant his weary steps echoed dolefully, but the sound was soon followed by the rattling of his carriage wheels as he was borne away at a gallop.

'Messieurs,' said the President when silence was restored, 'is the Count of Morcerf guilty of felony, treason, and dishonour?'

'Yes,' was the unanimous reply of all the members.

Haydee was present to the end of the meeting; she heard the verdict passed on the Count, but neither pity nor joy was depicted on her features. Covering her face with her veil, she bowed to the councillors and left the room with queenly tread.

29

Albert was resolved to kill the unknown person who had struck this blow at his father. He had discovered that Danglars was making inquiries through his correspondents concerning the surrender of the castle of Janina, and he now proposed to his friend Beauchamp to accompany him to an interview with the banker, since, in his view, it was unfitting that such a solemn occasion should be unmarked by the presence of a witness.

When they reached Danglars' house the young man was announced, but, on hearing Albert's name, the banker, cognizant of what had taken place the previous evening, refused to see him. It was too late, however; he had followed the footman, and, hearing the instructions given, pushed open the door and entered the room, followed by Beauchamp.

'Pray, monsieur, is one not at liberty to receive whom one chooses?' cried the banker. 'You appear to have forgotten yourself sadly.'

'No, monsieur,' said Albert coldly; 'there are certain circumstances, such as the present one, when one is compelled to be at home to certain persons, at least if one is not a coward – I offer you that refuge.'

'Then what do you want of me?'

'All I want of you,' said Albert, 'is to propose a meeting in some secluded spot where we shall not be disturbed for ten minutes; where, of the two men who meet, one will be left under the leaves.'

'I warn you, monsieur, that when I have the misfortune to meet a mad dog, I kill it,' said Danglars, white with fear and rage, 'and far from thinking myself guilty of a crime, I should consider I had rendered a service to society. Therefore, if you are mad and try to bite me, I shall kill you without mercy. Is it my fault that your father is dishonoured?'

'Yes, it is your fault, you scoundrel,' replied Morcerf.

'My fault! Mine?' cried Danglars. 'You are mad! Do I know anything about the history of Greece? Have I travelled in those parts? Was it upon my advice that your father sold the castle of Janina and betrayed . . .'

'Silence!' roared Albert. 'You did not bring this calamity on us directly, but you hypocritically led up to it. Who wrote to Janina for information concerning my father?'

'It seems to me that anyone and every one can write to Janina.'

'Nevertheless, only one person wrote, and you were that person.'

'I certainly wrote. If a man's daughter is about to marry a young man, it is surely permissible for him to make inquiries about the young man's family. It is not only a right, it is a duty.'

'You wrote knowing full well what answer you would receive,' said Albert.

'I assure you,' cried Danglars with a confidence and security which emanated perhaps less from fear than from his feeling for the unhappy young man, 'I solemnly declare that I should never have thought of writing to Janina. What do I know of Ali Pasha's adversities?'

'Then someone persuaded you to write?'

'Certainly. I was speaking about your father's past history to someone and mentioned that the source of his wealth was still a mystery. He asked where your father had made his fortune. I replied: "In Greece." So he said: "Well, write to Janina."'

'Who gave you this advice?'

'Why, none other than your friend, the Count of Monte Cristo. Would you like to see the correspondence? I can show it you.'

'Does the Count of Monte Cristo know what answer you received?'

'Yes, I showed it him.'

'Did he know that my father's Christian name was Fernand, and his family name Mondego?'

'Yes, I told him a long time ago.'

Then many a detail forgotten or unobserved presented itself to Albert's mind. Monte Cristo knew all since he had bought Ali Pasha's daughter, yet, knowing all, he had advised Danglars to write to Janina. After the answer had been received he had yielded to Albert's desire to be introduced to Haydee; he had allowed the conversation to turn on the death of Ali, and had not opposed the recital of her story (doubtless after giving her instructions in the few Romaic sentences he spoke, not to let Morcerf recognize his father); besides, had he not begged Morcerf not to mention his father's name before Haydee? There could be no doubt that it was all a premeditated plan that Monte Cristo was in league with his father's enemies.

Albert took Beauchamp aside and expounded these views to him.

'You are right,' his friend said. 'In all that has happened Monsieur Danglars has only done the dirty work. You must demand satisfaction of Monsieur de Monte Cristo.'

Albert turned to Danglars with the words: 'You must understand, monsieur, I am not taking definite leave of you. I must first ascertain from the Count of Monte Cristo that your accusations against him are justified.'

Bowing to the banker, he went out with Beauchamp. Danglars accompanied them to the door, renewing his assurance that he had not been actuated by any motive of personal hatred against the Count of Morcerf.

They drove to number thirty, Avenue des Champs-Élysées, but the Count was in his bath and could not see anyone. Albert ascertained from Baptistin, however, that he would be going to the Opera that evening.

Retracing his steps, he said to Beauchamp: 'If you have anything to do, Beauchamp, do it at once. I count upon you to go to the Opera with me this evening and if you can bring Château-Renaud with you, do so.'

On his return home, Albert sent a message to Franz, Debray, and Morrel that he would like to see them at the Opera that evening. Then he went to his mother, who, since the events of the previous evening, had kept to her room and refused to see anyone. He found her in bed overwhelmed at their public humiliation. On seeing Albert, she clasped his hand and burst into tears. For a moment he stood silently looking on. It was evident from his pale face and knit brows that his determination for revenge was gaining in force.

'Mother, do you know whether Monsieur de Morcerf has any enemies?' Albert asked.

Mercédès started; she noticed the young man did not say 'my father'.

'My son,' she replied, 'people in the Count's position always have many secret enemies. Furthermore, the enemies one is cognizant of are not always the most dangerous.'

'I know that, and for that reason, I appeal to your perspicacity. You are so observant that nothing escapes you. You remarked, for instance, that at the ball we gave Monsieur de Monte Cristo refused to partake of anything in our house.'

Mercédès raised herself on her arm. 'What has Monte Cristo to do with the question you asked me?'

'You know, Mother, Monsieur de Monte Cristo is almost an Oriental, and in order to reserve for themselves the liberty of revenge, Orientals never eat or drink in the house of an enemy.'

'Do you wish to imply that Monte Cristo is our enemy, Albert?' cried Mercédès. 'Who told you so? Why, you are mad, Albert! Monsieur de Monte Cristo has shown us only kindness. He saved your life and you yourself presented him to us. Oh, I entreat you, my son, if you entertain such an idea, dispel it, and I advise you, nay I beg of you, to keep on good terms with him.'

'Mother, you have some reason for wishing me to be friendly with this man,' replied the young man with a black look.

'I?' said Mercédès.

'Yes, you,' replied the young man. 'Is it because he has the power to do us some harm?'

Mercédès shuddered, and, casting on him a searching glance, said: 'You speak strangely and appear to have singular prejudices. What has the Count done to you?'

An ironical smile passed over Albert's lips. Mercédès saw it with the double instinct of a woman and a mother and guessed all, but, being prudent and strong, she hid both her sorrows and her fears.

Albert took leave of his mother and went to his room to dress. At ten minutes to eight Beauchamp appeared; he had seen Château-Renaud, who promised to be at the Opera before the curtain rose.

It was not until the end of the second act that Albert sought Monte Cristo in his box. The Count, whose companion was Maximilian Morrel, had been watching the young man all the evening, so that when he turned round on hearing his door open, he was quite prepared to see Albert before him, accompanied by Beauchamp and Château-Renaud.

'A welcome visit!' said the Count, with that cordiality which distinguished his form of salutation from the ordinary civilities of the social world. 'Good evening, Monsieur de Morcerf.'

'We have not come here to exchange banalities or to make false professions of friendship,' returned Albert. 'We have come to demand an explanation of you, Count.'

The quivering voice of the young man was scarcely louder than a whisper.

'An explanation at the Opera?' said the Count, with the calm tone and penetrating look which characterize the man who has complete confidence in himself. 'Unfamiliar as I am with the customs of Paris, I should not have thought this was the place to demand an explanation.'

'Nevertheless, when people shut themselves up and will not be seen on the pretext that they are in the bath, we must not miss the opportunity when we happen to meet them elsewhere.'

Albert had raised his voice to such a pitch when saying these last words that everyone in the adjoining boxes and in the corridors heard him.

'Where have you come from, monsieur?' said Monte

Cristo, outwardly quite calm. 'You do not appear to be in your right senses.'

'So long as I understand your perfidies and make you realize that I will be revenged, I am reasonable enough,' said Albert in a fury.

'I do not understand you, and even if I did, there is no reason for you to speak in such a loud voice. I am at home here, and I alone have the right to raise my voice. Leave the box, Monsieur de Morcerf!' said the Count of Monte Cristo, as he pointed towards the door with an admirable gesture of command.

Albert understood the allusion to his name in a moment, and was about to throw his glove in the Count's face when Morrel seized his hand. Leaning forward in his chair, Monte Cristo stretched out his hand and took the young man's glove, saying in a terrible voice:

'I consider your glove as having been thrown, monsieur, and I will return it wrapped round a bullet. Now leave me, or I shall call my servants to throw you out!'

Utterly beside himself with anger, and with wild and bloodshot eyes, Albert stepped back; Morrel seized the opportunity to shut the door. Monte Cristo took up his glasses again as though nothing out of the ordinary had happened. The man had, indeed, a heart of iron and a face of marble.

'How have you offended him?' whispered Morrel.

'I? I have not offended him – at least not personally.'

'But there must be some reason for this strange scene.'

'The Count of Morcerf's adventures have exasperated the young man.'

'What shall you do about it?'

'What shall I do? As true as you are here I shall have killed him before the clock strikes ten tomorrow morning. That is what I shall do.'

Morrel took the Count's hands in his; they were so cold and steady that they sent a shudder through him.

'Ah, Count,' said he, 'his father loves him so.'

'Tell me not such things!' cried Monte Cristo, with the first signs of anger that he had yet shown. 'I would make him suffer!'

Morrel let Monte Cristo's hand fall in amazement. He saw it was useless to say anything more. The curtain which had been raised at the conclusion of the scene with Albert was dropped once more, and a knock was heard at the door.

'Come in,' said Monte Cristo, in a voice devoid of all emotion.

Beauchamp entered.

'Good evening, Monsieur Beauchamp,' said Monte Cristo as though this was the first time he had seen the journalist that evening. 'Pray be seated.'

Beauchamp bowed, and, taking a seat, said: 'As you saw, monsieur, I accompanied Monsieur de Morcerf just now. I have to make the necessary arrangements for the duel.'

'I am quite indifferent on that score,' replied the Count of Monte Cristo. 'It was unnecessary to disturb me in the middle of an opera for such a trifling matter. Tell the Viscount that although I am the one insulted, I will give him the choice of arms and will accept everything without discussion or dispute. Send me word this evening to my house, indicating the weapon and the hour. I do not like to be kept waiting.'

'Pistols the weapon, eight o'clock the hour in the Bois de Vincennes,' said Beauchamp.

'Very well,' said Monte Cristo. 'Now that all is arranged, pray let me listen to the opera and tell your friend Albert not to return this evening. Tell him to go home and sleep.'

Beauchamp left the box perfectly amazed.

'Now,' said Monte Cristo, turning towards Morrel. 'I may reckon on you, may I not? The young man is acting blindfolded and knows not the true cause of this duel, which is known only to God and to me; but I give you my word, Morrel, that God, Who knows it, will be on our side.'

'Enough,' said Morrel. 'Who is your second witness?'

'I do not know anyone in Paris on whom I could confer the honour except you, Morrel, and your brother-in-law. Do you think Emmanuel will render me this service?'

'I can answer for him as for myself, Count.'

'Very well, that is all I require. You will be with me at seven o'clock in the morning?'

'We shall be there.'

30

Monte Cristo waited, as he usually did, until Duprez had sung his famous *Follow me*, then he rose and went out, followed by Morrel, who left him at the door, renewing his promise to be at his house, together with

Emmanuel, at seven o'clock the next morning. Still calm and smiling, the Count entered the brougham and was at home in five minutes. On entering the house, he said to Ali: 'Ali, my pistols inlaid with ivory!' and no one who knew him could have mistaken the tone in which he said it.

Ali brought the box to his master, who was beginning to examine them when the study door opened to admit Baptistin. Before the latter could say a word, a veiled woman who was following behind him, and who through the open door caught sight of a pistol in the Count's hand and two swords on the table, rushed into the room. Baptistin cast a bewildered look on his master, but upon a sign from the Count, he went out, shutting the door behind him.

'Who are you, madame?' the Count asked of the veiled woman.

The stranger looked round her to make sure they were alone, then, throwing herself on to one knee and clasping her hands, she cried out in a voice of despair:

'Edmond, you will not kill my son!'

The Count started, and, dropping the weapon he held in his hand, uttered a feeble cry.

'What name did you pronounce then, Madame de Morcerf?' said he.

'Yours!' she cried, throwing back her veil. 'Your name which I alone, perhaps, have not forgotten. Edmond, it is not Madame de Morcerf who has come to you. It is Mercédès.'

'Mercédès is dead, madame. I know no one now of that name.'

'Mercédès lives, and not only lives, but remembers.

She alone recognized you when she saw you, and even without seeing you, Edmond, she knew you by the very tone of your voice. From that moment she has followed your every step, watched you, feared you. She has no need to seek the hand that has dealt Monsieur de Morcerf this blow.'

'Fernand, you mean, madame,' returned Monte Cristo, with bitter irony. 'Since we are recalling names, let us remember them all.'

He pronounced the name of Fernand with such an expression of venomous hatred that Mercédès was stricken with fear.

'You see, Edmond, I am not mistaken. I have every reason to say: "Spare my son!"'

'Who told you, madame, that I have evil designs against your son?'

'No one, but alas, a mother is gifted with second sight. I have guessed everything. I followed him to the opera this evening, and, hiding in another box, I saw all that occurred.'

'If you saw everything, madame, you also saw that Fernand's son insulted me in public,' said Monte Cristo with terrible calmness. 'You must also have seen,' he continued, 'that he would have thrown his glove in my face but that one of my friends held back his arm.'

'Listen to me. My son has discovered your identity; he attributes all his father's misfortunes to you.'

'Madame, you are under a misapprehension. His father is suffering no misfortune; it is a punishment, and it is not inflicted by me, it is the work of Providence.'

'Why should you take the place of Providence? Why

should you remember when He forgets? In what way do Janina and the Vizier concern you, Edmond? What wrong has Fernand Mondego done you by betraying Ali Tebelin?'

'As you infer, madame, that is all a matter between the French officer and Vasiliki's daughter and does not concern me. But if I have sworn to take revenge, it is not on the French officer or on the Count of Morcerf; it is on Fernand, the fisherman, the husband of Mercédès the Catalan.'

'What terrible vengeance for a fault for which fate alone is responsible! I am the guilty one, Edmond, and if you take revenge on someone, it should be on me, who lacked the strength to bear your absence and my solitude.'

'But do you know why I was absent? Do you know why you were left solitary and alone?'

'Because you were arrested and imprisoned, Edmond.'

'Why was I arrested? Why was I imprisoned?'

'I know not,' said Mercédès.

''Tis true, you do not know; at least, I hope you do not. Well then, I will tell you. I was arrested and imprisoned because on the eve of the very day on which I was to be married, a man named Danglars wrote this letter in the arbour of La Réserve, and Fernand, the fisherman, posted it.'

Going to a writing-desk, Monte Cristo opened a drawer and took out a discoloured piece of paper and laid it before Mercédès. It was Danglars' letter to the Procureur du Roi.

Filled with dismay, Mercédès read the following lines:

The Procureur du Roi is herewith informed by a friend to the throne and to religion that a certain Edmond Dantès, mate on the *Pharaon* which arrived this morning from Smyrna after having touched at Naples and Porto Ferrajo, has been entrusted by Murat with a letter for the usurper and by the usurper with a letter for the Bonapartist party in Paris. Corroboration of this crime can be found either on him, or at his father's house, or in his cabin on board the *Pharaon*.

'Good God!' exclaimed Mercédès, passing her hand across her forehead wet with perspiration. 'This letter . . .'

'I bought it for two hundred thousand francs, Madame,' said Monte Cristo. 'But it is cheap at the price since it today enables me to justify myself in your eyes.'

'What was the result of this letter?'

'You know it, madame. It led to my arrest. But what you do not know is how long my imprisonment lasted. You do not know that I lay in a dungeon of the Château d'If, but a quarter of a league from you, for fourteen long years. On each day of those fourteen years, I renewed the vow of vengeance I had taken the first day, though I was unaware that you had married Fernand, and that my father had died of hunger.'

'Merciful heavens!' cried Mercédès, utterly crushed.

'That is what I learned on leaving my prison fourteen years after I had been taken there. I have sworn to revenge myself on Fernand because of the living Mercédès, and my deceased father, and revenge myself I will!'

'Are you sure this unhappy Fernand did what you say?'

'On my oath it is so. In any case it is not much more odious than that, being a Frenchman by adoption, he passed over to the English; a Spaniard by birth, he fought against the Spanish; a hireling of Ali's, he betrayed and assassinated Ali. In the face of all this, what is that letter you have just read? The French have not avenged themselves on the traitor, the Spaniards have not shot him, and Ali in his tomb has let him go unpunished; but I, betrayed, assassinated, cast into a tomb, have risen from that tomb by the grace of God, and it is my duty to God to punish this man. He has sent me for that purpose and here I am.'

'Then take your revenge, Edmond,' cried the heart-broken mother falling on her knees, 'but let your vengeance fall on the culprits, on him, on me, but not on my son!'

'I must have my revenge, Mercédès! For fourteen years have I suffered, for fourteen years wept and cursed, and now I must avenge myself.'

'Edmond,' continued Mercédès, her arms stretched out towards the Count, 'ever since I knew you, I have adored your name, have respected your memory. Oh, my friend, do not compel me to tarnish the noble and pure image that is ever reflected in my heart! If you knew how I have prayed for you, both when I thought you living and later when I believed you dead. Oh, believe me, Edmond, guilty as I am, I too have suffered much!'

'Have you seen your father die in your absence?' cried Monte Cristo, thrusting his hands into his hair. 'Have you seen the woman you loved give her hand to your rival while you were pining away in the depths of a dungeon?'

'No, but I have seen him whom I loved about to become my son's murderer!'

Mercédès said these words with such infinite sadness and in such tones of despair that they wrung a sob from the Count's throat. The lion was tamed, the avenger was overcome!

'What do you ask of me?' he said. 'Your son's life? Well then, he shall live!'

'Oh, Edmond, I thank you!' cried Mercédès, taking the Count's hand and pressing it to her lips. 'Now you are the man of my dreams, the man I have always loved! I can own it now.'

'It is just as well, for poor Edmond will not have long to enjoy your love,' replied Monte Cristo. 'Death will return to its tomb, the phantom to darkness!'

'What is that you say, Edmond?'

'I say that since you so command me, I must die!'

'Die! Who said that? Who told you to die? Whence come these strange ideas of death?'

'You cannot suppose I have the least desire to live after I have been publicly insulted, before a theatre full of people, in the presence of your friends and those of your son, challenged by a mere child who will glory in my pardon as in a victory?'

'But the duel will not take place, Edmond, since you pardon my son.'

'It will take place,' said Monte Cristo solemnly, 'but it will be my blood instead of your son's that will stain the ground.'

Mercédès screamed and rushed up to Monte Cristo, but suddenly she came to a halt.

'Edmond,' said she, 'I know there is a God above,

for you still live and I have seen you. I put my whole trust in Him to help me, and in the meantime I depend upon your word. You said my son would live and you mean it, do you not?'

'Yes, madame, he shall live,' said Monte Cristo.

Mercédès looked at the Count with eyes full of admiration and gratitude.

'You see that, though my cheeks have become pale,' she said, 'and my eyes dull and I have lost all my beauty, that, though Mercédès is no longer like her former self, her heart has remained the same. Farewell, Edmond, I have nothing more to ask of Heaven; I have seen you, and you are as noble and as great as in the days long past. Farewell, Edmond, farewell, and thank you.'

The Count made no reply. Mercédès opened the door, and had disappeared before he had woken from his painful and deep reverie into which his thwarted vengeance had plunged him. The clock on the Invalides struck one as the rumbling of the carriage which bore Mme de Morcerf away brought the Count of Monte Cristo back to realities.

'Fool that I am,' said he, 'that I did not tear out my heart the day I resolved to revenge myself!'

The night wore on. The Count of Monte Cristo knew not how the hours passed, for his mental tortures could only be compared to those he had suffered when, as Edmond Dantès, he had lain in the dungeon of the Château d'If. History was repeating itself once more, only the external circumstances were changed. Then his plans were frustrated at the eleventh hour through no action on his part; now, just as his schemes for revenge were materializing, he must relinquish them for ever, solely because he had not reckoned with one factor – his love for Mercédès!

At length as the clock struck six he roused himself from his dismal meditations, and made his final preparations before going out to meet his voluntary death. When Morrel and Emmanuel called to accompany him to the ground, he was quite ready, and, outwardly at least, calm. They were the first to arrive, but Franz and Debray soon followed. It was not until ten minutes past eight, however, that they saw Albert coming along on horseback at full gallop, followed by a servant. He pulled up his horse, jumped down, and, throwing the bridle to the servant, walked up to the others. He was pale and his eyes red and swollen; it was easily seen he had not slept all night. There was about his whole demeanour an unaccustomed sadness.

'Thank you, messieurs, for having granted my request!' he said. 'Believe me, I am most grateful for this token of friendship.' Noticing that Morrel had stepped back as he approached, he continued: 'Draw nearer, Monsieur Morrel, to you especially are my thanks due!'

'I think you must be unaware that I am Monsieur de Monte Cristo's second,' replied Morrel.

'I was not certain, but I thought you were. All the better; the more honourable men there are here, the better pleased shall I be.'

'Monsieur Morrel, you may inform the Count of Monte Cristo that Monsieur de Morcerf has arrived,' said Château-Renaud. 'We are at his service.'

'Wait, messieurs, I should like a few words with the Count of Monte Cristo,' said Albert.

'In private?' Morrel asked.

'No, before everyone.'

Albert's seconds looked at each other in surprise. Franz and Debray began whispering to each other, while Morrel, overjoyed at this unexpected incident, went in search of the Count, who was walking with Emmanuel a short distance away.

'What does he want?' asked Monte Cristo.

'I only know that he wishes to speak to you.'

'I hope he is not going to tempt me with fresh insults.'

'I do not think that is his intention,' was Morrel's reply.

The Count approached, accompanied by Maximilian and Emmanuel, his calm and serene mien forming a strange contrast with the grief-stricken face of Albert, who also advanced towards his adversary. When three paces from each other they stopped.

'Messieurs, come nearer,' Albert said. 'I do not want you to lose a word of what I have to say to the Count of Monte Cristo.'

'I am all attention, monsieur,' said the Count.

'I reproached you, monsieur, with having made known Monsieur de Morcerf's conduct in Epirus,' began Albert in a tremulous voice, which became firmer as he went on. 'I did not consider you had the right to punish him, however guilty he might be. Yet today I know better. It is not Fernand Mondego's treachery towards Ali Pasha that makes me so ready to forgive you, it is the treachery of Fernand the fisherman towards you, and the untold sufferings his conduct has caused you. I therefore say to you, and proclaim it aloud, that you were justified in revenging yourself on my father, and I, his son, thank you for not having done more.'

Had a thunderbolt fallen in the midst of his listeners, it would not have astonished them more than did Albert's declaration. Monte Cristo slowly raised his eyes to heaven with an expression of gratitude; he could not comprehend how Albert's proud nature could have submitted to this sudden humiliation. He recognized in it Mercédès' influence, and understood now why the noble woman had not refused the sacrifice which she knew would not be necessary.

'Now, Monsieur,' continued Albert, 'if you consider this apology sufficient, give me your hand. In my opinion the quality of recognizing one's faults ranks next to the rare one of infallibility, which you appear to possess. But this confession concerns me alone. I have acted well in the eyes of man, but you have acted well in the eyes of God. An angel alone could have saved one of us from death, and that angel has appeared, not to make us friends, perhaps, but at least to make us esteem each other.'

With moistened eyes and heaving bosom, Monte Cristo extended his hand to Albert, who pressed it with respectful awe as he said: 'Messieurs! Monsieur de Monte Cristo accepts my apology. I was guilty of a rash act, but have now made reparation for my fault. I trust the world will not look upon me as a coward because I have followed the dictates of my conscience.'

31

The Count of Monte Cristo bowed to the five young men with a sad smile, and, getting into his carriage, drove away with Maximilian and Emmanuel. Albert stood wrapped in deep and melancholy thought for a few moments, then suddenly loosing his horse from the tree around which his servant had tied the bridle, he sprang lightly into the saddle and returned to Paris at a gallop. A quarter of an hour later he entered his house in the Rue du Helder. As he dismounted from his horse, he thought he saw his father's pale face peeping from behind the curtain of his bedroom. Albert turned away his head with a sigh and went to his own apartments. Once there, he cast a last lingering look at all the luxuries that had made his life so easy and happy from his childhood, and began to pack a few things.

When he had finished, his thoughts turned to his mother, and as no one was there to announce him, he went straight to her bedroom, but, distressed by what he saw and still more by what he guessed, he paused on the threshold.

As though one mind animated these two beings, Mercédès was doing in her room what Albert had been doing in his.

'What are you doing, Mother dear?' he asked.

'What have you been doing?' was her reply.

'Oh, Mother!' cried Albert, almost too overwhelmed

to speak. 'It does not affect you as it does me. No, you surely cannot have taken the same resolutions as I have! I am come to inform you that I am leaving this house . . . and you?'

'I am leaving it, too, Albert,' replied Mercédès. 'I must confess, I had reckoned on being accompanied by my son. Was I mistaken?'

'Mother, I cannot let you share the life I have chosen. I must live henceforth without name and without fortune; to start my apprenticeship, I must borrow from a friend my daily bread till I can earn it myself. So I am going from here, Mother, to Franz, to ask him to lend me the small sum of money I think will be necessary. From today I have done with the past, and I will accept nothing from it, not even my name, for you understand, do you not, Mother, that your son could not bear the name of a man who should blush before every other man?'

'Albert, my son, had I been stronger, that is the advice I should have given you,' said Mercédès. 'Your conscience has spoken to you when my enfeebled voice was still; follow its dictates, my son. You had friends, Albert; break with them, but, for your mother's sake, do not despair. Life still has its charms at your age, for you can barely count twenty-two summers, and as a noble character such as yours must carry with it a name without blemish, take my father's. It was Herrara. Whatever career you pursue, you will soon make this name illustrious. When you have accomplished this, my son, make your appearance again in a world rendered more beautiful by your past sufferings.'

'I shall do as you wish, Mother,' the young man said. 'Your hopes are mine. God's anger cannot follow us, you who are so noble and I who am so innocent. But since we have taken our resolution, let us act with all speed. Monsieur de Morcerf left the house about an hour ago. The opportunity is therefore propitious, and we shall be relieved of the necessity of giving any explanations.'

'I am ready,' said Mercédès.

Albert ran into the boulevard for a cab to take them away. He thought of a nice little furnished house in the Rue des Saints-Pères where his mother would find a humble, but comfortable lodging. As the cab drew up at the door and Albert alighted, a man approached and handed him a letter. Albert recognized the Count of Monte Cristo's steward.

'From the Count,' said Bertuccio.

Albert took the letter and read it; then, with tears in his eyes and his breast heaving with emotion, he went in to find Mercédès and handed it to her without a word.

Mercédès read:

ALBERT

While showing you that I have discovered the plans you are contemplating, I hope to prove to you also that I have a sense of what is right. You are free, you are leaving the Count's house, taking with you your mother. But remember, Albert, you owe her more than your poor noble heart can give her. Keep the struggle to yourself, bear all the suffering alone and save her the misery that must inevitably accompany your first efforts, for she has not deserved even one fraction of the misfortune that has this day befallen her.

I know you are both leaving the Rue du Helder without taking anything with you. Do not try to discover how I know it; it is enough that I do know it.

Listen, Albert, to what I have to say. Twenty-four years ago, I returned to my country a proud and happy man. I had a sweetheart, Albert, a noble young girl whom I adored, and I was bringing to her a hundred and fifty louis which I had painfully amassed by ceaseless toil. This money was for her, and, knowing how treacherous the sea is, I buried the treasure in the little garden behind the house in Marseilles which your mother knows so well.

Recently I passed through Marseilles on my way from Paris. I went to see this house of sad memories. In the evening I took a spade and dug in the corner where I had buried my treasure. The iron chest was still in the same place: no one had touched it. It is in the corner that is shaded by a beautiful fig tree my father planted on the day of my birth.

By a strange and sad coincidence this money, which was to have contributed to the comfort of the woman I adored, will today serve the same purpose. Oh! Understand well my meaning. You are a generous man, Albert, but maybe you are blinded by pride or resentment. If you refuse me, if you ask another for what I have the right to offer you, I can but say it is ungenerous of you to refuse what is offered to your mother by one whose father was made to suffer the horrors of hunger and despair by your father.

Albert waited in silence for his mother's decision after she had finished reading the letter.

'I accept,' said she.

Placing the letter against her heart, she took her son's arm and went down the stairs with a step that surprised her by its firmness.

Meanwhile Monte Cristo had also returned to town with Emmanuel and Maximilian, and was sitting wrapped in thought when the door suddenly opened. The Count frowned.

'Monsieur le Comte de Morcerf,' announced Baptistin, as though this name was excuse enough for his admittance.

'Ask Monsieur de Morcerf into the salon.'

When Monte Cristo joined the General, he was pacing the length of the floor for the third time.

'Ah, it is really you, Monsieur de Morcerf,' said Monte Cristo calmly. 'I thought I had not heard right.'

'Yes, it is I,' said the Count, with a frightful contraction of the lips which prevented him from articulating clearly.

'I only require to know now to what I owe the pleasure of seeing the Count of Morcerf at such an early hour,' continued Monte Cristo.

'You had a meeting with my son this morning, monsieur?'

'You knew about it?'

'I also know that my son had very good reason to fight you and to do his utmost to kill you.'

'He had, but you see that, nothwithstanding these reasons, he did not kill me; in fact he did not fight.'

'No doubt you made some sort of apology or gave some explanation?'

'I gave him no explanation, and it was he who apologized.'

'But to what do you attribute such conduct?'

'To conviction; probably he discovered there was one more guilty than I.'

'Who is that man?'

'His father!'

The General smiled grimly and said, 'I came to tell you that I look upon you as my enemy. I have come to tell you that I instinctively hate you, that I seem to have known and hated you always! As the young men of this generation no longer fight, it is for us to do so. Are you of this opinion?'

'I am always ready, monsieur.'

'You understand that we shall fight till one of us drops?' said the General, clenching his teeth in rage.

'Till one of us drops,' repeated the Count of Monte Cristo, slowly nodding his head.

'Let us go, then; we have no need of seconds.'

'Indeed, it were useless,' replied Monte Cristo. 'We know each other so well.'

'No, no', exclaimed the General. 'I am known to you, but I do not know you, adventurer sewn up in gold and precious stones! In Paris you call yourself the Count of Monte Cristo, in Italy Sinbad the Sailor, in Malta – who knows? I have forgotten. It is your real name I now ask and wish to know, so that I may pronounce it in the field when I plunge my sword into your heart.'

The Count of Monte Cristo turned a ghastly colour; his wild eyes were burning with a devouring flame; he bounded into the adjoining room, and, within a second, tearing off his tie, his coat, and his waistcoat, had put on a small sailor's blouse and a sailor's hat, from under which his long black hair flowed.

He returned thus attired, and, with his arms crossed, walked up to the General, who had wondered at his sudden disappearance. On seeing him again his teeth chattered, his legs gave way under him, and he stepped back until he found a table against which to lay his clenched hand for support.

'Fernand!' cried Monte Cristo, 'I need but mention one of my many names to strike terror into your heart. But you guess this name, or rather you remember it, do you not? For, in spite of all my grief and tortures, I show you today a face made young by the joy of vengeance, a face that you must often have seen in your dreams since your marriage with – Mercédès.'

With head thrown back and hands stretched out, the General stared at this terrible apparition in silence; then, leaning against the wall for support, he glided slowly along it to the door through which he went out backwards, uttering but the one distressing and piercing cry: 'Edmond Dantès!'

With a moan that can be compared with no human sound, he dragged himself to the yard, staggering like a drunken man, and fell into his valet's arms. 'Home! Home!' he muttered.

The fresh air and the shame he felt at having given way before his servant made him pull himself together, but the drive was a short one, and the nearer he got to his house the greater was his anguish.

A few paces from his door, the carriage stopped, and the Count alighted. The door of the house was wide open; a cab, whose driver looked his surprise at being called to this magnificent residence, was stationed in the middle of the yard. The Count looked at it in terror, and, not daring to question anyone, fled to his room.

Two people were coming down the staircase, and he had only just time to hide himself in a room near by. It was Mercédès, leaning on her son's arm. They were both leaving the house. They passed quite close to the unhappy man, who, hidden behind a door-curtain, felt

Mercédès' silk dress brush past him and the warm breath of his son on his face, as he said:

'Have courage, Mother! Come away, this is no longer our home.'

The words died away and the steps were lost in the distance. The General drew himself up, clinging to the curtains with clenched hands, and the most terrible sob escaped him that ever came from the bosom of a father abandoned at the same time by his wife and his son.

Soon he heard the door of the cab closed and the voice of the coachman, followed by the rumbling of the lumbersome vehicle as it shook the windowpanes. He rushed into his bedroom to see once more all that he had loved on earth; the cab passed, and neither Mercédès' nor Albert's heads appeared at the door to take a last farewell of the deserted house, or to cast on the abandoned husband and father a last look of farewell and regret.

At the very moment when the wheels of that cab passed under the arched gate, a report was heard, and dark smoke issued through the glass of the bedroom window, which had been broken by the force of the explosion.

32

On leaving Monte Cristo, Morrel walked slowly toward Villefort's house. Noirtier and Valentine had allowed him two visits a week, and he was now going to take advantage of his rights.

Valentine was waiting for him. Almost beside herself with anxiety, she seized his hand and led him to her grandfather. She had heard of the affair at the Opera and its consequences, and, with her woman's instinct, had guessed that Morrel would be Monte Cristo's second.

One can understand with what eagerness all details were asked, given, and received, and the expression of indescribable joy that appeared in Valentine's eyes when she learned the happy issue of the terrible affair.

'Now, let us speak of our own affairs,' said Valentine, making a sign to Morrel to take a seat beside her grandfather while she sat on a hassock at his feet. 'You know Grandpapa wants to leave this house? Do you know what reason he has given?'

Noirtier looked at his granddaughter to impose silence on her, but she was not looking at him; her eyes and smiles were all for Morrel.

'Whatever the reason may be that Monsieur Noirtier has given, I am sure it is a good one!' exclaimed Maximilian.

'He pretends that the air of the Faubourg Saint-Honoré does not suit me!'

'Monsieur Noirtier may be right too,' said Morrel. 'You have not looked at all well for the past fortnight.'

'Perhaps not,' replied Valentine, 'but my grandfather has become my physician, and, as he knows everything, I have the greatest confidence that he will soon cure me.'

'Then you are really ill, Valentine?' Morrel asked anxiously.

'Oh not really ill; I only feel a little unwell, nothing more.'

Noirtier did not let one of Valentine's words escape him.

'What treatment are you following for this strange illness?'

'A very simple one,' said Valentine. 'Every morning I take a spoonful of my grandfather's medicine; that is, I commenced with one spoonful, but now I take four. Grandfather says it is a panacea.'

'But I thought this medicine was made up especially for Monsieur Noirtier?' said Morrel.

'I know it is, and it is very bitter,' replied Valentine. 'Everything I drink afterwards seems to have the same taste.'

Noirtier looked at his granddaughter questioningly.

'Yes, Grandpapa, it is so,' she replied. 'Just now before coming to you I drank some sugared water; it tasted so bitter that I left half of it.'

Noirtier made a sign that he wished to say something. Valentine at once got up to fetch the dictionary, her grandfather following her all the while with visible anguish. As a matter of fact, the blood was rushing to the girl's head, and her cheeks became red.

'Well, this is singular,' she said, without losing any of her gaiety. 'I have become giddy again. It is the sun shining in my eyes.' And she leaned against the window.

'There is no sun,' replied Morrel, more concerned by the expression on Noirtier's face than by Valentine's indisposition. He ran towards her.

'Do not be alarmed,' she said with a smile. 'It is nothing and has already passed. Really, Maximilian, you are too timid for an officer, a soldier who, they say, knows not what fear is,' said Valentine with a spasmodic movement of pain, and she burst into harsh, painful laughter. Her arms stiffened, her head fell back on her chair, and she remained motionless.

The cry of terror which was imprisoned in Noirtier's throat found expression in his eyes. Morrel understood he was to call for help. The young man pulled at the bell; the maid, who was in Valentine's room, and the servant who had taken Barrois' place came rushing in immediately.

Valentine was so cold, pale, and inanimate that the fear that prevailed in this accursed house took possession of them, and they flew out of the room shouting for help. At the same moment, Villefort's voice was heard calling from his study: 'What is the matter?'

Morrel looked questioningly at Noirtier, who had now regained his composure, and indicated by a look the little room where Morrel had already taken refuge on a similar occasion. He was only just in time, for Villefort's footsteps were heard approaching. He rushed into the room, ran up to Valentine and took her in his arms for an instant, calling out the while: 'A doctor! Monsieur d'Avrigny! No, I will go for him myself,' and he flew out of the room.

Morrel went out by the other door. A dreadful recollection chilled his heart; the conversation between Villefort and the doctor which he had overheard the night Mme de Saint-Méran died came back to his mind. These were the same symptoms, though less acute, that had preceded Barrois' death. On the other hand Monte Cristo's words seemed to resound in his ears: 'If you have need of anything, Morrel, come to me. I can do much,' and, quicker than thought, he sped from the Faubourg Saint-Honoré to the Champs-Élysées.

In the meantime Villefort arrived at the doctor's house in a hired cabriolet, and rang the bell so violently that the porter became quite alarmed and hastened to open the door. Without saying a word, Villefort ran up the stairs. The porter knew him and let him pass, calling after him: 'In his study, monsieur, in his study!' Villefort pushed open the door.

'Doctor,' cried Villefort, shutting the door behind him, 'there is a curse on my house!'

'What!' cried d'Avrigny, outwardly calm though inwardly deeply moved. 'Is there someone ill again?'

'Yes, Doctor,' said Villefort, clutching at his hair.

D'Avrigny's look said: 'I told you so,' but his lips slowly articulated the words: 'Who is dying in your house now? What new victim is going to accuse us of weakness before God?'

A painful sob broke from Villefort's lips. He went up to the doctor and, seizing his arm, said: 'Valentine! It is Valentine's turn!'

'Your daughter!' cried the doctor with grief and surprise.

'You see you were mistaken,' said the magistrate. 'Come and see her on her bed of torture and ask her forgiveness for having harboured suspicion against her.'

'Each time you have summoned me, it has been too late,' said d'Avrigny. 'No matter, I will come. But let us hasten. You have no time to lose in fighting against your enemies.'

'Oh, this time you shall not reproach me with weakness, Doctor. This time I shall seek out the murderer and give him his desserts.'

'Let us try to save the victim before thinking of

vengeance,' said d'Avrigny. The cabriolet which had brought Villefort took them both back at a gallop just as Morrel knocked at the Count of Monte Cristo's door.

The Count was in his study, and, with a worried look, was reading a note Bertuccio had just brought him. On hearing Morrel, who had left him barely two hours before, announced, he raised his head.

'What is the matter, Maximilian?' the Count asked. 'You are quite white, and the perspiration is rolling down your forehead.'

'I need your help, or rather, fool that I am, I thought you could help me where God alone can help!'

'I am all attention,' said the Count, smiling.

'Well, then, I will begin. One evening I was in a certain garden. I was hidden behind a clump of trees so that no one was aware of my presence. Two people passed close to me – allow me to conceal their names for the present. They were talking in a low voice, but I was so interested in all they said that I did not lose a word of their conversation. Someone had just died in the house to which this garden belonged. One of the two persons thus conversing was the owner of the garden, the other was the doctor. The former was confiding his fears and troubles to the latter, for it was the second time in a month that death had dealt such a sudden and unexpected blow in this house.'

'What reply did the doctor make?' asked Monte Cristo.

'He replied . . . he replied that it was not a natural death, and that it could only be attributed to . . .'

'To what?'

'To poison.'

'Really?' said Monte Cristo with a slight cough. 'Did you really hear that?'

'Yes, I did, and the doctor added that if a similar case occurred again, he would be compelled to appeal to justice. Well, death knocked a third time, yet neither the master of the house nor the doctor said anything. In all probability it is going to knock for the fourth time. In what way do you think the possession of this secret obliges me to act?'

'My dear friend,' said Monte Cristo, 'you are telling me something that everyone of us knows by heart. Look at me; I have not overheard any confidence, but I know it all as well as you do, and yet I have no scruples. If God's justice has fallen on this house, turn away your face, Maximilian, and let His hand hold sway. God has condemned them, and they must submit to their sentence. Three months ago it was Monsieur de Saint-Méran, two months ago it was Madame de Saint-Méran, today it is old Noirtier or young Valentine.'

'You knew about it then?' cried Morrel in a paroxysm of terror that made Monte Cristo shudder. 'You knew it and said nothing?'

'What is it to me?' replied Monte Cristo, shrugging his shoulders. 'Do I know these people? Must I lose the one to save the other? Indeed not, for I have no preference between the guilty one and the victim.'

'But I . . . I love her!' cried Morrel piteously.

'You love whom?' exclaimed Monte Cristo, jumping on to his feet and seizing Morrel's hands.

'I love her dearly, madly; I love her so much that I would shed all my blood to save her one tear. I love Valentine de Villefort, whom they are killing, do you hear? I love her, and I beseech you to tell me how I can save her.'

Monte Cristo uttered a wild cry, which only those can conceive who have heard the roar of a wounded lion.

Never had Morrel beheld such an expression; he shrunk back in terror. As for Monte Cristo, he closed his eyes for a moment after this outburst, and, during these few seconds, he restrained the tempestuous heaving of his breast as turbulent and foamy waves sink after a shower under the influence of the sun.

This silence and inward struggle lasted about twenty seconds, and then the Count raised his pale face.

'Behold, my dear friend, how God punishes the most boastful and unfeeling for their indifference in the face of terrible disasters,' he said. 'I looked on unmoved and curious. I watched this grim tragedy developing, and, like one of those fallen angels, laughed at the evil committed by men under the screen of secrecy. And now my turn has come, and I am bitten by the serpent whose tortuous course I have been watching – bitten to the core.'

A groan escaped Morrel's lips.

'Come, come, lamenting will not help us. Be a man, be strong and full of hope, for I am here, I am watching over you. I tell you to hope! Know once and for all that I never lie and never make a mistake. It is but midday and you can be grateful, Morrel, that you have come to me now instead of this evening or tomorrow morning. Listen to what I am going to tell you. It is midday, and, if Valentine is not dead now, she will not die!'

'How can you say that when I left her dying!'

Monte Cristo pressed his hand to his forehead. What was passing through that mind heavy with terrible secrets? What was the angel of light, or the angel of darkness, saying to that implacable human mind? God alone knows.

Monte Cristo raised his head once more, and this time his face was as calm as that of a sleeping child.

'Maximilian, return quietly to your home,' he said. 'I command you to do nothing, to take no steps, to let no shadow of sorrow be seen on your face. I will send you tidings. Go!'

'Count, you frighten me with your calm. Have you any power over death? Are you more than man? Are you an angel?'

The young man who would shrink from no danger now shrank from Monte Cristo in unutterable terror. Monte Cristo only looked at him with a smile mingled with sadness which brought the tears to Morrel's eyes.

'I can do much, my friend,' replied the Count. 'Go, I need to be alone . . .'

Conquered by the prodigious ascendancy Monte Cristo exercised on all around him, Morrel did not even attempt to resist. He shook the Count's hand and went out.

In the meantime Villefort and d'Avrigny had made all possible haste. When they returned Valentine was still unconscious, and the doctor examined her with the care called for by the circumstances and in the light of the secret he had discovered. Villefort awaited the result of the examination, watching every movement of the doctor's eyes and lips. Noirtier, more eager for a verdict than Villefort himself, was also waiting, and all in him became alert and sensitive.

At last d'Avrigny slowly said: 'She still lives!'

'She is saved?' asked the father.

'Since she still lives, she is.'

At this moment d'Avrigny met Noirtier's eyes, which sparkled with such extraordinary joy that he was startled and stood for a moment motionless, looking at the old man, who, on his part, seemed to anticipate and commend all he did.

The doctor laid the girl back on her chair; her lips were so pale and bloodless that they were scarcely outlined against the rest of her pallid face.

'Call Mademoiselle de Villefort's maid, if you please,' he said to Villefort.

Villefort left his daughter's side and himself went in search of the maid. Directly the door was shut behind him, the doctor approached Noirtier.

'You have something to say to me?' he asked.

The old man blinked expressively.

'To me alone?'

'Yes.'

'Very well, I will stay with you.'

Villefort returned, followed by the maid, and after them came Mme de Villefort.

'What ails the dear child?' she exclaimed with tears in her eyes, and affecting every proof of maternal love as she went up to Valentine and took her hand.

D'Avrigny continued to watch Noirtier; he saw the eyes of the old man dilate and grow large, his cheeks turn pale, and the perspiration break out on his forehead.

'Ah,' said he involuntarily as he followed the direction of Noirtier's eyes and fixed his own gaze on Mme de Villefort, who said: 'The poor child would be better in bed. Come and help me, Fanny.'

M. d'Avrigny saw an opportunity of being alone with M. Noirtier and nodded his assent, but forbade anyone to give her to eat or drink except what he prescribed. Valentine had returned to consciousness, but her whole frame was so shattered by the attack that she was unable to move and scarcely able to speak. D'Avrigny followed the invalid, wrote his prescriptions, and told Villefort to take a cab and go himself to the chemist's, have the prescriptions made up before his eyes, and wait for him in the girl's room. After renewing his instructions that Valentine was not to partake of anything, he returned to Noirtier and carefully closed the doors. Ascertaining that no one was listening, he said: 'Come now, you know something about your granddaughter's illness.'

'Yes,' motioned the old man.

'We have no time to lose. I will question you, and you will answer.'

Noirtier made a sign that he agreed.

'Did you anticipate the accident that has occurred to Valentine today?'

'Yes.'

D'Avrigny thought for a moment, then, drawing closer to Noirtier, said: 'Forgive me what I am going to say, but no stone must be left unturned in this terrible predicament. You saw Barrois die. Do you know what he died of?'

'Yes,' was the reply.

'Do you think he died a natural death?'

Something like a smile showed itself on Noirtier's immovable lips.

'Then the idea occurred to you that Barrois had been poisoned?'

'Yes.'

'Do you think the poison was intended for him?'

'No.'

'Now do you think that the same hand that struck Barrois in mistake for someone else has today struck Valentine?'

'Yes.'

'Then she will also succumb to it?' d'Avrigny asked, looking attentively at Noirtier to mark the effect these words would have on him.

'No,' he replied with an air of triumph which would have bewildered the cleverest of diviners.

'You hope, then? What do you hope?' said the doctor with surprise.

The old man gave him to understand that he could not answer.

'Ah, yes, it is true,' murmured d'Avrigny, and turning to Noirtier again: 'You hope that the murderer will grow weary of his attempts?'

'No.'

'Then do you hope that the poison will not take effect on Valentine?'

'Yes.'

'Then in what way do you think Valentine will escape?'

Noirtier fixed his gaze obstinately on one spot; d'Avrigny followed the direction of his eyes and saw that they were fixed on a bottle containing his medicine.

'Ha, ha,' said d'Avrigny, struck by a sudden thought. 'You conceived the idea of preparing her system against this poison?'

'Yes.'

'By accustoming her to it little by little?'

'Yes, yes, yes!' replied Noirtier, delighted at being understood.

'In fact, you heard me say there was brucine in your medicine, and wished to neutralize the effects of the poison by getting her system accustomed to it?'

Noirtier showed the same triumphant joy.

'And you have achieved it, too!' exclaimed the doctor. 'Without this precaution Valentine would have died this day, and no one could have helped her. As it is her system has suffered a violent shock, but this time, at any rate, she will not die.'

A supernatural joy shone in the old man's eyes as he raised them to Heaven with an expression of infinite gratitude. Just then Villefort returned.

'Here is what you asked for, Doctor,' said he.

'Was this medicine made up before you? It has not left your hands?'

'Just so.'

D'Avrigny took the bottle, poured a few drops of its contents into the palm of his hand, and swallowed them.

'It is all right,' said he. 'Now let us go to Valentine. I shall give my instructions to everyone, and you must see that no one disregards them.'

At the time that d'Avrigny returned to Valentine's room, accompanied by Villefort, an Italian priest, with dignified gait and a calm but decided manner, rented for his use the house adjoining that inhabited by M. de Villefort. It is not known what was done to induce the former occupiers to move out of it, but it was reported that the foundations were unsafe; however, this did not prevent the new tenant from moving in with his humble furniture at about five o'clock in the afternoon of the same day. The new tenant's name was Signor Giacomo Busoni.

Workmen were summoned at once, and the same night the few passers-by were astonished to find carpenters and masons at work repairing the foundations of this tottering house.

33

Valentine was confined to her bed; she was very weak and completely exhausted by the severe attack. During the night her sick brain wove vague and strange ideas and fleeting phantoms, while confused forms passed before her eyes, but in the daytime she was brought back to normal reality by her grandfather's presence. The old man had himself carried into his granddaughter's room every morning and watched over her with paternal care. Villefort would spend an hour or two with his father and child when he returned from the Law Courts. At six o'clock Villefort retired to his study, and at eight o'clock Monsieur d'Avrigny arrived, bringing with him the night draught for his young patient. Then Noirtier was taken back to his room, and a nurse, of the doctor's choice, succeeded them. She did not leave the bedside until ten or eleven o'clock, when Valentine had dropped off to sleep, and gave the keys of the room to M. de Villefort, so that no one could enter the room except through that occupied by Mme de Villefort and little Edward.

Morrel called on Noirtier every morning for news of

Valentine, and, extraordinary as it seemed, each day found him less anxious. For one thing, though she showed signs of great nervous excitement, Valentine's improvement was more marked each day; then, again, had not Monte Cristo already told him that if she was not dead in two hours, she would be saved? Four days had elapsed, and she still lived!

The nervous excitement we mentioned even pursued Valentine in her sleep, or rather in that state of somnolence which succeeded her waking hours. It was in the silence of the night that she saw the shadows pass which come to the rooms of the sick, fanning their fever with their quivering wings. At one time she would see her stepmother threatening her, at another time Morrel was holding his arms out to her, or again she was visited by beings who were almost strangers to her, such as the Count of Monte Cristo; during these moments of delirium even the furniture appeared to become animated. This lasted until about two or three o'clock, when she fell into a deep sleep from which she did not wake until the morning.

One evening after Villefort, d'Avrigny, and Noirtier had successively left her room, and the nurse, after placing within her reach the draught the doctor had prepared for her, had also retired, carefully locking the door after her, an unexpected incident occurred.

Ten minutes had elapsed since the nurse left. All at once Valentine dimly saw the door of the library, which was beside the fireplace in a hollow of the wall, slowly open without making the least sound. At any other time she would have seized the bell-pull to call for help, but nothing astonished her in her present state. She was aware that all the visions that surrounded her were the children of her delirium, for in the morning there was no trace of all these phantoms of the night.

A human figure emerged from behind the door. Valentine had become too familiar with such apparitions to be alarmed; she simply stared, hoping to see Morrel. The figure continued to approach her bed, then it stopped and appeared to listen with great attention. Just then a reflection from the night-light played on the face of her nocturnal visitor. 'It is not he,' she murmured, and waited, convinced that she was dreaming and that the man would disappear or turn into some other person. She noticed the rapid beating of her pulse, and remembered that the best means of dispelling these importunate visions was to take a drink of the draught which had been prescribed by the doctor to calm these agitations. It was so refreshing that, while allaying the fever, it seemed to cause a reaction of the brain and for a moment she suffered less. She, therefore, reached out her hand for the glass, but as she did so the apparition made two big strides to her bed and came so close to her that she thought she heard his breathing and felt the pressure of his hand. This time the illusion, or rather the reality, surpassed anything she had yet experienced. She began to believe herself fully awake and alive, and the knowledge that she was in full possession of her senses made her shudder.

Then the figure, from whom she could not divert her eyes and who appeared desirous of protecting rather than threatening her, took the glass, went over to the light and looked at the draught as though wishing to test its transparency and purity. But this elementary test did not satisfy him, and the man, or rather phantom, for he trod so gently that the carpet deadened the sound of his steps, took a spoonful of the beverage and swallowed it. Valentine watched all this with a feeling of stupefaction. She felt that it must all disappear to give place to another picture, but, instead of vanishing like a shadow, the man came alongside the bed, and, holding the glass to her, he said in an agitated voice: 'Now drink!'

Valentine started. It was the first time any of her visions had spoken to her in a living voice. She opened her mouth to scream: the man put his finger to his lips.

'The Count of Monte Cristo!' she murmured.

'Do not call anyone and do not be alarmed,' said the Count. 'You need not have the slightest shadow of suspicion or uneasiness in your mind. The man you see before you (for you are right this time, Valentine, it is not an illusion) is as tender a father and as respectful a friend as could ever appear to you in your dreams. Listen to me,' he went on, 'or rather, look at me. Do you see my red-rimmed eyes and my pale face, paler than usual? That is because I have not closed my eyes for an instant during the last four nights; for the last four nights have I been watching over you to protect and preserve you for our friend Maximilian.'

The sick girl's cheeks flushed with joy. 'Maximilian,' she repeated, for the sound of the name was very sweet to her. 'Maximilian! He has told you all then!'

'Everything. He has told me that you are his, and I have promised him that you shall live.'

'You have promised him that I shall live? Are you a doctor then?'

'Yes, and believe me, the best one Heaven could send just now.'

'You say you have been watching over me?' Valentine asked uneasily. 'Where? I have not seen you.'

'I have been hidden behind that door,' he said. 'It leads to an adjoining house which I have rented.'

Valentine bashfully turned her eyes away and said with some indignation: 'I think you have been guilty of an unparalleled indiscretion, and what you call protection I look upon as an insult.'

'Valentine, during this long vigil over you,' the Count said, 'all that I have seen has been what people have come to visit you, what food was prepared for you, and what was given you to drink. When I thought there was danger in the drink served to you, I entered as I have done now and emptied your glass, substituting a health-giving potion for the poison. Instead of producing death, as was intended, this drink made the blood circulate in your veins.'

'Poison! Death!' cried Valentine, believing that she was again under the influence of some feverish hallucination. 'What is that you say?'

'Hush, my child,' said Monte Cristo, placing his finger to his lips. 'I said poison and I also said death, but drink this.' The Count took from his pocket a phial containing a red liquid, of which he poured a few drops into a glass. 'When you have drunk that, take nothing more tonight.'

Valentine put out her hand but immediately drew it back in fear. Monte Cristo took the glass, drank half of its contents and handed it back to Valentine, who smiled at him and swallowed the rest.

'Oh, yes,' said she, 'I recognize the flavour of my

nightly drinks – the liquid which refreshed and calmed me. Thank you.'

'This has saved your life during the last four nights, Valentine,' said the Count. 'But how have I lived? Oh, the horrible nights I have gone through! The terrible tortures I have suffered when I saw the deadly poison poured into your glass and feared you would drink it before I could pour it away!'

'You say you suffered tortures when you saw the deadly poison poured into my glass?' replied Valentine, terror-stricken. 'If you saw the poison poured into my glass, you must have seen the person who poured it?'

'Yes, I did.'

Valentine sat up, pulling over her snow-white bosom the embroidered sheet still moist with the dews of fever, to which were now added those of terror.

'Oh, horrible! You are trying to make me believe that something diabolical is taking place; that they are continuing their attempts to murder me in my father's house; on my bed of sickness even! Oh no, it cannot be, it is impossible!'

'Are you the first one this hand has struck, Valentine? Have you not seen Monsieur de Saint-Méran, Madame de Saint-Méran, and Barrois fall under this blow? Would not Monsieur Noirtier have been another victim but for the treatment they have been giving him for nearly three years which has accustomed his system to this poison?'

'Then that is why Grandpapa has been making me share all his beverages for the past month?'

'Had they a bitter flavour, like half-dried orange-peel?'

'Oh, yes, they had.'

'That explains all,' said Monte Cristo. 'He also knows there is someone administering poison here, perhaps he even knows who the person is. He has been protecting you, his beloved child, against this evil. That is why you are still alive after having partaken of this poison, which is as a rule unmerciful.'

'But who is this . . . this murderer?'

'Have you never seen anyone enter your room at night?'

'Indeed I have. I have frequently seen shadows pass close to me and then disappear, and even when you came in just now I believed for a long time that I was either delirious or dreaming.'

'Then you do not know who is aiming at your life?'

'No. Why should anyone desire my death?'

'You will see this person,' said Monte Cristo, listening.

'How?' asked Valentine, looking round her in terror.

'Because you are not delirious or feverish tonight, you are wide awake. Midnight is just striking; this is the hour murderers choose. Summon all your courage to your assistance; still the beatings of your heart; let no sound escape your lips, feign sleep, and you will see, you will see!'

Valentine seized the Count's hand. 'I hear a noise,' said she. 'Go quickly.'

'*Au revoir*,' replied the Count, as with a sad smile he tiptoed to the door of the library. Before closing the door, he turned round once more and said: 'Not a movement, not a word, pretend you are asleep.' With this fearful injunction, the Count disappeared behind the door, which he closed noiselessly after him.

*

Valentine was alone. Except for the rumbling of distant carriages, all was still. Valentine's attention was concentrated on the clock in the room, which marked the seconds, and she noticed that they were twice as slow as the beating of her heart. Yet she was in a maze of doubt. She, who never did harm to anyone, could not imagine that anyone should desire her death. Why? To what purpose? What harm had she done that she should have an enemy? There was no fear of her falling asleep. A terrible thought kept her mind alert: there existed a person in the world who had attempted to murder her, and was going to make another attempt. What if the Count had not the time to run to her help! What if her last moment were approaching, and she would see Morrel no more!

This train of thought nearly compelled her to ring the bell for help, but she fancied she saw the Count's eye peering through the door, and at the thought of it her mind was overwhelmed with such shame that she did not know whether her feeling of gratitude towards him could be large enough to efface the painful effect of his indiscreet attention.

Thirty minutes, which seemed like an eternity, passed thus, and at length the clock struck the half-hour; at the same moment a slight scratching of finger-nails on the door of the library apprised Valentine that the Count was still watching.

Then Valentine seemed to hear the floor creaking on the opposite side, that is to say, in Edward's room. She listened with bated breath; the latch grated, and the door swung on its hinges. Valentine had raised herself up on her elbow, and she only just had time to lay herself down again and cover her eyes with her arms. Then trembling, agitated, and her heart heavy with indescribable terror, she waited.

Someone approached her bed and touched the curtains. Valentine summoned all her strength and breathed with the regular respiration which proclaims tranquil sleep.

'Valentine,' said a low voice.

A shudder went through the girl's whole frame, but she made no reply.

'Valentine,' the same voice repeated.

The same silence: Valentine had promised not to waken. Then all was still except for the almost noiseless sound of liquid being poured into the tumbler she had just emptied. Then from the vantage ground of her arm she risked opening her eyes a little and saw a woman in a white dressing-gown emptying some liquid from a phial into her tumbler. It was Mme de Villefort!

When Valentine recognized her stepmother she trembled so violently that the whole bed shook. Mme de Villefort instantly stepped back close to the wall, and from there, herself hidden behind the bed-hangings, watched attentively and silently for the slightest movement on Valentine's part. Summoning all her willpower to her assistance, the sick girl forced herself to close her eyes. Hearing Valentine's even breathing once more and reassured thereby that she was asleep, Mme de Villefort stretched out her arm once more, and, hidden as she was behind the curtains at the head of the bed, emptied the contents of the phial into Valentine's tumbler. Then she withdrew, but so quietly that not the least sound told Valentine that she was gone.

Soon the scratching of the fingernails on the library door roused the poor girl from the stupor into which she had fallen, and she raised her head with an effort. The door noiselessly turned on its hinges, and the Count of Monte Cristo appeared again.

'Well,' he asked, 'do you still doubt?'

'Alas!'

'Did you recognize her?'

Valentine groaned as she answered: 'I did, but I still cannot believe it! What am I to do? Can I not leave the house? . . . Can I not escape?'

'Valentine, the hand that pursues you now will follow you everywhere; your servants will be seduced with gold, and death will face you disguised in every shape and form; in the water you drink from the well, in the fruit you pluck from the tree.'

'But did you not say my grandfather's precautions had made me immune from poisoning?'

'From one kind of poisoning, but, even then, not large doses. The poison will be changed or the dose increased.'

He took the tumbler and put his lips to it.

'You see, it has already been done. She is no longer trying to poison you with brucine but with a simple narcotic. I can recognize the taste of the alcohol in which it has been dissolved. If you had drunk what Mme de Villefort has just poured into this tumbler, you would have been lost.'

'Oh, dear!' cried the young girl. 'Why does she pursue me thus? I cannot understand. I have never done her any harm!'

'But you are rich, Valentine; you have an income of two hundred thousand francs; what is more, you are keeping her son from getting this money.'

'Edward? Poor child! Is it for his sake that all these crimes are committed?'

'Ah, you understand at last. But I have foreseen all her plots, and so your enemy is beaten. You will live, Valentine, you will live to love and be loved; you will live to be happy and make a noble heart happy. But to attain this, you must have confidence in me. You must take blindly what I give you. You must trust no one, not even your father.'

'My father is not a party to this frightful plot, is he?' cried Valentine, wringing her hands.

'No, and yet your father, who is accustomed to juridical accusations, must know that all these people who have died in your house have not died natural deaths. Your father should have watched over you; he should be where I am now; he should have emptied this tumbler, and he should have risen up against this murderer.'

'I shall do all I can to live, for there are two persons in the world who love me so much that my death would mean their death – my grandfather and Maximilian.'

'I shall watch over them as I have watched over you,' said Monte Cristo. Then he went on: 'Whatever happens to you, Valentine, do not be alarmed. Though you suffer and lose your sight and hearing, do not be afraid; though you awaken and know not where you are, fear not; even though on awakening you find yourself in some sepulchral vault or coffin; collect your thoughts quickly and say to yourself: "At this moment a friend is watching over me, a father, a man who desires our happiness, mine and Maximilian's."'

Valentine gave him a grateful look and became submissive as a little child. Then the Count took from his waistcoat pocket the little emerald box, and, taking off the lid, put into Valentine's right hand a pill about the size of a pea. Valentine took it into her other hand and looked earnestly at the Count. There was a look of grandeur almost divine in the features of her sure protector. He answered her mute inquiry with a nod of assent.

She placed the pill in her mouth and swallowed it.

'Now goodbye, my child,' said he. 'I shall try to gain a little sleep, for you are saved!'

Monte Cristo looked long at the dear child as she gradually dropped off to sleep, overcome by the powerful narcotic he had given her. Taking the tumbler, he emptied three quarters of its contents into the fireplace, so that it might be believed Valentine had drunk it, and replaced it on the table. Then, regaining the door of his retreat he disappeared after casting one more look on Valentine, who was sleeping with the confidence and innocence of an angel at the feet of the Lord.

34

The night-light continued to burn on the mantelpiece; all noise in the streets had ceased and the silence of the room was oppressive. The door of Edward's room opened, and a head we have already seen appeared in the mirror opposite: it was Mme de Villefort, who had come to see the effects of her draught. She paused on the threshold and listened; then she slowly approached the night-table to see whether Valentine's tumbler was empty.

It was still a quarter full, as we know. Mme de Villefort took it and emptied the rest of the draught on to the embers, which she disturbed to facilitate the absorption of the liquid; then she carefully washed the tumbler, and, drying it with her handkerchief, placed it on the table.

At length she drew aside the curtain, and, leaning over the head of the bed, looked at Valentine. The girl breathed no more; her white lips had ceased to quiver, her eyes appeared to float in a bluish vapour and her long black eyelashes veiled a cheek as white as wax. Mme de Villefort contemplated this face with an expression eloquent in its impassivity. Lowering the quilt, she ventured to place her hand on the young girl's heart. It was still and cold. The only pulsation she felt was that in her own hand. She could not doubt that all was over. This terrible work was done; the poisoner had nothing more to do in the room. She retired with great precaution, fearing even to hear the sound of her own footsteps.

The hours passed, until a wan light began to filter through the blinds. It gradually grew brighter and brighter, till at length every object in the room was distinguishable. About this time the nurse's cough was heard on the staircase, and she entered the room with a cup in her hand.

One glance would have sufficed to convince a father or a lover that Valentine was dead, but this mercenary woman thought she slept.

'That is good,' she said, going up to the night-table;

'she has drunk some of her draught, the tumbler is three-quarters empty.' Then she went to the fireplace, rekindled the fire, made herself comfortable in an armchair and, though she had but just left her bed, took advantage of the opportunity to snatch a few minutes' sleep.

She was awakened by the clock striking eight. Astonished to find the girl still asleep, and alarmed at seeing her arm still hanging out of bed, she drew nearer. It was not until then that she noticed the cold lips, blue fingernails and still bosom. She tried to place the arm alongside the body, and its terrible stiffness could not deceive a nurse. With a horrified scream, she rushed to the door, crying out: 'Help! Help!'

'Help? For whom?' asked the doctor from the bottom of the stairs, it being the hour he usually called.

'What is the matter?' cried Villefort, rushing out of his room. 'Do you not hear the cry for help, Doctor?'

'Yes, let us go quickly to Valentine,' replied d'Avrigny.

But before the father and doctor could reach the room, all the servants who were on the same floor had rushed in, and, seeing Valentine pale and motionless on the bed, raised their hands heavenward and stood rooted to the spot with terror.

'Call Mme de Villefort! Wake Mme de Villefort!' shouted the Procureur du Roi from the door, for he seemed almost afraid to enter the room. But, instead of obeying, the servants simply stared at d'Avrigny, who had run to Valentine and taken her in his arms.

'This one too!' he murmured, letting her fall back on to the pillow again. 'My God! My God! When will it cease!'

Villefort rushed in. 'What do you say, Doctor?' he called out. 'Oh, Doctor . . . Doctor . . .'

'I say that Valentine is dead!' replied d'Avrigny in a voice that was terrible in its gravity.

M. de Villefort staggered as though his legs had given way under him, and he fell with his head on Valentine's bed.

Just then Mme de Villefort, with her dressing-gown half on, appeared. For a moment she stood on the threshold and seemed to be interrogating those present, at the same time endeavouring to summon up a few rebellious tears. Suddenly she stepped, or rather bounded, toward the table, with outstretched hands. She had seen d'Avrigny bend curiously over the table and take the tumbler she was sure she had emptied during the night. The tumbler was one-quarter full, just as it had been when she threw its contents on to the embers. Had Valentine's ghost suddenly confronted her, she would not have been more alarmed. The liquid was actually of the same colour as that which she had poured into the tumbler and which the girl had drunk; it was certainly the poison, and it could not deceive M. d'Avrigny, who was now examining it closely. It must have been a miracle worked by the Almighty, that, notwithstanding all her precautions, there should be some trace left, some proof to denounce the crime.

While Mme de Villefort remained as though rooted to the spot, looking like a statue of terror, and Villefort lay with his head hidden in the bedclothes oblivious to everything, d'Avrigny went to the window in order to examine more closely the contents of the tumbler. Dipping his finger into it, he tasted it.

'Ah!' he murmured. 'It is no longer brucine. Let me see what it is!'

He went to one of the cupboards, which was used as a medicine-chest, and, taking some nitric acid, poured a few drops into the liquid, which instantly turned blood-red.

'Ah!' said d'Avrigny in a tone which combined the horror of a judge to whom the truth has been revealed and the joy of the student who has solved a problem.

For an instant Mme de Villefort was beside herself; her eyes flared up and then dulled again; she staggered towards the door and disappeared. An instant later the distant thud was heard of a body falling. Nobody paid any attention to it, however. The nurse was intent on watching the chemical analysis, and Villefort was still prostrate. Only M. d'Avrigny had watched her and had noticed her departure. He raised the door-curtain, and, looking through Edward's room, perceived her stretched unconscious on the floor of her own room.

'Go and attend to Madame de Villefort; she is not well,' he said to the nurse.

'But Mademoiselle de Villefort?' stammered the nurse.

'Mademoiselle de Villefort has no further need of help: she is dead!'

'Dead! Dead!' moaned Villefort in a paroxysm of grief which the novelty of such a feeling in this heart of stone made all the more terrible.

'Dead, did you say?' cried a third voice. 'Who says that Valentine is dead?'

The two men turned round and perceived Morrel standing at the door, pale and terrible in his grief.

This is what had happened. Morrel had called at his

usual hour to obtain tidings of Valentine. Contrary to custom, he found the side door open.

In a turmoil of doubt and fear he flew up the stairs and through several deserted rooms until he reached Valentine's chamber. The door was open, and the first sound he heard was a sob. As through a mist, he saw a black figure on his knees and lost in a mass of white drapery. Fear, a terrible fear, rooted him to the spot.

It was at this moment that he heard a voice say: 'She is dead!' and a second voice repeat like an echo: 'Dead! Dead!'

Villefort rose, almost ashamed at being surprised in such a paroxysm of grief. The terrible office he had held for twenty-five years had placed him far outside the range of any human feeling. He looked at Morrel in a half-dazed manner.

'Who are you,' said he, 'that you are unaware that one does not enter a house where death reigns? Go, go!'

Morrel stood still; he could not take his eyes from the disordered bed and the pale figure lying on it.

'Do you hear me? Go!' cried Villefort, while d'Avrigny advanced towards Morrel to persuade him to leave.

Dazed, the young man looked at the corpse, the two men, and the room; then he hesitated for a moment and opened his mouth to reply, but could not give utterance to any of the thoughts that crowded in his brain; he thrust his hand in his hair and turned on his heels. D'Avrigny and Villefort, distracted for a moment from their morbid thoughts, looked at each other as though to say: 'He is mad.'

But in less than five minutes they heard the stairs

creaking under a heavy weight and perceived Morrel carrying Noirtier in his chair up the stairs with almost superhuman strength. Arrived at the top, Morrel set the chair down and wheeled it rapidly into Valentine's room. Noirtier's face was dreadful to behold as Morrel pushed him towards the bed.

'Look what they have done!' cried Morrel, resting one hand on the arm of the chair he had just wheeled up to the bedside, and with the other one pointing to Valentine.

In response to Morrel's words, the old man's whole soul seemed to show itself in his eyes, which became bloodshot; the veins of his throat swelled, and his neck, cheeks, and temples assumed a bluish hue. D'Avrigny rushed up to the old man and made him inhale a strong restorative.

'They ask me who I am, monsieur, and what right I have to be here!' cried Morrel, seizing the inert hand of the paralytic. 'Oh, you know! Tell them! Tell them!' And the young man's voice was choked with sobs. 'Tell them that I was betrothed to her; tell them she was my darling, the only one I love on earth.' And looking like the personification of broken strength, he fell heavily on his knees before the bed which his hands grasped convulsively. His grief was such that d'Avrigny turned his head away to hide his emotion, and Villefort, attracted by the magnetism which draws us towards such as have loved those we mourn, gave his hand to the young man without asking any further explanations.

For some time nothing was heard in the room but sobs, imprecations and prayers. Yet one sound gained the mastery over all the rest; it was the harsh and heart-rending breathing of Noirtier. With each intake it seemed as though his very lungs must burst asunder. At length Villefort, who had, so to say, yielded his place to Morrel and was now the most composed of them all, said to Maximilian: 'You say that you loved Valentine and that you were betrothed to her. I was unaware of your love for her, as also of your engagement. Yet I, her father, forgive you, for I see that your grief is deep and true. Besides, my own grief is too great for anger to find a place in my heart. But, as you see, the angel you hoped to possess has left us. Take your farewell of her sad remains. Valentine has now no further need of anyone but the priest and the doctor.'

'You are mistaken, monsieur,' cried Morrel, rising on to one knee, and his heart was pierced with a pang sharper than any he had yet felt. 'You are quite wrong. Valentine, as I judge from the manner of her death, not only needs a priest but also an avenger. Send for the priest, Monsieur de Villefort; I will be her avenger!'

'What do you mean, monsieur?' murmured Villefort, trembling before this new idea of Morrel's.

'What I mean is that there are two personalities in you: the father has done enough weeping, it is now time that the magistrate bethought him of his duty.'

Noirtier's eyes gleamed, and d'Avrigny drew nearer.

'I know what I am saying,' continued Morrel, reading the thoughts that were revealed on the faces of those present, 'and you all know as well as I do what I am going to say. Valentine has been murdered!'

'You are mistaken, monsieur,' replied Villefort. 'No crimes are committed in my house. Fate is against me, God is trying me. It is a horrible thought, but no one has been murdered.'

'I tell you that murder has been committed here!' cried the young man, lowering his voice but speaking in a very decided tone. 'This is the fourth victim during the past four months. I declare that they attempted to poison Valentine four days ago but failed owing to Monsieur Noirtier's precautions. I declare that the dose has now been doubled or else the poison changed, so that their dastardly work has succeeded. You know all this as well as I do, for this gentleman warned you, both as a friend and a doctor.'

And then it was d'Avrigny's turn.

'I, too, join Monsieur Morrel in demanding justice for the crime,' said he. 'My blood boils at the thought that my cowardly indifference has encouraged the murderer.'

'Have mercy! Oh, my God, have mercy!' murmured Villefort, beside himself.

Morrel raised his head, and, seeing that Noirtier's eyes were shining with an almost supernatural light, he said: 'Wait a moment, Monsieur Noirtier wishes to speak. Do you know the murderer?' he continued, turning to the old man.

'Yes,' replied Noirtier.

'And you will help us to find him?' cried the young man. 'Listen, Monsieur d'Avrigny, listen!'

Noirtier threw the unhappy Morrel a sad smile, one of those smiles expressed in his eyes which had so often made Valentine happy, and demanded his attention. Then having, so to say, riveted his questioner's eyes on his own, he looked towards the door.

'Do you wish me to leave the room?' asked Morrel sadly.

'Yes,' looked Noirtier.

'Alas! Alas! Have pity on me!'

The old man's eyes remained relentlessly fixed on the door.

'May I at least come back again?'

'Yes.'

'Am I to go alone?'

'No.'

'Whom shall I take with me? The doctor?'

'Yes.'

'But will Monsieur de Villefort understand you?'

'Yes.'

'Have no fear, I understand my father very well,' said Villefort, overjoyed that the inquiries between him and his father were to be made privately.

D'Avrigny took the young man's arm and led him into the adjoining room. At length, after a quarter of an hour had elapsed, a faltering footstep was heard, and Villefort appeared on the threshold. 'Come,' said he, leading them back to Noirtier.

Morrel looked fixedly at Villefort. His face was livid; large drops of perspiration rolled down his face; between his teeth was a pen twisted out of shape and bitten to half its natural length.

'Messieurs,' said he in a voice choked with emotion, turning to d'Avrigny and Morrel, 'give me your word of honour that this terrible secret shall remain buried for ever amongst ourselves.'

The two men stirred uneasily.

'But the culprit! . . . the murderer! . . .' cried Morrel.

'Fear not, justice shall be done,' said Villefort. 'My father has revealed to me the name of the culprit, and, though he is as anxious for revenge as you are, he entreats you even as I do to keep the crime a secret. If my father makes this request, it is only because he knows that Valentine will be terribly avenged. He knows me, and I have given him my word. I only ask three days. Within three days the vengeance I shall have taken for the murder of my child will be such as to make the most indifferent of men shudder.' As he said these words, he ground his teeth and grasped the lifeless hand of his old father.

'Will this promise be fulfilled, Monsieur Noirtier?' Morrel asked, while d'Avrigny questioned him with his eyes.

'Yes,' signalled Noirtier with a look of sinister joy.

'Then swear,' said Villefort, joining d'Avrigny's and Morrel's hands, 'swear that you will spare the honour of my house and leave it to me to avenge my child!'

D'Avrigny turned round and gave a faint 'Yes' in reply, but Morrel pulled his hand away and rushed towards the bed. Pressing his lips to Valentine's mouth, he fled out of the room with a long groan of despair.

When he had gone, d'Avrigny asked Villefort whether he desired any particular priest to pray over Valentine.

'No,' was Villefort's reply. 'Fetch the nearest one.'

'The nearest one is an Italian priest who lives in the house next to your own,' replied the doctor. 'Shall I summon him?'

'Pray do so.'

'Do you wish to speak to him?'

'All I desire is to be left alone. Make my excuse to him. Being a priest, he will understand my grief.'

D'Avrigny found the priest standing at his door and went up to him saying: 'Would you be good enough to render a great service to an unhappy father who has lost his daughter? I mean Monsieur de Villefort, the Procureur du Roi.'

'Ah, yes, I know that death is rife in that house,' replied the priest in a very pronounced Italian accent.

'Then I need not tell you what service it is that he ventures to ask of you?'

'I am coming, monsieur,' replied the priest, 'and I venture to say that no prayers will be more fervent than mine.'

D'Avrigny led the priest into Valentine's room without meeting M. de Villefort, who was closeted in his study. As soon as they entered the room Noirtier's eyes met those of the priest, and no doubt something particular attracted him, for his gaze never left him. D'Avrigny recommended the living as well as the dead to the priest's care, and he promised to devote his prayers to Valentine and his attentions to Noirtier.

The abbé set to his task in all seriousness, and as soon as d'Avrigny had left the room, he not only bolted the door through which the doctor had passed, but also the one leading to Mme de Villefort's room – doubtless that he might not be disturbed in his prayers or Noirtier in his grief.

The Abbé Busoni watched by the corpse until daylight, when he returned to his house without disturbing anyone. When M. de Villefort and the doctor went to see how M. Noirtier had spent the night, they were greatly amazed to find him sitting in his big armchair, which served him as a bed, in a peaceful sleep, with something approaching a smile on his face.

35

Before paying his last respects to Valentine, Monte Cristo called on Danglars. From his window the banker saw the Count's carriage enter the courtyard, and went to meet him with a sad though affable smile.

'Well, Count,' said he, holding out his hand. 'Have you come to offer me your condolence? Have you noticed that people of our generation – pardon me, you are not of our generation, for you are still young – people of my generation are not lucky this year. For example, look at our puritan, the Procureur du Roi, whose whole family are dying in a most mysterious fashion, the latest victim being his daughter. Then again there is Morcerf, who is dishonoured and killed by his own hand, while I have lost my daughter as well.'

'Your daughter?'

'Yes, she has gone away with her mother, and, knowing her as I do, I am sure she will never return to France again. She could not endure the shame brought on her by Morcerf.'

'Still, my dear Baron,' said Monte Cristo, 'such family griefs, which would crush a poor man whose child was his only fortune, are endurable to a millionaire.'

Danglars looked at the Count out of the corner of his eye; he wondered whether he was mocking him or whether he meant it seriously. 'Yes,' he said, 'it is a fact; if wealth brings consolation, I should be consoled, for I am certainly rich. That reminds me,' said he, 'when you came in, I was drawing up five little bills; I have already signed two, will you excuse me while I sign the other three?'

'Certainly, Baron.'

There was a moment's silence broken only by the scratching of the banker's pen.

'Are they Spanish, Hayti, or Neapolitan bonds?' said Monte Cristo.

'Neither the one nor the other,' replied Danglars with a self-satisfied smile. 'They are bearer bonds on the Bank of France. Look there,' he added, 'if I am the king, you are the emperor of finance, but have you seen many scraps of paper of this size each worth a million?'

The Count took the scraps of paper which the banker proudly handed him and read:

To the Governor of the Bank of France.
Please pay to my order from the deposit placed by
me with you the sum of one million in present currency.

BARON DANGLARS

'One, two, three, four, five!' counted Monte Cristo. 'Five millions! Why, you are a regular Croesus! It is marvellous, especially if, as I suppose, the amount is paid in cash.'

'It will be.'

'It is truly a fine thing to have such credit and could only happen in France. Five scraps of paper worth five millions: it must be seen to be believed.'

'Do you discredit it?'

'No.'

'You say it in such a tone . . . But wait, if it gives you pleasure, accompany my clerk to the bank, and you will see him leave with treasury bills to that amount.'

'No,' said Monte Cristo, folding the five notes, 'indeed not. It is so interesting that I will make the experiment myself. My credit with you amounted to six millions: I have had nine hundred thousand, so that I still have a balance of five million, one hundred thousand francs. I will accept the five scraps of paper that I now hold as bonds, on the strength of your signature alone; here is a general receipt for six millions which will settle our account. I made it out beforehand because, I must confess, I am greatly in need of money today.'

With one hand Monte Cristo put the notes into his pocket, and with the other presented the receipt to the banker.

Danglars was terror-stricken.

'What!' he stammered. 'Do you intend taking that money, Count? Excuse me, it is a deposit I hold for the hospitals, and I promised to pay it this morning.'

'That is a different matter,' said Monte Cristo. 'I do not care particularly about these five notes. Pay me in some other way. It was only to satisfy my curiosity that I took these, so that I might tell everyone that, without any advice or even asking for five minutes' grace, Danglars' bank had paid me five millions in cash. It would have been so remarkable! Here are your bonds, however. Now give me bills of some other sort.'

He held out the five bonds to Danglars, who, livid

to the lips, stretched out his hand as the vulture stretches out its claw through the bars of its cage to seize the piece of meat that is being snatched from it. All of a sudden he changed his mind, and with a great effort restrained himself. A smile passed over his face and gradually his countenance became serene.

'Just as you like,' he said.

Monte Cristo put the five bills into his pocket again.

'Yes,' said Danglars. 'Certainly keep my signatures. But you know no one sticks to formalities more than a financier does, and as I had destined that money for the hospitals it appeared to me, for a moment, that I should be robbing them by not giving them just those five bonds: as though one franc were not as good as another.' And he began to laugh, loudly but nervously. 'But there is still a sum of one thousand francs?'

'Oh, that is a mere trifle. The commission must come to nearly that much. Keep it and we shall be quits.'

'Are you speaking seriously, Count?' asked Danglars.

'I never joke with bankers,' replied Monte Cristo with such a serious air that it was tantamount to impertinence, and he turned towards the door just as the footman announced M. de Boville, Treasurer General of Hospitals.

'Upon my word,' said Monte Cristo, 'it appears I was only just in time for your signatures – another minute and I should have had a rival claimant.'

The Count of Monte Cristo exchanged a ceremonious bow with M. de Boville, who was standing in the waiting-room and was at once shown into M. Danglars' room. The Count's stern face was illuminated by a fleeting smile as he caught sight of the portfolio the Treasurer General carried in his hand. He found his carriage at the door and drove to the bank.

In the meantime the banker advanced to meet the Treasurer General with a forced smile on his lips.

'Good morning, my dear creditor,' he said, 'for I am sure it is the creditor.'

'You are quite right, Baron,' said M. de Boville. 'I come in the name of the hospitals; through me the widows and orphans have come to ask you for an alms of five millions! Did you receive my letter yesterday?'

'Yes.'

'Here is my receipt.'

'My dear Monsieur de Boville,' began Danglars, 'if you so permit, your widows and orphans will be good enough to wait twenty-four hours, as Monsieur de Monte Cristo, who has just left me . . . You saw him, I think, did you not?'

'I did. Well?'

'Well, Monsieur de Monte Cristo took with him their five millions.'

'How is that?'

'The Count had unlimited credit upon me opened by Messrs Thomson and French, of Rome. He came to ask me for five millions right away, and I gave him cheques on the bank. You can well understand that if I draw ten millions on one and the same day, the Governor will think it rather strange. Two separate days will be quite a different matter,' he added with a smile.

'What?' cried M. de Boville in an incredulous tone. 'You paid five millions to the gentleman who just left the house! Five millions!'

'Yes, here is his receipt.'

M. de Boville took the paper Danglars handed him and read:

Received from Baron Danglars the sum of five million francs, which he will redeem at will from Messrs Thomson and French of Rome.

'It is really true then,' he said. 'Why, this Count of Monte Cristo must be a nabob! I must call on him, and get a pious grant from him.'

'You have as good as received it. His alms alone amount to more than twenty thousand francs a month.'

'How magnificent! I shall set before him the example of Madame de Morcerf and her son.'

'What is that?'

'They have given their whole fortune to the hospitals. They say they do not want money obtained by unclean means.'

'What are they to live on?'

'The mother has retired to the provinces, and the son is going to enlist in the Spahis. I registered the deed of gift yesterday.'

'How much did they possess?'

'Oh, not very much. Twelve to thirteen thousand francs. But let us return to our millions.'

'Willingly,' said Danglars, as naturally as possible. 'Do you require this money urgently?'

'Yes, our accounts are to be audited tomorrow.'

'Tomorrow? Why did you not tell me so at once? Tomorow is a long time hence. At what time does the auditing take place?'

'At two o'clock.'

'Send round at midday, then,' said Danglars with a smile.

'I will come myself.'

'Better still, as it will give me the pleasure of seeing you again.' With which they shook hands, and M. de Boville left. He was no sooner outside than Danglars called after him with great force, 'Fool!' Then he added: 'Yes, yes, come at noon; I shall be far from here.'

Then he double-locked the door, emptied all the cash drawers, collected about fifty thousand francs in bank notes, burnt several papers, placed others in conspicuous parts of the room, and finally wrote a letter which he sealed and addressed to Baroness Danglars.

Taking a passport from his drawer, he looked at it, muttering: 'Good! It is valid for another two months! Farewell, faithless wife! Farewell, Paris!'

36

As the *cortège* carrying Valentine's body was leaving Paris, a carriage drawn by four horses came along at full speed and suddenly stopped. Monte Cristo alighted and mingled in the crowd who were following the hearse on foot. When Château-Renaud and Beauchamp perceived him, they also alighted from their carriages and joined him. The Count's eager eyes searched the crowd; it was obvious that he was looking for someone. At length he could restrain himself no longer.

'Where is Morrel?' he asked. 'Do either of you gentlemen know?'

'We have already asked ourselves that question. No one seems to have seen him.'

The Count remained silent but continued to look around him.

They arrived at the cemetery. Monte Cristo peered into every clump of yew and pine, and was at length relieved of all anxiety: he saw a shadow glide along the dark bushes and recognized him whom he sought. This shadow crossed rapidly but unseen to the hearse and walked beside the coffin-bearers to the spot selected for the grave. Everyone's attention was occupied, but Monte Cristo saw only the shadow, which was otherwise unobserved by all around him. Twice did the Count leave the ranks to see whether the man had not some weapon hidden under his clothes. When the procession stopped, the shadow was recognized as Morrel. His coat was buttoned up to his chin, his cheeks were hollow and livid, and he nervously clasped and unclasped his hands. He took his place against a tree on a hillock overlooking the grave, so that he might not miss one detail of the service.

Everything was conducted in the usual manner, though Monte Cristo heard and saw nothing; or rather, he saw nothing but Morrel, whose calmness and motionlessness were alarming to him, who could read what was passing through the young man's mind.

The funeral over, the guests returned to Paris. When everyone had gone, Maximilian left his place against the tree and spent a few minutes in silent prayer beside Valentine's grave; then he got up, and, without looking back once, turned down the Rue de la

Roquette. Monte Cristo had been hiding behind a large tomb, watching Morrel's every movement. Dismissing his carriage, he now followed the young man on foot as he crossed the canal and entered the Rue Meslay by the boulevards.

Five minutes after the door had been closed on Morrel, it was opened again for Monte Cristo. Julie was in the garden watching Penelon, who, taking his position as gardener very seriously, was grafting some Bengal roses.

'Ah, is that you, Count!' she cried with the delight each member of the family generally manifested every time he made his appearance there.

'Maximilian has just come in, has he not?' asked the Count.

'I think I saw him come in,' replied the young woman, 'but pray call Emmanuel.'

'Excuse me a minute, madame, I must go up to Maximilian at once. I have something of the greatest importance to tell him.'

'Go along, then,' she said, giving him a charming smile.

Monte Cristo soon ran up the two flights of stairs that separated Maximilian's room from the ground floor; he stood on the landing for a moment and listened; there was not a sound. As is the case in most old houses, the door of the chamber was panelled with glass. Maximilian had shut himself inside, and it was impossible to see through the glass what was happening in the room, as a red silk curtain was drawn across. The Count's anxiety was manifested by his high colour, an unusual sign of emotion in this impassive man.

'What am I to do?' he murmured, as he reflected for a moment. 'Shall I ring? Oh, no, the sound of a bell announcing a visitor often hastens the resolution of those in the position in which Maximilian must now be; then the tinkling of the bell will be accompanied by another sound.' He was trembling from head to foot, and, with his usual lightning-like rapidity in coming to a decision, he suddenly pushed his elbow through one of the panes of the door, which broke into a thousand pieces. Raising the curtain, he saw Morrel at his desk with a pen in his hand. He started up with a jump when he heard the noise made by the broken glass.

'I am so sorry,' said the Count. 'It is nothing; I slipped, and in doing so pushed my elbow through your door. However, I will now take the opportunity of paying you a visit. Pray, do not let me disturb you.' Putting his hand through the broken glass, he opened the door.

Obviously annoyed, Morrel came forward to meet the Count, not so much with the intention of welcoming him as of barring his way.

'It is your servant's fault,' said Monte Cristo, rubbing his elbow. 'Your floors are as slippery as glass.'

'Have you cut yourself?' Morrel asked coldly.

'I do not know. But what were you doing? Were you writing with those ink-stained fingers?'

'Yes, I was writing,' replied Morrel. 'I do sometimes, though I am a soldier.'

Monte Cristo went farther into the room, and Morrel was compelled to let him pass.

The Count looked around him.

'Why are your pistols on your desk beside you?' said he, pointing to the two weapons.

'I am going on a journey.'

'Maximilian,' Monte Cristo, 'let us lay aside our masks. You can no more deceive me with your exterior calmness than I can mislead you with my frivolous solicitude. You no doubt understand that to have acted as I have done, to have broken a pane of glass, intruded on the privacy of a friend, I must have been actuated by a terrible conviction. Morrel, you intend to take your life!'

'Well, and if I have decided to turn this pistol against myself, who shall prevent me?' cried Morrel, passing from his momentary appearance of calmness to an expression of violence. 'When I say that all my hopes are frustrated, my heart broken, and my life worthless, since the world holds no more charms for me, nothing but grief and mourning; when I say that it would be a mercy to let me die, for, if you do not, I shall lose my reason and become mad; when I tell you all this with tears of heart-felt anguish, who can say to me: "You are wrong?" Who would prevent me from putting an end to such a miserable existence? Tell me, Count, would you have the courage?'

'Yes, Morrel,' said Monte Cristo, in a voice which contrasted strangely with the young man's excitement. 'Yes, I would.'

'You!' cried Morrel with an angry and reproachful expression. 'You who deceived me with absurd hopes! Count of Monte Cristo, my false benefactor, the universal saviour, be satisfied, you shall see your friend die . . .'

With a maniacal laugh, he rushed towards the pistols again. Pale as a ghost, his eyes darting fire, Monte Cristo put his hand over the weapons saying: 'And I repeat once more that you shall not take your life!'

'And who are you that you should take upon yourself such an authority over a free and rational being?'

'Who am I?' repeated Monte Cristo. 'I will tell you. I am the only man who has the right to say to you: "Morrel, I do not wish your father's son to die today!"'

Morrel, involuntarily acknowledging the Count's ascendancy over him, gave way a step.

'Why do you speak of my father?' he stammered. 'Why bring my father's memory into what I am going to do today?'

'Because I am the man who saved your father's life when he wanted to take it as you do today! Because I am the man who sent the purse to your sister and the *Pharaon* to old Monsieur Morrel! Because I am Edmond Dantès!'

Morrel staggered, choking and crushed; his strength failed him, and with a cry he fell prostrate at Monte Cristo's feet. Then all of a sudden his true nature completely reasserted itself; he rose and flew out of the room, calling out at the top of his voice:

'Julie! Julie! Emmanuel! Emmanuel!'

Monte Cristo also attempted to rush out, but Maximilian would sooner have let himself be killed than let go of the handle of the door, which he shut against him. Upon hearing Maximilian's shouts, Julie, Emmanuel, Penelon, and several servants came running up the stairs in alarm. Morrel seized Julie by the hand, and, opening the door, called out in a voice stifled with sobs: 'On your knees! On your knees! This is our benefactor, this is the man who saved our father, this is . . .' He was going to say 'Edmond Dantès,' but the Count restrained him. Julie threw herself into the

Count's arms, Emmanuel embraced him, and Morrel once more fell on to his knees. Then this man of iron felt his heart swelling within him, a burning flame seemed to rise in his throat, and from thence rush to his eyes; he bowed his head and wept. For a while nothing was heard in the room but weeping and sobbing; a sound that must have been sweet to the angels in Heaven!

At last the Count, realizing that he must make one final struggle against his friend's grief, took Julie's and Emmanuel's hands in his, and said to them with the gentle authority of a father: 'My good friends, I pray you, leave me alone with Maximilian.'

Julie drew her husband away, saying: 'Let us leave them.'

The Count stayed behind with Morrel, who remained as still as a statue.

'Come, come!' said the Count, tapping him on the shoulder with his burning fingers. 'Are you going to be a man again?'

'Yes, since I am again beginning to suffer.'

The Count's forehead wrinkled in apparent indecision. 'Maximilian! Maximilian!' said he. 'The ideas to which you are giving way are unworthy of a Christian.'

'Oh, do not be afraid!' said Morrel, raising his head and smiling at the Count with a smile of ineffable sadness. 'I shall make no attempt on my life. My grief itself will kill me!'

'I tell you to hope, Morrel,' insisted the Count.

'Ah! You are trying to persuade me, you are trying to inspire me with the belief that I shall see Valentine again.'

The Count smiled.

'My friend, my father!' cried Morrel excitedly. 'The ascendancy you hold over me alarms me. Weigh your words carefully, for my eyes lighten up again and my heart takes on a fresh lease of life.'

'Hope, my dear friend!' repeated the Count.

'Ah, you are playing with me,' said Morrel, falling from the heights of exaltation to the abyss of despair. 'You are doing the same as those good, or rather selfish, mothers who calm their children's sorrow with honeyed words because their cries annoy them. No, my friend. I will bury my grief so deep down in my heart and shall guard it so carefully from the eyes of man that you will need have no sympathy for me. Goodbye, my friend, goodbye!'

'On the contrary,' said the Count. 'From now onward, you will live with me and not leave me. In a week we shall have left France behind us.'

'Do you still bid me hope?'

'I do, for I know of a remedy for you.'

'You are only prolonging my agony. Have pity on me, Count!'

'I feel so much pity for you that if I do not cure you in a month to the very day, mark my words, Morrel, I myself will place before you two loaded pistols and a cup of the deadliest poison – a poison which is more potent and prompt of action than that which killed Valentine.'

'Do you promise me this?'

'I not only promise it, I swear it,' said Monte Cristo, giving him his hand.

'Then on your word of honour, if I am not consoled in a month, you leave me free to take my life, and, whatever I may do, you will not call me ungrateful?'

'In a month to the day, and it is a date that is sacred to us. I do not know whether you remember that today is the 5th of September? It is ten years ago today that I saved your father when he wanted to take his life.'

Morrel seized the Count's hands and kissed them, and the Count suffered him to do it, for he felt that this homage was due to him.

'In a month,' continued Monte Cristo, 'you will have before you on the table at which we shall both be seated, two trusty weapons and a gentle death-giving potion, but in return you must promise me to wait until then and live.'

'I swear it!' exclaimed Morrel.

Monte Cristo drew the young man towards him and held him for a few minutes in close embrace.

'Well, then, from today you will live with me; you can occupy Haydee's rooms, and my daughter will be replaced by my son.'

'Haydee?' said Morrel. 'What has happened to Haydee?'

'She left last night.'

'To leave you for ever?'

'To wait for me . . . Make ready to join me at Rue des Champs-Élysées and now let me out without anyone seeing me.'

37

It will be remembered that the Abbé Busoni stayed alone with Noirtier in the chamber of death. Ever since the day on which he had conversed with the priest, Noirtier's despair had given way to complete resignation, to the great astonishment of all who knew his deep affection for Valentine.

The assizes were to be opened in three days, and Villefort spent most of his day closeted in his study preparing his cases, which afforded him the only distraction from his sorrow. Once only had he seen his father. Harassed and fatigued, he had gone into the garden and, deep in gloomy thought, he paced the avenues, lopping off with his cane the long, withering stalks of the hollyhocks, which stood on either side of the path like the ghosts of the brilliantly coloured flowers that had bloomed in the season just passed. All of a sudden his eyes were involuntarily attracted towards the house, where he heard the noisy play of Edward, who had come home from school to spend the Sunday and Monday with his mother. At the same time he perceived Noirtier at one of the open windows, to which he had had his chair wheeled so that he might enjoy the last warm rays of the sun.

The old man's eyes were riveted on a spot which Villefort could only imperfectly distinguish, but their expression was so full of hatred, venom, and impatience that the Procureur du Roi, ever quick to read the impressions on that face that he knew so well, turned out of his path to discover the object of that dark look. He saw Mme de Villefort seated under a clump of lime-trees nearly divested of their foliage. She had a book in her hand which she laid aside from time to time to smile at her son or to return to him his ball, which he persisted in throwing into the garden from the salon. Villefort turned pale, for he understood what was passing through his father's mind. Noirtier continued to look at the same object, but suddenly his eyes were turned from the wife to the husband, and Villefort himself had to submit to the gaze of those piercing eyes, which, while changing their objective, had also changed their language, but without losing their menacing expression.

'Yes, yes!' Villefort replied from below. 'Have patience for one day more. What I have said shall be done!'

These words seemed to calm Noirtier, for he turned away his eyes. Villefort, on the other hand, tore open his coat, for it was choking him, and, passing his hand over his brow, returned to his study.

The night was cold and calm; everybody in the house had gone to bed as usual. Only Villefort once more remained up and worked till five o'clock in the morning. The first sitting of the assizes was to take place the next day, which was a Monday. Villefort saw that day dawn pale and gloomy.

He opened his window; a red streak traversed the sky in the distance, and seemed to cut in two the slender poplars which stood out in black relief against the horizon.

Involuntarily his glance fell on the window where he had seen Noirtier the previous evening. The curtains were drawn, yet his father's image was so vividly impressed on his mind that he addressed himself to the closed window, as though it were open and he still beheld the menacing old man.

'Yes,' he muttered, 'yes, it shall be done!'

His head dropped upon his chest, and, with his head thus bowed, he paced his room several times till at last he threw himself on a settee, not so much because he wanted to sleep as to rest his tired and cold limbs. By degrees everybody in the house began to stir. From his room Villefort heard all the noises that constitute the life of a house: the opening and shutting of doors, the tinkle of Mme de Villefort's bell summoning her maid, and the shouts of his boy, who woke fully alive to the enjoyments of life, as children at that age generally do.

The breakfast-hour arrived, but M. de Villefort did not make his appearance. The valet entered his room.

'Madame desires me to remind you that it has struck eleven o'clock, monsieur, and that the sitting begins at noon,' he said.

For a moment Villefort remained silent, digging his fingernails into his cheek, the paleness of which was accentuated by his ebony black hair.

'Tell madame that I wish to speak to her,' he said at length, 'and that I request her to wait for me in her room. Then come and shave me.'

'Yes, monsieur.'

The valet returned almost immediately, and, after having shaved Villefort, helped him into a sombre black suit. When he had finished, he said: 'Madame said she would expect you, monsieur, as soon as you were dressed.'

'I am going to her.'

With his papers under his arm and his hat in his hand, he went to his wife's room. He paused outside for a moment to wipe his clammy forehead. Then he pushed open the door.

Mme de Villefort was sitting on an ottoman impatiently turning over the leaves of a newspaper which

Edward, by way of amusing himself, was tearing to pieces before his mother had time to finish reading it.

'Ah, here you are,' she said, with a calm and natural voice. 'But you are very pale! Have you been working all through the night again? Why did you not come and breakfast with us?'

Mme de Villefort had asked one question after another in order to elicit one single answer, but to all her inquiries M. de Villefort remained as cold and mute as a statue.

'Edward, go and play in the salon,' he said, looking sternly at the child. 'I wish to speak to your mother.'

Mme de Villefort trembled as she beheld his cold countenance and heard his resolute tone, which presaged some new disaster. Edward raised his head and looked at his mother, and, seeing she did not confirm his father's orders, proceeded to cut off the heads of his lead soldiers.

'Edward, do you hear me? Go!' cried M. de Villefort, so harshly that the child jumped.

Unaccustomed to such treatment, he rose, pale and trembling, but whether from fear or anger it was difficult to say. His father went up to him, took him in his arms and, kissing him, said: 'Go, my child, go!'

Edward went out, and M. de Villefort locked the door behind him.

'Oh, heavens! What is the matter?' cried the young woman, endeavouring to read her husband's inmost thoughts, and forcing a smile which froze M. de Villefort's impassibility.

'Madame, where do you keep the poison you generally use?' the magistrate said slowly without any preamble, as he placed himself between his wife and the door.

Madame's feelings were those of the lark when it sees the kite over its head making ready to swoop down upon it. A harsh, stifled sound, which was neither a cry nor a sigh, escaped from her lips, and she turned deathly white.

'I . . . do not understand,' she said, sinking back on to her cushions.

'I asked you,' continued Villefort in a perfectly calm voice, 'where you hide the poison by means of which you have killed my father-in-law, my mother-in-law, Barrois, and my daughter Valentine.'

'Whatever are you saying?' cried Mme de Villefort, clasping her hands.

'It is not for you to question, but to answer.'

'My husband or the judge?' stammered Mme de Villefort.

'The judge, madame, the judge.'

The pallor of the woman, the anguish in her look, and the trembling of her whole frame, were frightful to behold.

'You do not answer, madame?' cried her terrible examiner. Then, with a smile which was more terrifying than his anger, he added: 'It must be true since you do not deny it.'

She made a movement.

'And you cannot deny it,' added Villefort, extending his hand towards her as though to arrest her in the name of the law. 'You have accomplished these crimes with impudent skill; nevertheless, you have been able to deceive only those who were blinded by their affection for you. Ever since the death of Madame de Saint-Méran have I known that there was a poisoner in my house – Monsieur d'Avrigny warned me of it.

After the death of Barrois – may God forgive me! – my suspicions fell on someone, an angel, for I am ever suspicious, even where there is no crime. But since the death of Valentine there has been no doubt in my mind, madame, or in that of others. Thus your crime, known by two persons and suspected by many, will be made public. Moreover, as I told you just now, I do not speak to you as your husband, but as your judge!'

The young woman hid her face in her hands.

'Oh, I beg of you, do not trust to appearances,' she stammered.

'Are you a coward?' cried Villefort in a contemptuous tone. 'Indeed, I have always remarked that poisoners are cowards. Is it possible, though, that you are a coward, you who have had the awful courage to watch the death agony of three old people and a young girl, your victims? Is it possible that you are a coward, you who have counted the minutes while four people were slowly done to death? Is it possible that you, who were able to lay your plans so admirably, forgot to reckon on one thing, namely, where the discovery of your crimes would lead you? The poisoner shall go to the scaffold whoever she may be, unless she was cautious enough to keep for herself a few drops of the deadliest poison.'

Mme de Villefort uttered a wild scream, and a hideous and invincible terror laid hold of her distorted features.

'Oh, do not fear the scaffold, madame,' resumed the magistrate. 'I do not wish to dishonour you, for in doing so, I should bring dishonour on myself. On the contrary, if you have heard me correctly, you must understand that you are not to die on the scaffold! So, where is the poison you generally use, madame?'

She raised her arms to Heaven, and wringing her hands in despair, exclaimed: 'No, no! You could not wish that!'

'What I do not wish, madame, is that you should perish on the scaffold, do you understand?' replied Villefort.

'Have mercy!'

'What I demand, madame, is that justice shall be done. My mission on earth is to punish,' he added with a fierce look in his eyes. 'I should send the executioner to any other woman were she the Queen herself, but to you I am merciful! To you I say: "Madame, have you not put aside a few drops of the most potent, the swiftest, and deadliest poison?"'

'Oh, forgive me! Let me live! Remember that I am your wife!'

'You are a poisoner.'

'For heaven's sake . . .! For the sake of the love you once bore me! For our child's sake! Oh, let me live for our child's sake!'

'No! No! No! I tell you. If I let you live, you will perhaps kill him like the rest.'

'I kill my son?' cried the desperate mother, throwing herself upon Villefort. 'I kill my Edward? Ha, ha!' She finished the sentence with a frightful laugh, a mad, demoniacal laugh, which ended in a terrible rattle. She had fallen at her husband's feet! Villefort bent down to her.

'Remember, madame,' he said, 'if justice has not been done when I return, I shall denounce you with my own lips and arrest you with my own hands!'

She listened panting, overwhelmed, crushed; only her eyes had any life in them, and they glared horribly.

For a moment the magistrate appeared to feel pity for her; he looked at her less sternly, and, slightly bending towards her, he said: 'Goodbye, madame, goodbye!'

This farewell fell upon Mme de Villefort like the knife of an executioner, and she fainted.

The judge went out and double-locked the door behind him.

The Court had risen, and as the Procureur du Roi drove home through the crowded streets, the tumultuous thoughts of the morning surged through and through his weary brain. The carriage stopped in the yard. He stepped out and ran into the house. When passing Noirtier's door, which was half open, he saw two men, but he did not trouble himself about who was with his father; his thoughts were elsewhere. He went into the salon – it was empty!

He rushed up to her bedroom. The door was locked. A shudder went through him, and he stood still.

'Héloïse!' he cried, and he thought he heard some furniture move.

'Héloïse!' he repeated.

'Who is there?' asked a voice.

'Open quickly!' called Villefort. 'It is I.'

But, notwithstanding the request and the tones of anguish in which it was made, the door remained closed, and he broke it open with a violent kick.

Mme de Villefort was standing at the entrance to the room which led to her boudoir. She was pale and her face was contracted; she looked at him with a terrifying glare.

'Héloïse! Héloïse!' he cried. 'What ails you? Speak!'

The young woman stretched out her stiff and lifeless hand.

'It is done, monsieur,' she said with a rattling which seemed to tear her very throat. 'What more do you want?' And with that she fell her full length on the carpet. Villefort ran up to her and seized her hand, which held in a convulsive grasp a glass bottle with a gold stopper. Mme de Villefort was dead!

Frantic with horror, Villefort started back to the door and contemplated the corpse.

'My son!' he called out. 'Where is my son? Edward! Edward!'

He rushed out of the room calling out, 'Edward! Edward!' in tones of such anguish that the servants came crowding round him in alarm.

'My son – where is my son?' asked Villefort. 'Send him out of the house! Do not let him see . . .'

'Monsieur Edward is not downstairs, monsieur,' said the valet.

'He is probably playing in the garden. Go and see quickly.'

'Madame called her son in nearly half an hour ago, monsieur. Monsieur Edward went to madame and has not been down since.'

A cold sweat broke out on Villefort's forehead; his legs gave way under him, and thoughts began to chase each other across his mind like the uncontrollable wheels of a broken clock.

'He went into Madame de Villefort's room?' he murmured, as he slowly retraced his steps, wiping his forehead with one hand and supporting himself against the wall with the other.

'Edward! Edward!' he muttered. There was no answer. Villefort went farther. Mme de Villefort's body was lying across the doorway leading to the boudoir in which Edward must be; the corpse seemed to guard the threshold with wide staring eyes, while the lips held an expression of terrible and mysterious irony. Behind the body the raised curtain permitted one to see into part of the boudoir: an upright piano and the end of a blue satin sofa. Villefort advanced two or three steps, and on this sofa – no doubt asleep – he perceived his child lying. The unhappy man had a feeling of inexpressible joy; a ray of pure light descended into the depths in which he was struggling. All he had to do was to step across the dead body, take the child in his arms, and flee far, far away.

He was no longer the exquisite degenerate typified by the man of modern civilization; he had become like a tiger wounded unto death. It was not prejudice he now feared, but phantoms. He jumped over his wife's body as though it were a yawning furnace of red-hot coals. Taking the boy in his arms, he pressed him to his heart, called him, shook him, but the child made no response. He pressed his eager lips to the child's cheeks – they were cold and livid; he felt the stiffened limbs; he placed his hand over his heart – it beat no more. The child was dead.

Terror-stricken, Villefort dropped upon his knees; the child fell from his arms and rolled beside his mother. A folded paper fell from his breast; Villefort picked it up and recognized his wife's handwriting, and eagerly read the following:

You know that I have been a good mother, since it was for my son's sake that I became a criminal. A good mother never leaves her son!

Villefort could not believe his eyes, and thought he must be losing his reason. He dragged himself towards Edward's body, examined it once more with the careful attention of a lioness contemplating its cub.

Then a heart-rending cry escaped his breast. 'God!' he murmured. 'It is the hand of God!'

Villefort rose from his knees, his head bowed under the weight of grief. He, who had never felt compassion for anyone, decided to go to his father so that in his weakness he would have someone to whom he could relate his sufferings, someone with whom he could weep. He descended the little stairs with which we are acquainted, and entered Noirtier's room.

As he entered, Noirtier appeared to be listening attentively, and as affectionately as his paralysed body would permit, to Abbé Busoni, who was as calm and cold as usual. On seeing the abbé, Villefort drew his hand across his forehead. The past all came back to him, and he recollected the visit the abbé had paid him on the day of Valentine's death.

'You here?' he said. 'And why have you come today?'

'I have come today to tell you that you have made abundant retribution to me and from today I shall pray God to forgive you.'

'Good heavens!' cried Villefort, starting back with a look of terror in his eyes. 'That is not Abbé Busoni's voice!'

'No,' said the abbé, and as he tore off his false tonsure his long black hair fell around his manly face.

'That is the face of Monte Cristo!' cried Villefort, a haggard look in his eyes.

'You are not right yet. You must go still further back.'

'That voice! That voice! Where have I heard it before?'

'You first heard it at Marseilles twenty-three years ago, on the day of your betrothal to Mademoiselle de Saint-Méran.'

'But what did I do to you?' cried Villefort, whose mind was struggling on the borders between reason and insanity and had sunk into that state which is neither dreaming nor reality. 'What have I done? Tell me! Speak!'

'You condemned me to a slow and hideous death; you killed my father; you robbed me of liberty, love, and happiness!'

'Who are you then? Who can you be?'

'I am the ghost of an unhappy wretch you buried in the dungeons of the Château d'If. At length this ghost left his tomb under the disguise of the Count of Monte Cristo, and loaded himself with gold and diamonds that you might not recognize him until today.'

'Ah! I recognize you! I recognize you!' cried the Procureur du Roi. 'You are . . .'

'I am Edmond Dantès!'

'You are Edmond Dantès!' cried the magistrate, seizing the Count by the wrist. 'Then come with me!' He dragged him up the stairs, and the astonished Monte Cristo followed him, not knowing where he was leading him, though he had a presentiment of some fresh disaster.

'Look, Edmond Dantès!' said Villefort, pointing to the dead bodies of his wife and son. 'Are you satisfied with your vengeance?'

Monte Cristo turned pale at the frightful sight. Realizing that he had passed beyond the bounds of vengeance, he felt he could no longer say: 'God is for me and with me.' With an expression of indescribable anguish, he threw himself on the child's body, opened his eyes, felt his pulse, and, rushing with him into Valentine's room, locked the door.

'My child!' de Villefort called out. 'He has taken the body of my dead child! Oh, curse you! Curses on you in life and death!'

He wanted to run after Monte Cristo, but his feet seemed rooted to the spot, and his eyes looked ready to start out of their sockets; he dug his nails into his chest until his fingers were covered with blood; the veins of his temples swelled and seemed about to burst through their narrow limits and flood his brain with a deluge of boiling fire. Then with a shrill cry followed by a loud burst of laughter, he ran down the stairs.

A quarter of an hour later the door of Valentine's room opened, and the Count of Monte Cristo reappeared. Pale, sad of eye, and heavy of heart, all the noble features of that usually calm face were distorted with grief. He held in his arms the child whom no skill had been able to recall to life. Bending his knee, he reverently placed him beside his mother with his head upon her breast. Then, rising, he went out of the room and, meeting a servant on the staircase, asked: 'Where is Monsieur de Villefort?'

Instead of replying, the servant pointed to the garden. Monte Cristo went down the steps, and, approaching the spot indicated, saw Villefort in the midst of his servants with a spade in his hand digging the earth in a fury and widely calling out: 'Oh, I shall find him. You may pretend he is not here, but I shall find him, even if I have to dig until the day of the Last Judgement.'

Monte Cristo recoiled in terror. 'He is mad!' he cried.

And as though fearing that the walls of the accursed house would fall and crush him, he rushed into the street, doubting for the first time whether he had the right to do what he had done.

'Oh, enough, enough of all this!' he said. 'Let me save the last one!'

On arriving home he met Morrel, who was wandering about the house in the Champs-Élysées like a ghost waiting for its appointed time to enter the tomb.

'Get yourself ready, Maximilian,' he said to him with a smile. 'We leave Paris tomorrow.'

'Have you nothing more to do here?' asked Morrel.

'No,' replied Monte Cristo, 'and God grant that I have not already done too much!'

38

The next day the Count came to fetch Morrel from his sister's house.

'I am ready,' said Maximilian. 'Goodbye, Emmanuel! Goodbye, Julie!'

'Let us be off,' said the Count.

'Before you go, Count, permit me to tell you what the other day . . .'

'Madame,' replied the Count, taking her two hands, 'all that you can tell me in words can never express what I read in your eyes, or the feelings awakened in your heart, as also in mine. Like the benefactors of romances, I would have left without revealing myself to you, but this virtue was beyond me, because I am but a weak and vain man, and because I feel a better man for seeing a look of gratitude, joy and affection in the eyes of my fellow beings. I will leave you now, and I carry my egoism so far as to say: "Do not forget me, my friends, for you will probably never see me again!"'

'Never see you again!' exclaimed Emmanuel, while the tears rolled down Julie's cheeks.

He pressed his lips to Julie's hand and tore himself away from this home where happiness was the host; he made a sign to Morrel, who followed him with all the indifference he had manifested since Valentine's death.

'Restore my brother to happiness again,' Julie whispered to Monte Cristo.

He pressed her hand as he had done eleven years ago on the staircase leading to Morrel's study.

'Do you still trust Sinbad the Sailor?' he asked with a smile.

'Oh, yes.'

'Well, then, sleep in the peace and confidence of the Lord.'

The post-chaise was waiting; four vigorous horses were shaking their manes and pawing the ground in their impatience. Ali was waiting at the bottom of the steps, his face bathed in perspiration as though he had been running.

'Well, did you see the old gentleman?' the Count asked him in Arabic.

Ali made a sign in the affirmative.

'And did you unfold the letter before him as I instructed you to do?'

The dumb slave again made a sign in the affirmative.

'What did he say to you, or rather, what did he do?'

Ali placed himself under the light so that his master might see him, and in his intelligent manner he imitated the expression on the old man's face when he closed his eyes in token of assent.

'It is well, he accepts,' said Monte Cristo. 'Let us start!'

They travelled for ten leagues in complete silence, Morrel wrapped in dreams and Monte Cristo watching him dream.

'Morrel,' said the Count at length, 'do you regret having come with me?'

'No, Count, but in leaving Paris . . .'

'If I had thought your happiness was to be found in Paris, I should have left you there.'

'Valentine is laid at rest in Paris, and I feel as though I were losing her for a second time.'

'Maximilian, the friends we have lost do not repose under the ground,' said the Count; 'they are buried deep in our hearts. It has been thus ordained that they may always accompany us. I have two such friends. The one is he who gave me being, and the other is he who brought my intelligence to life. Their spirits are ever with me. When in doubt I consult them, and if I ever do anything that is good, I owe it to them. Consult the voice of your heart, Morrel, and ask it whether you should continue this behaviour towards me.'

'The voice of my heart is a very sad one,' said Maximilian, 'and promises nothing but unhappiness.'

The journey was made with extraordinary rapidity;

villages fled past them like shadows; trees, shaken by the first autumn winds, seemed like dishevelled giants rushing up only to flee as soon as they had reached them. They arrived at Chalon the next morning, where the Count's steamboat awaited them. Without loss of time the two travellers embarked, and their carriage was taken aboard.

The boat was almost like an Indian canoe, and was especially built for racing. Her two paddle-wheels were like two wings with which she skimmed the water like a bird. Even Morrel seemed intoxicated with the rapidity of their motion, and at times it almost seemed as though the wind, in blowing his hair back from his forehead, also momentarily dispelled the dark clouds that were gathered there. Marseilles was soon reached. As they stood on the Cannebière a boat was leaving for Algiers. Passengers were crowded on the decks, relatives and friends were bidding farewell, some weeping silently, others crying aloud in their grief. It was a touching sight even to those accustomed to witnessing it every day, yet it had not the power to distract Morrel from the one thought that had occupied his mind ever since he set foot on the broad stones of the quay.

'Here is the very spot where my father stood when the *Pharaon* entered the port,' he said to the Count. 'It was here that the honest man whom you saved from death and dishonour threw himself into my arms; I still feel his tears on my face.'

Monte Cristo smiled. 'I was there,' he said, pointing to a corner of the street. As he spoke a heart-rending sob was heard issuing from the very spot indicated by the Count, and they saw a woman making signs to a passenger on the departing boat. The woman was veiled. Monte Cristo watched her with an emotion which must have been evident to Morrel had his eyes not been fixed on the boat.

'Good heavens!' cried Morrel. 'Surely I am not mistaken. That young man waving his hand, the one in uniform, is Albert de Morcerf.'

'Yes,' said Monte Cristo. 'I recognized him.'

'How can you have done? You were looking the other way.'

The Count smiled in the way he had when he did not wish to answer. His eyes turned again to the veiled woman, who soon disappeared round the corner of the street. Then, turning to Maximilian, he said: 'Have you nothing to do in the town?'

'Yes, I wish to pay a visit to my father's grave,' replied Morrel in a lifeless voice.

'Very well, go and wait for me; I will join you there.'

'You are leaving me?'

'Yes . . . I also have a visit of devotion to make.'

Morrel let his hand fall into the one the Count held out to him; then, with an inexpressibly melancholy nod of the head, he took his leave of the Count and directed his steps toward the east of the town.

Monte Cristo stayed where he was until Maximilian was out of sight, then he wended his way to the Allées de Meilhan.

In spite of its age the little house, once inhabited by Dantès' father, still looked charming and not even its obvious poverty could deprive it of its cheerful aspect. It was to this little house that the veiled woman repaired when Monte Cristo saw her leaving the departing ship. She was just closing the gate when he turned the corner of the street.

He entered without knocking or announcing himself in any way. At the end of a paved path was a little garden that caught all the sunshine and light, and its trees could be seen from the front door. It was here Mercédès had found, in the spot indicated, the sum of money which the Count's delicacy of feeling had led him to say had been deposited in this little garden for twenty-four years.

Monte Cristo heard a deep sigh and, looking in the direction whence it came, he beheld Mercédès sitting in an arbour covered with jasmine with thick foliage and slender purple flowers; her head was bowed, and she was weeping bitterly. She had partly raised her veil and, being alone, was giving full vent to the sighs and sobs which had so long been repressed by the presence of her son.

Monte Cristo advanced a few steps, crunching the gravel under his feet as he trod. Mercédès raised her head and gave a cry of fear at seeing a man before her.

'Madame, it is no longer in my power to bring you happiness,' said the Count, 'but I offer you consolation. Will you deign to accept it from a friend?'

'In truth I am a most unhappy woman, and all alone in the world,' replied Mercédès. 'My son was all I had, and he too has left me.'

'He has acted rightly, madame,' replied the Count. 'He is a noble-hearted soul who realizes that every man owes a tribute to his country; some their talents, others their industry, others their blood. Had he remained beside you, he would have led a useless life. In struggling against adversity, he will become great and powerful and will change his adversity into prosperity. Let him remake a future for himself and for you, madame, and I venture to say you are leaving it in safe hands.'

'I shall never enjoy the prosperity of which you speak,' said the poor woman, shaking her head sadly, 'but from the bottom of my heart I pray God to grant it to my son. There has been so much sorrow in my life that I feel my grave is not far distant. You have done well, Count, in bringing me back to the spot where I was once so happy. One should wait for death there, where one has found happiness.'

'Alas!' said Monte Cristo. 'Your words fall heavily on my heart, and they are all the more bitter and cutting since you have every reason to hate me. It is I who am the cause of all your misfortunes; why do you pity me instead of reproaching me?'

'Hate you! Reproach you, Edmond! Hate and reproach the man who saved my son's life, for I know it was your intention to kill the son of whom Monsieur de Morcerf was so proud, was it not? Look at me and you will see whether I bear the semblance of a reproach against you.'

The Count looked up and fixed his gaze on Mercédès, who, half rising from her seat, stretched her hands towards him.

'Oh, look at me,' she continued in tones of deep melancholy. 'My eyes are no longer bright, as in the days when I smiled upon Edmond Dantès, who was waiting for me at the window of this garret where his father lived. Since then many sorrowful days have passed and made a gulf between that time and now. Reproach you! Hate you, Edmond, my friend! No, it is myself that I hate and reproach!' she cried, wringing her hands and raising her eyes to heaven. 'Ah, but I have been sorely punished . . . I had faith, innocence, and love – everything that makes for supreme happiness, yet, unhappy wretch that I am, I doubted God's goodness!'

Monte Cristo silently took her hand.

'No, my friend, do not touch me,' she said, gently withdrawing it. 'You have spared me, yet of all I am the most to blame. All the others were prompted by hatred, cupidity, or selfishness, but cowardice was at the root of all my actions.'

Mercédès burst into tears; her woman's heart was breaking in the clash of her memories. Monte Cristo took her hand and kissed it respectfully, but she knew that it was a kiss without feeling, such as he would have imprinted on the marble statue of a saint.

'No, Mercédès,' said he, 'you must form a better opinion of yourself. You are a good and noble woman, and you disarmed me by your sorrow; but behind me there was concealed an invisible and offended God, Whose agent I was and Who did not choose to withhold the blow I had aimed.'

'Enough, Edmond, enough,' said Mercédès. 'Now bid me farewell. We must part.'

'Before I leave you, Mercédès, is there nothing I can do for you?' asked Monte Cristo.

'I have but one desire, Edmond – my son's happiness.'

'Pray to God, who alone disposes over life and death, to spare his life, and I will do the rest. And for yourself, Mercédès?'

'I need nothing for myself. I live, as it were, between

two graves. The one is that of Edmond Dantès, who died many years ago. Ah, how I loved him! The other grave belongs to the man Edmond Dantès killed; I approve of the deed, but I must pray for the dead man.'

Monte Cristo bowed his head under the vehemence of her grief. 'Will you not say *au revoir* to me?' he said, holding out his hand.

'I do say *au revoir*,' Mercédès replied 'and that is a proof that I still hope.'

She touched the Count's hand with her own trembling fingers, ran up the stairs, and disappeared from his sight. Monte Cristo left the house with heavy steps. But Mercédès did not see him; her eyes were searching in the far distance for the ship that was carrying her son towards the vast ocean. Nevertheless her voice almost involuntarily murmured softly: 'Edmond! Edmond!'

The Count went with a heavy heart from the house where he had taken leave of Mercédès, in all probability never to see her again, and turned his steps towards the cemetery where Morrel was awaiting him.

Ten years previously, he had also sought piously for a grave in this same cemetery, but he had sought in vain. He who had returned to France with millions of money had been unable to find the grave of his father, who had died of hunger. Morrel had had a cross erected, but it had fallen down, and the sexton had burnt it with the rubbish. The worthy merchant had been more fortunate. He had died in the arms of his children, and by them had been laid beside his wife, who had preceded him into eternity by two years.

Two large marble slabs, on which were engraved

their names, were standing side by side in a little railed-in enclosure shaded by four cypresses.

Maximilian was leaning against one of these trees staring at the two graves with unseeing eyes. He was obviously deeply affected.

'Maximilian, it is not on those graves you should look, but there!' said the Count, pointing to the sky.

'The dead are everywhere,' said Morrel. 'Did you not tell me so yourself when you made me leave Paris?'

'On the journey, Maximilian, you asked me to let you stay a few days at Marseilles. Is that still your wish?'

'I have no longer any wishes, Count, but I think the time of waiting would pass less painfully here than anywhere.'

'All the better, Maximilian, for I must leave you, but I have your word, have I not?'

'I shall forget it, Count, I know I shall.'

'No, you will not forget it, for you are, above all things, a man of honour, Morrel; you have sworn to wait and will now renew your oath.'

'Have pity on me, Count, I am so unhappy!'

'I have known a man unhappier than you, Morrel.'

'What man is there unhappier than he who has lost the only being he loved on earth?'

'Listen, Morrel, and fix your whole mind on what I am going to tell you. I once knew a man who, like you, had set all his hopes of happiness upon a woman. He was young; he had an old father whom he loved, and a sweetheart whom he adored. He was about to marry her, when suddenly he was overtaken by one of those caprices of fate which would make us doubt in the goodness of God, if He did not reveal himself later by showing us that all is but a means to an end. This man was deprived of his liberty, of the woman he loved, of the future of which he had dreamed and which he believed was his, and plunged into the depths of a dungeon. He stayed there fourteen years, Morrel. Fourteen years!' repeated the Count. 'And during those fourteen years he suffered many an hour of despair. Like you, Morrel, he also thought he was the unhappiest of men, and sought to take his life.'

'Well?' asked Morrel.

'Well, when he was at the height of his despair, God revealed Himself to him through another human being. It takes a long time for eyes that are swollen with weeping to see clearly, and at first, perhaps, he did not comprehend this infinite mercy, but at length he took patience and waited. One day he miraculously left his tomb, transfigured, rich and powerful. His first cry was for his father, but his father was dead! When his son sought his grave, ten years after his death, even that had disappeared, and no one could say to him: "There rests in the Lord the father who so dearly loved you!" That man, therefore, was unhappier than you, for he did not even know where to look for his father's grave.'

'But then he still had the woman he loved.'

'You are wrong, Morrel. This woman was faithless. She married one of the persecutors of her betrothed. You see, Morrel, that in this again he was unhappier than you.'

'And did this man find consolation?'

'At all events he found peace.'

'Is is possible for this man ever to be happy again?'

'He hopes so.'

The young man bowed his head, and after a moment's silence he gave Monte Cristo his hand saying: 'You have my promise, Count, but remember . . .'

'I shall expect you on the Isle of Monte Cristo on the 5th of October, Morrel. On the 4th, a yacht named the *Eurus* will be waiting for you in the Port of Bastia. Give your name to the captain, and he will bring you to me. That is quite definite, is it not?'

'It is, Count, and I shall do as you say. You are leaving me?'

'Yes, I have business in Italy. I am leaving you alone with your grief.'

'When are you going?'

'At once. The steamboat is waiting for me, and in an hour I shall be far from you. Will you go with me as far as the harbour?'

'I am entirely at your service.'

Morrel accompanied the Count to the harbour. The smoke was already issuing from the black funnel like an immense plume. The boat got under way, and an hour later, as Monte Cristo had said, the same feather of white smoke was scarcely discernible on the horizon as it mingled with the first mists of the night.

39

It was about six o'clock in the evening; an opalescent light through which the autumn sun shed a golden ray descended on the sea. The heat of the day had gradually diminished into that delicious freshness which seems like nature's breathing after the burning siesta of the afternoon, and a light breeze was bringing to the shores of the Mediterranean the sweet perfume of trees and plants mingled with the salt smell of the sea.

A small yacht, elegant in shape, was drifting in the evening air over this immense lake, like some swan opening its wings to the wind and gliding through the water. It advanced rapidly, although there seemed hardly sufficient wind to ruffle the curls of a young maiden.

Standing on the prow, a tall dark man was watching the approach of land, a cone-shaped mass, which appeared to rise out of the water like a huge Catalan hat.

'Is that Monte Cristo?' he asked of the skipper in a voice full of sadness.

'Yes, Your Excellency,' replied the latter. 'We are there.'

Ten minutes later, with sails furled, they anchored a hundred feet from the little harbour. The cutter was ready with four oarsmen and the pilot. The eight oars dipped together without a splash, and the boat glided rapidly onward. A moment later they found themselves in a small natural creek and ran aground on fine sand.

'If Your Excellency will get on to the shoulders of two of our men, they will carry you to dry land,' said the pilot. The young man's answer was a shrug of complete indifference as he swung himself out of the boat into the water.

'Ah, Excellency!' cried the pilot. 'That is wrong of you! The master will scold us.'

The young man continued to follow the two sailors, and after about thirty steps reached the shore, where he stood and peered into the darkness. Then he felt a hand on his shoulder, and a voice startled him by saying: 'Good evening, Maximilian. You are very punctual.'

'It *is* you, Count!' cried the young man, delightedly pressing Monte Cristo's two hands in his.

'Yes, and, as you see, as punctual as you are. But you are drenched, my friend; come, there is a house prepared for you, where you will forget cold and fatigue.'

The sailors were dismissed, and the two friends proceeded on their way. They walked for some time in silence, each busy with his own thoughts. Presently Morrel, with a sigh, turned to his companion: 'I am come,' said he, 'to say to you as the gladiator would say to the Roman Emperor: "He who is about to die salutes you."'

'You have not found consolation then?' Monte Cristo asked, with a strange look.

'Did you really think I could?' Morrel said with great bitterness. 'Listen to me, Count, as to one whose spirit lives in heaven while his body still walks the earth. I am come to die in the arms of a friend. It is true there are those I love, my sister and her husband, Emmanuel, but I have need of strong arms and one who will smile on me during my last moments. I have your word, Count. You will conduct me to the gates of death by pleasant paths, will you not? Oh, Count, how peacefully and contentedly I shall sleep in the arms of death!'

Morrel said the last words with such determination that the Count trembled.

Seeing that Monte Cristo was silent, Morrel continued: 'My friend, you named the 5th of October as the day on which my trial should end. It is today the 5th of October . . . I have but a short while to live.'

'So be it,' said Monte Cristo. 'Come with me.'

Morrel followed the Count mechanically, and they had entered the grotto before he perceived it. There was a carpet under his feet; a door opened, exhaling fragrant perfumes, and a bright light dazzled his eyes. Morrel paused, not venturing to advance. He mistrusted the enervating delights that surrounded him. Monte Cristo gently drew him in.

He sat down, and Morrel took a seat opposite him.

'I have your word, Count,' said Morrel coldly. Taking out his watch, he added: 'It is half-past eleven.'

'Morrel, consider. You would do this thing before my eyes? In my house?'

'Then let me go hence,' replied Maximilian gloomily. 'Otherwise I shall think that you do not love me for myself but for yourself.'

'It is well,' said the Count, whose face had brightened at these words. 'You wish it, and you are firmly resolved on death. You are certainly most unhappy, and, as you say, a miracle alone could save you. Sit down and wait.'

Morrel obeyed. Monte Cristo rose and went to a cupboard, and unlocking it with a key which he wore on a gold chain, took out a small silver casket wonderfully carved; the corners represented four bending women symbolical of angels aspiring to Heaven.

He placed the casket on the table, and, opening it, took out a small gold box, the lid of which opened by the pressure of a secret spring. This box contained an oily, half-solid substance of an indefinable colour. It was like an iridescence of blue, purple, and gold.

The Count took a small quantity of this substance with a gold spoon and offered it to Morrel while fixing a long and steadfast glance upon him. It was then seen that the substance was of a greenish hue.

'This is what you asked for and what I promised to give you,' said the Count.

Taking the spoon from the Count's hand, the young man said: 'I thank you from the bottom of my heart. Farewell, my noble and generous friend. I am going to Valentine and shall tell her all that you have done for me.'

Slowly, but without any hesitation, and waiting only to press the Count's hand, Morrel swallowed the mysterious substance the Count offered him.

The lamps gradually became dim in the hands of the marble statues that held them, and the perfumes seemed to become less potent. Seated opposite to Morrel, Monte Cristo watched him in the shadow, and Morrel saw nothing but the Count's bright eyes. An immense sadness overtook the young man.

'My friend, I feel that I am dying.'

Then he seemed to see Monte Cristo smile, no longer the strange, frightening smile that had several times revealed to him the mysteries of that profound mind, but with the benevolent compassion of a father towards an unreasonable child.

Overcome, Morrel threw himself back in his chair, and a delicious torpor crept into his veins; he seemed to be entering upon the vague delirium that precedes the unknown thing they call death. He endeavoured once more to give his hand to the Count, but it would not move; he wished to articulate a last farewell, but his tongue lay heavy in his mouth like a stone at the mouth of a sepulchre. His languid eyes involuntarily closed, yet through his closed eyelids he perceived a form moving which he recognized in spite of the darkness that seemed to envelop him.

It was the Count, who was opening a door. Immediately a brilliant light from the adjoining room inundated the one where Morrel was gently passing into oblivion. Then he saw a woman of marvellous beauty standing on the threshold. She seemed like a pale and sweetly smiling angel of mercy come to conjure the angel of vengeance.

'Is heaven opening before me?' the dying man thought to himself. 'This angel resembles the one I have lost!'

Monte Cristo pointed to the sofa where Morrel was reclining. The young woman advanced towards it with clasped hands and a smile on her lips.

'Valentine! Valentine!' Morrel's soul went out to her, but he uttered no sound; only a sigh escaped his lips and he closed his eyes.

Valentine ran up to him, and his lips opened as though in speech.

'He is calling you,' said the Count. He is calling you in his sleep. Valentine, henceforth you must never leave him, for, in order to rejoin you, he courted death. Without me you would both have died; I give you to each other. May God give me credit for the two lives I have saved!'

Valentine seized Monte Cristo's hand, and in a transport of irresistible joy carried it to her lips.

'Oh, yes, yes, I do thank you, and with all my heart,' said she. 'If you doubt the sincerity of my gratitude, ask Haydee, ask my dear sister Haydee, who, since our departure from France, has helped me to await this happy day that has dawned for me.'

'Do you love Haydee?' asked Monte Cristo, vainly endeavouring to hide his agitation.

'With my whole heart.'

'Well, then, I have a favour to ask of you, Valentine,' said the Count.

'Of me? Are you really giving me that happiness?'

'Yes, you called Haydee your sister; be a real sister to her, Valentine; give to her all that you believe you owe to me. Protect her, both Morrel and you, for henceforth she will be alone in the world.'

'Alone in the world?' repeated a voice behind the Count. 'Why?'

Monte Cristo turned round.

Haydee was standing there pale and motionless, looking at the Count in mortal dread.

'Tomorrow you will be free, my daughter,' answered the Count. 'You will then assume your proper place in society; I do not wish my fate to overcloud yours. Daughter of a prince! I bestow on you the wealth and the name of your father!'

Haydee turned pale, and, in a voice choking with emotion, she said: 'Then you are leaving me, my lord?'

'Haydee! Haydee! You are young and beautiful. Forget even my name and be happy!'

'So be it!' said Haydee. 'Your orders shall be obeyed, my lord. I shall even forget your name and be happy!' and stepping back she sought to retire.

The Count shuddered as he caught the tones of her voice which penetrated to the inmost recesses of his heart. His eyes encountered the maiden's, and he could not bear their brilliancy.

'My God!' cried he. 'Is it possible that my suspicions are correct? Haydee, would you be happy never to leave me, again?'

'I am young,' she replied. 'I love the life you made so sweet to me, and I should regret to die!'

'Does that mean to say that if I were to leave you . . .?'

'I should die? Yes, my lord.'

'Do you love me then?'

'Oh, Valentine, he asks me whether I love him! Valentine, tell him whether you love Maximilian!'

The Count felt his heart swelling within him; he opened his arms, and Haydee threw herself into them with a cry.

'Oh, yes, I love you!' she said. 'I love you as one loves a father, a brother, a husband! I love you as I love my life, for to me you are the noblest, the best, and the greatest of all created beings!'

'Let it be as you wish, my sweet angel,' said the Count. 'God has sustained me against my enemies and I see now He does not wish me to end my triumph with repentance. I intended punishing myself, but God has pardoned me! Love me, Haydee! Who knows? Perhaps your love will help me to forget all I do not wish to remember! Come, Haydee!'

Throwing his arms round the young girl, he shook Valentine by the hand and disappeared.

An hour or so elapsed, and Valentine still stood beside Morrel, breathless, voiceless, with her eyes fixed on him. At length she felt his heart beat, his lips parted to emit a slight breath, and the shudder which announces a return to life ran through his whole frame. Finally his eyes opened, though with an expressionless stare at first; then his vision returned and with it the power of feeling and grief.

'Oh, I still live!' he cried in accents of despair. 'The Count has deceived me!' Extending his hand towards the table, he seized a knife.

'My dear one!' said Valentine with her sweet smile. 'Awake and look at me!'

With a loud cry, frantic, doubting, and dazzled as by a celestial vision, Morrel fell upon his knees.

At daybreak the next day Morrel and Valentine were walking arm in arm along the seashore, while Valentine related how Monte Cristo had appeared in her room, how he had disclosed everything and pointed to the crime, and finally how he had miraculously saved her from death by making believe that she was dead.

They had found the door of the grotto open and had gone out whilst the last stars of the night were still shining in the morning sky. After a time, Morrel perceived a man standing amongst the rocks waiting for permission to advance, and pointed him out to Valentine.

'It is Jacopo, the captain of the yacht!' she said, making signs for him to approach.

'Have you something to tell us?' Morrel asked.

'I have a letter from the Count for you.'

'From the Count!' they exclaimed together.

'Yes, read it.'

Morrel opened the letter and read:

MY DEAR MAXIMILIAN,

There is a felucca waiting for you. Jacopo will take you to Leghorn, where Monsieur Noirtier is awaiting his granddaughter to give her his blessing before you conduct her to the altar. All that is in the grotto, my house in the Champs Élysées, and my little château at Tréport are the wedding present of Edmond Dantès to the son of his old master, Morrel. Ask Mademoiselle de Villefort to accept one half, for I beseech her to give to the poor of Paris all the money which she inherits from her father, who is now insane, as also from her brother, who died last September with her stepmother.

Tell the angel who is going to watch over you, Morrel, to pray for a man who, like Satan, believed for one moment he was the equal of God, but who now acknowledges in all Christian humility that in God alone is supreme power and infinite wisdom. Her prayers will perhaps soothe the remorse in the depths of his heart.

Live and be happy, beloved children of my heart, and never forget that, until the day comes when God will deign to reveal the future to man, all human wisdom is contained in these words: Wait and hope!

Your friend,

EDMOND DANTÈS, Count of Monte Cristo

During the perusal of this letter, which informed Valentine for the first time of the fate of her father and her brother, she turned pale, a painful sigh escaped from her bosom, and silent tears coursed down her cheeks; her happiness had cost her dear.

Morrel looked around him uneasily.

'Where is the Count, my friend?' said he. 'Take me to him.'

Jacopo raised his hand towards the horizon.

'What do you mean?' asked Valentine. 'Where is the Count? Where is Haydee?'

'Look!' said Jacopo.

The eyes of the two young people followed the direction of the sailor's hand, and there, on the blue horizon separating the sky from the Mediterranean they perceived a sail, which loomed large and white like a seagull.

'Gone!' cried Morrel. 'Farewell, my friend, my father!'

'Gone!' murmured Valentine. 'Goodbye, my friend, my sister!'

'Who knows whether we shall ever see thèm again,' said Morrel, wiping away a tear.

'My dear,' replied Valentine, 'has not the Count just told us that all human wisdom is contained in the words "Wait and hope!"'